Camelot Games
by
Frank V. Costanza

I0615391

Pearl River Publishing Group presents

Pearl River Publishing Group

Camelot Games
by
Frank V. Costanza

This work previously published under the penname, Oliver F. Chase

---

1. http://www.bookcoverdesign.us/

2. http://www.bookcoverdesign.us/

Dedication

To my wife, Jane, who works on our farm and makes wonderful the nature outside my window. All the while, I sit in air conditioning or heat inventing imaginary heroes and other people.

I may need to think again.

Frank

Chapter 1

The second shotgun blast exploded against the bare concrete.

"Stop, for God's sake!" Scott McHale yelled and dropped to the dusty concrete floor.

No answer. He squinted to see in the building's shadows. "Look, we're only doing an inspection. I'm the architect."

Maybe an overzealous security guard. After several incidents of gang-fueled vandalism, the last security company was fired.

No reply, then fast, scuttling footsteps from nearby. Scott looked around the thick column just as the overweight building inspector accompanying him broke and ran for the stairs.

Scott yelled. "Marvin. Christ, get back here."

Three quick pistol shots and the inspector went down. His face smacked the floor like a dropped halibut. Blood smeared across his cheeks.

That is not a security guard.

Across the bare concrete space, Marvin Engels rolled onto his back and grunted. "Scott ... help me, please."

McHale peeked around the corner. Viscous crimson blood soaked the inspector's shirt front. He worked a cell phone from a jeans pocket and dialed 9-1-1.

"Shots fired at the Scholarplex. Man down."

"Scott?" Theo Haines, county dispatcher and an old friend from a different life.

"Theo, thank God. We're in trouble here. Pinned down by at least two active shooters."

"Okay, help is on the way. Which building?"

McHale gulped air and looked around as if for the moment he had forgotten where he was. "Middle school, third floor. Southernmost staircase, next to the ballfield."

"Stay on the line, Scott." The dispatcher's professional manner helped calm the chaos.

McHale breathed hard. He was no stranger to maniacs with guns. The phone slipped easily into the top shirt pocket.

He buttoned the flap and called out, "How you doing, Marvin? That's Joe on the phone. He'll be up here in a minute."

McHale tossed a chunk of broken porcelain into the stairwell, then ran at full speed for the next pillar. A bullet careened unseen into the shadow.

A wild shot into the staircase. Amateurs. There was no Joe.

Engels moaned in wet rasps as tears streaked his bloodied face. Wide eyes searched around the empty floor as his ham-sized leg pumped dark blood in a spreading pool.

Arterial flow.

A part of McHale's brain recalled his own bullet wound, the searing pain, months in rehab. He broke cover and dropped to Engels' side. The inspector was a big man. McHale staggered a step as he hefted him over a shoulder. The jostling elicited a scream. McHale moved a dozen steps then pressed against the wide concrete pillar. A siren sounded miles from across the desert floor. Another shot.

McHale ran for the staircase. He captured both wrists and never slowed jumping two steps at a time.

McHale reached the ground floor.

Between grunting and moaning, Engels managed to utter a few words. "I'm going to die."

"No, you're not. Hang in there, damn it."

McHale could barely breathe as he slammed through the fire exit. The sun-bright parking lot had him squinting and scrambling for his key fob. The back doors popped and he pushed Engles into the back seat.

"Sorry, Marvin, sorry."

McHale ran to the driver's side. The old Explorer burst into life as if realizing the danger. No backing up. Instead, he slammed the front wheels over the curb and floored the engine. This time, Engels had not protested the jostle.

McHale yelled toward his shirt pocket. "Theo? Still there?"

The voice crackled. "Go ahead."

The truck bounced off the hard-pack soil and squealed onto the asphalt.

McHale said, "At least two shooters. One shotgun and a pistol."

He rounded the second corner and headed for the highway. The truck strained. A county patrol car, wigwagging headlights with blue flashers tore past and didn't slow. McHale slammed on his brakes. Engels shrieked, sliding forward in the seat. The police car disappeared behind him.

"Shit. He went on by."

The dispatcher's voice. "Rookies, Scott. Sorry. Medical is on their way, but they're up in Mojave. It'll be at least thirty minutes."

McHale pushed the gas to the floor. "Okay. I'm on my way to County, ETA twenty minutes."

He turned and eyed Engels' blood-soaked pants. "Press on the wound, Marvin. You've got to slow the bleeding."

But Engels only groaned.

McHale reached over the seat back. The SUV swerved threatening to rollover. He recovered and accelerated. His hand found the wound. "You got to put your hands here, Marvin. See? Press down until it hurts."

"It hurts."

"Press down harder, damnit."

He felt Engels take over. "Now, hold it there. I've got to drive."

Ten tense minutes slipped by with only engine roars and moaning from the back.

When the freeway's hospital exit sign came into view, he hit the ramp and accelerated through the light. The Explorer threatened to flip on every bounce of broken roadway.

Engels stopped moaning.

McHale glanced in the rearview mirror. "Two minutes buddy. Hang in there."

The Explorer bumped through the last light. Another block. He dodged and passed other cars before they banged up the hospital's emergency ramp.

He held the horn down, slammed the car into park. He ran to the other side and pulled the back door. Sightless eyes stared up.

"No. You will not die."

He pulled Marvin to the pavement, locking his mouth over the bloody man's own. Attendants ran. One found a gurney. McHale did not stop. Ribs cracked as he leaned his muscled body into the man's flabby chest.

When a third white uniform pushed him aside, McHale fell back. An errant swipe across his cheek left a macabre image caught by a man with a cell phone camera.

The admissions clerk returned to his side. "My God, Scott. Are you hurt?"

He shook his head and rose. "No, I'm okay."

Then he remembered. He pulled his cell phone from the shirt pocket.

"Theo?"

"I'm here. How's Marvin?"

McHale looked into the eyes of the clerk.

"The doctor's with him now."

"I guess, I don't know, Theo. What in the world just happened?"

"You did what you could."

"I'm afraid it wasn't enough."

The clerk helped him stand and walk into the waiting room.

Drained, he fell into a plastic chair. "I got to go. Thanks, Theo." He disconnected and hit the speed dial.

He needed to hear Angie's voice.

• • • •

In the parking lot, a man watched, his cell phone faithfully recording a death and a birth of sorts. After the din had died down, he flicked the off button and approached the waiting black Yukon.

Wesley Teague handed the phone over. "Here you go, Mr. Dearborn."

"Big Jim" was the longtime chief commissioner of the Muroc County Board of Supervisors. His corpulence filled the driver's seat with thick arms and a gut that touched the steering wheel.

Dearborn stabbed buttons and watched the entire sequence. All had been caught by the video.

He blew satisfied cigar smoke out an open window. "This is good. Get me the 9-1-1 tape."

Teague took his spot in the passenger seat. "Yes, sir. No problem." Wiry and not particularly tall, the younger man emanated prowess and danger that kept others at bay.

Big Jim watched the video one more time, savoring and nodding a sage head. "Yep. I couldn't have planned this any better."

Teague did not reply. A laconic reticence, his trademark, served him well.

Dearborn sent both windows up. "Get this to your people and onto social media. Tonight. Anonymously of course. Make that dumb bastard Scott McHale an even bigger hero than he thinks he already is."

"Yes, sir."

Dearborn put the truck into gear. "And it only cost us a building inspector. You know. I never liked that Engels anyway."

Teague said nothing.

Chapter 2

Scott

The furor over warring drug gangs and the death of an innocent man faded with the next news cycle. Despite their proximity to Los Angeles, Scott McHale's video hit fifty thousand times in the first hour before You Tube suspended its replay as overly graphic and inappropriate. The notoriety had not helped his project progress. They remained stalled with little hope of breaking the logjam of late and no-show subcontractors and material unavailability. Credit had seemingly become a thing of the past.

McHale slit a rare payment envelope from the county.

"Money?" Brian Peterson tried Groucho Marx's eyebrows but failed. "Any in there for me?"

"You bet."

McHale scribbled his name on the back and pushed the check over.

Brian shook his head in horror. "No, no. Don't do that."

"Hey, you're not a one-man company like me. You've got to survive, and this won't even cover two days of labor. For right now, it's all I can do. I'm tapped out."

Brian glanced at the yellow message slip on Scott's desk. The county supervisor had called.

"We're due for a break here, Scott. Tell that Dearborn guy, I don't want to get fired. We need this job. Both of us."

"Nobody said anything about us getting fired. This is just a meeting. I'm sure it's going to be okay."

Peterson's lineman position years ago in high school football had given McHale the scampering room to become the hometown hero. When the time came for college, no team offered a scholarship to a dime-a-dozen blocker like Peterson like they did for the quarterback.

Peterson did not take his eyes off the message slip. "That guy has declined every meeting you asked for. Don't forget, he was quoted in the paper saying we were 'snake bit.' Then all of a sudden, he calls? Geez. Barely a month ago Marvin Engels died on our job. What else could it be except the hatchet? He was just lining up our replacement before he drops the hammer."

McHale watched his longtime friend run a thick workman's hand over a short blond scalp.

"I don't think this afternoon's meeting is going to be that bad. Right now, we need to figure out how to get another thousand tons of slurry on credit we don't have."

Both men tipped their coffee cups in thought knowing nothing short of manna from heaven could save them now.

At four o'clock, McHale parked the Explorer at the county offices. He pulled a wrinkled off-the-rack Penney's sport jacket from the back seat hook and tightened his necktie.

With a pull at the glass doors, he glanced up to the gods of good luck. "Here goes nothing."

He knocked.

"Come!"

Big Jim rose with a booming bonhomie, his clothes stretched with bulky muscle easing through middle age. "Scotty. How are you? Have a drink."

McHale shook his head. "No thanks."

Now suddenly, he expected the worst, just like Peterson. All he wanted was a simple yes or no answer. Did he still have the project?

Big Jim shrugged at the rebuff. "Suit yourself. I'm going to top off this bad boy."

The commissioner's desk and high, padded leather chair dominated the cool, glass-enclosed room. The row of spots highlighted trophies, loving cups, and pictures of a bare-chested James Dearborn in two-decades-old photos. In one, Big Jim accepted a champion's brass belt as a superheavyweight boxer. He did not let others forget he had fought the best and never went to his knees. From his first election in the valley, Big Jim ran unopposed. A news reporter once called him the "Monarch of the High Desert." The man soon found work elsewhere. Dearborn worked best in the dark and behind the curtains.

Dearborn spoke at the corner bar, keeping his back to McHale. "Tell me. Don't drink, or just don't drink with me?"

McHale fought his tightening gut. "I drink, sir, but my mother expects me for dinner. She raises hell if alcohol is on my breath."

He forced a smile. "I pick the fights I can win, Mr. Dearborn. I've never won with my mother."

Big Jim was unamused. "That's smart. Win the fights you pick because I don't give a shit what anybody says. Nobody can stand a loser."

He pointed to the couch. "Grab a seat, Scotty. Let's get to know one another."

In his middle years now, Dearborn had added fifty pounds to his fighting weight. Today, he was no less formidable than when he had knocked the champion down. Twice.

McHale sat.

Amber whiskey swirled as he settled behind the giant desk. "How's the Scholarplex coming along? I know about your troubles, and now you got a murder. I don't think that's ever happened on one of our projects before."

McHale had rehearsed before coming. "The project is sound, Mr. Dearborn. The idea was good, and the outcome will be a legacy."

Epicanthic folds hid a gray steel gaze. "Good answer ... for a politician. Doesn't work well for the project manager, though. You're behind schedule and I haven't seen this month's numbers yet. Are you over budget, too?"

McHale knew he should not have blocked the man's jab. "Yes, but it's manageable. We have got troubles where we shouldn't, and I haven't a clue why."

Dearborn smiled and drained the liquor. "You sure about that drink?"

Another forced smile. "Mr. Dearborn, if you could cure these problems with two fingers of scotch, I'd be glad to have a drink. My mom would understand."

Big Jim nodded, as if in thought. "Okay, Scotty. You got a deal."

McHale blinked his surprise, watching the man rock off the chair and pour a second glass.

Big Jim handed the tumbler over and dropped his bulk onto the cushion next to a surprised McHale. "So, tell me about that Bronze Star you got. Is that real, or just one of those presents to make your generals feel good?"

McHale considered the man next to him, the taunt and innuendo, and thought about his decision to join the California National Guard. He'd lost his scholarship because a not-so-innocent party stunt broke a teammate's leg. Both were red-shirted. He eventually lost his scholarship with mediocre grades. So, he grew bored and angry with himself so joined the guard to go to flight school. Fifteen months later he flew a Blackhawk against an Afghanistan Taliban position that turned out to be heavily defended by the Taliban. In the ensuing fight, he rescued another crew shot down and transported wounded ground soldiers throughout the night. He hadn't quit that night, and he wasn't going to quit now.

"I suppose the generals always look good giving away medals. As for mine, we also earned a combat 'V' for valor. Helicopters are flown by a crew, Mr. Dearborn. Good crews are good teams, and I had a good one that night."

Big Jim eyed McHale then took a drink. "I can get the project moving, but the murder will take a bit more. The idiots at City Hall need to do their thing, but I'll handle them, too."

He let a dribble cross his gullet in McHale's silence. "What's it worth to you to kick this Scholarplex in the ass and get it going?"

"I'm not sure what you mean."

The big man harrumphed. "If that's true, I'm wasting my time."

The soft words had the grit of every school yard bully McHale had ever known. "But I'll explain so even you can understand. My name will be on the building someday. I'll make damn sure of it. I'm prepared to step in and go all the way for you. You're the project boss so you'll get credit for bringing this in. Without me though, I guarantee the work won't get done. I've got the juice, and you got the need. This is no different than finding the right plumber, understand? Hire me to get the job moving. I'll make the problems go away. Simple as that."

Big Jim worked his heavy lips for a moment, tasting and savoring his own words. McHale got the feeling he had not been the only one with a rehearsed speech.

The clock clicked a paced staccato in the silent room.

It was McHale's move. "I don't understand what's in this for you. Why wouldn't you just fire Brian and me, and bring Jove Construction in here to wrap things up? Your name will still be on the building."

Big Jim examined his drink for a moment, the ghost of a grin behind the man's eyes. "That's a damn good question, but you're not making a deal with the devil. Just the opposite. Think of me as the world's greatest customer service guy. I only exist to please you. And to get this project the hell done. Got it?"

McHale looked down at his untouched glass. "I need help, Mr. Dearborn. I need whatever help you can offer. We're building a beautiful square mile of buildings and gyms. The roads and concrete alone will delay us past September. The middle school is stopped dead in its tracks, and now it's a crime scene the county won't release. I'll go under, no matter how this turns out. Brian Peterson might survive, but he's already lost more than he can afford—"

Big Jim held up a hand. "Let's be clear on one thing. I don't give a shit about Brian Peterson. I'm talking to you."

McHale nodded. "Your call, but I do care. My company will implode the first time I try to bid on something new, because I don't have any reserves left. I'm only trying to save my reputation now. What can I do to earn your help?"

Big Jim upended his glass and clanged the tabletop. "You just did, Scotty. From now on, you call me Big Jim. All my friends do. Drink up and grab a mint. Then get the hell out of here and let me get to work."

Chapter 3

Scott

Sitting inside the project's construction trailer, McHale pushed the memory of the evening with Dearborn to the back of his mind. The project had sailed. No, the project rocketed. Subcontractors arrived early and eager. If Brian's crew ran into a supply glitch, a second supplier waited as if clairvoyant with the right materials, a county approval number, and warranty paperwork already filed. If a sub ran into a problem, no one complained, and the next sub showed on time whether or not McHale remembered to call.

And of course, paychecks rolled in. He hit each of the bonus gates in May and June. He refused to count the money refilling his daughter's education fund for fear of cursing the good fortune. McHale judged the classrooms, lab, and music hall. The cafeteria was already equipped and only awaited perishables and students. Even the football team ran scrimmages on new practice greens.

The McHale family planned a vacation for late August using a rental Cessna. He had only logged a few hundred flying hours since cashing in on his military time and earning a private pilot endorsement years ago. Up until recently, tight budgets meant no extra money, but now, they can afford the occasional treat. He smiled at the thought and closed the airplane rental website just as Big Jim Dearborn's luxurious Yukon rolled to a stop.

McHale opened the metal trailer door.

Big Jim called out. "Scotty!"

"Hi, Mr. Dearborn. Good to see you again." Only a few people called him Scotty and usually only the ones who hadn't bothered to become friends.

The man seized McHale's hand with a meaty grip. "Let's go for a ride. And for the last damn time, call me Big Jim."

"Will do, sir." McHale extracted his fingers and climbed in.

"Show me my legacy."

"Certainly. Want to see the middle school first?"

Neither man noticed the heat off the desert floor.

"Tech school. I understand the auto shop was installed last week."

The air conditioning blew hard from dash vents against the outside temperature.

McHale pulled his seatbelt on. "Pretty impressive equipment that's getting me lots of comments and questions. And the huge storage building, wow. What's the county need with something the size of two football fields?"

"Uh-huh."

A wide expanse of gritty dirt and irrigated green separated the two sites. Big Jim didn't bother with the roads but took off across the open fields of caliche.

He stopped the truck in the open field. "Let's walk a bit. I wanted to be out of earshot from snoops."

McHale joined him in the hundred- and five-degree heat.

Big Jim chewed the end of a cigar as his coattails flapped. "So, how're you getting along?"

McHale knew the man read every weekly report. "The project is good, really good. We're ahead of schedule and labor hasn't filed a grievance in six months. Whatever you're doing is working well."

"Uh huh." Big Jim waited.

McHale crushed the skin between his eyebrows. "Things are going great, but I'm all grown up now. And I know magic is just a trick."

"Good. Magic is also for idiots. I'm happy you know the difference. We're walking."

He turned toward a fescue mat laid earlier in the month. Sprinklers sent water arcing in the sunlight. The cushion sprung with each footfall.

"My grandniece, Becky Lawton, knows Joy. Becky says your daughter's a good kid. That's a good thing. Children see through adult bullshit, so I trust what Becky tells me."

The sound of Joy's name from Dearborn's mouth bothered McHale. He said nothing.

"I don't bring families into these things, either, Scotty, not unless I have to."

McHale tamped down his irritation. "I've met most of Joy's friends, sir. I don't recall Becky."

Dearborn spat on the grass and wiped tobacco left over from his cigar. "Not surprising. She's going to Our Lady in Santa Barbare. They did summer volunteer work together. She doesn't get to the Antelope Valley that often."

"I see."

"I checked Angie out, too. The work she did for the summer migrants was good. Good press. We can use that. Both your gals are okay."

McHale felt a chill work up his backbone. Big Jim grinned. "Don't worry about being a little pissed, Scotty. You wouldn't be much of a man if you didn't want to take me on. But don't try it."

Big Jim swigged from a small flask and screwed the lid back on. "I checked out your family and your past. I've had a team of detectives checking out your relatives. Hell, boy, they even checked out your third-grade schoolteacher." He laughed in the afternoon wind. "Is it really true the big-ass Black FBI agent is your best friend?"

McHale didn't like the path of the conversation but kept his temper. "It's true, he is. And he's Joy's godfather. I love Ken Litton like I love my brothers."

Big Jim examined McHale's face and walked again. "No offense, so get down off your high horse. My only question is, will the fact he's a fed hurt you?"

The dry desert soil crunched under their feet as they left the carpet of grass. "I don't understand. Hurt me? We're only a month from the punch list."

"Uh huh. Are you familiar with Charles Campanella?" Big Jim cupped his body against the wind and lit the soggy cigar.

"Sure, I know the name."

Big Jim laughed. "Well, forget his name. He's going to resign at the end of term. Health reasons. Because I'm going to ruin it if he doesn't. You're going to run in his place. I'm going have the governor endorse you as soon as we make the announcement. Campanella will endorse you too, of course. His constituency is thirty-five percent Hispanic. Your last name is kind of a problem, but I don't see it as too big a deal, especially when we put Angie and your mother onstage. You speak Spanish, right?"

McHale stopped walking. "Whoa, whoa. You got my mom on a stage, and I don't have the first idea of what the heck you're talking about."

A moment ebbed on Big Jim's face as he turned to look at McHale. "What I'm talking about is getting your Latino ass to Congress. We got twelve months to get you known outside the county. We ain't got time to put you though the State's legislature to learn the ropes. The only way we're going to make the timetable is to get your butt in gear and get your face and blue eyes known. What the hell is with the eyes, anyway?"

He held up a hand to stop McHale. "Never mind. So, why is this so goddamn tough to understand?"

McHale growled his answer. "Ever think about asking me?"

Big Jim watched him for a moment, then grew tranquil, dangerous. "I already did when you came whining to me. I busted my ass getting your broken-down project going. The next goddamn thing you'll have to learn is to roll with the story. Think before you open your mouth and prove I'm digging in the right goddamn garden."

Standing a head taller, lean, and muscular, McHale forced himself to slow down. He took stock of the man mocking him.

"All right, Mr. Dearborn. You chose correctly for a lot of reasons. But pardon me if sometimes you need to spell things out."

Big Jim started walking. "The world moves fast in politics and I'm always on the lookout for talent. This half of California is mine, my responsibility, and I've got to deliver.

Marvin might've died, but you did your Desert Storm thing, and the newspapers loved you. Even the *LA Times* ran your story when the video went viral. Good stuff. I just wished you had a more Mexican name. Scott McHale sounds white bread, like television reruns."

Blood rushed in McHale's ears as he fought his Latino temper. He hated the idea of failing, but now it seemed he could do no wrong and that bothered him, too. But Angie knew everything. She accepted success as his and urged him to do the same.

Big Jim watched closely. "So, what's it going to be Scotty? Are you in or out?"

McHale let a long moment pass, then decided. "In."

Big Jim boomed. "Ha! You're a funny one. This is already happening. Oh, yeah. Cancel that goddamn vacation. You got work to do."

Chapter 4

Angie

That night, McHale broke the news over the dinner table. Joy asked a dozen high schooler questions he couldn't answer. Angie sat back, listening, subdued and thoughtful. She watched her husband and daughter chatter happily. The more they talked, the further her misgivings slipped into memory.

The phone rang halfway through the meatloaf. Angie answered. The Antelope Valley Press wanted to confirm the rumor for the morning news.

McHale waved his hand and pointed to himself. Big Jim had already briefed him on what to say.

Her accent came out thicker than usual. "I will tell Mr. McHale you're on the line."

He gave her a quizzical look and took the phone. "Scott McHale."

A familiar voice. "Hey, Scott. It's Henry from the Antelope Valley Times." Henry Wittington had been a year ahead of him in high school. "We've been told that you plan to enter the Congressional race this fall. Care to comment?"

"You must have great sources, buddy. You didn't pay him already, did you?"

A hardy laugh. "Is that a denial?"

McHale glanced up at his two ladies. "Look. I'd like to talk about it, but this will have to wait. I'm really sorry."

"Booyah! Thanks for confirming. You know, Scott, I always faked you out on field, too."

Angie waggled a finger at him and mouthed the words, "Quit it."

Scott just grinned.

The reporter persisted. "Come on Scott. Tell me the story. For old times' sake."

"There's no story, but there is dinner on the table. Let me get back to it."

"Hey, no sweat, but don't give it to any else. We're friends, remember."

"Of course, we are. 'Night Henry."

Dearborn had explained that a mystery created great publicity and sales. San Bernardino's ABC Channel 7 called next, followed by KCAL 9. McHale answered each, never varying the story.

The family finally gave up on dinner as the phone continued to ring and took their dishes to the kitchen. Joy returned to her school project, skipping down their narrow hallway.

Angie tossed him the keys to the old Explorer. "Can you spare the time, Mr. Congressman? I need to see Papi's new trees."

The phone began to ring again. "Don't have to ask me twice."

The forty-minute drive took them into the San Joaquin valley and a dirt road where a stand of three-hundred-year-old Joshua trees marked the property's corner. She slipped out and opened the gate for the dirt road and a small overlook where stars filled the quiet desert night.

He turned on the seat. "What do you think? I mean really think. This is a commitment for both of us ... all three of us."

She poked his ribs. "You will make a wonderful president, and I will make a great First Lady."

"I'm serious, babe. This is a hell of a fork in our road."

"It is. And, if you think our life was unsettled with your construction business, just wait until you take the oath of office. The vagaries of life have a way of upsetting even the best of plans."

"You think it'll be that big a change?"

She already knew the answer. "I think it's about time a real Latino couple got to Washington and Pennsylvania Avenue."

He chuckled. "This is a freshman job in Congress. And they're only hiring for two years."

He hung an elbow out the window thinking his wife had never looked so animated and lovely.

"Have you thought about what I am to do while you run the country? I'm not now nor will I ever be a stay-at-home wife and mom. Those days are long gone. If you do this, Scott, I will expect to be involved and active. Can you manage that?"

His smile dropped as the realization dawned on him. "You're right. This needs to be both of us. But not behind the scenes. Out in front for the world to see. The voters will have to choose both of us. You will have to give up the Assistant District Attorney's job."

Angie took his hand. "I agree. You're going to be great, Scott. You're honest and hardworking. You're probably good-looking enough. Joy and I will form your first election committee. We will be your refuge, keep your secrets, and be your team. And we will find opportunities for all of us."

He switched off the engine and focused a thousand miles away.

"My God, Angie we will be unstoppable."

• • • •

She put her back against the car's door as he dreamed.

"You know, Scott, I'm not going to rain on your parade, and I agree, but we can never forget who we are and where we came from. Sorry to be the serious one, because recognition brings temptation. Big recognition brings the devil. They will not be just the ones who laugh at your jokes or the ones always wanting to shake your hand. We must learn to separate them from real people. This will take both of us and we must be vigilant. I know what I'm talking about."

She hated that he had to witness her own failures. At one time, everyone knew her name, too. She led cheers in high school and did the same at Stanford. She served as Graduate Student Council President and later, editor for the Law Review. She had a perfect academic record and once shared the cover of Glamour magazine with two other Miss California finishers.

Accomplishments and adulation came naturally although it had not always been so. Born to a single parent, her grandparents took her in when her mother died in a traffic accident. Her father was already gone. She came to live on the family's modest twenty-acre pistachio farm in the San

Joaquin Valley. Eventually, her grandfather and grandmother were able to scrimp and save and buy tiny parcels of abandoned marginal land that finally totaled nearly three hundred acres. Most were farms on the brink of collapse. This did not scare her grandparents. Hard work and luck turned dusty waste land into the San Joaquin Valley's largest privately held pistachio conglomerate.

Angie adored her grandparents and worked alongside them for most of their twelve-hour days. She drove the family truck, made deliveries of parts to broken down equipment, fixed the equipment, ran the irrigation, and kept the family books. She learned the importance of commitment, accuracy, ambition, and honesty. Her grandmother died suddenly after Angie's fourteenth birthday. The loss nearly crushed her spirit and would have except for her grandfather. Together, they hired when they needed to, lengthened already long days, and split more duties. Angie managed most of the outlying acreage, hired and fired employees, and continued to lead an active high school and college life. Her grandfather never missed one of Angie's games, award ceremony, plays, or conferences. He imbued in her the appreciation of austerity and a focus on personal achievement as a way to frame and understand the world that awaited her.

After finishing second on the dean's list at UC Davis Law, big-name Los Angeles firms sent their svelte, high heeled and handsome young associate attorneys to recruit her. The attention threatened to turn her head. She quickly because a focal center as firms competed for her commitment. Cold reality came to her when a recruiter casually mentioned that she must never to underestimate the power of her loveliness or Latina heritage.

Angie owned mirrors. She knew what others wanted to see. Even her grandmother had warned her beauty was as much a blessing as a taskmaster. After the wining and dining, she realized the enormous pressure on associate lawyers. Beneath their professional surface, an anxiety and instability nested. The work did not scare her, nor did the expectation that her face would be that of the law firm. She already knew veneer hid most truths.

While weighing the various firms and their possibilities, she chanced on a local advertisement for the public defender's office. She applied, and two months later, Angela Molina returned home to Kern County.

Before she finished the second successful year as the public defender, she met Scott McHale. He accompanied a friend who found himself crosswise with the sheriff. She discovered he was the reformed bad-boy college dropout, football player hopeful for her alma mater's rival, and a war hero. He was also Latino, handsome, and with inquiring blue Anglo eyes who worked construction all day and studied engineering at night. A year later, they married, with two unhappy families filling local church pews and a baby well on its way.

In the dark of the Explorer's front seat, she touched his chin. "Did you ever think something like this could happen?"

"Never in my foggiest, Angie. You're the one who should be running for congress. Lawyer, smart, beautiful."

"I don't disagree but you're not half bad yourself. I'm sure Big Jim had his minions drag out all your past. What about your skeletons, Mijo? Old girlfriends, stuff that will embarrass?"

He laughed. "I'm Mr. Dull, remember?"

She smiled. "Stick with that story."

"Well, that's a heck of an endorsement."

"Hey, I'm a voter too. You'll have to prove yourself."

He pulled her closer and fingered the top button on her blouse. "Oh, I can prove myself alright."

"Big talk, gringo."

He laughed and nuzzled.

She held on tightly.

Chapter 5

Scott

True to his word, in a month Congressman Tino Campanella announced he would retire and pursue other ventures. The press conference was held in the county's small meeting hall at Big Jim's direction. The diminutive room gave the impression of a larger crowd.

At his summons, McHale rose and centered himself at the podium introducing his mother, Angie, and their nervous high schooler, Joy.

He turned back to the audience. "I am very honored to be here with you this evening. When the state committee asked me to run, and I'll admit this right up front, I was pretty darn scared. Congressman Campanella has a terrific record of public service and has given no small measure of his life to benefit our community throughout the Inland Empire. And I'd like to thank him for that."

McHale turned and began to clap, then stepped over and shook the man's limp hand. Campanella refused to make eye contact.

My first political enemy.

McHale returned to the podium. "Let's not forget progress starts at home. We need to manage our own local affairs and not depend on big government. I'll bring the decisions back home to the community, encourage local growth, more jobs, and good schools. Prosperity will follow. Everyone will share not only the burden of working hard, but the benefits too."

A man in the back applauded. Several others joined in.

"We have a special guest tonight. Please say hello to the Honorable Ms. Twila Crawford, US Congressional Representative from District 1." A tall, striking woman rose from the chair next to the taciturn Campanella. She smiled, inclined her head toward McHale, and resumed her seat. "Congresswoman Crawford leads the efforts in Washington to bring energy decision-making back to the community. She's eliminating out-of-date hydro dams and inefficient electrical systems while capping our rates.

The same clap led the group.

"If left unchecked, utility rates will grow out of control and our energy decisions will be dictated by out-of-state investment bankers, leaving us victims instead of entrepreneurs. Bringing decisions home means we create jobs and drive out crime. Then, we can take back our streets." His words grew in volume, surprising several reporters.

He began to improvise. "Yes. Take-back-our-streets. That's the name we'll put to a plan to encourage businesses and go after the gangs, the thugs, and the misery brokers. Either they go meekly back to where they came from, or they will go to our jails."

More hands clapping. The group from the back didn't have to initiate this time.

"There's no middle ground. We will not allow gangs to prey on our children."

A second camera lifted from the floor as the applause grew again.

A voice picked up the chant. "Take back our streets," repeated over and over again.

"This is our country, our land, and our heritage. And this is our duty. With your help, and that of God's, I will go to Washington and find solutions. This I promise."

When the applause died down, he surprised his audience by repeating the salient parts of the speech in Spanish. His words translated well for the media.

By month's end, McHale appeared several more times on front covers and evening news interviews. The "Take Back Our Streets" initiative gained momentum even in San Diego, well outside of his district and a hundred miles away.

For the next nine months McHale worked twelve-hour days, finishing the Scholarplex by day and meeting civic leaders, bloggers, and neighborhood clubs at night. In early November, he beat a retired movie start opponent by one of the narrowest margins in memory and went to bed as a first-term US congressman.

Chapter 6

Scott

The time between election and swearing-in became even busier. The governor cut the Scholarplex's ribbon the week before Thanksgiving. Scott and Angie spent three quick days in DC, renting a tiny apartment and meeting with constituents before returning home. Juliette Pearson, a staffer on loan from the California state committee, and Big Jim Dearborn arrived to organize the election's aftermath of contributor acknowledgements and benefit parties.

A pretty, blonde dynamo, Juliette handled phones and issued orders like a general. Angie and she often sat together, *strategizing* as they enjoyed saying, figuring out seating arrangements, and sharing intelligence on attendees.

On the night before they left for Washington, Angie found McHale in a quiet spot in the Knights of Columbus hall. "Going over your speech?"

He looked up and smiled. "It's more like a stump speech with an opening prayer."

She knew he usually avoided public displays of his religion "You okay with that? Maybe you can have Father Julio step in for you. They're going to be expecting a little ...hmm, deeper than what you do for the protestant prayer breakfasts."

McHale grimaced. "I'm going to have to do this. The monsignor has already made it clear he's expecting great things. I can't bypass this one."

She watched him thoughtfully. "I'm on my way out right now. How about if I send Juliette to listen? She might have a better feel."

He was about to say no when Juliette walked in. "I can help. I've stolen a prayer from Edmund Muskie—"

McHale laughed. "How in the world did you know? Don't answer that. But Maine's senator from the 70s? Oh, brother."

She put her lips together in a pout. "Give an attribute if you must, but no one will know you're plagiarizing."

He sighed as Angie laughed and patted her shoulder. "Good girl. Make him practice." She waved walking out the back.

"Here, sir." She sat and handed him the three short paragraphs. "It's not plagiarized but rewritten for today's voter."

He read quickly. "This is really good, and please, call me Scott." He caught her scent of roses and lime, and instinctively slid an inch away.

She closed the gap, touching arm to arm, hip to hip. Her eyes met his, her expression straightforward and confident. "I'm listening. Read and tell me what's uncomfortable or just not you."

McHale couldn't be sure if there was a double message in there or not.

He stood. "Okay. I'll be standing at the podium."

She waved him on. "I'll write up any changes when you're done."

The evening's Muskie prayer with California variations fit perfectly as an introduction to his speech.

After dinner, Juliette came quickly up, bouncing on her toes. "That was just so awesome, sir. Really."

She bounced away, as two church deacons looked on.

He agreed the speech had gone well. He almost hated to admit to himself, but speeches and "politicking" as Big Jim would say, came naturally. He never felt forced or artificial and he enjoyed banter.

Later, after both he and Angie had gone to bed, McHale's mobile rang.

"Want to run in the morning?"

He shook sleep from his head. "Hey, Ken. How you doing?"

"Don't answer a question with a question, Mr. Congressman. You gonna run with me or not?"

McHale laughed and propped up a pillow. Angie stirred, so he lowered his voice. "Can we make it early? I know how you FBI agents like to lounge around in bed, but I've got to fly to DC tomorrow."

The baritone chuckle was trademark. "Oh, I think my butt can meet you at the 'Plex, say oh-six hundred. How about you?"

McHale smiled. "Oh, all right. I'll wait until then. See you there."

When he arrived, the dash clock read five-fifteen. The sun barely lit the eastern horizon and Ken Litton already stretched against a post.

McHale locked the Explorer's door. "Special Agent Litton. Is it true you routinely squander the public's money on booze and broads?"

"I categorically deny any such allegation." Litton kept the pace of his warm-up. "That's a phrase you might try and memorize, Congressman."

McHale dropped to the transplanted grass. "So, how are things?"

The early morning's temporary coolness would soon be lost in the coming day.

"Oh, good, I guess. We got a new tight-ass SSRA from DC who's been all over my files for the last two weeks." Litton's rock-hard muscles glistened in the security light.

"I thought you were the senior dude at the Resident Agency."

"Get with the lingo, McHale. This is a GS-14 Supervisory Resident Agent. Not a bad bump in the wallet."

McHale glanced over with a grin. "Are you thinking about it?"

Litton walked backward on the tips of his fingers. "Give it up, punk. Time to run."

McHale stood too, bouncing on the balls of his feet. "Tell me the truth. You going for a promotion?"

Litton laughed. "You can't hide, Congressman. Let's run."

McHale was six-one, but Litton stood two inches taller and twenty fat-free pounds heavier. The trot began slow but wouldn't last long.

McHale trailed as they started up a rise. "So, when do you decide to go for the gold?"

The caliche turned loose as each struggled with sandy footfalls.

Litton took a moment. "I applied for DC a month ago—"

"A month? What the hell. You never told me."

"I don't tell you everything. We aren't married."

"Yeah, yeah. And thank God for that. What's Anne Marie say?"

They topped the mound as Litton pointed a finger. The tail of a rattler disappeared into the low brush.

"Got'm." McHale quickened his stride to give the shy snake a wider berth. "When?"

"Sixty days. Got the letter last night."

"The evil twins take DC. Ha! Think they're ready for us?"

Litton laughed as they wound single file down the path. McHale fell back into an easy pace for the next mile.

Litton called over his shoulder. "Doing okay?"

McHale grunted.

"Good, 'cause we're stepping it up here."

"I'm with you." McHale stretched his stride to match Litton's.

He watched as Highway 14 twisted into the far hills. The high-desert town of Cantil never strayed far from his thoughts, or the late night he had stopped a weaving family sedan. Instead of an elderly couple making their way home at two in the morning, three Cartel drug runners ambushed and left him to die on the cold blacktop. The merciful biology of the human brain erased much of that traumatic night from his gunshot memory.

McHale watched sweat-glistened black arms pump as he fell behind. A train climbed the Tehachapi foothills hooting its approach to an unguarded crossing. Wind turbines wheeled across the valley floor, an obligatory blight marring the vista.

Litton disappeared over the rise, doubling back to the start point. McHale stretched his legs, trying in vain to close the distance.

On that horrific night, Ken Litton was a young patrol officer. When the dispatcher's calls to McHale fell into an empty night, he'd headed that way. No other deputies were on duty in the north desert's hundreds of square miles. Twelve minutes later, Litton came upon the blue rotating roof lights and an unconscious, gunshot McHale. The wild, no holds-barred drive to Muroc's hospital took more than the golden hour as life seeped away. Of course, McHale only later heard about the drive topping the patrol car's speedometer and Litton who promptly collapsed in the ER. He regretted missing that part of the night. His friend failed to swear the nurses to secrecy.

Litton slowed his pace and McHale finally caught up. They trotted, then walked the last half mile. Both panted from a good run.

Litton stretched his muscled shoulders. "So, what's the deal with this Jim Dearborn?"

McHale used his T-shirt to wipe his face. "He's the reason the state committee even knows about me."

Litton said nothing and stretched hamstrings against Explorer.

McHale tossed Litton a bottle of water and kept one for himself. "Big Jim pushed my name and probably called in all sorts of favors. So, I sort of owe him. What are you thinking?"

He had asked himself the same question a hundred times. As a Latino in a state with seven million voting sons and daughters of immigrants, he understood his advantages. And with a beautiful wife like Angie, the reasons for Big Jim's choice seemed clear enough.

Litton's non sequitur however, confused him. "I see you and the wife have a website now. I Googled it the other day. She's very impressive. You, not so much."

McHale grinned but Litton was not smiling. "Is there something you're not saying?"

"A minority in the limelight isn't easy, Scott. People will always watch you, wait for you to stumble, make some minor transgression, then point like they'd always known we weren't good enough for their white guy club." He turned his head to meet the other's eyes.

"Hey, easy there on my white half, buddy."

But Litton would not be cajoled. "Just 'cause the white man stole your country a couple hundred years ago, doesn't mean squat when you leave here. My people were stuffed in slave ships, but that'll only get you so far, too. The reception you get in DC will be smiles to your face but watch out for the backstabbers. Just like the O'Jays told our parents."

McHale reminded himself Litton fought his way into the Bureau. Now he poised for another fight on the promotion ladder. "I'll remember."

"So, answer the question. How did Big Jim convince the committee to go with an unknown from little Muroc County?"

Litton tossed the empty water bottle into his gym bag and began a set of silent sit-ups.

McHale joined him. "I don't know what Big Jim thinks. Maybe he's just looking for a pretty face."

Litton didn't return the silly grin, so McHale grew serious. "We've got some problems out here. I know you know about this stuff. Like the Earth First movement? Domestic terrorists spiking trees that give Twila Crawford fits. You remember her, right?"

Litton grunted.

"Well, she works with him, too."

"Dearborn's in this thing for himself, Scott. You got to watch him."

"I thought that was your job."

Neither man laughed as they finished and stood. The sun crested the far desert mountains, rays beating hot spikes on their skins.

McHale spoke. "You're sounding pretty dire. What do you know I don't?"

Litton slammed the trunk on the Bureau Dodge Charger. "I know there's a lot of something going on behind closed doors and it scares the crap out of me. You're going to be one of about five hundred people who make the country's tough decisions, Scott. I'm just hoping Big Jim isn't sitting in your seat."

"It'll be me, Ken. I promise you that. Big Jim supports but the decisions are going to be mine." He felt a twinge of anger grow unbidden from down deep.

Litton eyed his friend for a long moment. "Good enough for me. I have to get to work. Thanks for the run."

McHale watched Litton's taillights disappear on the new blacktop. Even with the growing heat, a chill tickled his backbone.

Chapter 7

Scott

Three elections to the house and a successful run for the United States Senate had grayed McHale's hair at the temple. His handsome face, accentuated by celebrated blue eyes, remained untouched. The Cessna Citation Jet, a patron's business airplane, taxied at the direction of the lanky lineman's two orange flashlight wands. A moment later, both turbine engines wound down.

Sylvia Flores, a quiet, diminutive, and dynamic administrative assistant paused her iPad. "You only have an hour, Senator. We still have a conference call tonight, and of course, you don't want to be late for Angie at Muroc's airport."

McHale maintained his equanimity. "Thanks for the reminder, but this shouldn't take long."

With a sigh, she touched the save icon and looked up. "The San Francisco office sent an email reminding you to call Senator Swanson's aide in the morning. You know his presidential exploration committee is in full swing. This is important."

"Sure thing." He barely listened, undoing his seat belt and swinging around long legs.

She glanced outside. "That's Rusty out there, Senator. I don't recall his last name. You sent his support request to Juliette."

The grinning lineman hurried up and dropped the passenger door to poke his head inside. "Welcome, Senator. Good to see you again."

"Hello, Rusty." McHale handed over his computer briefcase from the storage rack. "How are things going?"

The young man grinned, taking the case and standing back as McHale stepped out.

"Awesome, sir. Totally. I got into the Army helicopter program. Just like you. Did you know?"

"Hey, that's terrific." The conversation came back to him.

"And I got you to thank for it."

McHale stretched his tight back. "You've got nothing to thank me for. The country needs fine young people. I think you'll make a fine officer."

Rusty laughed. "Tell that to my dad, the master sergeant. He's pissed at you and still wants me to go to college. Of course, after your secretary talked with him, he's not so pissed."

For a moment, McHale was confused. "You mean Juliette Pearson?"

"Yeah, that's her." The young man flushed and looked at the ground. "Dad and I met her at your office."

McHale's aides, like Juliette, collected requests and complaints, handling the vast majority without his knowledge. Her wide eyes and bewitching face flashed into his consciousness. He promptly set the image aside.

Dangerous ground, there.

"I'm glad she could help but you still need to get the degree. I spent time in the army's warrant officer program myself, and the successful guys got the sheepskins."

"Oh, for sure. Everyone knows about you rescuing all those guys with a Blackhawk, Senator. That's why I want to get in."

"Tell your dad you're going to get a degree. Keep me out of trouble."

"No problem." He eyed the briefcase in his hands. "I'll carry this for you."

"Hand it over, dude. I can schlep my own gear."

Another lineman pulled up in the golf cart. McHale slung the case strap over a shoulder. "You guys go ahead. I need to stretch my legs."

Several dozen people stood at the cyclone fence, many holding cell phones high over their heads taking videos. He wanted to look young and fresh. Even though the polls showed his approval rating ten points ahead of last year, no one should be allowed to escape without getting to know him personally.

McHale worked the crowd, shaking hands and holding mobile phones for selfies. After detouring to spend time across the border in Arizona, they were behind schedule, and yet, he maintained his famous relaxed and unhurried persona. He was a frequent visitor to the Western Central Grid Facility, a twenty-year construction project in Deer Creek, Arizona. Early in his first term as a junior congressman, Big Jim had involved him in the Facility's planning and financing. And now, after a decade of quiet progress, the nuclear facility will soon power a huge swath of the southwest throughout the century. The WCG would be an unparalleled economic win and a major political bonanza for McHale thanks to Big Jim Dearborn.

In ten minutes, he'd made his way to private offices inside the terminal building.

He closed the door behind him and nodded at the room's only other occupant. "Good turnout for eight o'clock on a school night."

Dearborn worked his fleshy jaw. "Yeah, well you aren't the reason they're here. Free beer and food bring out the cockroaches. You're late."

"Sorry, Big Jim. Couldn't be helped."

The door opened and closed behind Wes Teague, Dearborn's shadow. McHale nodded as the man took his place by the shaded window.

McHale set his computer down. "Theo Haines said to say hello."

Dearborn's hooded gray eyes glanced at McHale. "Theo, huh? Is he still dispatching ... where ... Arizona?"

"Arizona yes, but not dispatching. He was reelected sheriff of Pima County. Second time."

Headlights crossed the glass. Teague walked for the door. "He's here. I'll bring him through the side. Too many cameras on the ramp."

When the room was empty, McHale sat next to his mentor. "You know, Big Jim, this has all the trappings of inside-the-Beltway shenanigans. Those are reporters out there. They might be filling their faces, but I'm sure they're not opposed to pulling overtime if they get a sniff of what's happening."

"Wes will take care of it. Six o'clock would have been better." McHale didn't answer. "Oh well. This guy wasn't one of your backers, but he can be now. He's on the president's shortlist for a federal magistrate's position in the 9th District, so he's looking for support. You're on the committee, so you must be distant *and* cooperative, and damn careful what you promise."

McHale stood and pointed to the hall. "Stomach. Be back in a moment."

"Damn it, Scotty."

Several minutes later, McHale stepped back into the room drying his hands on a paper towel. Dearborn conferred with Teague at the window while a slender and young Hispanic man sat holding his overcoat in both hands. He looked like a candidate readying for a job interview.

McHale had already read the man's resume. Near the top of his Stanford Law class, two years in the Public Defender's Office, three years as a District Attorney in LA County, and only recently joined the bench in the Bay Area's Alameda Family Court. With the exception of his youthful undergraduate and experiments in social action politics, the young man poised for a jump into the Federal Judicial system.

"Very sorry, Judge Nieto. Queasy stomach." The two men shook hands as McHale switched to Spanish. "Fast food is not home cooking. Does me in all the time, although if the truth were known, I'd like to avoid coming home just now." He grinned at his own self depreciating joke. "Got an election coming in a couple years. Maybe you can help?"

The direct approach surprised the man. "Well, ah sure, Senator."

"Excellent." McHale switched back to English. "I appreciate you meeting us, Judge. I know this couldn't have been convenient."

Nieto replied in English. "Not at all."

McHale sat beside the Judge. "I can't believe we've never met. I don't know how many times it's been on my calendar to give you a call."

Nieto quickly found his own political footing after McHale's surprising request for help. "Well, I think that would be unexpected. I was pretty vocal in favor of the other guy last time."

McHale nodded in agreement. "You were and for good reason. I'm the right guy, Judge, don't get me wrong. But if I wasn't making myself clear, that's on me, not you."

Nieto measured him.

McHale pretended not to notice. "I've followed your career. Decisions in family court are tough ones. When it was needed, you brought the hammer down. I respect that. When you can, compassion. That's admirable *and* courageous. Even if I didn't agree all the time."

Nieto grinned. "I think Abraham Lincoln warned us about trying to please everyone."

McHale leaned into the conversation matching with a smile. "Old Abe stole that one from Aesop, you know. But I agreed with him before, and I agree with *you* now."

For the next twenty minutes, the two men talked the looming power generation crisis. McHale described in knowledgeable detail from the Western Central Grid facility. Favorable rulings would help the bumps sure to come.

Nieto favored the environmentalists and was unconvinced about a looming power shortage. "I can't help but believe market makers manufactured the talk about crisis. This will help them get their bonds sold. We have power. Yet, we don't bring down last century's hydro dam that doomed the fish and forever changed our land. We need conservatism to balance out-of-control capitalism."

And there it was. Nieto staked his lingering belief in the Marxist activism of his youth. McHale was afraid of just that. Now, he needed to find out just how pedantic was the Judge.

Dearborn shifted nearby but didn't speak. No other sound in the room. Nieto glanced from McHale to Dearborn, his expression growing more firm with conviction.

Wes Teague cleared his throat. "Our flight plan has a 2100 departure, Senator."

McHale stood, as if reluctant, and reached out a hand. "Judge? Thank you for your sharing and your candor. Could you hang around just a moment? I'm going to check with the pilots. Maybe we can extend for a few more a few minutes." He smiled with blue eyes twinkling.

Nieto's nodded even though his brow beaded with sweat. He knew the judgeship rapidly slipped away.

Teague followed McHale out of the room.

Dearborn stood and took the empty chair. "Have a seat, Judge. Let's talk a minute."

Before long, McHale strode into the room. He looked at the two men deep in conversation. "I'm sorry, gentlemen. We've got some weather, and they'll need the extra few minutes if we've got to shoot the approach."

Nieto stood quickly. His brown eyes reminded McHale of doomed animals in the rancher's feedlots. "Yes, of course. I understand."

Dearborn leaned back and watched out the window.

McHale extended his hand, thinking the man needed to hide his emotions better. "Thanks again for coming out here to meet me. I'm really pleased with your nomination, and I'll do everything I can on committee to see the process is swift and simple. I'm sure the votes are all there. Is there anything I can do for you, Your Honor?"

Nieto breathed in short, staccato mouthfuls. "No. You've done quite enough already."

"Excellent. Just excellent."

• • • •

A slender, lovely figure waved as the business jet stopped on its destination parking spot. A gust of cold desert wind whipped the onlookers.

McHale left out the air stairs and pulled his greeting party into an embrace.

Angie gently pushed him away. "Careful, gringo. Cameras are everywhere and I wouldn't want to make the grandmammas blush."

"I've missed you. A lot."

She laughed and held onto his forearms. "I can tell. Do you need my coat?"

She turned as Sylvia stepped down helped by the senator. "Mrs. Flores. I hope you're planning to spend the night at our home."

Angie saw the refusal rising. "Please. You and I can share all the dirt before this lazy bum is out of bed tomorrow morning."

Sylvia sighed gratefully. "Thank you, ma'am. That will save me a drive into Santa Clarita." She glanced at the people standing by the fence. "I'll wait in the car."

Angie turned to him "You've been gone too long. Again."

"The DC apartment is so lonely without you."

A hired non-descript Lincoln waited. No fanfare. This was home and he felt the weight of the east coast life lift from his shoulders.

He squeezed her hand. "We've lost some momentum with the inspector general's report that nailed IGT construction. They're just plain greedy. Doesn't Griswold realize there's plenty of work to go around?"

She turned with him for the fence and the ever-present cameras. "Does this take him off the list of approved contractors?"

He puffed out air. "A one-year penalty and he'll be back. I'd rather he'd never work for us again at any price, but this is up to the GAO. But I just don't like grifters."

She switched easily to Spanish. "And yet you work with them every day. You're a good man, Scott. I can help put the pressure on the committee for the last of this years' funding."

"That's really going to help. Sylvia and you can review and maybe we can avoid IGT's lawsuit. We need to finish strong so there's no holdup in committee."

"You were always a strong finisher, as I recall."

He laughed and relaxed back into English. "I hope that means what I think it means."

"You can find out tonight if you don't dawdle here too long." She squeezed and released his hand.

He waved to several waiting people. "Joy is at home, right? I want to hear all about the residency interview, but first I need to ..."

"Go, go. We'll talk about Joy later."

He kissed her cheek and headed into the small hometown crowd. Teague stood nearby, hands against his belt, jacket unzipped despite the chill.

A quarter of an hour later, Angie sat beside McHale in the Lincoln's backseat as they left the airport. Teague drove with Sylvia beside him. Both had the McHale's absolute trust.

Angie turned in her seat. "Joy is certain she aced the interview."

He grinned with pride. "I should hope so. She's got a half-dozen offers from some very prestigious—"

"Scott..." The warning tone stopped him.

"I'm just saying Georgetown or even Boston General might be better in the long run."

She lightly put her hand on his. "Undergrad and medical school in San Diego were full-ride scholarships. Joy knew we needed financial help then. She believes going somewhere else now would be disloyal."

McHale had lost this argument before, but he pursued it anyway. "I appreciate her attitude; I really do and there's nothing wrong with UCSD. But as a matter of record, the best jobs—"

"Might as well drop it. You lost this one before and she can be just as stubborn as you."

He looked out the window. "The least I can do is give Jim Robinson a call tomorrow ..."

"No, you won't. Not unless you'd like to feel the wrath of Joy. This is her decision, her pathway, and you, Senator McHale, are just an observer. Not a participant."

He pulled Angie close. "You should be the politician. You're much better at this than me."

"I'm not as pretty as you."

He turned and looked into her dark Hispanic eyes. "Now, that's just not true. Most guys just have to keep watch on their randy neighbors. The entire American male population wants to get you in the sack."

She laughed and jutted a chin forward. "Stop with the dirty talk."

They fell into a comfortable silence. The little town slept as traffic lights blinked yellow and red. The off-ramp rounded and turned up the valley, passing young orchards struggling in the desert.

"I love it here, Angie. DC's great and I like our Georgetown apartment, but my heart is here."

"This, I know. Everyone leaves but eventually comes home again. Just like you. Tell me, when you become president, will you have your library here, or in the San Joaquin nearer my family's farm?"

He turned to look at her in the shaded dark of the car. "Let's not get too far ahead of ourselves."

"I can read the papers. I know what they're saying about you. The national convention isn't far off and you're on the shortlist to give a speech."

"Right. At two o'clock in the morning."

She wasn't smiling now. "Maybe, but next time it'll be the keynote. Barack Obama gave the keynote in 2004 as a first-term senator and an unknown. He wowed the world, and you're twice the speaker he ever was. Plus, you're a war hero and a cop hero and a businessman—"

"Maybe, but we've got an internal challenge that could derail the dream. You know our party needs a minority female in this decade. I'll have to face Lora in the Senate primary next year. Even if I'm the incumbent, the party machine could make her unbeatable."

"Now you stop that. Lora Lu is a pretty photogenic little flake with a tree-hugger background and a weird campaign manager. She's riding a wave at the moment that won her Nancy Pelosi's old congressional seat, but you're the steady hand. Juliette and I have talked. We can find dirt when we need it."

He blinked away his surprise. "You ... you talked to Juliette about the presidential ticket?"

"Sure. And other things. Why not? You don't think for a moment you're in this alone, do you?"

The car's interior hid his face, and he was thankful. "I just didn't know you two were...you know, talking."

"I talk to lots of people, Scott. I must. Get your head on straight. How else would I know about Lu in the Bay Area? Don't forget California is as traditional as the rest of the country once you're away from the big cities. Juliette's been keeping an eye on Lora Lu for a long time now. Besides, with Joy as an established doctor, you and me with the Latino heritage, and your record? Ha. Lu can be beaten even without uncorking her past."

McHale watched the sleeping middle-class neighborhood. "I guess you've thought this all through."

She intertwined her fingers with his. "Of course, I have. Now's the time to find something to neutralize the new-face appeal. We don't want to lose her, because you'll need the Asian vote, and she might be useful in the future. We just need to slow her down a bit. Tap the brakes."

"If I'm slated for something later, she needs to be electable."

"Oh, Scott. Don't be naïve. In politics, everything can be taken back when you have the media on your side. And, right now, you do. We need a meeting with Lu to explain the facts of life. Sylvia can set it up for you and Juliette. They're friends. That should take the edge off a bit."

The Towncar turned in the drive. McHale and Angie waited as Teague popped the trunk and Sylvia made her way to the house.

McHale flipped through his mental calendar. "I'll call Juliette in the morning and have her set up a meeting with Lora Lu for Monday. I'll rent the Cessna 340 and fly to Hayward. Maybe, Wes can come with me."

She squeezed his hand as the trunk lid came down. "Keeping Big Jim in the loop is good thinking. See? You're getting the hang of this political stuff."

He let out a long breath without commenting on the desert night, his favorite distraction.

Angie watched him. "You okay, Scott?"

He grinned back. "Sure. Why not? I'm just beat."

They walked the flagstone curve several feet behind Teague. McHale didn't need Lora Lu's high jinks especially now and wished he'd never mentioned tamping down his own replacement. Wrangling the late-night convention spot in two years was tough and cost him plenty of political capital. Several committee members had been putting pressure on to join in a condemnation of the sitting president, but so far, he'd resisted.

Tomorrow. He would think about this tomorrow. For now, he only wanted a shower, a drink, and Angie.

• • • •

Several months later, Lora Lu, the former non-profit CEO and now current congresswoman from California's Twelfth District answered closed door questions from the Federal Trade Commission. A particularly robust breach of security had occurred, and the FBI's cybersecurity unit had conducted an audit. Revealed in the investigation were several stolen documents with both Chinese Communist and Lu's 501(c) fingerprints. The San Francisco media, unfriendly toward Lu broke the story. McHale immediately offered her a vigorous defense after mean-spirited speculation caused a national uproar. His presence on friendly media cameras and news shows soon put the matter to rest as simply more propaganda, misinformation, and sensationalism by political foes. The FBI quietly backed off.

Chapter 8

"You stink, Senator."

Sylvia did not look up from her Washington DC desk as deft fingers cut and pasted the obituary into McHale's iPad. A dozen other must-reads accompanied the death notice of a junior congressman's father-in-law. With an easy second-term senatorial win now under his belt, Sylvia kept her boss up to speed with the newsworthy tidbits of an established, serious lawmaker.

"I trust that's a reflection on my hygiene and not yesterday's floor speech."

She didn't look up. "Take it any way you like it. Former President George W ran every morning and never showed up in the office without a shower."

"Yes, ma'am. Sorry." McHale snatched the tablet and slipped through his office door and into the small bathroom. Thanks to his machinations, the primary threat from Lora Lu never materialized and he'd beaten the other party's candidate by a wide margin. His star rose even higher as the media looked more and more to Scott McHale for national leadership on the media issues of the day.

He waited for the water to run hot as he scanned the *Post*'s sports section. He didn't care about athletics but sometimes needed a conversation icebreaker. Juliette's power grid analysis from the West Coast appeared in a new PDF icon. He smiled and tossed the tablet onto the chair as he stepped into the shower.

McHale heard his outside office door open. Angie called out, "It's just me, Scott. I need a few minutes."

He answered. "Are you alone?"

"Yes...?"

"I can give you more than just a few minutes ... if you like."

He heard the door to the shower room open, and then close. The lock clicked. The rustle of cloth, and after a minute the shower door opened. Her dark hair was pulled behind the ears with a string of pearls her sole remaining attire.

"Oh, my goodness, Senator McHale. What do we have here? Were you expecting me or Mrs. Flores?"

He grinned and touched the soft skin around her breast. "I was sort of hoping for you. My God, you're more beautiful every day."

She stepped into the shower and for a few minutes, the world outside disappeared.

McHale dried second on the towel. By the time he walked out, she sat on the settee rolling a lipstick closed. A letter on White House stationery lay open on the coffee table.

He grinned. "Is that the invitation to lunch with the First Lady?"

She placed the cosmetics in her bag. "Yes."

"Not bad for the grandson and daughter of Chicano field hands."

"Language, dear. Latino, not Chicano. And my grandpa owns the pistachio farm. Someday, that will be ours as well."

McHale pulled at the tie's knot and settled onto the leather sofa. An electric fireplace filled one short wall with books on either side.

He pushed the White House envelope with a finger. "You're due, Angie. You know that. Who the hell else spends ten unpaid hours a day on the boards of directors for National Public Radio, the Red Cross, and Smithsonian, and then has time for the American Heart Association after dinner?"

She smiled at him.

He looked thoughtful. "But you know the real question is, how do we keep it going? I know it's better to be lucky than good–"

"Stop that, Scott. They love you, that's how you'll keep everyone looking at you. Don't give them anything they don't want." She straightened her skirt and leaned back. "You just need to pay attention to the polls and keep your eye on the presidential prize."

He smiled. "Never utter those words outside our walls. Not yet anyway. Naked ambition is not something the public appreciates."

She watched him closely. "This will soon be our time, Scott. I know it. They know it. All we have to do is convince you."

He chuckled. "I love you, babe. Screw the world. I just want to sit here with you."

A knock at the door, and McHale glanced at the Seth Thomas on the wall.

"And the world awaits." She stood and picked up the letter, opening the door to Sylvia Flores. "He's all yours until tonight, then he's mine again."

• • • •

At four a.m., the next morning, a yellow and black taxi stopped at the brick apartments. Cold pattering rain challenged a mist hanging in the bare branches. Angie touched his neck under an amber porch light. The glow of their lovemaking remained.

He kissed her gently. "Aren't you getting a little tired of all these trips?"

"Can't chair the Red Cross every day from Washington. Sometimes, you just have to do, what you have to do."

"I'd rather have you here with me."

"That's sweet, but it's only for two weeks. You'll be okay without me, right?"

"I'll miss you, but I heard there's two girls to every boy in DC."

"That's Surf City, and seventy years ago. Those guys are in retirement homes now." She pulled back, her lovely face serious in spite of the repartee. "You need to go back to bed. Skip the run today. Dark circles are growing under your beautiful eyes."

He kissed her lips. "You worry too much, Angie. Be careful in Minneapolis. It'll be cold for a Latina like you."

"Two blond boys for every girl, or so I hear."

They stood for a moment, cheek to warm cheek, and then she hurried down the steps.

McHale did not go back to bed. Instead, he turned on Fox, NBC, and the local CBS as more coffee brewed. He decided they'd need a larger place. A brownstone to hold a thirty-person cocktail party. Something with a back porch and a lawn. He'd put Mrs. Flores ... no, Juliette on it, first thing today. With a DC spring only a couple of months away, a housewarming with new leaves and short grass would be just the showcase he needed. The sessions' landmark legislation would soon be coming to the floor, and a patio should make the arm-twisting more pleasant.

He would need to invite the vice president, too. Reciprocate for the weekend's upcoming meeting. He wondered what the man would want with him, one of the opposition's most vocal critics of the current administration. McHale would have refused the invitation except Mrs. Flores left a note saying the VP asked him to come an hour early for a private meeting.

He wondered. Time to check out the competition.

Chapter 9

Scott

On the third Saturday night following his meeting with the vice president, McHale adjusted the tie on his tux and smiled down at his phone.

Snapchat, the untraceable text service, vibrated. A scribbled note read: *Being stupid cost Ted Kennedy. Drop Earth First.*

He chuckled and glanced at Wes Teague, his chief of staff, downloading his speech into the teleprompter. But the man did not look up. He also had no sense of humor.

The message disappeared. The writing was unfamiliar, maybe Juliette's.

He sighed and would try to remember to skip the line in his speech. Maybe. After all this time, he wondered why Dearborn did not just accept the fact he liked notes, not prepared statements. The speech he had sent to California for review included the VP's suggestions, and then, came back with so many strikeouts, McHale never finished reading. He expected Teague to tattle and decided he could live with the rebukes.

An hour later, the dinner crowd clapped at his introduction. For five minutes, he rambled through pleasant DC claptrap and a few jokes while dishes clattered, and people settled down. He arrived at his moment and covered the podium-mounted prompter screen with a sheet of paper.

"I'd like to switch gears a bit and address our power crisis."

He gripped both sides of the podium, capturing the room's attention.

"What, you say? We don't have a crisis. Sorry, but we do. As I look around the room, every person here will still be here, God willing, in 2030s. Why is the year important? Because in the not-so-distant future, forty of our ninety-nine nuclear reactors will be history. Forty.

"Did you know thirty percent of all our electricity comes from those ninety-nine reactors? That leaves us with seventy percent, right? So, what's the big deal? Add the remaining nukes to our wind and solar, and there isn't a crisis. Green is good, I grant you. Of course, nuclear power doesn't stop giving if the wind doesn't blow or the winter days are cloudy. And it is there without checking the tide tables. With apologies to my brethren a hundred miles to the west, there is no coal smoke, either. With a flip of a switch, nuclear power is available more than ninety-nine percent of the time. It is cheap and reliable, and safe, and we didn't drop nine billion dollars a year to subsidize nuclear power like we did the wind. Take note. Nine billion is one heck of a lot of money, even in DC."

Several people laughed. McHale smiled but did not join in.

"Right now, the world's leading academics, as well as many Americans say climate change is the biggest threat we face, and we humans are responsible. I'm not here to argue science, but even if only a little bit is true, I'd like to point out nuclear power provides sixty percent of our country's carbon-free electricity.

"Right now, Arizona's Deer Creek Complex or as it's known in legislation, the Western Central Grid, is stopped dead in its tracks. Why? Not because of danger. No person in this country has ever been seriously injured in a nuclear accident. Yucca Mountain is certified to take the waste and will be open for the next one hundred thousand years. That's a long time."

McHale stopped and smiled at the audience.

"Heck, that's even longer than Senator Ripley is old."

Laughter at the expense of McHale's archrival from Vermont rolled across the room.

He held up his hand and smiled. "I like Don Ripley, so don't get me wrong. He's not here to defend himself, so I won't take any more cheap shots. Besides, we have a great relationship, and I love arguing with him. I state the facts, and he reads me a bedtime story."

More laughter.

McHale couldn't help himself and glanced at Teague. The man proved as unreadable as ever. "Let me give you more facts ..."

For twenty minutes, McHale recited from memory, then closed the speech book he'd never used.

"In less than ten years, the United Arab Emirates surpassed the US in energy production and now sells to its neighbors. They're using our proven technology, and our American companies with our safety standards. *What is wrong with us?*"

Two hundred pairs of eyes riveted on him. A camera clicked. Teague kept his gaze down and on his iPad.

"I've talked too long. Let me wrap this up by saying we guarantee our future by finishing the last reactors at the Western Central Grid. If we don't, we're in trouble. America is great because we are a nation of entrepreneurs. Let's fuel free-market innovation with cheap power and support commercial energy diversity. Progress and the health of our planet are not and have never been mutually exclusive concepts."

He finished with platitudes designed to gentle bruised egos and soothe wounds as he tuned out the applause. Teague shut off the recording app. The consummate politician, McHale then waded into the crowd and shook hands for another half hour.

"Can I walk with you, Scott?" Twila Crawford stood near the exit doors with her hand extended, blocking his retreat. Northern California's tall, lovely representative took his elbow and walked beside him as he gathered his coat. She leaned close, her long brunette hair brushing his cheek. "Our mutual friend asks you to call him this evening. Your cell phone is apparently not working."

McHale understood why Twila stopped conversations whenever she walked into a room. She was breathtaking. "I turn it off when I'm talking with folks."

Her large eyes twinkled. "Interesting idea, Senator. Do you think it'll catch on? And yet, he still wants to talk to you."

On this night, she wore a dark blue cocktail dress showing off long legs in high stiletto pumps and a deep dip over intriguing breasts. A solitaire diamond necklace topped the ensemble and drew one's eyes.

McHale sighed and wondered if he had underestimated the blowback. "I get it. Big Jim doesn't want me out front on the WCG again, but he's not right on this one. You've got to get the appropriation bill out of committee, Twila. You and I both know that piece needs to come to the floor for a vote."

"Yes, we do. And the plan is that I'll carry the water and take the criticism from my tree huggers. I can stand the heat. You can't."

"I know, and I appreciate it." He found it difficult to let go of the project after so many years as front man.

He helped with her light jacket.

She turned to him. "So, why haven't you? Don't you trust me?"

"Of course, I trust you. There's more to this than just making electricity. We need to forget the new aircraft carrier the Navy wants and use the money to replace our power grid with equipment *not* installed by Thomas Edison."

Twila smiled. "You might want to talk this out with Jimmy. He doesn't make his decisions based on right and wrong. He makes them with a plan in mind. That plan includes you."

She drew close and touched his forearm. He could smell the sweet aroma of her perfume.

"He a chess master, Scott. The move we see today may cost him his Queen, but in the end, he's still got a King and the game. The pawn you knocked over tonight means you don't trust him. I'm telling you he doesn't make mistakes, and he's watching you and the next few years. You have to be careful about the two of us. This is our future you're messing with."

McHale's frustration grew. "And what of right and truth? Doesn't that count for something? I feel like his mouthy little puppet, sitting on committee, having my strings pulled and watching the words fall out of my mouth."

Twila offered her most appealing smile. "Down, boy. We don't disagree. You've got to get your head straight and listen to Jimmy. Bigger issues are at stake. Like tonight. Did you read the text?"

He watched her in silence.

"I thought so. I'm just passing on what Jimmy's telling us. You're the shining star, Scott. You're going to go national, but you've got to listen when he talks."

For a moment, he debated telling Twila much of tonight's speech came from the opposition party and the VP. Instead, he would let it go and take the heat. And why did she call Big Jim – Jimmy?

"He's waiting on your call."

"Thanks. Sometimes, I get wrapped a little tight about people piddling on our future."

Twila smiled and patted his arm. "You're important to everyone's future. You've got to be smart and hold on to your friends, new and old."

She walked away, heels tapping the travertine, her body fitting well the curve of the evening dress. He stopped at the bar, asked for a double bourbon, then moved to a hotel alcove.

Dearborn answered and did not bother with McHale's explanation. "Listen, Scotty. We've got bigger fish to fry right now. I don't care about Twila's bill or getting the WCG moving again, because it's DOA for this term. We killed it a week ago, so all that crap you spouted tonight was for nothing."

The VP thought otherwise. "You killed it? Why?"

Dearborn did not like answering questions. "The bill had riders. Fifteen billion over five years was the right number, but not when you dilute it with other people's crapola. We'll have this thing in our hip pocket in the fall. You can't do it. Especially if you're all alone out there."

McHale heard the threat and said nothing.

"With the right bill and two houses, it won't matter what the VP told you, the president will sign. Got it?"

McHale gulped his drink and signaled for another. "I'm hearing you."

"Good, 'because you don't do enough of that."

"I need time to think this through—" The waiter picked up his empty glass.

Dearborn countered quickly. "No, you don't. The money will be there once the budget passes. Now, I got Vegas to deal with."

The phone clicked.

McHale fought down his anger. How the hell did he know about the VP's words in the talk tonight? And what the hell was Las Vegas, anyway?

He glanced at the new glass placed before him and dropped two twenties on the bar grabbing his keys off the kiosk shelf.

A moment later he stood under a low sky reflecting the distant city's glow. Two after-dinner mints sat in his coat pocket. If the police stopped him, they would not smell the liquor. His Senate ID card lay tucked next to his driver's license if he needed preferential treatment ... just in case. The three-year-old Buick purred as he drove slowly toward the freeway onramp.

A white four-door Ford sedan started and traced McHale's route a half-mile behind. Nearly alone on Interstate 66, he glanced in the rearview mirror at the lone pair of headlights. Setting the cruise control at fifty-seven, he moved into the right lane and concentrated on staying between the white lines.

At the next ramp, he signaled a turn for Tyson Corners and pulled into a hotel parking lot. A sleepy attendant snapped to attention and stepped to his door.

"Evening sir. Staying with us? Shall I get your luggage?"

"Give me a moment, will you?"

McHale leaned on the window and into the shadows of the portico. He hit his autodial. Thirty minutes from home. Damn those headlights. He watched as a late-night traveler pulled into the lot.

A soft tone rang. "Angie?"

"Scott? What time is it?"

"Late. Eleven-thirty. Twelve."

"Where are you?"

He took a deep breath. "The Westin off 66. Tee— too many martinis, I'm afraid."

"Are you in trouble?"

"No, no sweetheart. I pulled off the interstate. Getting caught would be a pretty miserable mistake." He touched the down window button to breathe cold air. "Sorry, babe."

Angie spoke quickly. "I'll be there in a half hour. You did the right thing. You're probably not as bad as you think."

"So, I should come home?"

"Absolutely not. I'll be there. And don't drink coffee. You'll just be wide awake and probably get frisky."

They both laughed, but the mirth fell away.

She said, "You remember I've got a nine a.m. out of Dulles. I'm heading home tomorrow. Doctor Joy's birthday." The silence told the truth. "No worries. I'm on the way."

"Geezus. Things are ... so busy." He trailed off thinking he had missed too many birthdays. Days flew by he could never get back.

Angie spoke. "Is there something else?"

"No, no." He thought of Dearborn, but pictured Twila in the lobby walking away. "Just feeling sorry for myself. Go figure. The *Times* this morning called me and you the New Camelot. I think the moniker is going to stick. Can you believe it?"

"No, I do not, and neither should you. Don't let them pander or it'll never stop until they find some dirt. I'll be there as quick as I can."

He sighed "Okay. Bring a bottle of champagne for my pity party. Woe is me." He paused. "Listen, Angie. Instead of a cab in the morning I can drive you to the airport."

"I'll do you one better. My suitcase is packed now. I'll call a cab, so you can drop me and go to the office. I'll bring you a change of clothes. Get us a room and *don't* drive."

He said goodbye and punched the phone's button. Mist dappled the windshield into patterns of reflected security light. A quick click and the engine died as he leaned against the headrest. His heart always swelled when Angie pulled together a solution. The guilt at his errant thoughts of Twila twisted a knife in the same heart.

The next thing he knew, someone tapped at the glass. He turned the key and let the window down.

"Got a date, sailor?" Angie smiled.

Across the parking lot, the white Ford's headlights came on and Twila drove for the freeway.

• • • •

The sun warmed McHale's steering wheel even though the day stayed cool. Angie had been gone nearly a week now, and he wasn't sleeping well.

His mobile rang through the Buick's system as the big engine accelerated from the light.

"Hello?"

"Scotty?" Dearborn's voice boomed inside the car. "I just told Sylvia to pass me your research from last week's speech. She told me to call you. What the hell's with that? Did she forget where her bread's buttered?"

"Morning Big Jim. It's early in California. Can't sleep?"

The man ignored the question. "Are you going to tell Sylvia or not? You'll get to take credit later, if need be, but I'm resurrecting Lora Lu, so we need to get her up to speed."

His antennae immediately rose. "What for?"

"Jesus Christ!" The iPhone over modulated with the angry volume. "Your damn speech from last week if you can call it that. I made crystal goddamn clear then I wanted you to concentrate on other things. I know the idiot VP gave you a nuke to drop on the environmental crap."

McHale held his temper. "Fine. I still want to be on the sponsor—"

"No."

McHale felt the anger work its way into his neck. "Listen—"

"No, you listen, god damn it. This is nickels and dimes. Lu will be able to use your stuff to dig herself out of the hole from a couple of years ago with the Feds. The environmentalists already think they love her. They need to really love her like they love Twila. Do we have a communication problem here?"

Dearborn didn't wait for the answer. "I hope like hell I'm getting through."

McHale smiled. He would need this marker one day but was not about to make it too easy. "This will be a very delicate thing, Big Jim. I spoke off the cuff and used some of the White House's stats."

"Yeah, yeah, so I heard. You wouldn't have this problem if you'd say what you write, instead of making it up as you go."

McHale did not give him the satisfaction. "I'll need to walk a fine line here ...."

"You do that better than most." The accusation was not meant to be kind or complimentary.

McHale signaled a turn. "What else can I do for you?"

Big Jim blew a breath into the phone "Oh, for Christ's sake. Don't get your panties in a bunch. You'll get honorable mention somewhere down the road, and hell, if it works out, you might even get bragging rights for mentoring a bright new up-and-comer party faithful."

McHale had heard all this before.

"By the way, Scotty. You're aware the chairman's going to make his decision on the keynote speech ...sub rosa, of course."

The speech to end all political speeches.

Scott spoke up and into the car's microphone. "That's quite a plum this time. Good ol' Senator Swanson from the Big Apple's really stirring them up in the hinterlands. He sounds good, like he can unseat Pruitt. My convention speech last time was at eleven p.m. ... Pacific Time. Prime time for late night comedians in California. A shit timeslot, Big Jim."

"That was experience, and you did good on the podium. Even those assholes at Fox played a clip. Look, Scotty. I'm sorry if I'm being tough on you. I've been up half the night kissing rings. You're in by the way."

Silence.

"Did you hear me? I said you got the convention's keynote next year in August."

McHale half coughed; half exclaimed. "Holy shit! That's great."

The light changed. He didn't move. A driver honked.

Dearborn roared with laughter. "You better believe it's great. I spent every goddamn favor in my back pocket for this. And you want to fight me over the VP's research?"

"What research?"

Dearborn snorted. "Okay, Scotty. That's what I wanted to hear. You got sixteen months to work on this speech and stay out of trouble."

"I hear you, Big Jim."

"If those Chicago boys can get an unknown neighborhood organizer with a name like Barack Hussein Obama elected President of the United States right in the middle of a god damn war with the towelheads, a Latino named Scotty McHale will be a breeze."

The line went dead. McHale pulled the Buick behind a massive, high cube truck double-parked and delivering on 6th Street. He looked at the food supplier's logo without seeing. Horns honked. He ignored them, too. His mind twirled in the land of dizzy, recalling the glitz and pageantry of last cycle's national convention. All of a sudden, an eventual presidency did not seem so far away.

The phone buzzed again. Big Jim continued as if he had not hung up. "I'm sending Wes over to you this week with my list. You need to listen closely because there's some syncing you and I need to do. No mistakes this time."

Dearborn began to rattle instructions. McHale wasn't curious about the list. Pruitt, the other party's first-term incumbent president, and his pandering VP, trailed Senator Swanson in the national polls. Too bad because Swanson had a lot of big city baggage from New York the party tried to ignore. Big Jim knew where all the bodies were buried and even though McHale wasn't privy to his plans, knew the party elite would not hold back. With McHale's squeaky-clean record, they might even draft him without having to be a primary debate target. Instead of waiting four years like Obama, he could sweep by Swanson and his machine from New York. Pushback from other candidates, and the fact the West Coast did not particularly like the ex-NYC mayor, gave him, Scott McHale, the eminently likable dark horse, a chance.

As the senator, he could head up the California delegation and push for a favorite-son nomination. He needed to have lunch with the Florida senator, Swanson's prime rival and a great VP choice. Could he step into the convention without the deals and promises everyone else made? Maybe. Except to Dearborn, of course.

"Are you still there, for Christ's sake?"

"I'm here, Big Jim."

"Good. It's pretty important you take this to heart. You've got a real shot here, Scotty. A chance to shine. The dos and don'ts will mean everything in the next year. Sometimes you only get one opportunity, like Romney. You got to be ready to step up and take it. I've got you scheduled for every goddamn meeting and confab with every group with a special interest in the county. You'll be talking to cops, Jews, evangelicals, blacks, and Muslims. I've also got some major hands-across-the-aisle stuff to make you look like the Boy Scout you are. The PM in the UK and Israel are going to host ..."

"How do you know these people?" McHale interrupted feeling out of breath.

"Because I do. Who the hell cares? That's how all this works, but you got to listen to me."

"I'm listening."

"Good. By the time I get done, people will think they've known you all their lives. We don't want people to see you for the first time in August at the keynote. We want them asking why the hell you're not the one on the ballot. You got it?"

"Yes. Got it."

"By the time Angie walks across the convention stage and gives you a big kiss, everyone's got to be wet and trembling."

"Wait a second. Angie? That's reserved for candidates."

"Exactly. And no one except the dipshits will miss the inference. Especially Swanson, so for now, steer clear of that bottom feeder."

McHale sucked in a deep breath.

"After Angie does her thing, you're going to have them talking and comparing you to Swanson and the rest of the field in every backroom there. That pompous prick doesn't stand a chance. You're the new prince of Camelot. The Washington Post said so. The first ballot's guaranteed to be deadlocked. The right people will be saying your name in Miami and it's going to spread like wildfire. Are you starting to catch my drift here, Scotty? President, not just the keynote, and not VP to the Florida guy. This is a West Coast steal."

"Yes, sir."

"Good, 'cause the excitement is going to make this convention look like Harding in 1920 and Carter in '76. Only bigger. Delegates will be released and looking for a hero." He paused. "Guess who they're going to choose? So now do you understand why you must start listening?"

No words came to McHale's dry mouth. Someone honked again, and he waved them around. Workers glanced his way.

"Well, ye-haw, folks, I finally found a way to shut you up. Now, I'm going to the major news outlets. Today is the first day of you moving your ass out of obscurity and into the daylight. Stand by and keep your mouth shut until I say so. Don't go having sidebars with senators from Florida, got me?"

• • • •

McHale stood in the office fifteen minutes later, grinning, excitement oozing. "Do we have any coffee made? God, I'm ready to take on the world."

Sylvia smiled back. "I can see that. And yes. The pot's been on for an hour." She eyed her boss. "Did you catch the canary this morning, Senator?"

He wanted to hug her and spin around the office. Of course, he didn't, but instead put his briefcase on the table and straightened his tie. "No canaries, Mrs. Flores. But could you see if Mrs. McHale is in her hotel? I need to speak with her before the Red Cross meeting, if I can."

"Yes, sir. Do you recall Juliette Pearson will be joining our group next week?"

The San Francisco office manager. He had let it slip from his mind. "That's great. Thanks for the reminder."

"And you also have a meeting with Twila Crawford this morning."

The air seeped from his balloon. "Twila, right. Eleven?"

"Ten. And William Brannigan from Lockheed Martin Aircraft is waiting."

He snapped his fingers. "Ah, that one, I remembered." He pushed open his door. "Bill. Great to see you! How's the family?"

• • • •

The following Saturday morning, McHale put away his reading and woke Angie. They made love and lay together as the morning light traced its way through the blinds. She dozed, until his fingers worked their way across the bed.

Angie slapped and rolled away with a laugh. "Doesn't *middle aged man* mean anything to you?"

"I can work on that image."

"Shower and quick."

They drove her Camry to Front Royal Airport where his Cessna 180 four-seater sat fueled on the black tarmac. The windless blue sky promised a good day to fly. After a quick preflight and takeoff, the high-wing single engine airplane climbed and turned southwest. Buried in the half-million acres of the dense Nantahala National Forest and tucked away in a corner of North Carolina, the little village of Murphy hid from most of the world.

The town was home to Hal and Marge Burckhardt, California transplants and Angie's friends from her Bakersfield High School days. The couple owned the Sunrise Bed and Breakfast and for three days, Scott and Angie walked the Appalachian Trail talking and planning, dreaming of a far different future than most. During the evenings, a drink on the back porch in the mountain air made them all but forget about Big Jim Dearborn.

• • • •

McHale spent the next two weeks writing his Keynote speech between meetings. On the Friday before a three-day weekend, Twila Crawford called for an appointment. He hurried from the Senate Judiciary Committee meeting.

"I'm running late, Twila. Sorry." He pulled open the office door. "Please, sit. Iced tea?"

She nodded and crossed slim ankles while he filled glasses from a small refrigerator. At nearly six feet and with sculpted muscles, her presence, whether in the congressional gym or the floor of the House, made her a considerable force.

She took a taste. "I got a call from Wes before he headed to Mexico."

McHale leaned back and swallowed before returning the glass to the coaster.

This was news to him. "Deer Creek and the Western Central Grid, I hope."

She had paid particular attention to her makeup with a deep red gloss accentuating her lips. A sign she expected an interview outside the chambers.

"Yes, from Deer Creek. But the funding will come out of the omnibus bill this fall. No one can know until it's a done deal. There'll be enough money to test reactors number five and six and bring two and three online full time. But not number four."

He reacted. "Why not? Isn't that the one that overlays Texas?"

"It is, but Big Jim has a schedule. He doesn't want the surprise he's planning for President Pruitt until it's due."

"Does this mean we'll start on seven and eight?"

"Patience says Big Jim. There's money, but I need a couple of hundred million first." She looked up, her wide gray eyes humorless. "And it's your fault."

"What do you mean?"

Her voice carried an edge. "Oh, I don't know. Maybe what you said last year? Like, 'The dams north of Marin County are dead. They just don't know it yet.' I've been whittling that down for months. What a thing to say, Scott."

"I said it was putting the cart before the horse. We're killing energy output, and *still* we haven't brought on a fraction of WCG's potential. What's the big rush with bringing these dams down anyway? Where the hell is the power for electric vehicles going to come from?"

"Western Central Grid wasn't the only thing you talked about."

He grinned. "I might've referred to some pork, but that's just jabbing Swanson. He's a big boy. He can take it."

She didn't return the smile.

He grew serious. "Look, Twila. I understand the environmentalist thing and Lora Lu's rise, but you tell me why speed is all of a sudden so important. Do you and Jane Fonda have inside information on a coming earthquake or something?"

Twila's face remained deadpan. "Or something."

He leaned back silently watching her over his glass.

"I'm sensing some resistance here, Scott. Jimmy said you'd be onboard."

"Onboard, yes. Brain dead, no. I've got to live with all these promises."

Twila leaned forward. "You know, Senator, much of this is already written in stone, but not everything. You're the architect of the Western Central Grid. I'm just the pen and the money. Lots of little things will come my way, like Jimmy loves to say. I'm going to make some important friends. They'll become your friends, too. Just remember electricity is the new gold. Everything in the future requires clean energy. The climate nazis be damned. You need to remember that and open a bank account."

She smoothed her skirt across muscled thighs, fingertips sensing then creasing the material under his gaze.

He glanced out the window. A view of the Mall might be his someday if he could swallow his pride and get in step. "I will sponsor, endorse, and encourage my senatorial colleagues to support the House's WCG ... omnibus measure."

For a moment, McHale thought he saw a flicker in Twila's unreadable face.

She looked up from her leather satchel. "Good. You understand we'll coordinate our moves and our utterances. Like Jimmy says. No missteps now."

McHale nodded.

"This is good for me, too, make no mistake. I'll be running essentially unopposed next election. Lora has a lock if we need her. Your endorsement will cement my place with the House Finance Committee."

"Then, my seat?"

Her eyes held his. "Your job would be nice, I suppose, but Jimmy won't talk about it. Maybe a low-level position in your cabinet one day, but don't cry for me. Tom and I are getting what I want."

McHale wasn't about to cry. He did wonder though. She rarely mentioned her college professor husband.

"Jimmy wants it this way, and what he wants, he gets. You understand, right?"

He said nothing.

Chapter 10

Scott

"Senator?" Juliette stood in the doorway to the large office. "This came for you in the FedEx. And I've got those NRC notes."

She held a manila folder and a flash drive.

"Hi. Come on in. Just finishing." He accepted the folder and slipped the drive from Dearborn into his top desk drawer.

He looked at the Nuclear Regulation Committee meeting notes. "This is good stuff. Did you do the summary?"

"Yes, it wasn't hard. I have a new friend on the staff."

"Oh?"

"Yeah. He's a little young but I think he likes me."

"You're well versed in nuclear power?"

She nodded and looked at another folder of papers. "Sorry about Mr. Teague, sir, but as far as I know, he went to Cabo for some R&R. A long weekend."

Wes had returned from Mexico but been tight lipped about who he met and what he did. McHale had asked Juliette to learn what she could.

He leaned back and smiled her way. "Okay, thanks. No big deal."

McHale discovered to his surprise most women in the DC Mixmaster seemed to resent Juliette. He thought she must make wives suspicious, and their husbands think of beach parties. Blond and lovely in the special,

California-tanned way, she had grown up in politics, especially McHale politics. She had been with the team since nearly the beginning of his congressional career.

It was funny though, but just lately, she seemed to have come into her own in DC. She had always been attractive. Now he noticed she was confident, and poised, and turned heads wherever she went. Sometimes when she accompanied him to a committee or another meeting, he felt a twinge at the stares of others in the corridors. Paternal protectiveness, he reasoned. He was responsible for her and yet after only two months in DC, she knew the ropes and the pitfalls as well as anyone. Sylvia Flores and Angie were notable exceptions to other skeptical women.

"Are you interested in attending the National Academy graduation dinner? Theo Haines will walk the stage tonight and Angie's still in LA." He loosened the knot in his tie. The afternoon rush of traffic to leave DC would start in an hour. "You'll face having to eat dinner with three hundred horny cops a couple of months away from home, but I'll be there to safeguard you."

"Three hundred cops sound okay. Toss in my boss giving a stump speech, and I'm not so sure."

McHale grinned. "Oh, hurt me."

"I don't know, Senator. They'll be expecting Angie. I'll disappoint them."

"Nah, you'll be okay. Ken and Anne Marie Litton will be there. So, what do you say? The Hostage Rescue Team and rubber chicken?"

"I like the HRT, and I'll try the chicken, but I will *never* marry a politician."

"Good thought, but please don't tell Angie."

She headed for the door as he had another thought. "I'd appreciate it if you stayed close to your source on the NRC. That could be important for us."

"Yes, sir."

Marine Corps Base Quantico sprawled over a hundred thousand acres near the giant Virginia-Maryland curve in the Potomac River. Home to twenty thousand Marines and their families, the main base hosted a small airfield and the presidential helicopter fleet. The FBI built a training enclave in a remote part of the base fifty years ago, expanding into buildings, shooting ranges, classrooms, and gyms. A city-block replica of the Chicago street where John Dillinger died served to train agents and conduct the Bureau's local business. The tan brick, multistoried complex of over twenty structures connected with enclosed glass walkways and had become known to insiders as the gerbil palace. A person could enter through the admin offices and need not feel outside air for months except on the pistol range or the track.

The pool car dropped McHale and Juliette at a wire enclosure near the periphery of the compound. The squat buildings and helicopter hangar served as home to the FBI's famous Hostage Rescue Team. Senator McHale, a frequent visitor to the team and the Academy, was promptly forgotten when Juliette stepped out of the car.

"We use paintball gun technology but fired from very real Glock and MP-10 sub machine guns." The commander, Dick Robillard, stood erect and trim and enjoyed showing off the team's abilities. "Our agents use ballistic helmets, face shields, and vests but the rounds still sting like the dickens if you're hit."

They climbed a human maze to overhead, raised catwalks, from where they could watch agents silently round corners and clear interior rooms. Nearby, other agents, playing terrorists, waited and listened. The "bad guys" would shoot the hostages at the first sign of an attack. One look at the seriousness on both sides had onlookers holding their breaths.

Silent close-quarter battle lines drew together. A "terrorist" agent's face shield suddenly exploded with pink paint from a silenced weapon. A second "terrorist" shouted and ran for the room holding the blindfolded manikins. More fluorescent pink paint exploded on his back. He sat down to wait. A hidden "terrorist" sprayed down the hallways and doors. Everyone played for real, neither side giving up territory. Agents moved as another bad guy dropped. Handcuffs and a pat down. A terrorist sprang from a closet and fired twice. He dropped when hit by return fire but not before a single, glancing "bullet" scuffed an assaulter's boot.

Juliette drew her first breath in several minutes. "Oh my God."

Robillard did not smile. "This isn't over yet."

A helicopter suddenly roared mere feet over their heads giving her a start. Hurricane-force winds beat down the assault team and the observers. Ropes from either side of the cabin dropped and the team hooked up. Two men clipped the "injured" man and the combatant onto the chests of other members. With the wave of an arm, the helicopter lifted eight dangling bodies hundreds of feet into the air, then nosed over and flew away. Men trailed behind like puppets on strings. From the assault's inception to the helicopter's diminishing rotor noise, less than five minutes had elapsed.

McHale watched the helicopter escape low over the treetops, the dangling bodies quickly out of harm's way. A thrill ran up his neck, the recollection of missions like this with him at the controls, a young national guardsman deployed in the dangerous mountains of Afghanistan. This was why he loved to come and hangout with the HRT operators and their pilots.

The commander stepped up. "Our initial brief said we were deep in enemy territory and the hostages were being held in a captured hi-rise apartment building."

McHale failed to keep his knowing smile neutral. "You took terrorists, right? High value, or a leader?"

The commander answered with clipped words. "Yes, sir. That's exactly right."

McHale glanced over the other's shoulder at a grinning Ken Litton. "I'm impressed, Dick. Wonderful job, as always. Thank you. Can you and your men join us in the Boardroom for a debrief?"

"Sorry, sir. Work to do."

A disappointed McHale maintained an even expression. "Sure. No problem." He then spent the next twenty minutes shaking hands and talking with the team as he made his way to the car.

A quick tour of the Academy ended at the theater and the graduates to-be. McHale again spent time mingling. Across the room, he spotted an old friend.

Theo Haines claimed he was the last sheriff of the last "rootin' tootin', real goddamn western stretch of land in the United States." That's how the Pima County lawman described it whenever he got the chance. Twenty years ago, he was the Muroc County dispatcher on duty the night McHale lay dying on a stretch of lonely California desert highway. A few years later, Haines took the call when Marvin Engels died in the backseat of McHale's Explorer.

Since then, at six foot four and nearly two hundred and fifty pounds, Theo Haines had worked his way through the ranks of the Pima County Arizona sheriff's office. An innovator with friends in high places, he drove tipsy wives of local banker's home, then called in the favor when the department needed new bulletproof vests. He also reserved a space as the first man through the door with a shotgun when raiding a meth lab. When the media and photographers arrived at high-profile crime scenes, Theo Haines stood in front, giving praise to the men and women who brought criminals to justice. Of course, his men also warned new recruits never, ever to get between the sheriff and a camera.

When the ceremonies got underway, Haines opened his commencement speech with a ten-minute recounting of the night McHale lay dying. No one breathed as he retold the story of a lone patrol car racing at over a hundred and twenty miles an hour to beat the last minutes of the golden hour of life.

Haines turned to the senior FBI Section Chief. "Stand up, Ken. Let these guys get a look at you."

Litton shook a finger at Haines and stood.

Haines dismissed Litton's growl with a good-natured wave. "Yeah, yeah. You told me not to say anything embarrassing. You should've known that'd never happen. Besides, this is *my* graduation. You got to give me some love. You too, Scott...Senator. Please stand up." Several hundred people laughed and clapped for the hero who saved the life of a young police officer, and the one saved who became a United States senator.

Haines led the hand clapping. "That was a tough call to make, and some mighty fine driving. Of course, we had to scrap the patrol car afterwards, and fire them both."

Laughter.

"Fortunately, we found Ken another job. The FBI said they'd hire him, and we ain't taking him back." Polite hoots from the police graduates. "If you buy me a beer tonight, I'll tell you how Ken shared some space in the emergency room himself that night." He grinned at the big FBI agent. More laughter.

Haines grew serious. "Sometimes the fates smile on us even when we don't deserve it." He turned and looked at McHale. "Every once in a blue moon, the right man steps up and is willing to give of himself in the fight for a nation. He bares his chest and takes all the arrows meant for us. These are the real heroes. Thank God, we all got lucky that night and we got to keep ours." He smiled at Litton. "Thank you, Ken, for saving Scott."

When the clapping ceased, Haines drew himself up. "Our cartel enemies dealt not in drugs, but power and money. They don't care how they get it—guns, explosives, people, vice—it doesn't matter. Make no mistake, this country is nothing more than a cash cow to the cartel and the criminal profiteers living among us ..."

• • • •

Later that evening after the official function, a relaxed and informal class and guests sat at the FBI Academy's Boardroom. McHale and Haines accepted two longneck beers standing in the near-empty bar.

"Hell of a speech, Theo. Looking for a job in Washington?"

Perpetually baby-faced and with a slick, pink head, Haines laughed. "You've got enough blowhards in DC without me. Present company excepted, of course."

McHale laughed. "Oh sure. Thanks, so much."

Haines hiked a cowboy boot onto the foot rail and smoothed a large mustache. "I'm really glad you could make it. I wanted to know how the plan is coming to finish up the WCG in Deer Creek. We're actually having some brownouts down in little ol' Pima County. El Paso and Amarillo both had downright failures. Cooked two old substations. You could get a lot of pressure off of me with some cash to replace those things."

"Time, my friend. We need more time to work the bill." Scott thumbnailed an inch of beer bottle label and said no more.

Haines got the message. "Come on. Let's sit."

They moved to a table. McHale glanced at Juliette, in conversation with Ken and Anne Marie Litton and several National Academy graduates. Juliette sparkled as the center of attention.

Haines followed McHale's gaze. "I'll help you rescue her in a few minutes. First, we need to talk."

They took a table near a wall-sized window with a black forest beyond.

Haines's good humor disappeared. "You still pushing on this single-point failure of our electrical grid, right?"

"Not working for the newspapers, are you?"

Haines harrumphed at his friend's caution.

McHale nodded. "I'm still in favor, sure. But the legislation's been tied to dam reclamation in two dozen states on both coasts. That's slowing it down to a snail darter's pace."

Haines ignored the attempt at environmental humor. "Good, because you're not the right guy to carry the message. No offense, but maybe the lady from up north is better suited. The law's going to piss off lots of people all over the country. The progressives and tree-huggers will be looking to jam it up someone's behind. Doesn't match their commitment to solar and wind power."

"I'm reminded of my shortcomings every day, Theo. My colleagues dance around it, and Big Jim Dearborn has a radar in my bedroom. If I dream about the WCG, he's texting me before I can get out of bed."

Haines snorted. "That guy gives me a pain in my ass, but in this case, he's right."

As a Marine with two Purple Hearts from Fallujah, Haines had clashed more than once with Big Jim. "Listen, Scott. This bill is going to be part of a much bigger plan. I don't always agree with that guy, but in this case, you best listen."

"What have you heard? What am I missing here?"

The big man wiped at his smooth head. "I was talking to Wesley Teague on Sunday. He came out and watched us shoot our qualification course. We only had ten minutes because of my makeup constitutional law class, but he made a strong case. He told me to keep it to myself but screw him. He's a water boy and I wanted you to know."

"Thanks, but know what? Why'd he come way out here to talk? He owns a phone."

Haines clenched his jaw. "Yeah, well, maybe it means more when the guy looks you in the eye and calls in a favor."

McHale was confused. Teague might be his chief of staff, but he still worked for Dearborn. "Hold on. You're telling me that Big Jim's calling in a favor to convince me to drop my funding work?"

Haines worked the muscles in his jaw. "That's what this boils down to. He wants me to make sure you drop it. I guess you aren't playing nice. You're using your own goddamn mind to make decisions. What a novel thought."

The big sheriff leaned back and exhaled to the ceiling before continuing. "Shit. I don't like using friendships like this. I don't have the whole story, Scott. I listened to Teague, and he made sense. You've got some big opportunities coming your way, or so I hear, and frankly, this country needs you. Coming down hard on the side of common sense, before the voters get there, will stop you dead. Teague, and I guess Dearborn, could be looking out for your best interests. Shit, I don't know. I'm just sayin'. They could have me fooled, dead to rights."

McHale looked surprised.

Haines laughed. "Yeah, well. I don't believe it either, but I do believe in you doing the right thing ... if you get the opportunity. That's all I'm talking about. You being in the right place at the right time is damn important. The WCG becoming operational, beyond just a couple of reactors, will break the hold on our light switch, for sure. A few oil bigwigs will lose some money in Arabia, so you have to be careful. Those guys got rich being ruthless."

Haines swigged at his beer. "Hey, I got nothing against fossil fuels, so don't lump me in with the crazies. But in Arizona, we're five hundred miles away from any wellhead and nothing comes cheap anymore. So, let's close the deal on the WCG. We need the power if we're ever to crack the energy ceiling, and the nukes are the only way I figure we'll break the habit."

McHale leaned forward. "It's coming, Theo. Maybe sooner than we think."

"Good. Just keep an eye on Big Jim and Wes, 'cause they're watching out for themselves, not you."

McHale leaned back in his chair. "You got all this from Wes Teague in ten minutes?"

Haines harrumphed. "Give me some credit here. I can read. You have got to protect yourself. This screwed-up country might need you for something other than putting your pretty face on TV."

"Now you are thinking of Angie. She's got that department covered."

"A beautiful First Lady she will be."

McHale jerked up in surprise.

Haines chortled and taped his longneck Coors to McHale's bottle. "You think you're the only one who has tea leaves?"

Juliette picked that moment to approach the table. "Senator? Sheriff?"

"Hello, darlin'." Haines rose and stretched out his arms.

She moved in for a bear hug. "It's good to see you, Theo. Loved your speech."

McHale stood, a little nonplused. "I knew you guys were friends, but ..."

Haines dismissed him with a wave. "Lots of late nights and early mornings on your campaign trail, Senator."

She murmured into the big man's shoulder. "Forget him, Theo. When the senator's working, he's single-minded. He doesn't see anything or hear anybody unless it votes."

McHale looked between the two. "Tell me that's not a bad thing."

Theo grinned and released her. Juliette's easy grace gave McHale a moment's pause. She indeed possessed the quintessential look as well as a finely honed political sense.

She turned to McHale. "We need to get the pool driver back, sir."

"Right, right." He held out a hand to Haines. "Congratulations on being a National Academy grad. Let's not allow so much time to pass again."

"It won't." He turned to Juliette. "And you darlin', you take care of this boy."

"He's a handful. But between Angie and me, we'll manage."

Chapter 11

Scott

Typical Washington dinner. A lot of formality and protocol and short on relaxation. Angie had left in the morning for a speech to the veterans in Chicago. She planned to return this afternoon, but they had disagreed on something silly. Angie left a voice message on his mobile phone saying she would meet the lawn contractors in Lancaster to fix their home's sprinkler system. The system had been limping along for more than two months now.

After that, she would let him know her schedule. Even if she remembered their dinner invitation, he doubted it would have mattered. Angie was angry. He wanted to tell her the topic was less important than the resolution and not worth the argument. He intended to add an apology but would not happen. She would be in the air until too late to call. By the time he could excuse himself, she would be in transit, or in bed. The dearth of hacker security made using the airphone service too risky and he was not willing to chance a leak.

McHale then made a quick phone call to Sylvia, asking if Juliette could substitute for Angie. Family matters back home he explained. The VP's Chief of Staff agreed to the substitution. He knew Juliette and besides, at this late hour, an empty seat or a repositioned layout at the table would be insulting.

Juliette sat in Angie's spot strategically placed because the Consult's wife spoke no English. Julliette was fluent in

Spanish and carried the evening well. From the DC point of view, the evening had been worth the expense of beef Bourguignon. For McHale, he escaped an embarrassing and politically damaging faux pas.

McHale drove Juliette in his Buick to the Observatory for the evening. Easier and faster than having to checkout and then return a staff car to the pool. He intended to briefly stop at her at townhouse on the way home.

The offer of a beer had him squeezing the Buick into the crowded residential street. Now she tapped down a rounded red oak staircase, changed from a breath snatching black evening dress into a light blue sweater and gray skirt. Both alluring and desirable, alarm bells sounded in his head as long legs captivated his eyes. He rose from the couch.

"I just had to get out of those clothes, Scott. Too confining. You don't mind, do you? I couldn't wait to unwind."

"You look great. You always do." Scott meant to be glib yet sincere. Now, he suddenly regretted what sounded to his ears as a come-on. As usual, Juliette waved away the compliment.

"How can you stand the tuxedo? Loosen your tie, for God's sake. Relax. Take off your jacket."

He wondered why his sudden discomfort. They had worked one-on-one too many times to count.

"Yeah, thanks. You impressed the hell out of the Consul's wife. Every time you spoke, your end of the table stopped to listen."

She laughed. "Now, you stop that. I'll have notes on her comments for you in the morning. That third glass of wine got her pretty worked up."

A twitch at the corner of her mouth.

"Sit down, and stay awhile, for goodness sake. I've got an Autumn Ale getting cold in the freezer. You deserve a few minutes. I mean, you work harder than any half-dozen senators put together."

The plush couch felt welcome, and he relaxed into its cushions.

She flipped on a play list of Angie and his favorites.

He tossed his jacket to the chair. "Hey, good tunes."

"Glad you like it. I stole it from you."

"That's Angie's stuff actually but I really like it, too." He decided any danger signals were his own misinterpretations. She bustled in the kitchen.

"A beer sounds good, actually. Even if I'm not so sure I deserve it."

She stood in the walkway, her animated blue eyes wide. "Well, I am. You know all us staffers talk...gossip really. It seems to me that senators use this time away like a vacation. Half-ass politics. They golf, BS with their friends, divvy up their political contributions, and do taxpayer-paid fancy dinners."

She handed him a cool bottle before retreating back into the kitchen. "Not that I mind the dinners and standing in for Angie. I like being your date for the evening."

The sip of beer caught in his throat. He barely kept from spewing into the empty living room.

He glanced around but did not think Juliette saw.

He breathed out of his mouth forcing himself to slow down. He downed a swallow, demanding that his heart slow, too.

What had he and Angie even bickered about? The subject did not seem so important now. His date that night should have been his wife. He should be at home shoulder to shoulder on his own couch with Angie.

And yet, Juliette's body captured his attention. Muscles moved under her clothes. Her profile...

The thought tickled hairs on the back of his neck.

Noise clattered. "Like goat cheese?"

His response was more like clearing the throat. "Yes, sure. Look, I really appreciate what you did tonight. You gave up a night on the town for me."

"It was nothing."

She waited.

"And the seating. That couldn't have been easy. I've heard about the ambassador's wife, an ex-communist. You know what they say. Just like the Mafia: once you're in, you're never out again."

He caught her reflection in the kitchen's black window and wondered if she was watching herself in the dark glass.

She turned her head to see the reflection into the living room and caught him. He dropped his eyes and swallowed beer.

From the kitchen. "You know, Angie would have done this tonight much better."

He did not answer. He watched her reflection fit cheese and crackers on the small plate. She was no dummy. When he had promised her Angie's place on invitations in return for loyalty from Dearborn, she checked off a goal from her list. She as much had told him.

What had he been thinking? Juliette was ambitious and besides, playing with Big Jim's beautiful protégée was a magnesium fire. Once lit, it would burn forever. He vowed to be more careful and not let this relationship get out of hand.

She stepped in with the snacks and two more beers.

"I'd better not, Juliette. I need to drive home."

She smiled. "Whatever you think but two beers are not going to get you drunk."

It was an odd way of saying things. "Sure, maybe one more sip."

She tipped her bottle neck toward his empty. "In that case, s*alud*."

For a moment, their gazes met.

He picked up the fresh beer bottle. "*Salud*."

But he looked away first. They chewed on crackers in the silence for several moments.

She straightened her skirt. "Would you like something more than nibblers? You know it will only take me a moment."

"Another time ... I'm beat, thanks."

He placed the nearly full beer on the table. Her eyes, a bright blue was so unlike Angie's deep, sexy brown impenetrable gaze. He heart beat hard deep in his chest.

Juliette ignored his cautious glance and slathered a cracker. "Here try this."

Quick fingers passed his head feint and stopped an inch from his mouth.

Roses and lime scent wafted over him. His eyes dropped to her full round breasts.

He bit and chewed. The food burned. He could not swallow. His stomach suddenly cramped, and he doubled over.

Her eyes widened. "Scott? Are you okay?"

He wiped his mouth, but his stomach clutched causing to clutch with an involuntary grunt.

"I'm okay. Maybe cheese didn't agree with me."

She quickly tasted the green peppers and pimento mix. "I thought you'd like this. You know, it's Mexican and all, but it *is* kind of spicy."

Rapid breathing made his words come out staccato. "No, it's okay. I drank my beer too fast."

"You're exhausted, my God. You need to rest. I've got a guest room."

His eyes widened. "Juliette. I can't do that. Any perception of impropriety ..."

She laughed. "Impropriety? Oh, please. That was gone when we both came in here at midnight."

"What?" Panic spread across his features. "I was just dropping you off. Besides, I parked the Buick on the street. You wouldn't do that if this were something else."

She took a cracker but did not bite. "I think most of the people in DC have enough on their plates not to worry about us. Besides, if you leave and scratch that Queen Mary of a car trying to get through these tight little spaces, they might have to call the cops. And then where will we be? I shudder to think if Big Jim or the *Post* finds out. That would be hell to pay. And you do have the big speech coming up."

She laughed and drank her beer. "Besides, who says this is innocent?"

He gulped air. "A taxi. Uber. I'll leave the Buick here. You can drive it to work tomorrow. Or pick me up."

She leaned away, adjusting her sweater, her breasts so round and supple beneath the fuzzy material. "Oh, good. Shall I wear an 'A' on my chest, too? No, my dear Scott. Sleep for an hour, and then go home. Anything else is just plain silly. We're adults here, and you're nervous as a cat. Slow down. This was a working dinner. Besides, I'm just messing with you. I love Angie and nothing is going to happen. Unless of course..." She allowed a bit more of the naughty to emerge from behind those soft eyes.

"Juliette..."

Her face took on a theatrical playfulness. "What *are* you thinking, Senator McHale? You're old enough to be my ... big brother's best friend." She batted her eyes.

He stood. "I've got to go."

She reached out a hand that touched his thigh. He jumped back as if a thousand volts had shocked him. A table bumped, and the beer bottle clattered over. Foam spewed in a crazy circle.

She stood too. "My God, Scott. Are you okay? I was just kidding."

He fought for calm. "Jesus. I'm sorry. Must have been the fancy food tonight. My head is spinning. Look at the mess I've made."

She had a hand on his arm, steadying him. "I can call 9-1-1."

"No. God, no. I just need the bathroom."

The sweater rode high on her creamy stomach. Her belly button met his gaze. He looked up, "Bathroom. Quick."

"Upstairs. On the left."

He pulled himself up the steps and into the little room.

Juliette watched as he went, then gently shut the half-bath door under the staircase.

"Everything okay, Scott? I'm coming up."

She took the stairs humming Marilyn Monroe's rendition of "Happy Birthday, Mr. President."

Chapter 12

Scott

Juliette didn't come to work the next day. When Sylvia Flores asked if McHale knew any reason why, he played dumb and then tried to call her.

Christ. He did not need a complication like this. *Why doesn't she answer her mobile?* Angie remained in Chicago after sending him a text that she needed to work on an issue. He knew nothing about a problem there and decided he did not want to know if she was just avoiding him.

He also didn't want to think about the sprinkler repair guys.

After lunch in the Senate cafeteria, he tried Juliette's number again. The phone didn't ring this time and instead went straight to voicemail.

Dead battery. Broken phone.

Anxiety churned his stomach. Forty-eight hours and still no answer from either Juliette or Angie.

The next morning, he stepped into the wide Senate chamber's alcove. The hearing would begin without him.

He punched numbers into his cell.

"FBI."

"Agent Litton, please."

"This is SAC Litton."

"I thought you were in charge of the New York office now, Special Agent. You don't have a secretary, or is she out buying donuts?"

His words sounded hollow in a strained mind.

"I'm the Special Agent in Charge, Senator. There are several SACs in this office. I work for New York's Assistant Director in Charge. You'd think by now a politician of your standing would understand how the world's premier law-enforcement agency works. By the way, we don't eat donuts. They're reserved for the real cops."

"It's good to hear your voice, Ken. How is everything there?"

"Busy place, New York."

"You volunteered, right?"

A deep baritone laugh filled the small phone.

"Volunteerism is a loose turn of phrase at FBIHQ. I got lucky and pulled an assignment close enough to commute home on weekends. I used to have this friend who said he'd get me a pay raise. That'd help with the airline tickets. Whatever happened to that guy?"

McHale folded into the banter. "He used your extra money to buy votes. Come on, Ken. You didn't believe me, did you?"

"You're right. So, to what do I owe this honor? If you're heading my way, I'm catching the big silver bird to Reagan in a couple of hours. I'll be down in your part of the country."

"I was counting on it. Dinner. You and me. Angie's out of town. I could pick you up and we can head to Anthony's. My treat."

The street jargon dropped. "I'm going to be hard-pressed tonight, Scott. My young man booked the family for a meeting with the teachers, and Anne Marie and I are splitting duty with Meagan's recital."

"Bad news at school?"

"No, not really. He's only in trouble around me. Apparently, he's got the school fooled into thinking he's some sort of Machiavellian Adonis or something. They made him class president."

McHale fought to relax. "Obviously, this is his godfather's influence. Congratulations, Ken. That's terrific."

"It'll mean I'm booked until late."

"No problem, how about a run and lunch tomorrow?"

"Soccer first thing in the A.M. Sorry, man. I'm tied up all day Saturday. I've got an agent's retirement party that night. Can you come to the game, or maybe join us for church on Sunday before I catch the shuttle back?"

"I would but Angie's coming in." He lied, unable to tell even his best friend the truth. He added casually. "Maybe I'll slide up your way sometime."

Immediate concern sounded in Litton's voice. "Whoa, there. Is there something going on?"

McHale realized his mistake. "No, no. It's nothing."

"Nothing, huh? You call and scare the bejesus out of me."

"Hey, nothing really."

"You promise?"

"Sure, thing. I'll catch you later."

McHale hit the disconnect as breath left his chest. His pen point traced a circle around three names on his scratchpad: Twila Crawford, Juliette Pearson, and Big Jim Dearborn. Two beautiful women and their medieval protagonist.

Chapter 13

Scott

Juliette contacted Sylvia Flores nearly four weeks after the dinner with McHale. The call originated in the senator's San Francisco office and used one of the non-secure numbers. She offered no explanation except to say Dearborn expected Juliette to work on McHale's reelection committee.

Ten minutes later, the diminutive woman stood in front of McHale. Her head tilted back to meet him eye to eye. He felt like a recruit in basic training.

Her lips barely moved. "I'm the office manager, Senator. Personnel issues go through me. We agreed on that years ago."

"Yes, Mrs. Flores. I know and I'm sorry. Juliette was distraught. I don't think I ever knew the whole story, but I do approve of this change of venue. I over stepped and I'm sorry."

He knew his explanation bordered on the mealy mouth. In truth, he knew nothing about this supposed transfer and wondered if Dearborn did. He doubted it.

Mrs. Flores studied him closely for a minute. "All right. I'll take care of it. But next time—"

"There won't be a next time. I promise."

She nodded and left, and he fell into his chair, exhaling in relief.

If it wasn't for people and their issues, the job of senator would be a breeze.

His mood lifted, grateful Juliette and temptation moved to the other coast.

An hour later, he was caught up on marking a copy of House legislation and three cups of coffee.

The intercom on McHale's desk buzzed. "Senator? Your wife is on the phone."

He snatched the receiver. "Hi Honey. How are you?"

"Fine, and you were going to tell me if you're coming home this week."

Their squabble since the Ecuadorian ambassador's dinner resulted in his promise to take a couple of days off mid-session. He'd forgotten. Of course.

"I don't know."

Silence answered.

"Angie, I don't mean to be a dickhead. I've got a lot on my mind and it's a critical time around here."

"Okay."

He hated it when they were out of sync. "Did you see the caucus write-ins? I got two percent in Iowa. I'm not even on the ballot. Ha. That was your two percent."

"Thank you."

His stomach churned acid. "Just thanks? Come on. How can you be not overjoyed when the master of the universe apologizes to you?"

She sighed. "If that was an apology, you're right about the dickhead part."

"Now you're killing me."

He sensed the end to their month-long spat.

Her voice did not relax the tension. "I know there's a lot happening, but you need to come home. Now. It's time to walk in the desert and recharge the batteries. You're distracted and this is not a good time to lose your focus. Everyone needs unwinding time and recharging time."

He suddenly recalled Twila Crawford's twice repeated invitation. He wanted to avoid a face-to-face with Big Jim especially now that Juliette opted to return to San Francisco. But Angie was right. He needed her to anchor him again.

"Okay. I can do it."

Angie didn't hide her astonishment. "Really? When?"

"Hold on." He punched a button. Sylvia answered in her clipped professional voice. "Mrs. Flores? Would you check the calendar next week to see if I can clear a couple of days?"

"Going home?"

"I'm really thinking about it. Twila Crawford wanted me to take a look at the project layout in Humboldt. I could go and still have an extra-long weekend at home. How does it look?"

She answered immediately. "Your calendar is clear. Or it will soon be. I'll call Mrs. Crawford's office and set it up. I'll also check with the Whip's office, but I don't think there's anything critical until week after next. That's a five-day weekend, Senator. Don't be back here until Wednesday night."

He grinned. "Yes ma'am, and thanks. Why don't you come, too? Get us two tickets."

"No. I'll hold down the fort and you spend time with the family. I'll go with you next time."

"Thank you."

But she had already hung up to make arrangements.

He punched the other line. "Angie? I'm coming home."

• • • •

The one-day diversion to the town of Arcata on Northern California's wild and windy north coast would justify the trip and the weekend. He pushed hard through the following days, keeping himself and his staff moving at a breakneck pace. Even the two college-aged pages hustled to near exhaustion to get the senator on the road to the airport.

Twila met him at the American baggage counter inside San Francisco International.

He took her outstretched hand. "This is a pleasant surprise."

A team of reporters stood at a distance, recording the event.

"The pleasure is mine, Senator."

She smiled and half turned. The cameras caught both images. "Actually, I'm your ride to Marin County. I hope you don't mind."

"Heck, no. Driving in the Bay Area is always a challenge for me."

Wes Teague stood nearby.

McHale gave a wave. "Hi, Wes. Looks like the gang's all here."

At Dearborn's insistence, Teague had become the senator's chief of staff.

"Just doing advance work for your tour, sir."

Twila took his elbow and headed toward the VIP area. "We have an open evening but a full day tomorrow."

Teague trailed behind.

As the Lincoln pulled away from the curb, she leaned in. "I know you're tired, but I need a few minutes before you check into the hotel. I understand we all love our plausible deniability, but we need to brief you on some new developments."

McHale's stomach clutched wondering if his dalliance with Juliette had been discovered. And so quickly, too. He brought a prepared but untested story to mind. He would insist on the innocence. The night in Georgetown would be more difficult, but not impossible. How in the world had they caught him already?

He sounded breathless in his own ears. "What's this about? I like plausible deniability."

She turned in her seat. "For God's sake, Scott. Relax and stop looking so guilty. Unless of course you really are. I just wanted to take a quick facilities tour. Won't take long."

Dots sparkled behind his eyes as he fought hyperventilation.

Twila touched his clammy wrists. "Are you okay? I just need to run a few docs passed you on our drive."

She handed him a plastic bottle of water. He spun the top loose and then promptly dropped it on the floor. Instead of retrieving the cap, he drained a third of the drink.

"Take her easy, Cowboy. We still have a long day."

He smiled weakly. "Flying. Always gets me."

"Strange coming from a pilot."

"You'd think so, but I can't do anything sitting in the tube. I'd rather be upfront."

The car merged into traffic.

In a few moments, McHale fought his breathing to something approaching normal. The middle of his chest ached so he arched his back to release the pressure.

"Really, Scott. You lost all your color. Are you sure you're okay?"

He grinned without enthusiasm. "Ha, Ha. You almost had me making Nixon's speech all over again." He pulled at the corners of his suit jacket. "Say, do you mind if we put business aside for a few minutes? I'm beat."

She knew the pressures and yet, had never seen him fold up before. "Need that nap, right? Sure, I'll even be quiet for a few minutes."

"Thanks, Twila. You're a pal."

"Uh-huh. You must have done something really bad. But hey. I don't judge."

He barely got out the words. "What more could a guy ask."

Twenty-minutes later, they crossed the Golden Gate on Highway 101 and turned off in Novato.

When the tires reported a changed road surface, McHale straightened and took a deep breath. "Ah. That was great. Thanks, you two. Much appreached."

He looked around and knew if they were headed to the hotel, they had taken the long way. He kissed his run goodbye. They climbed the wine-growing hills until two-lane twisting ceased as Teague signaled at road leading to a farmhouse. The rough macadam kicked up cinnamon dust for more minutes. Grape trestles and overhanging coast live oaks accompanied them off the tourist track. The rented

Lincoln Town Car finally pulled into a long unused employee parking lot above a running creek freed of its dam.

McHale could see water-stained red bricks and concrete stands of rubble from demolition shoring the creek's sides.

Twila swung in the seat beside him. "This is what we're doing to old dams all over the state."

He'd seen reclamation before but not like this. Instead of land returned to its natural beauty, high barbed wire and a new, half city block-sized metal building stood partially hidden by tall sycamores and white alder. He recalled a similar though much larger metal structure near a sun farm and the Scholarplex three hundred miles south. Cameras and military sensors topped steel-reinforced pillars looking down and toward the surrounding cleared acres. The defunct dam's switching station provided a view for several soldiers from the creek's far side. A military police Humvee waited nearby. A soldier manned the machine gun atop the olive-drab vehicle.

McHale was a little taken aback. "I hope they know we're friendly."

Teague answered from the front seat. "They were briefed, sir. We need to remain on our side of the creek."

He snorted. "No problem there."

He turned to Twila. "What's going on here and why is our National Guard standing post? The governor didn't authorize this."

"You outed the soldier boys a couple of years ago in a speech if I recall. I think Jimmy might have told you not to mention them."

McHale recalled the gaffe. "Yeah. He never forgets to remind me."

The unmoving Humvee driver and gunner watched him. They did not threaten, but then neither did they welcome him.

Twila glanced toward her passenger. "You've got something like this close to your home, too. You remember the technical school, right? You do know what's in the steel building."

"I've seen it of course, but it was finished after I left. The mirror farm is nearby, so I assumed it did something to do with the solar energy efficiency and storage."

Her chuckle held no mirth. "Oh, it makes for better efficiency all right. Much better. There are more of these little facilities, Scott. Lots more all around the state. I'm getting the feeling you had no idea."

"You're right, I didn't. Obviously, this groups has something to do with power. I mean we have a substation right next door. What are they? Geothermal? Surely not solar around here in the cloudy north. I don't see any panels. I did see the reconciled DC budgets with entries I didn't recognize. Is this one of them?"

"That's good. Jimmy said you'd be interested. He wants to talk with you about all this. I'm just the dumb tour guide."

"You're not the dumb anything, Twila. What is this?"

But she shook her head. "Jimmy was very clear. Show you, answer no questions, and deliver you to the hotel in Petaluma. He'll meet us tomorrow evening after we tour my district."

"Not tomorrow evening. I'm catching the shuttle into Van Nuys. Why don't you just tell me? Secrets will be the death of us all."

Teague started the car and pulled back onto the country lane. Twila caught McHale's eye as she turned to stare out her side glass window. No one spoke on the drive to the hotel.

He waited twenty minutes in the room, sitting on the bed as a deep twilight turned to indigo. He picked up the phone and called the front desk.

"Do you have the keys for my rental car?"

• • • •

McHale slowed the Taurus in the Sunset District as scuds of a moist chilling breeze drifted beneath the streetlights. The upscale neighborhood rebuilt after the quake of 1989 never lost its early turn-of-the-twentieth-century aura.

A light showed against the curtains on the second floor. He had been here before in a limo to pick her up. Then, the blinds whisked to one side accompanied by a wave and a smile. Tonight, the window remained opaque with a light shining somewhere behind.

He shut the engine off and cracked the driver's side glass. He let the fantasy consume him, images in spite of his vow to avoid temptation.

Long moments passed until suddenly the window banged next to his head. McHale reared back as yellow eyes and a grizzled mop of uncut, filth invested hair filled the wet open space.

A homeless man. "What the hell?"

"Spare change." Stained talon fingers hooked over the edge of the opening, yanking and pulling.

"Stop that. You'll break the window."

"Give me your spare change." The brute of a man pulled and pushed oblivious to the fragile glass.

McHale hastily waded bills and tossed them through the opening. "Go on now. Leave me alone."

The man swayed and knelt. McHale sent the window back up. The bulk of the man's shadow stumbled away in the dappled light.

McHale's breath slowed as his gaze locked on Juliette's silhouette framed in the window. He couldn't look away. She didn't either. He turned the key. She never moved. The engine caught and he drove off into the night.

A few unseen moments later, the curtain dropped back into place.

Chapter 14

Scott

"Hello?" The same soft voice that first sparked his soul so many years ago moved him today. "I'm sorry but we're not here to take your call. Please leave a message and the time you called."

"Hey babe. I'm in the Bay Area for Twila's tour. We should be back to the airport by four. I'll catch the shuttle from San Fran to Burbank. I'm guessing we'll be on the ground at six. If you get this, call me back and I'll tell you which flight. No worries if you can't make it. I can grab a rental car and drop it later. I'll be back sooner if I can talk the pilot into dropping me at Muroc County. The weather's really lousy here."

When McHale looked up, Wes Teague's dour unsmiling face watched him.

Teague looked back at the podium. "I think the Mayor is almost finished."

"Right, thanks."

As they climbed the small stage, Twila broke off from a group of sixth graders and followed.

"Ladies and gentlemen. Senator Scott McHale and Congresswoman Twila Crawford." He stepped aside, raising his hands into a clap.

Cell phones and cameras recorded.

McHale waved and took the microphone first. "Good morning, all. Thank you for coming out. I'll only take a minute or two because I'm just the warm-up act ... I get it

... you're here to see Twila." The remark got him a few hoots and another round of applause.

He smiled. "Since 2000, our north Californian population has slid by a hundred thousand people, our jobs decreased by twelve percent, and our prices jumped by twenty-two percent. Our average income has slipped for three years in a row. And the value of our homes?" He shook his head for emphasis. "The price will break your heart. For those of us who live paycheck to paycheck, and I'm one of you with a full-time family farm in the San Joaquin and a second job in Washington, fifteen percent of our buying power is gone. And worst of all, we keep shipping our future to China with two-dollar-an-hour labor. What in the world is up with that?" Calls and claps. "We are hurting, our state is hurting, and this must stop."

A few more cheered and shouted encouragement.

"Just as important, our infrastructure for power generation, roads, and bridges is falling apart, and this hurts our commerce. What factory wants to build a plant in a place where schools barely scrape along, and the roads will break an axle from potholes? This has got to stop. Too much of our blood is invested in these lands. Your congresswoman is not taking this lying down."

The sudden cheer forced him to stop. Twila raised both arms over her head and pranced like Rocky.

He turned back to the audience with a broad smile. He had wanted to make a call for cheap energy, a synthesis of all the fuels including fossil, but Big Jim stripped out the reference. This time he decided to listen.

He waited a moment, then continued. "You have my promise. Twila and I will not fail you. We will not be turned back from our joint legislation to keep American jobs in America. To regain energy independence and to bring our jobs and our companies home. Thank you for stopping by this morning."

He nodded at the Mayor who moved to introduce the congresswoman.

Twila clapped as she stepped to the microphone. Fifteen minutes later, the audience rose when she finished.

McHale gestured to Teague as he reached the bottom steps. "Are we headed for Novato?"

"I can check but I believe there's another stop, sir."

McHale's jaw worked for a moment. "Okay. Find out if the pilot can drop me at Muroc County tonight. I'll cover the hotel and the bar bill."

"I'll check, sir."

Twila caught Scott's eye, holding the keys up for him to see. He nodded, shook hands, then walked to where she stood.

She smiled. "Jimmy censoring your speeches?"

There it was again. 'Jimmy.'

"In a manner of speaking, I suppose. He still won't let me chip away at the House's tight fists. One day we're going to regret letting our infrastructure go to hell."

"Baby steps, Scott. Baby steps."

"Think trillions of dollars when we turn into a third world country. Think China, for God's sake."

She ignored his plea. "One more stop, so I hope you don't mind. A quick town hall at the Red Bluff Airport. We'll be in the air for home by six."

The shuttles ran every hour. He forced equanimity into his voice. "In for a penny."

• • • •

The small business jet leveled off after a bumpy climb out of Red Bluff. Teague unbuckled first and moved forward to crouch next to McHale.

"Sir? I spoke with the pilot. They will be out of crew duty time when we arrive at Novato. They can call ahead to the dispatcher and see if another crew can meet you."

The airplane belonged to a donor, an LA construction company. "Thanks anyway. I'll grab a limo and head over the bridge."

"Ms. Crawford is speaking at the Rotarian tonight in Marin. If you wanted to spend the evening in Petaluma, you could speak at their meeting."

"As attractive as that is, Wes, I don't think so. I'm bushed and Angie's at home. I'm going to spend the evening with her."

The other man's expression remained unreadable.

McHale tried to hide his irritation. "I'm going home tonight. The work day is over."

"Mr. Dearborn sent some papers with Juliette. She's your ride to Oakland."

His breath hitched. "Okay."

Teague nodded and moved back to his seat.

McHale watched the storm's clag through the tiny porthole. An old drunk had spared him last night's idiocy. Now, it seemed fate would force him to face Juliette, anyway. So be it. This had to stop.

He rose and slipped between the pilots' seats.

The captain pulled an ear free of his headset. "Sorry we can't get to Muroc Regional, Senator."

"No problem." McHale glanced at the small weather display. "The coastal stuff looks pretty intense. When's it going to get to the Bay Area?"

"It's there, sir. The weather guessers missed this one so late in the season. They've already got'm stacked up trying to get into Oakland and San Fran. We're lucky to get into Navato."

"Okay, thanks." McHale tried to hide his unhappiness.

When he returned to his seat, Twila touched his shoulder. "You can give me a hand with the Rotarians. You'll spend hours just trying to get to the airport. Jimmy will be there, and you know he wants to talk."

He gave her his best grin. "I've already called home. I don't want to disappoint Angie, and he'll understand."

Her face showed she did not. "For your sake and mine, I hope you know what you're doing."

The seat belt sign chimed as they buffeted in gray, wet clouds. The landing bounced and splashed and ended with the copilot's apology.

"The air's got rocks tonight, folks. Sorry. It's raining pretty hard, and we have cars coming to the airplane. Stay dry and wait for your ride."

As a Crown Victoria pulled up, the rain grew even more intense. Wes and Twila ducked under an umbrella and slipped into the backseat. McHale moved to the rear fold-down seat to wait. A bright green Volkswagen stopped at the stairs.

He called to the cockpit. "Thanks for the flight today, guys."

They waved as he hurried down the steps.

Juliette beamed from the driver's side. "Hello, again."

The tips of her ash-blond hair curled against powder smooth skin. She looked rested and relaxed. He felt tired and drawn.

"Nice of you—"

She interrupted, the smile never leaving her face. "We need to talk."

"I need to get to the airport."

"I'll take you and we can talk on the way."

"Please, Juliette. Just drop me at a cab stand."

"That's silly, Scott. A cab will cost two hundred dollars. Besides, Big Jim sent you documents to read. I'll drive. You work. No problem."

Calling him "Scott" was an intimacy and a discussion he did not want.

Rain pounded on the Beetle's convertible's canvas roof. "Please just drop me in San Rafael, Juliette. I think we both know why."

"I'm a big girl. I'm also disappointed but I can live with that. Me dropping you at a cab stand is a useless show. I can have you in Oakland in an hour. What could happen?"

They pulled into traffic with the Pacific rain reducing their speed and visibility.

He accepted a small towel and wiped his face. She drove as he read. The windshield wipers barely kept up. Construction overflow left muddy rivers and flashing-yellow warning barricades across the tricky road. More than once, he jerked his head out of the documents as the VW fishtailed on slick pavement.

"This is really bad and we're not going to make the next shuttle anyway. Let's grab a coffee. Maybe some of the worst will pass."

She nodded, her lips pressed together and signaled for the exit. They splashed up to a Seattle's Best Coffee shop.

He pointed at a sign. "There's a drive-through. We don't need to get wet."

She turned in the seat, watching him closely. "I'll drop you at the airport, Scott. Is that what you really want? If it is, okay. But you were parked outside my building last night. What the *hell*?"

"That was a mistake, I'm sorry. But now I know you're okay. You left DC without saying a word."

Her eyes widened in anger. "'I'm okay?' Really? What did you want me to do? You send me all these signals. I'm not saying you flirted ... but you do. Your eyes want me, but you don't want me. I want you, but you're a coward. You came to my apartment, for God's sake. Where I sleep. Where my bed is. What am I supposed to think?"

"I'm sorry, Juliette."

Her angry voice rose against the hard-falling rain. "You're a bastard and I'll take you to the airport, if that's what you really want. And then I'll never come back to DC. I don't want you ever calling me or coming around me. You keep Angie away from me."

She suddenly pounded the steering wheel with both fists.

"God damn it, Scott. I can't take seeing you every day, having you undress me with your eyes, and then watch you go home to your wife."

Her vehemence shocked him. "Juliette. Please. I was tempted. I just...I don't know what to tell you."

Juliette's rueful laugh lacked humor. "You don't know? You do when she's away, though, don't you? You're full of charm. You expect me to take her place, to go to your dinners, sit with fat bitch wives of fat politicians. The only problem is when the evening's over, I get nothing out of it. We're both adults. What's wrong with that?"

"Juliette, that's enough–"

"No, Scott, it's not nearly enough. What I feel for you is not wrong. I know you feel the same and I can't help that you're married. I'm willing to accept that. What I don't understand is why you're not. This is done all over the world."

"Juliette–"

She smiled and placed his hand on her breast. "You know this is what you want."

Chapter 15

Scott

"Oh, Scott. Are you at the airport?"

McHale thought how much he loved her excited anticipation every time he heard it. He steeled himself for what would come next.

"I'm going to be stuck in the Bay Area tonight, Angie. It's a real mess."

"I saw on the news. What phone is this?"

"Comfort Inn across the bridge from Oakland. My cell battery's almost dead."

He relaxed a bit when she gently chided him. "And no charger, right? I told you to hire an aide when Juliette left. Where's Wes?"

"With Twila and Big Jim in Petaluma."

"Oh, and you didn't go so you could come home."

He felt the anxiety tighten his chest. "Yes. That was the plan."

She filled the silence. "I'm disappointed you won't be home tonight, and I do have an awful lot to do tomorrow. Of course, now, I won't have to drive my date home early ..."

He knew the routine but the tension inside him fought the levity. "Tell that octogenarian he needs to get back to the nursing home."

"If you insist. You are after all a United States senator, and I suppose rank has its privileges."

His stomach tightened to the size of an olive pit. "You bet."

"Scott, what's wrong?"

She knew him too well. "Nothing, babe. It's just been a long day."

Angie's voice remained unsure. "Okay. See you in the morning then. Love you."

"Love you, too."

He hung up and sat on the edge of the bed.

A knock at the door. He saw Juliette through a break in the curtains, long blond hair whipping in the wet night.

He waited. She knocked again and smiled, holding up a six-pack of Heinekens.

He opened the door. "No, Juliette. We've been through this."

She breezed past him and put the beer, her keys, and an opener on the desk. "Have one, Scott. And for God's sake, relax."

"Juliette. We can't do this. The optics–"

She patted the bed as a tiny line of mascara ran from under one wet eye. "Of course we can. Sit with me."

He held the open door. Wind gusts blew water inside, quickly sopping the rug.

Her smile didn't falter as she unbuttoned the top of a soaked blouse. "We've already done this so many times. I've imagined you with me. You've imagined it too. Don't lie. You've been inside me, making love to me in your mind, haven't you?"

"Please, don't."

"Please don't what?" Her voice purred as she rotated her head back and forth.

"Juliette–"

She leaned back on the pillow, pulling up bare and silky knees. "This isn't love, you silly goose. I'm not stupid. I know you can never leave Angie. This is how the most powerful men in the world get what they need, what they must have. Close the door, Scott."

A glance told him she wore nothing underneath. He stepped out of the line of view.

The next blouse button fell to her agile fingers. "At first, I didn't understand, but now I do. Your kind seduces women because you're dominant, virile. It's in your nature to couple. Once you were a great conquistador, taking only the most beautiful women. No one blamed JFK for doing what he did. I want to be Rihanna to my DiCaprio. What's wrong with that?"

A coy smile twisted her lips as wind rattled the windows and pushed against the closing door.

He stepped to the desk and pulled a green bottle from the carton. She blinked large eyes. Her blouse opened. She wore no bra.

He worked the top off the bottle. His eyes didn't leave hers.

She slowly, seductively worked her hips until muscular thighs sent the skirt to the floor.

He took a long drink and toppled the bottle on the tabletop. Without a backward glance, he picked up the key to her room and walked out the door.

• • • •

He awoke with a start. The chair remained wedged under the door to her motel room. A glance to his watch. Only an hour since he'd laid down his head. The sounds of the storm undulated against the motel walls.

A second bang outside shocked his lethargy aside. Glass broke in the night.

He pulled the curtain aside as the raging rain blurred amid the parking lot's rocking streetlamps and twisting signs. Foaming beer and green glass shards ran into the overflowing gutter. Juliette stalked away unsteadily raising her middle finger.

Why hadn't he seen this coming? He needed to do something and ran into the downpour.

"Juliette, wait. Don't drive, it's late. Go back to your room. My room..."

Wet hair stuck to her cheeks. Her face set in an ugly mask of rage. "You're a fool. This will cost you. Big Jim will make you pay." She worked the key fob then sat in the green compact pulling the door closed against the intense wind.

His voice was lost in the buffeting air. "Come back inside. We can talk this out."

She sent the window down. "You're so pathetic, Scott. You're just another pretty whore doing what he's told. I thought you were different. Go to hell."

Two spaces away, a young couple unloading a minivan pretended not to hear.

She rolled the window up and accelerated backwards. He jumped clear to save his toes. A splash filled his sockless shoes as her taillights bounced over the curb and disappeared into the night.

The couple did their best to ignore the show as he returned to his room. The door, of course was locked. He went next door where beer and broken glass lay.

He lifted the hotel's phone watching the black bay beyond churn into a white froth.

Damage control. Wes' number rang then rang more. No machine. No answer. He redialed. Same result.

Finally, he stretched out on the bed. Her bed. A unique California roses and lime scent. His mind screamed with the night. The terror of his mistakes played in his head.

Where the hell was Wes? He dialed as the cell battery level blinked red. The number rang and the phone died. Nothing. McHale rolled onto his side, eyes wide and unseeing.

An hour into the gray dawn, McHale listened to an army of sirens as the city woke to the damage. He still didn't know what he would tell Angie.

She would find out. He was sure of it. He needed to tell her first.

The promises made to Juliette hadn't included sleeping with her ... but of course, they had, or at least that's what he let Juliette conclude. He played around the edges of his own desire and deluded himself into believing he could balance the young woman's ambition against his own. When he ran to her DC apartment bathroom and vomited like a nervous virgin, he forced himself to confront a reality about himself. He was a coward and afraid to join the power merchants. He had no place in the midst of the elite.

And now, Juliette knew his story. Scott brought this nightmare onto himself. His secrets, the worst of which was his spinelessness. Leading troops into enemy guns had never been the issue. He wanted no part of political nightmares. How do others exist? How do they sleep at night.

Juliette maneuvered the delivery of papers yesterday. She realized his showing up on her street last night had been the final clue. And then, of course, he backed out and she knew and then, rubbed his face into the excrement of his own reticence.

The hotel phone rang. The dead cell phone lay on the floor.

He had finally fallen asleep and now, gravel filled his voice "Hello?"

"Scott?"

His eyes shot open. "Angie. Are you okay?"

"I was going to ask you the same thing. There was no answer in your room. Isn't this Juliette's room?"

He caught his breath. "No, it's m-mine. The front desk probably just screwed up. I rented two rooms."

The pause was long enough to leave him uncomfortable.

She spoke first. "Where is Juliette?"

"She left. I think maybe she got a phone call from Big Jim."

Another uncomfortable pause.

"And left you?"

Nothing gelled in his fuzzy mind. "I haven't called the airport, yet. Have you watched the news?"

Her sigh was a long time in coming. "Well, it's not good. There's a lot of damage and I think there were some deaths from mudslides."

He could think of nothing.

"You need to contact the mayor's office, Scott. Maybe put in an appearance."

He swallowed some warm beer. "The mayor. Yes. Not necessarily a photo op, but a show of support."

"Yes, that's good. I'll get ahold of the LA office right now. I've already tried our Bay Area office, but the phones are out. Do you think the satellite phones ..."?

McHale barely listened to the rest as Angie planned his participation in the aftermath. He let the opportunity to tell the truth pass and be buried in his heart. Perhaps providence had given him a way to avoid honesty. He promised to become a better person, if only...

"Can you be ready in an hour?"

He focused. "A little wet, but yes."

"I'll have Mario grab an extra shirt and suit from the office and pick you up. In the meantime, we'll scan the news and find out where the mayor is going to be. I assume you'll want a few minutes alone with her before the cameras are on."

"Uh, yeah."

"Okay. I'll have the emergency management people get you briefed up. Don't upstage her royal highness with facts. Play second fiddle. This is her city even if she plans to run against you. She'll hate you for it."

"Good advice. Thanks."

She hesitated. "You don't sound like yourself. I can always tell Mario to drop you at the airport if you're not feeling up to this."

"No. I'm good. Really. It's the smart play. I'm just tired. No sleep."

"You won't be alone. A haggard look will serve you well. Too bad I'm not there with you. We could turn this around."

He released pent up breath. "Truer words were never spoken. God, I love you."

Chapter 16

Scott

A month after the violent California storm, the tailwheel on the Cessna 180 touched down a few moments after the mains. McHale relaxed the yoke and touched the toe brakes.

Paula tapped the control wheel. "Fly 'er all the way to the hangar, Scott. Come on, now."

"Right." He corrected for the crosswind as they turned off the runway.

"Better."

Paula served as the airfield's resident flight instructor and his longtime friend. "Don't forget: Tail draggers are like women. You treat 'm nice to get 'm going, and you damn well better treat 'm nice when you're all done."

"Yes, ma'am." He smiled at her bawdy trademark humor.

He had heard nothing more from Juliette but still smarted from sitting through two performances of Big Jim wearing him out. In the first round, McHale explained over the phone why he didn't stay in Petaluma the night after Twila's northern California tour. A month later, Big Jim and Wesley Teague met him at an Alexandria hotel room. For nearly an hour, McHale listened anew about political flesh flailed from Big Jim's backside on the behalf of his candidacy.

Paula looked at the flight shack. "I think someone's looking for you."

Two men stood beside a dark government sedan at his hangar door.

She pointed away. "Park on the flightline near the pilot lounge. I'll have Tony top it off and put her back in the barn."

McHale eyed the men. Cop was written all over both. "The job never slows down."

"Go grab a coffee, take a breather, and I'll send them your way."

He sighed. "Thanks, Paula."

"Thank me by putting a check on the counter when you leave. Momma needs a new pair of shoes."

He laughed and pulled the brake handle. "Sure thing."

He didn't have long to wait. The men following him into the airport lounge.

The lead police officer stood beside his chair. "I'm Nathan Truax, DC Metropolitan PD.

McHale rose and extended his hand. "Good to meet you."

The man accepted the handshake. "My partner, Detective Sergeant Reginald Smythe."

The shorter man nodded and made it clear he didn't want to shake hands. He looked more like he wanted to make an arrest with his narrow face and darting eyes.

Ringing from McHale's belt stopped with the mute button.

Truax moved to sit opposite. "No problem if you want to get that."

"Messages, Detective. Can't get them in the air, so they catch up with me once we're back in range."

Truax nodded. "We're getting some information for the San Francisco police. Doing them a favor."

McHale wetted his lips with the coffee. "Really? I know the SFPD Chief. I wonder why he didn't just call me. What do you need?"

Smythe took up the questioning. "You were in California a couple months ago, right?"

McHale looked over. "I'm back and forth all the time. I'm from California so you'll have to be more specific."

"You know Juliette Pearson?"

"Of course. She used to be on our staff."

Truax spoke. "When did you see her last?"

McHale's mind raced to that night in the San Raphael Comfort Inn as he tried to understand what was going on.

His first lie. "I'd need to check my calendar. I don't know the exact date."

Smythe pressed. "But you saw her last in California, right?"

McHale faced the smaller detective. "Yes. Last time I saw her, we did a one-day talking tour with Congresswoman Crawford. She brought some documents to the airport for me."

"And then?"

"And then, I spent a long weekend at home." McHale glanced between the detectives. "What's this about?"

Truax tapped his notebook. "Can you give me a rundown of your schedule?"

"Off the top of my head, no." McHale knew he could, but alarm bells were sounding, and he needed to slow down and think.

Smythe set his phone between them. "Give us what you remember. Okay if we record this? I got a terrible memory."

McHale looked between the two police officers. "I don't mind, but first tell me what my schedule has to do with the San Francisco Police Department."

Truax shrugged. "They're questions, senator. You were there for a storm, I believe."

"That's true. Wild weather. A lot of damage."

McHale recounted the flight from Petaluma to Crescent City, talked about the storm and spending the night in San Raphael, and the next day touring with the mayor before catching the shuttle home. He talked about the rainstorm and renting two rooms at a freeway-side motel. "Much better detail will come from my travel voucher. Mrs. Flores will have those."

Truax rolled a shoulder. "Can I get a copy?"

"Sure, but now please tell me what we're talking about."

Smythe flipped to a page in his own notebook and read in a nasal voice, "Missing person. Juliette Pearson. Age thirty-seven. Employed by Syntac Technologies. Former employee of the California state committee for the reelection of Scott —"

McHale felt the blood drain from his face. "Missing? Jesus, when?"

Paula came out of the kitchen with a pot of coffee. "Scott? What's going on?"

Smythe did not turn around. "Police business, ma'am,"

Truax held up a meaty hand, but McHale looked at Paula. "Juliette's missing."

"Oh no, Scott. What happened?"

McHale looked between the men. "What did happen?"

Truax looked momentarily nonplused. "Sorry, I don't know. We just got the lead—"

Paula slammed the coffeepot to the table. "Damn it all to hell. This country is getting worse every day. Every goddamn day! Does Angie know?"

The two detectives glanced at one another.

McHale gathered himself. "I don't know if she does."

He looked at Truax. "Has anyone spoken with my wife yet? Juliette's a close family friend."

Truax looked at Smythe. "I don't know that answer."

Smythe ignored the other's concern. "When did you hear from her last, Senator?"

McHale tried to calm the roiling in his stomach. "Well, she left our office, I don't know, maybe three months ago. Mrs. Flores and she traded emails all the time. She'd been key to our California office for years."

"But she left DC, right?" Truax resumed his dispassionate tone. "Your office here would have been like a promotion, the big show. Then, suddenly, she steps down. That's kind of unusual."

McHale wrinkled his forehead. "Well, yes. I suppose that's true, but as a personnel matter, Detective, you understand I can't talk about it. She wasn't fired if that's what you're thinking. She eventually resigned and joined a commercial company. Maybe she wanted a change."

McHale cursed himself inwardly. Stupid thing to say as worked to regain his footing.

Truax closed his notebook. "I'd appreciate it if we could take a look at her emails, and maybe her office, too."

Surprised, McHale looked between the two men. "You mean now?"

Truax tucked his notebook away. "Yes. If we could, of course. I'd like to get this thing off my desk and send the report back to SFPD."

McHale often spent his Saturdays at the office. Sylvia would actually be the one inconvenienced.

"Okay. Anything I can do to help. I'll have my secretary meet us."

Smythe spoke up, his tone irritating, "Is that necessary? Can't you get into the computer?"

McHale considered the man for a moment, then finally found timbre for his voice. "Yes and no, Detective. I thought you wanted access to emails. I wouldn't know where or how to start looking into the archives. You're aware all congressional emails are maintained on protected servers, right?"

Truax gave his partner a subtle shake of the head. "Thank you, sir. That'll be fine. You can ride with me, and Detective Smythe can drive your car."

McHale looked from man to man. "No. Thanks. I'm fine. This is shock, but I can drive myself."

Paula watched; her forehead wrinkled with incredulity.

Truax shrugged. "Suit yourself, sir. Would you like Detective Smythe to drive with you?"

"Of course not."

McHale turned to Paula. "Thank you for the flight this morning."

She nodded in silence and a set jaw as he wrote out a check and gathered his jacket.

• • • •

McHale called Angie as the cars merged onto Interstate 66.

"Oh Scott, this is awful. Do we know anything more than she's missing?"

His confusion cleared moment by moment. "The detectives said they didn't know, but they're being cagey. I don't understand why. I'd assume at some point they'll give me more details."

"I need to call Gina Pearson. She must be going out of her mind. How long has Juliette been missing?"

"The cops aren't talking. Either they don't know, or this is how they work. Her mother should know, so call Gina, and maybe Big Jim."

McHale considered for a moment. "I know Juliette quit the office but maybe he's stayed in contact with her. Let him know what's happening. I'll be at the Senate Building in an hour ..." His voice trailed as a thought struck him.

"What is it?"

"I just realized these guys drove an hour out of their jurisdiction to gather me up. This isn't protocol. Even in the worst cases, these cops have some heavy-duty restrictions about interviewing members of Congress. The Senate leadership was probably told and approved."

"What do you mean?"

"It means when we hang up, you call Big Jim ASAP. I think Wes Teague's in town, and I need to get smart."

Her silence scared him.

When she spoke, her voice had an edge. "Smart about what? What's going on?"

"They wanted to know about the Petaluma trip with Twila. I think they're looking for a bogeyman."

Angie, the activist lawyer stepped up to the plate. "You'd better tell me what you told them."

He took a breath and glanced into the rearview mirror. The police officers maintained a close distance to his back bumper.

"I told them everything, Angie. Just like I told you."

Angie clipped her words, tight and fast. "Including the fact, she spent the night with you at the motel."

"Yes, of course, and that I rented two rooms. Angie, come on, I told you all this."

He had not told her how a beckoning and partially nude Juliette had driven him from his room.

He recognized her clipped words. "Yes, you did tell me. I didn't like it then, and I don't like it now. Perceptions are reality in our world. Not everyone is a straight arrow like you."

At least she still believed in him. "And if I could take back the night—"

"You can't. This kind of innuendo brings a terrible connotation even with aides in their mid-thirties. When the media grabs hold, some offices never recover."

"Geezus, Angie, I got it, all right?"

"Yeah, okay. I'll call Big Jim now."

"Thanks. Somehow, I feel better."

Several moments of quiet played against the road noise.

He spoke first. "These two cops really shocked me this morning."

"Which is why they drove to West Virginia to find you. No way they'd be allowed inside the Senate offices to pull this kind of crap."

She gathered her words into a vehement arrow. "Do not talk to them anymore without me there."

"You're thinking I was set up?"

"Of course, you're being set up. Take the time, now, to think about all the things you said. You need to remember for later. Write it down or record it—not in your iPhone. Don't share it. Don't tell anyone. Any notes you have can be subpoenaed. Especially electronic. Understand?"

"Yes. Okay."

Another long moment. "I don't sound very presidential, do I?"

"We all need help now and then. Even you."

"Right."

He watched the road as faster cars passed him. He pressed the accelerator and put the speed control on.

Her voice grew softer. "Are you okay?"

"Yeah. I think so." The tightness in his bowels reminded him of the time just before a combat operation.

"Did you fly this morning?"

He appreciated her diversion. "Yes. Paula gave me some dual instructions. I'm pretty rusty."

"How long's it been? Three months?"

If he could just do the day over again and meet Big Jim in Petaluma—

She broke into his thoughts. "No cross-countries, Scott. No instruments without someone else. A qualified someone else."

He came back to the present. "Yes, boss. No chances."

"Don't patronize me."

"Sorry. I'll get more dual training."

She said nothing.

"And only in good weather, too, okay?"

"Okay. Call me after the detectives leave. If Gina Pearson wants company, I'm going to head up to the Bay Area. I'll be on my cell, then I'm coming to you. And no sharing. Listen to your lawyer."

"Okay. Love you."

"Love you, too."

McHale dialed Teague and hung up a minute later.

When they reached the Senate Office Building parking, the spaces were nearly empty. He took the one closest to the elevator. The detective's car pulled into a yellow zone.

Smythe jutted a jaw at his cell phone. "Who'd you call?" The tone of his voice took on an unpleasant echo in the wide, gray marble lobby.

The hulking Truax looked on, curious and unapologetic. McHale considered telling the officer to try remedial charm school, but decided he needed to be smart and not a smartass.

"My wife, Detective. She's in LA. Angie and Juliette have been friends for many years. Her friend is missing, and the cops out there haven't contacted her, but they want you to talk to me. What's up with that?"

The skinny detective stared. "I wouldn't know. I'm not running the case, am I?"

McHale looked away to tamp down his irritation.

Truax squinted at Smythe with a subtle shake of his head. "Sorry, sir. We just wondered, that's all."

"Yeah. I got it. My Chief of Staff Wesley Teague will be joining us. We needed to work for a couple of hours today, anyway. I'm sure this won't take that long."

His key unlocked the deadbolt and all three could hear the tapping of computer keys. "Hi Wes. That was fast."

Cold blue eyes glanced at the two sport jackets. "Thought I could get a start on things, sir. Are these the policeman assisting San Francisco?"

Truax held out his badge case. "Detectives."

"What division?"

Missing persons, McHale nearly said, then saw Truax working his jaw

"Homicide."

McHale spat incredulously. "What? You told me she was a missing person."

Truax turned to McHale. "And as far as I know, it still applies."

Teague waded in even though he'd only had the drive's hour to prepare. "If I see so much as a single leak, the hint of a rumor, a statement in the *Post*, you'll lose your jobs for lying your way into this office and misrepresenting yourselves to the Senator."

McHale held up a hand and faced Truax. "Wes, please. There's no need for that. Is this normal? I mean, to have homicide detectives investigating missing persons in California, and on a Saturday?"

Both officers regarded the stony faced Teague for a moment, then looked at McHale. "This is standard protocol based on San Francisco's *missing person* request."

McHale took a mental step back. "No. The requesting officers have assumed she was killed, and this is a murder investigation. You're not being forthcoming."

Truax stood his ground. "We never said that. We're assisting under extreme circumstances."

Wes Teague wasn't done either. "My promise remains, Detectives. Any word of this office's cooperation and I'll be speaking with the mayor. She and I are personal friends. You two have violated your own procedures, so you'd better be judicious when you report this information. You ambushed a United States Senator. That's not going to play well. I'll have a statement prepared in an hour."

Teague stared at both men, a force, and a threat. He continued. "As a courtesy, I'll courier a copy to the chief of police this afternoon. In his home. He can share if he wants. And, unless you have a warrant, I think we're done."

Smythe clearly enjoyed the confrontation. "We were invited to view McHale's calendar,"

Teague took firm control while his boss' face drained of color.

"That's *Senator* McHale, Detective, and this office will cooperate fully. Please send a request through proper channels."

Smythe pushed back. "Come now, *Mr.* Teague. We're only trying to gather a few facts here."

The big detective cleared his throat. "Senator McHale. Could you please tell us about your involvement with Ms. Pearson?"

Teague glanced at McHale. "Professional, Detective. Their relationship was professional. Please excuse us, now. I'll have something for your chief in an hour."

Teague's expression remained unchanged as the door closed behind the men.

He did not look at McHale as he returned to the keyboard. "I believe Mrs. McHale asked you to do something. Now would be a good time to get that done."

Chapter 17

Angie

Angie's head ached after a month of shoring up missed meetings and timetables in DC. For several days, she reviewed Scott and Sylvia Flores' calendars, finally archiving an acceptable copy in case the information became the subject of a subpoena. After a late evening flight to San Diego, she'd attended two critical planning meetings and this morning, a magazine interview. Now, she walked the dais answering questions feeling the fatigue of balancing her obligations and the quiet inquiries directly from the San Francisco Police. She was thankful Wes Teague had somehow prevented the media from grabbing the story about Juliette and her husband in San Raphael.

The ballroom held dozens of tables and over one hundred chairs. Many sitting before her wore the caps of American veterans' groups. Some wore business suits while others aloha shirts. T-Shirts occupied the last few rows.

The questions wound down as the general meeting came to a close.

A man raised his hand. "Mrs. McHale? As CEO of Veterans of California, you renegotiated the terms of our share pledge with a couple of national charitable collections. What I don't understand is why we've turned down some of the country's largest corporations. These are tried and true, generous companies. Can you explain?"

Angie recognized the man who made the same protest the night before.

"Certainly. Last year, we accepted nearly ten percent of our working capital from the three companies you're talking about. The remaining ninety was spread among a million donors who gave willingly and generously. Those first three however contributed with strings attached—"

The man interrupted. "But they gave a lot of money,"

"They did and would again if we asked them. But we will not."

A few persons mumbled in the audience.

She held up a hand. "Two of these companies receive their funds from social media giants as a pass through. Even though no one has yet asked, the finance committee was uncomfortable with an expectation of a future quid pro quo. The third is a Texas-based power conglomerate with a past history that is not in the best interest of the VOC."

A voice at nearby table. "Yeah, Brad. She's telling you those Texas folks cut their teeth with Enron. They're on work release from the old folks home and up to their old tricks."

A catcall from a side table had half the group laughing and the other half grumbling.

Angie was used to contentious meetings where everyone had an opinion and worked to quiet everyone down. "Please. We need to ask these tough questions. There's only so much support out there and I appreciate Brad bringing it up."

The room clapped their approval and an end to the forum.

A voice from the doors at the room's back. "Mrs. McHale. One last question."

Angie glanced at the clock feeling the jet lag fatigue. "Last one."

A young man stepped forward holding up his cell phone to record the answer. "Would you care to comment on the disappearance of your husband's female aide? And a follow up: Have the police finished questioning the senator?"

The room turned silent and chilled.

Angie answered without hesitation. "As soon as my husband's office was made aware of Juliette Pearson's disappearance, we opened our files and cooperated fully with the police. You know she left the office's employment many months ago for the private sector. When we found out she was missing, I visited Gina, her mother, but I don't know more. My husband phoned me as soon as he heard and was very upset. He is personally assisting the police with their investigation despite his busy schedule. You see, Juliette is more than just a former employee. She is a friend to our family and a particular friend to me since Scott's early political days."

She held up a hand to stop the man's next question. "Let's stop here. This is a tragic event, and Juliette has many friends who may not realize she's missing."

The young man ignored her and called out over the room's buzzing. "Isn't it true San Francisco homicide detectives are developing a case against your husband?"

The stunned room quieted.

Angie set her jaw. "That's nonsense. There's a better word for your suggestion, but I don't want to be on record giving you a story where there isn't one."

A veteran stood and approached the young man holding his camera phone. Another man assisted the first in closing the door to the questioner.

· · · ·

Angie's new aide, Susan Yancy drove the return trip in San Diego's afternoon rush. Six miles from their LAX exit, a tractor-trailer and Nissan minivan rubbed shoulders. Traffic came to a standstill.

Susan worked as Angie's assistant since they won the last senate reelection. "Ma'am? Do you mind if I listen to the radio? Jon and Kit are idiots of the LA airwaves and they're on. There's nothing like them in Portland. But music is okay, too...or no radio."

Susan had the unfortunate inability to lose the extra weight gained moving from one fad diet to another. She jogged, exercised regularly and only managed to move the weight around. Even her pretty red hair caused distress with its unruly cowlicks springing to life in any light breeze or momentary humidity. Had she been born five hundred years before; Susan would have been the toast of the Venetian waterways and hailed naked on the masters' canvases. But sadly, not in today's anorexic world.

Angie pulled back from her reverie. "Oh, of course not. I don't mind at all. I could use a little entertainment. The man in San Diego really got to me. How silly. Go ahead."

Her pretty round face flashed gratitude. "Oh good, thanks. They're *so* funny."

Angie leaned back to watch cars crawl ahead when someone was brave enough to drive the shoulder and chance a ticket. She knew of Jon and Kit and their brand of dark humor and edgy innuendo and was surprised Susan liked them.

"... and what about the beautiful California model-turned-Senate aide? Has anyone seen a picture of this arm candy?"

The other man, the one she thought might be Kit, laughed. "Oh, yeah. This gorgeous girl disappeared and nobody's talking. Even the senator's wife's is hiding behind storm troopers when someone asks the tough questions."

Jon agreed. "Hey, she no slouch either. We have Benjamin Hummel on the line, a freelance reporter and blogger who attended a rally for the Veterans of California charity in San Diego today."

Susan hit the off button. "Oh, God. I'm sorry."

"It's okay. I want to hear." Angie turned the radio back on.

"Brendon? Can you hear me now? How about telling us what happened at this high-level meeting."

The man laughed. "Bombshells, guys. I mean fireworks big-time. I managed to talk my way in where these veterans were celebrating some new funds discovered by the senator's wife. They were strategizing about using the old Enron cronies who were probably on work release. Would you believe it?"

Kit chimed in. "You mean those flipping thieves are still alive? Can she do that?"

The two jocks traded rejoinders and forgot the caller for a moment. "Those bastards screwed California for years.

And now you say the senator's wife's taking a page from *their* playbook? What the hell?"

Susan scrunched her fleshy shoulders behind the steering wheel. Angie sat straighter.

"Oh, yeah. Mrs. Scott McHale confirmed Enron used to be in bed with the vets."

Jon gave a hoot. "Hey, hey! This is a family show."

Kit joined in. "I wouldn't mind that duty. Angie McHale got a few years on her, but she's hot."

Susan reddened. "I'm really sorry—"

Angie shook her head and held up a finger.

Jon returned to the caller. "So, Brendon, tell us what happened."

The guest's voice scratched from a cell phone connection. "All I was trying to do was nail down what Mrs. McHale knew and when she knew it. I mean, this poor Pearson girl is missing after all, and it's the public's right to know ..."

Kit broke in. "Have you seen what Juliette Pearson looks like? Who can blame the senator for tapping that?"

"We've got thirty seconds here. What else you got?"

"As if that ain't enough."

Susan squirmed but Angie listened silently and analyzed.

"You'll want to hear this, because when I asked a simple question, like when her husband quit doing his aide, Angie's storm troopers threw me out. What's happened to the First Amendment?"

Jon chortled and cut the caller off. "Oh man! You've got to be kidding!"

Susan looked over. "That isn't true. They can't say something if it isn't true, can they?"

Angie smiled and reselected music. Their speed picked up as lane three opened. Scott sometimes used to spend more hours in Juliette's company than hers. Anyone else might damn him with the evidence, but she knew better.

Susan was near tears. "I'm sorry, Mrs. McHale. I would never have put the show on—"

"Please, Susan. Don't give it another thought. You're not responsible."

"Yes, ma'am."

"This is only the beginning you know."

A long pause. "Yes, ma'am."

Neither spoke as they entered the drive into the foothills. Angie wondered how Joy would take this slander about her father. So steady and firm a few hours ago, now life seemed poised at the brink. She wondered how a reporter's single question could rock their solid foundation. Her foundation. Had the power of McHale's office duped her? Perhaps her personal ambitions had skewered once-firm judgment.

No matter. She had to ensure her husband's survival at all costs.

Angie touched the young woman's hand and pointed at the turn-in. "Let's stop at Ralph's. Can you stay for dinner? I was thinking spaghetti and one of their readymade salads. I need the company unless you have other plans."

Susan smiled. "Sure, okay. I'd like that."

They locked the car and walked for the store.

Angie slowed and spoke carefully. "I wonder if you're up to a task. A favor really."

"Yes, certainly. Anything I can do. This is all so unfair."

Angie stopped under a transplanted sidewalk tree. "You're not well known in the Bay Area, and we need to do a bit detective work. Nothing dangerous. This is more like fact-finding. The radio program—"

"I didn't know they were going to use the meeting against you."

"They're just selling airtime, so don't worry. In a week, no one will even remember what they said today, but headlines today can sometimes be tomorrow's barometer. We need to know more and get in front of this thing. You're the one who can do this for us."

Susan squeezed her face into a smile. "Really? I want to do it. Do you think I can?"

"Yes, I do. Let's get our dinner and we can make a plan."

Chapter 18

Angie

Angie worked eighteen-hour days for the next three fielding inquiries and phone calls, taking selected interviews, and making statements for the media. When a Sunday news story surfaced of eleven illegal immigrants found dead in an abandoned tractor-trailer, the relentless pressure on the McHale household subsided.

Susan sat on their living room floor with paper work spread out around her. Her cup of tea with cream and double sugar was just the way she liked it.

"Angie? I can go to San Francisco tonight if you want me to,"

Her own cup was unadorned Indonesian black tea. "There's still a lot of publicity. I'm not sure if this would be the right thing to do now."

Susan's face fell. "I won't do anything to bring attention to me. I can start with missing persons and go from there. People don't really notice me."

Angie looked up, hearing the pain. "Oh, Susan. That's not true."

The younger woman shrank. "I didn't mean to sound like a pathetic loser, but it *is* true. You're spectacular, so beautiful. No one ever looks at the entourage, only the rock star. Besides, everybody loves a fat lady. Just not lately." She grinned self-consciously.

"You're a lovely young woman."

Susan laughed and set her cup down. "You sound like my mom, but that's just the way it is, and I accept it."

Angie shook her head. "I don't think any of us have to accept any such thing. We have choices."

Her eyes twinkled. "Does that include going to San Francisco for you?"

Angie laughed without reserve. "Yes, it does, my clever young friend. You're off to San Fran, but I'm taking you to the airport with a quick stop in between."

Before her flight, Angie and Susan parked in Nordstrom's lot. Two hours and a striking tan business suit and two skirt-and-blouse ensembles later, they turned into the LAX departure lanes. The added accessories, shoes, and pieces of costume jewelry nestled in a new suitcase, soon to reflect on Scott McHale's charge account.

The salesperson in Nordstrom even showed Susan how to pin back a few side and front curls to hide her unruly cowlick.

Angie looked to the passenger's seat. "Don't forget. This is my innocent husband's treat. You do your best."

"Yes, ma'am."

At the Southwest terminal, Susan bubbled, "Thank you so much for helping me with clothes. I'll pay you back."

"You look terrific. New clothes just bring out what was always there. I'll make sure Scott doesn't mind the bill, so no worries. Good luck and be careful. San Francisco is a lot different than our little town in the desert."

• • • •

Susan's second stop at the police department brought Inspector Tom D'Amico of the missing persons bureau into her life. Thin and tall, he stooped with rounded shoulders and veined powerful hands.

Looking up, Susan fixed her bright blue eyes on the police detective. Her thoughts were of a handsome Abe Lincoln.

He fumbled the paper a little. "I can give you our package on Ms. Pearson. Are you with the press?"

"Press? Oh, no. I'm with ..." The senator's name almost jumped out. "... myself. I'm an internet freelance journalist and thought my blog should have original facts. Not sieved through someone else."

D'Amico considered her answer and did not smile. "Well, that's admirable, I think. Getting the facts first is always a good idea." He pulled tri-folded papers from beneath the counter and selected the right one.

Incredulous, Susan stared at the fact sheet in her hands. "You're kidding, right? This is all the material?"

No way she could go home with this.

"Budget cuts, miss. Should be more, I know, but this is it."

Susan's disappointment showed with forehead wrinkles.

He added quickly. "I'm really sorry. Detectives are working the case, but we only release what they tell us."

Susan glanced at his nameplate on the metal desk. "Aren't you a detective, too? I heard they're coordinating with Washington DC."

"DC? Really? I didn't know. Are you from the senator's office?"

She'd always been a terrible liar and fell silent.

"I mean if you are, we're supposed to cooperate with the elected officials. And their staffs."

He offered his first tentative smile. "I don't know if there's anything else I can find out, but you could tell me what to look for and I can ask around. If you gave me a phone number, I could call you ... with the information, I mean."

She hesitated. This marked a first in her young life. A stranger asked for her phone number. She preferred not to think of it as work. He was interested in her, she was sure.

As the moment grew long, he swallowed embarrassed. "I didn't mean anything by it, miss. Give me a second, I'll call the precinct and see if there's anything."

The color rose in his face.

She worked a business card from her wallet. "Here's my number."

He smiled when he saw Veterans of California top the card. "Los Angeles?"

"Yes. But I live in Valencia."

He fumbled and reached for one of his own. "I'm Tom D'Amico."

She covered her mouth and pointed at his name plate. "Yes, I know."

They smiled at one another. "Oh, yeah, sorry. I'm on hold."

She nodded and took the card from his long, bony fingers.

After another minute, he mumbled and hung up. "The detectives are out."

"Oh."

"Even if they were there, Ms. Yancy, they can't really talk about it."

"Susan, please. Will they tell *you*?"

He looked doubtful. "Well, I suppose. But you couldn't write it in a blog."

Her eyes widened. "Oh, no. I'd never do that. I don't have a blog."

Five minutes, and already she'd blown her cover. "I fibbed, sorry. I work for the senator's wife."

D'Amico smiled. "Well, you had me fooled."

The sparkle in his eye told her otherwise.

Still, she didn't want to lose the moment. "I'll be here for a couple of days, Detective."

"Tom."

"Tom. I'm at the Holiday Express near the airport. Could you call me?" For a moment, she could hear her mother's warning voice.

The flush to his face made his delight evident. "Well, sure. I can do that."

"Oh, good." She wondered where to go next. "All right. I guess ... I'll head back."

"Yes, all right then."

His long face grinned as a fingernail clicked her card. "See you."

"See you."

She offered a tiny wave and walked through the dirty glass door. She glimpsed back and they shared a smile.

Susan lingered in Oakland and San Francisco for three more days. D'Amico called once, to say the case had been reassigned and had no new information. They talked and laughed for twenty minutes. She was disappointed when the conversation ended, and he hadn't asked her out.

The next day she finally flew back to LAX to help Angie with a Red Cross function. The following Sunday night, Susan checked into the same San Francisco Holiday Express and called his cell. Voice mail answered.

She went to the missing persons office the next morning as soon as the doors opened. D'Amico wasn't there. Instead, a middle-aged woman with huge hair and strong perfume sat at his desk, The detective had taken vacation time and would be back in a week. She examined Susan closely then returned to her newspaper on Tom's desk without another word.

For the rest of the day, Susan chased information from the senator's personnel files. Neighborhood stores, the place where Juliette had her hair cut, and even her high school in Beaumont. All leads ended with nothing new.

That evening, she called Angie from the café next door to the motel. "I've checked everyone in her file, and no one has seen her. She had been at her new job for about three months and was getting ready to move closer to work. Then, well ... she just sort of disappeared."

"You're doing a wonderful job. I'm so appreciative and I know Juliette's mother is, too. Have you spoken with Gina?"

Susan sipped at her soda. "Yes, ma'am. This morning."

"Okay, then. Do you know how much longer you'll be there?"

"I can come back—"

"No, no. Everything is fine here. I know you're staying up with email and appointments." Angie paused. "Have you spoken with the cute detective yet?"

"You mean—" She'd nearly blurted *Thomas*. "... Detective D'Amico?"

"Yes, I think that's the one you can't stop thinking about."

Angie laughed and Susan joined her.

"He's on vacation." The disappointment evident in her voice. "That's my luck for you. If it wasn't for bad, I'd have no..."

Just then, Thomas D'Amico walked through the front door and looked around. Susan was so surprised; she forgot all the guile gleaned from years of watching movies. She waved excitedly.

"Oh, Angie. He just walked in. What should I do?"

"Hang up and have fun for a change. No more work."

He returned the wave with ungainly arms.

"Gotta go."

She didn't bother waiting for Angie to answer.

"Sorry to bother your dinner, Ms. Yancy." He towered over the table, a grin creasing his long face, unable to hide his pleasure.

She tried not to gush. "You're not a bother. How in the world did you find me?"

She laughed and held up a hand. "No, no. Don't answer. Of course you could find me. You're a detective. Please, sit down. I thought you were on vacation."

"I am. I took some personal time so I could look into the Pearson woman's disappearance."

Her face grew warm. "Oh, my goodness. You did? Really? That's so nice. Do you want something to eat?"

D'Amico flushed with her unexpected adoration. "I don't think so. I'm not really ..." He hesitated seeing her disappointment. "Well. Maybe a Pepsi or something. I sort of ate a large lunch."

She remembered the unwrapped hoagie with pickle juice drippings and wilted lettuce on his desk the first day. "Not another submarine sandwich?"

He laughed. "Maybe you're the better detective."

She waved at the waiter. "Are you sure you don't want anything to eat? I'm on an expense account and we owe you."

They both smiled.

"I don't eat much."

She looked at her plate. "I wish I had your problem. I eat too much and all the wrong things."

"Well, that doesn't look like too much to me. I eat twice that much ... sometimes."

"But it doesn't put layers on you."

"Well, you neither."

He suddenly realized what he had said, and the color rushed his face. "Sorry."

The cleverness of a thousand Hollywood movies simply would not come to her. "You'd better call me Susan if we're going to get personal."

The tall detective nodded and withdrew a folder from his coat pocket. "I got a little something on Ms. Pearson. All unofficial and you can't tell anyone."

"What is it? What did you find?"

He placed the folded paper on the countertop. "This is a little gruesome, so tell me if I should stop."

She nodded.

"About a half-dozen bodies are fished out of the Bay each year. Normally, they're matched up pretty quickly with missing people. A woman's body was found several weeks ago by a fisherman and his son. There was no identification, because ... well." He took a breath. "She had been in the water for a very long time before she was found, and...she was decapitated."

Susan drew back.

"I'm sorry. I should never have told you."

She quickly recovered. "Yes, you should have. I just wasn't expecting that. I guess that means no dental records, right? What about fingerprints, then?"

"No. Whoever killed her ... cut off her hands and feet. And like I said, the death was a while ago."

Undeterred, Susan pressed. "DNA?"

He nodded seeming to approve of her strength. "Yes. They sent DNA along with samples for the toxicity screening when she was found. They rushed it, because ... well, because the senator's missing aide brought a big spotlight on the department."

She leaned toward him. "I can only imagine the awful pressure you must be feeling to solve this."

"Not me, Susan. I'm low on the detective totem pole. The homicide squad is spun up, though. They've got a half-dozen cops running leads."

"What did they find?"

D'Amico took a breath. "The DNA field test is a close-enough match to our control sample from Juliette's mother. Blood samples and such."

She felt breathless, lightheaded. "Oh, my God. Tell me."

"There's a better than average chance the woman was Juliette Pearson."

Susan pulled in a breath and silently turned to look out the window.

D'Amico was suddenly concerned. "Are you okay?"

She nodded. "It's just sad. I never knew her, really. I took her old job on Mrs. McHale's staff. I've seen lots of pictures. She was so beautiful."

D'Amico relaxed.

"You thought I was going to be a basket case, right? Actually, I'm pretty strong."

"I can see that."

Her own intuition sparked. "But there was something else, wasn't there?"

He nodded. "Yes. She had Ketamine in her system."

"The date-rape drug?"

"Wow. You should have been a cop. Something else, too. An indicator, HCG."

Susan screwed up her eyebrows and shook her head.

"Human chorionic gonadotrophin. She was pregnant."

She covered her mouth. "Oh, my God."

"She may not have even known. Sometimes women don't ... anyway, she was in the first trimester."

The doorbell chimed and two men stepped in, both with wide, heavy shoulders and blue-ink tattoos high on their necks. Neither Susan nor D'Amico turned to look.

He continued his thoughts. "It's a funny thing, really. The lab sent the results over, but when the lead detective tried to pull it up, there was nothing there. The computer crashed. In fact, the whole system went down. The captain called the state lab, but their database was corrupted, just like our servers. The morgue will have to send the DNA and tox off again, but now everything's going to be suspect."

"What do you mean?"

"Well, it's not a missing person anymore. We got a murder now, right? If it is Ms. Pearson. But here's the weird part. Her mom, Gina, won't give us another sample. They said she's pissed. Police incompetence. I think it's something else. Plus, you remember all the stuff in the OJ Simpson trial? To convict someone means no reasonable doubt. This case is really screwed up with reasonable doubt now."

"Wait. Do you mean there's a suspect?"

He tapped the table top with a long finger. "No, Susan. Not with a name yet, anyway. I just mean when we arrest this someone, there'll be another challenge. That's all."

Susan considered this, her straw slurping the last of the Pepsi. "Have you ever heard of something like this before, Tom?"

"Never. It's strange enough that the mom is making the homicide dicks get a warrant for her DNA. The fact files in both places disappeared is ... well, very strange. The files for hundreds of DNA cases are now pending again. It's like someone got in there and wiped everything clean. There's a hell of an uproar. It's a mess."

"Does that mean it might not be Juliette?" Susan's face hoped for reprieve.

"Well, they think it's her."

"What about the pregnancy DNA?"

"That's more problematic. Unless the father's in a database somewhere, you've got to get warrants to take someone's DNA."

"Can I tell Angie?"

He took a breath. "I've got eight months to my twenty years, then I'm leaving the force." He took her hand. "If you tell the senator's wife, she'll have to keep it a secret. Big-time secret. If they find out I leaked the information, it'll be my ass and maybe my pension."

She gripped his hand back. "I promise. Thank you for trusting me."

"You D'Amico?" A man's bulk filled the aisle next to their table, his accent street Spanish.

The detective dropped Susan's fingers and started to slide out of the booth. "Who're you?"

"You him or not?" The man's companion disappeared into the kitchen.

D'Amico reached under his jacket, but too late. Susan screamed as the gun's explosion sent brains, blood, and a spent bullet into the panel of glass.

Chapter 19

Scott

The media reported four people killed, including the manager and a cook cleaning a grill in the back kitchen. An act of unusual brutality said one reporter on the evening news. Even for the Bay Area. The off-duty police officer died of a single shot to the head. His gun, wallet, badge, and money were taken. The woman was shot as well, but not as cleanly. She escaped the booth and was hit several more times as she struggled across the tile leaving a crimson trail of her life's fluids. The others died, each with two rounds to the head. An execution. Wallets, purses, and the cash register were emptied.

Wes Teague spoke to reporters outside the Senate Office Building. His steel gaze and hardened posture urged the small crowd to retreat backwards and be respectful with any questions.

He read from a prepared script: "The senator is very naturally upset and angry. He left this afternoon to be with his wife and Susan's family in this most difficult time. Before boarding the airplane, the senator urged the formation of a task force aided by the FBI to hunt down the killers. He also called for Senate hearings into discovering the root of this festering evil in America's streets. He seeks recommendations from church, civic, and education leaders along with police chiefs and sheriffs. The demise of our society with illegal guns rampant in the streets and under the auspices of a weak federal government, must end. The deaths of four more people are a tragic loss for families and should be a rally siren for this nation. This is not just an attack on a senator's office and our government, but one aimed at our democratic way of life."

Teague passed out press releases.

Angie appeared in a taped statement from earlier in the day. The screen framed a lovely if strained face.

"My sympathies go out to Susan's family and her many friends. She was loved and respected by all of us. To be taken so young is a loss of epic proportions. I implore anyone with information to immediately contact your police department or the FBI. Please help us catch these killers. We need to do more, much more. My husband and I plead for your help. Do not let these monsters go free."

Three weeks later, Angie and McHale closed the deal on a refurbished brownstone sitting on 16th Avenue NW. The following day, the party's choice of McHale as keynote speaker for the following summer's presidential convention became public knowledge. Big Jim Dearborn called McHale—a most unusual gesture. The four-thousand-square-foot home with twelve-foot rustic copper ceilings held its first party two weeks later. Dearborn declined the invitation.

The DNA testing was completed in relative quiet at the Sacramento facility. A short time later, the computer-programmed refrigeration and preservation evidence system suffered a catastrophic failure. Left in ruins were criminal samples and a compromised record keeping system. Tainted evidence caused the state's attorney general to quickly dismiss twenty-seven pending murders, rapes, and incest cases. Several represented appeals with exculpatory evidence waiting only for a hearing. Experts scrambled but little could be done to save the incarcerated or to place blame where it belonged. The San Francisco Police Department's backlogged closed case squad received the Pearson matter a month later. Juliette's mother, Gina Pearson, left Pasadena and took a new position in a Chicago marketing firm.

Thomas D'Amico's older brother, a retired SFPD cop living in Oklahoma City, made a phone call to a friend in Sacramento. Two weeks later, a late-night call made it clear to him to drop the matter. Losing his pension might cripple the man's finances but Tommy was his little brother. Work began in earnest until one of the private detectives called on Susan Yancy's mother. She declined, assumed her maiden name, and left no forwarding address. The PI was killed a week later in a one car rollover on Highway 101 near Calabasas. The investigation was dropped.

· · · ·

McHale moved around the edge of his disheveled desk and eased into one of the winged chairs. His back ached from the mounting pressure of daily business and his chairmanship of the hearings on gun violence. Pushback from the gun lobbies and Second Amendment proponents, and his old campaign theme of "Take Back Our Streets," painted him in ways needing to be undone. Dearborn's angry phone calls and demands he distance himself from Party fringe elements did not help.

McHale stretched out his long legs and listened to the phones ring in the outer office. On the fourth, someone finally picked up. Two new assistants sat in the desk complex, making him miss Juliette's efficiency once more. In the back of his mind, he pictured himself convincing Big Jim Dearborn to start another search for Juliette. He could not believe she had simply disappeared.

He loosened his tie and undid a stiff shirt collar. A film of moisture coated his face, and his stomach churned from the hurried lunch. He yearned to run the Mall, catch the cool of the morning before DC turned into a baking swamp.

He tried earlier in the morning, but reporters in sneakers waited. They actually chased him a mile at four A.M. He finally gave in and for twenty minutes, held an impromptu news conference in running shorts and spandex, laying out a plan to take America back from lawlessness.

Dearborn exploded within an hour of Fox's airing of the story. "Why the hell are you spitting in the NRA's face? They're on our side, for Christ's sakes. I've already got damage control working from your last speech."

"Big Jim—"

"Jesus Christ, Scotty. You're killing me here."

That was this morning; now he sat weary in the late afternoon.

Sylvia Flores knocked gently and stood in the doorway. His mind was tired. He didn't want to answer. The big red leather chair would hide him.

"Senator?"

A fever lingered somewhere behind his throat. He wanted home, to be in the desert, on the farm. He wanted to break free of the ground in his Cessna and watch the wooded lands stretch out before him. Climb until the air grew smooth and the temperature frigid. He missed Angie. For years, she'd split her time between the California house, her charities, and their DC brownstone. It seemed now she was always someplace he wasn't.

He wanted to have a run with Ken. To go back to a simpler time, to go forward to something different.

Anywhere but here.

"Sir? Senator."

"Yes?" He swallowed hard. His top shirt button was open and his tie askew. Sweat glistened off his forehead. "I was just taking a moment."

"Are you ill, sir? You're pale."

"No, Mrs. Flores. I'm just beat to hell."

He smiled up at her concerned face and buttoned his collar. "I might be getting a cold, too. Really, I'm all right. Time for Senator Todd?"

"He sends his apologies, sir. He's been delayed in committee and wants to reschedule."

McHale unceremoniously flopped back into the cushions. "Thank goodness. Give him a slot next week, please."

"Sir? Congresswoman Crawford asked to see you for a few moments... if you're available. She's getting on a plane in two hours. I can call her office."

His face fell. "Okay. Fine."

He closed his eyes and fell asleep.

When he heard Twila's voice in the anteroom, he quickly pulled his jacket from the seat back and popped a Tic Tac. The door swung open, and he painted on his biggest smile.

"Twila, hi. Come on in. How are you?"

"I only need a minute, Scott. We've got to talk."

She stopped and looked at him more closely.

"You look like shit. Getting enough sleep?"

He snorted. "You look wonderful. As always."

Her eyes narrowed.

"Hey, I'm fine, Twila. What can I do for you?"

She fell into the chair across from his and crossed long legs. A small whirlwind always seemed to accompany her entrance.

"This whole power grid issue is getting out of hand and now, I've got a dozen questions coming at me because of your flip-flop on gun control."

She watched as he pushed the door closed and sat opposite her.

"There's no flip-flop—"

She waved a hand at him. "I don't know what else you'd call it. Where the hell is Wesley Teague?"

"At home. With the task force."

"At a time like this? Jesus. Now is every-man-on-deck time. We need Wes here."

She stood and paced. He remained silent, thinking fondly of those few minutes of sleep.

"Do you know Phil Henry in the Exchange? He's my biggest backer and a goddamn man-eating shark. He just refused to take my call. And do you know why?"

McHale's wasn't tracking. "No. Why?"

With a tiny knock, Sylvia looked around the door. "I'll be leaving now Senator. You remember I told you I had a dentist appointment at three."

McHale twisted on the couch to look at her. "Yes, of course, Mrs. Flores. Good night..." But the door closed behind her.

Twila waited a moment and listened.

Then she rose and twisted the thumb turn on the brass locks. "These walls are paper thin. We've got to watch what we say."

"What are you talking about?" His head swam making his eyes difficult to focus.

She looked sideways at him. "Probably the worst, but you'd know better than me."

He knew she loved the conversational advantage by bulldozing others. "Worst? Why don't you sit back down and explain so I can follow?"

She shook her head at him. "Geezus, but you're a cool one."

"Come on, Twila. I'm beat and you've got a plane to catch. Tell me what's going on."

"Well, the media's circling for one. And the cops are probably a mile ahead of them—"

"Over gun control?"

She looked at him as if he were crazy. "What's wrong with you? Jimmy's coming unglued, and he wants to know if you're implicated. How the hell am I supposed to figure that out?"

McHale screw up his forehead. "What are you talking about? Implicated in what?" His heart slammed heavy, sloshing beats.

She walked to the window. "I guess the cop who was killed with Susan had a brother who had friends in

Sacramento. They came up with some sort of anecdotal information and then quit the case. Well, that story and information got out. We need to nip this thing in the bud before some slaphappy junior G-man decides to bring you down. Jesus Christ, you men and your peckers. All this work could be for nothing."

"What in the hell are you talking about?" He fought to keep his voice even, and stood, lightheaded.

Twila squinted at him. "I'm talking Juliette Pearson's baby. They're saying somehow you got the cops to jack up the lab reports. Is it true?"

"What?" Blood rushed from his head as he reached for the chair back.

Twila paced. "You had Susan Yancy out there co-opting and charming the shit out of some homicide detective working on the missing persons case. Then all of sudden they're both gunned down and the killers drop off the face of the earth."

He ripped at his collar but couldn't find enough air. His mouth worked silently.

She looked out the window and did not see his struggles. "Then, California's whole computer system crashes." She turned. "The DNA evidence ... Scott?"

He pitched forward, eyes rolling white striking the chair and falling face first to the floor. With a shudder, he grew still.

Twila dropped to her knees. "Scott? Are you all right? Shit." She yelled. "Call 9-1-1."

Her hands pulled at his collar and tie.

A fist pounded the door as the knob twisted and rattled. Sweat glistened on his forehead. His mouth hung open. Twila ran and flipped the lock.

A young staffer gaped.

Twila yelled in his face, "Call 9-1-1. Now, goddamn it."

She kneeled next to him, decided he wasn't breathing, and slapped his cheek. Hard. Once, twice. He remained limp, lolling, unresponsive.

She locked their mouths together and forced air into chest.

The staffer ran back yelling into her cell, "Medical emergency...uh, Old Senate Office Building, second floor. Senator Scott McHale's office."

Ribbs cracked under Twila considerable muscles.

Chapter 20

Angie

When the bedside phone rang, Joy snatched it from the hook before her father stirred. Machines beeped as IVs ran into the backs of both hands.

"Hello?" Joy answered in a whisper.

"This is Jim Dearborn." The strident voice hurt her ears. "Who's this?"

"Hello, Mr. Dearborn. This is Joy McHale-Ransburg."

His greeting muted to match hers. "Well, hello, Joy. What are the doctors saying? I heard he's on the mend."

Joy never cared for Big Jim. She didn't like the way he always seemed to be watching her from his side vision.

"My dad is resting comfortably and doing much better. Thank you for asking."

"Good, good. Is your mother there?"

"She's taking a few minutes for herself, Mr. Dearborn."

"Ah. When are you going to call me Big Jim? You're all grown up now."

Joy's skin crawled at the base of her neck. "That's very nice of you, but you'll always be my daddy's wonderful friend and someone I call Mister."

Joy wondered for a moment if she could ever find her mother's grace. Her words sounded sincere unlike Joy's who reminded her of shaking a fishmonger's hand.

"Mom took a break to get a change of clothes. She'll be back in a couple of hours. I can have her call you or give you her cell number." Joy didn't doubt the man had her mother on speed dial.

"Good, good. Will you have her call me? It's pretty important, but I don't want to bother her now."

And the line went dead.

A weak voice from the bed. "Who was that?"

McHale might have been droopy eyed, but his skin glowed pink and full.

"Hi Daddy. You gave me a scare."

She leaned across the bed and gently rested her head on his chest.

He stroked dark hair. "So, I have to faint to get you to visit me, huh?"

"Oh, Dad."

"What happened, anyway? People dance in and out, but no one's told me much."

She lifted up to look at him. "Can you wait for your doctor? He'll be here soon, and Mom will be back in a little while, too."

McHale wiped a hand across his face as she propped a pillow under his head. "Sure, I can. But aren't you my doctor?"

She wasn't buying.

He relented. "Okay, okay. You got that hard head from your mother, you know. I'm not going anywhere and I'm really tired."

He closed his eyes. "It's nice to have you back, sweetie. God, I love you."

In a moment sleep took him, and Joy sat back adjusting his blanket. The image of life without her father flashed unbidden in her mind. She closed her own eyes, forcing the thought away.

• • • •

Even after the third day, the pale, green-painted walls reverberated with controlled bedlam. Mobile television cameras dropped off the shoulders of tired videographers. Walter Reed's senior department head stepped away from the bank of microphones and retreated into the hall behind the podium. The few print journalists tightened their coats in preparation of the afternoon thunderstorm. A last TV reporter hurried a pen through a script. She scanned her cards, then shifted to put the hospital's seal behind her.

She looked into the camera lens. "We are here at Walter Reed Hospital in Bethesda, Maryland where California Senator Scott McHale is resting comfortably. Dr. Sandy Glen described the cause as stress related cardiomyopathy, or as its often called, 'broken heart syndrome.' She said the condition is unusual for a man of Senator McHale's young age and obvious health, but not rare. Dr. Glen says this condition is often brought on by stress or even unusual physical exercise and can occur in athletes during intense exertion. Senator McHale is an avid runner and chairman of the President's Committee on National Physical Fitness, who just weeks ago ..."

The feed would include a clip of McHale and a group of nearly one thousand runners dressed in bright colors warming up for the Potomac River Half Marathon.

The reporter received a head nod from the cameraman and wrapped up.

"Doctors confirmed Senator McHale was given mouth-to-mouth resuscitation by Congresswoman Twila Crawford, also from California. The hospital staff remains guarded but say his prognosis is for a full recovery. Senator McHale was recently named keynote speaker in the upcoming presidential nominating convention in Miami. No word if this selection is in jeopardy.

"Viewers may recall Angie McHale's aide, Susan Yancy, was brutally murdered in an apparent drug-related robbery sparking renewal of Senator McHale's old campaign, 'Taking Back America's Streets.'

"This is Saundra Edgars from Walter Reed Military Hospital for American Headline News."

The young woman stopped and watched her cue cards as if they were about to talk back, then whipped her red hair to one side. The producer whispered into her ear microphone.

She exhaled and nodded to the cameraman. "Lenny says we're okay. They'll dub and edit this crap at the studio. You good?" The editor, doing double duty for a struggling news outlet in the dog-eat-dog news coverage void would voice-over the remaining footage.

The cameraman took the weight off his shoulder. "You don't look happy."

"I'm pissed they scratched my story and made me read this shit. There're some shenanigans going on. A high schooler could've written a better script."

Wet from a downpour, a man stood in the back of the room, the cell phone in his hand recording the video session. He seemed oblivious to the water dripping from his fedora.

The news personality pointed at the man. "Hey. Make him erase that. He's stealing our stuff."

He turned and caught the other's cold eyes.

Instead of stepping in, the cameraman zipped his jacket. "That's one bad dude, Saundra. Besides, what can you do? It's a free country."

She dropped her microphone into the coworker's bag. "My hero. I'm so out of here."

$$\bullet \ \bullet \ \bullet \ \bullet$$

Two days later, Dearborn sat in a wide, deep chair designed for people of girth. The kingmaker and businessman had grown to over three hundred pounds yet never seemed to slow down.

"They said you gave him the 'kiss of life,' Twila. Is that true?" The line of fat under his chin spilled over the open shirt and sprouting gray chest hair.

"What I did, I would do for anyone. Even you, Jimmy." Her tight, short skirt worked on muscular thighs.

He snorted laughter. "I wonder sometimes."

The political work of nearly two decades faltered as news stories and talk shows supercharged their audiences with bad reporting and purposeful misinformation.

And yet, the Kingmaker laughed as Rome burned.

She eyed him with suspicion. "You have something good going on, don't you?"

"Me? Nah, I'm just crying in my beer."

"I don't believe that for a second."

He wet his lips, his eyes sharp. "You could have saved me a lot of trouble, you know. Why didn't you just let him die?"

She said nothing but sipped the top of her amber drink.

He splashed more bourbon in his glass. "First, Juliette thinks she's in love. Then she up and quit without talking to me first. Then, nobody can find her until she pops up selling insurance or some such shit. Nobody knows what the hell is going on. Why don't we have this kind of trouble in your office, Twila?"

"The reason is obvious, Jimmy. I don't have a dick, and everyone's scared shitless of me."

He didn't laugh. "I think you're right."

She placed her glass on the low table. "Why can't I take McHale's place?"

"No. I got plans for you. They're dicey, though. Are you up for it?"

Twila held his gaze. "I'll do whatever you say. We've still got time, so I'm sure you'll let me in on this thing eventually. Scott might not have died, but he's just as good as dead. Fainting like a prissy little girl doesn't look very presidential."

Big Jim leaned his bulk forward. "You're a tough one."

Her rock-solid gaze didn't waver. "He needs to resign. I need to be in his seat. It's that simple."

Big Jim started a slow shake of his head. "Scotty will do as he's told but getting him to quit might be tough and end in chaos that even I can't manage. For right now, I want him where we can keep an eye on him. Let the furor settle down. Besides, what makes you think I could appoint you to his seat? That's the governor's job, not mine."

She smiled, shifting and re-crossing her legs. "If I was the incumbent senator and a weak titty-baby like our pistachio farmer, I'd have a lock on the off-year senatorial run."

"You're thinking too small, Twila."

She clicked her front teeth together and poured another inch of bourbon. "Really? I've never been accused of thinking small before. McHale's kind of a quitter, but not me."

"No, Twila. Until I'm ready, McHale stays under my thumb, and you stay in the shadows. I got bigger plans for you."

She laughed.

"You look good, Twila. Real good."

"And you're still as horny as an old goat. Won't you ever slow down?"

She stood and pushed the low table away, catching the twist switch on the table lamp. The room fell into a street-illuminated twilight as a zipper ratcheted and Big Jim Dearborn chortled. Twila Crawford murmured, and the room fell silent.

Chapter 21

Nieto

Judge Nieto's library in the gated-community home forced uninvited visitors into an alcove lined with books. Only a single chair behind a forbidding desk awaited the judge.

The others stood while the judge read. "What proof do you have *not* within the body of this affidavit to indicate probable cause of Senator McHale's involvement?"

His round Latino face looked over the top of reading glasses.

Mahan, the FBI agent assigned to the San Francisco Joint Task Force knew this line of questioning and did not fall into the trap. "None, Your Honor. What we know as evidence including exculpatory is fully contained within the detective's documents."

Two Bay Area police officers stood with the agent. The taller man, an African-American picked at his teeth. Nieto had seen this man before in his court. The antipathy was mutual. The third man watched out the window as if the document about to ruin a man's life meant nothing. All three were part of the hastily formed "Take Back America's Streets" campaign.

The agent began again. "We have a myriad of hunches, rumors, and innuendo, but what you have before you are solid facts. We're gathering more each day, but there's no allusion, speculation, or subjection in this document."

"Of course. Which is why I am getting this request at ten o'clock at night, and not Justice Thompson who normally handles your task force."

Nieto flipped a page and reread a passage, not bothering to look at the men.

Agent Mahan remained motionless. Of course, he had shopped judges but not for the usual reasons. Both men knew Nieto political leanings. Besides, they had waited until their assigned judge was on vacation. Mahan knew Nieto was their best chance to squash this and to have the task force escape scrutiny.

The judge pressed a thumb and forefinger under his glasses. "I fail to see sufficient facts to meet a Fourth Amendment test of probable cause to seize the senator's DNA. You might want to just ask him, but this request for a warrant is denied. Bring me something I can work with."

The taller cop coughed "Bullshit" under his breath.

Nieto looked up and frowned.

Agent Mahan quickly stepped forward. "Your Honor. Possibly the affidavit is not written clearly enough—"

He scowled toward the cop and turned to the FBI agent. "On the contrary. This one's a cut above what I normally see. The problem is not the document but the evidence. How do you connect the woman in the hotel with the senator? Or the mysterious shadowed figure on the coffee shop security tape in a driving rainstorm through a plate glass window? The parking lot witness is especially weak: a tired family finishing fourteen hours on the road in the middle of the same storm. Not one of their testimonies can stand alone.

It's only suspicious when put it together. And as you know 'reasonable suspicion' is not 'probably cause.'"

Nieto tiredly shook his head. "You obviously believe these people, but you need better than this. There's barely enough here to even disturb me tonight."

He held out the unsigned papers.

The shorter wiry lieutenant, silent until that moment, stepped forward. "Your Honor? We've placed McHale in the hotel. That's not in question. He is the lasso pulling this together. His wife told us about their phone conversation. I don't get it."

Nieto let the papers drop to the desktop. "This is not a debate. But for the sake of argument, I see the hotel record and the senator's *office* credit card paying for the rooms. The same card Ms. Pearson used during her employment that ended. Where is that card? Where are the charges? Nothing here conclusively places him in the hotel and in her room. And the desk clerk as corroboration? He can't remember a face as famous as McHale's. A bit unusual, don't you think? I appreciate the exculpatory FD-302 report. That shows me you're playing fair, but the fact he does not recognize one of the most famous faces in America doesn't help your case. You need a positive ID, not a negative or even a neutral one. You think McHale hide and let Pearson rent the rooms? Like in high school? No, no. You guys need better evidence. That's the bottom line."

Agent Mahan spoke. "We tried but the lab had that environmental problem three months after the storm."

The judge switched his gaze. "Correct. Lack of evidence, not to mention the disaster in the state's lab. A double whammy. Am I making myself clear? You guys need to do your own work and quit depending on science to do it for you. You're dismissed."

The Agent glanced at the two officers. "Yes, your honor."

The three let themselves out.

The judge waited for the front door to close and the alarm to reset. He picked up the phone. There was no need to look up the Muroc County number. The favor was now paid in full, and Neito intended to have his chit torn up.

Chapter 22

Scott

McHale's release from the hospital and transfer to his Georgetown brownstone caused little fanfare at one in the morning. After another week, Joy returned to California. Thanks to a husband with plentiful family resources, she left onboard a private jet from the Ransburg family's stable of airplanes, and so avoided the cameras, too.

Morning grey kept sunshine at bay in the exclusive neighborhood. He sat in a padded chair looking into his tiny private court of shrubs and evergreens. Angie clanged a dish inside the sink.

He turned to her. "Why don't you just ask me?"

"Because you'll tell me when you're ready."

She filled the carafe with filtered water. Fresh coffee grounds waited in the machine.

Silence greeted the patter of drizzle and the gurgling spew of the gutters. He wondered how life became so convoluted.

"Angie. I never slept with Juliette. I never kissed Juliette. I never touched Juliette, except in the course of our work. She had other friends ... boyfriends. I was not one of them."

Angie broke the lingering silence. "But?"

He hated that she knew and so didn't want to let the words loose in the room. "I can't say she wasn't attractive. Obviously, she is ... was. That's half the reason why Dearborn sent her to us, but I never gave in to temptation."

Angie gripped the carafe. "You were tempted, though, isn't that right? You flirted. You choose motel rooms next door to one another."

"Don't treat me like I'm on the stand."

She poured the water. "You'd better get used to it. The court of public opinion is going to have you on the stand twenty-four-seven for a long time to come."

"Yes, I thought she was pretty. *You* thought she was pretty. To most of the staff and Congress, she was ... poised for great things."

Angie glanced around. "You're kidding, right? *Poised for great things?* Because she was pretty? She had every man's attention, including apparently yours, wondering what she'd be like in bed. Who did she date, Scott? What was his name?"

The question took him back. "I ... I don't think I know."

"No, you don't, because she didn't date. Doesn't that seem a little strange to you?"

"I'm busy. Too busy to—"

"Why didn't she date if so many men found her attractive?"

He sighed. "I haven't the foggiest. I don't ... didn't go around asking what she did on her off time. I know she went out. She went to functions ... sometimes. She seemed to know people. I didn't keep track of her love life, Angie. The entire male population of Congress knew she was there. I just don't think there was one guy who was special to her."

"Nonsense. You know that special person. *You.* Just like you noticed all the others noticing her."

"For Christ's sake. What man wouldn't notice her?"

She returned to the sink. "Apparently not my man. Except I would've never believed it if someone had told me."

Her words crushed him. "Angie, I love you. I've always loved you."

When she turned this time, her face was hard. "You loving me is not the question here, Scott. The question is what the hell is going on with you. What went on with Juliette? What do the police have and why do they want a DNA swab?"

He looked up, his face incredulous. "What?"

"Your Judge Nieto denied the warrant, but that's only one jurisdiction."

He dropped his head into his hands.

"She left your employ months ago and got another job in San Jose." She placed two cups on the small counter. "If I'm going to help, you have got to trust me with the whole story. Everything. The good and the bad."

He spun the lock on the safe holding his conscience. "Everything, then."

She placed coffee in front of him and sat down.

His chest ached. He needed Angie. She was the smartest person he knew. Without her and her support, there could be no life.

He pushed the cup aside. "I've got to go back aways, to the time she worked in our San Fran office and for Dearborn. You knew that Juliette was his spy. She passed information back and forth. Her job let Big Jim and Wes Teague know what was happening in the office when they weren't around. I saw this as a problem at first, but not later."

"How could she not be a problem if she spied on you?"

His finger wiped at his dry lips. "Because Juliette changed her mind."

"Why would she do that?"

"I changed her mind." He watched his wife take in the information.

"In exchange for what? You?"

He held up his hand. "I never promised her anything like that. Not really. Juliette had ambitions. She wanted to be more than just an aide. I made it clear when you weren't in DC, she and I would go to social functions together. She'd get exposure to the movers and the shakers. I kept my promise, but then she got the wrong idea and came on to me. I should have realized ..."

He sighed, wanting the truth now, not some mealy-mouthed version.

"Maybe I did realize, but when you were gone, it was all so easy. I thought she'd come around. Find someone."

Angie's words were not kind or understanding. "Apparently not. This girl was only a few years older than Joy. She was a family friend, Scott, and yet you let her believe something that wasn't ever going to happen?"

"Yes, but please. Let me tell the whole story."

Angie's jaw muscles flexed under her smooth skin.

"Juliette knew my issues-like guns on the street. She helped by keeping her ears open and yeah, Dearborn probably got a lot of the same information as me. When she sat in on committee meetings and I wasn't there, she wrote up notes. She had contacts on other committees, and they shared information. She was smart and I was helping her. Remember that she dug up the dirt on Lora Lu that we didn't need to use. She talked about that, Lora Lu, I mean. She once asked me if I thought she could run for Lora Lu's seat on San Francisco's Board of Supervisors."

McHale stopped, the image of a headless, corpse floating in the bay weakening him.

"What'd you say?"

He gulped a deep breath. "I said yes, and I meant it. She was that good. Dearborn didn't mind planting Wes and Juliette in my office. Wes never talked to me. He was totally loyal to Big Jim. Juliette was loyal, too, but at least she helped me. What was I supposed to say, 'no'? Shit. She could run circles around Lu."

Angie rose and emptied her coffee into the sink. McHale's sat untouched. His fingers shook.

"This is too much strain on you. I understand better, even if I think you're wrongheaded. You should have talked to me about this. This is more than you leading some young woman astray. We have a problem, and it's not just that someone murdered Juliette. You left yourself vulnerable by trying to work behind Dearborn's back. What if Wes decided Juliette was reporting to you? Don't you think he'd turn her in? You're not adept enough to run a spy operation, Scott. That's just stupid and dangerous."

Her words stung. "I know you're right. I've gotten us into a hell of mess. And now, just when we're so close."

She pointed a finger. "We'll get through this, Scott, but no more secrets."

He nodded. "No more secrets. I promise."

• • • •

Angie flew home after cancelling her own agenda and spending nearly a month in his office. McHale kept his promise while avoiding the media and working hard to rebuild congressional and personal relationships. Whispered accusations followed his presence in the Capitol while aides and pages avoided being alone with him. Swanson surged in the polls and primaries. Few people talked about McHale's unlikely showing in the Iowa Caucus. Most called it ancient history.

Wesley Teague quietly became McHale's Chief of Staff after Angie resumed her charitable and NGO duties.

They wrapped up a meeting in his office with a snap of their iPad cases.

Teague stood. "You need some time off, Senator. We've got a busy summer coming up."

"It's a nice thought, Wes. We have a ten-day break coming. I can last."

"I know you can, sir. But I was thinking about a couple of days in contemplation before your appearance on the floor next week. Mr. Dearborn thinks you need it to clear your head. Everyone will be watching, and I've already heard C-SPAN will give you live as well as rebroadcast. You're going to get exposure but frankly, they'll want to see you implode. Same reason everyone watches car races, sir. For the blood and gore."

McHale leaned back in his chair. Wes was not usually so talkative.

"Waiting for the crackup, huh? Me taking some time sounds great but I'm not in the mood."

"Mr. Dearborn says this is up to you, but the keynote still has your name in the slot. Nothing has changed, which makes next week all the more important. Maybe a couple of days with someone other than your Beltway buddies will be therapeutic."

McHale watched the other man. He thought about the stares and whispers Ted Kennedy must have earned after Chappaquiddick. How did that man go on with his public career? The police had pretty much discounted his own involvement in Juliette's death. He wondered if the collective memory was really that brief.

Wes continued toward the door. "What about your family friends in North Carolina? Take your little airplane and go unwind."

Teague annoyed him with his unbroken, unblinking, pale-eyed stare. McHale dropped a pen to the desktop and smiled. Teague did not smile back. Of course.

His private line buzzed. "Can you excuse me, Wes? I really need to take this."

"Yes, sir." Teague left without another word.

"Hello?"

"Yo, buddy."

"Ken, hey. Great to hear from you. Still surviving in New York?"

The big FBI agent chuckled. "Catching the shuttle tomorrow morning. The real question is, do you still have a job? They are raking you over the coals, bro. Who'd you piss off?"

"The western world, I think. Poor Juliette and Susan."

"Oh, God yeah. That's really low. Boils my blood." He fell silent for several seconds. "Are you okay?"

"Sure,"

"What about this hospital thing? When I heard, I called Angie. I had a ticket in hand, but she told me to stay away. I guess an FBI SAC visiting would have really stirred up a hornet's nest."

"Ah, nobody believes you're a real FBI agent, Ken. You know that."

The other man laughed. "Yeah, yeah. Thanks. At least you still have your sense of humor."

"It's great to hear your voice. Someone who's not asking me when I quit beating my wife or in this case, doing my aide."

"Hey, guys in high places eventually get the spotlight jammed up their behinds, you know that. You're one of the good guys. You can weather this storm."

McHale smiled at his empty office and cancelled calendar. "I will. Thanks."

"For nothing. We still gonna get a run in on Saturday morning? Or, are you planning to turn tail on me?"

McHale made a quick decision. "I'm going to weasel, Ken. I'm about to call Hal in North Carolina and see if he's got a room at the B&B. A couple of days there will help me finish up the keynote and maybe get my head on straight for next week's Senate fight."

"Sounds good, but unfortunately, that'll mean I'll have to take the wife for a run."

"Too bad. I know how much you hate getting your ass kicked."

Chapter 23

Scott

The small airport was quiet at predawn. The sun's rays over the eastern horizon waited in most people's slumbering imagination, but not McHale. He arrived in the dark with a purpose. Paula was never an early riser, and today, he didn't want to be dissuaded from the flight.

McHale undid the hasp on the hangar door. The lock had been snapped backward, and he had to crane his neck around to read the combination.

Typical.

The airport boy who washed the planes had not paid attention. He pushed the tall doors to the side, the wings on the fifty-year-old classic clearing by only a few feet. The airplane was not usually a challenge to handcart to the apron when alone. This time, however, the effort left him winded and with a heaving chest. The FAA required every pilot to ground himself when a medical condition threatened his abilities. His certificate might be in jeopardy because of the hospitalization, even if Bethesda wrote it off as something other than a heart attack.

Stress, he told himself. Who wasn't stressed these days? He was feeling fine, and the flight was only two hours long.

He would avoid the FAA security restrictions around DC thus making a flight plan unnecessary. Except for Winchester's towerless airfield, and until he landed at towerless Andrews-Murphy airport, he did not need to talk with anyone. Radio calls were optional. Over the years he

192

had flown using this legal method for thousands of hours. He would be fine.

Stars blinked over the ridgeline, promising a smooth cruise, just as Wesley Teague had suggested. Hal Burckhardt's Sunset Bed and Breakfast would be a perfect place to relax before the floor speech next week.

The engine came to life with its oil warming in the cool night. If the few morning clouds didn't block his way, he'd cut diagonally down the invisible West Virginia border and fly south until the sun broke. By that time, the Blue Ridge mountain would disappear, replaced by the remote Nantahala's giant peaks. He flipped off the mini mag flashlight hanging around his neck and adjusted the instrument lighting. The glow sent chill bumps of pleasure up his spine. In less than ninety minutes, the sun would bump against civil twilight and the rest of the world would wake. He planned to arrive at midpoint over the range just as the day grew long enough to illuminate his way along the valleys of knifepoint ridges and hundred-foot-tall trees to the lodge.

He ran a finger down the checklist then released the parking brake to move away from the row of hangars. Because there was no tower, he habitually mumbled many memorized phrases to kill the silence and help fill his mind.

"November 2668Z cleared to taxi for Runway 32. South departure."

He clicked the automatic runway lights into operation using his transmitter. Twin lines of blue showed the yellow taxi lines while muted white globes marked the runway.

He halted short of a double yellow line and ran the engine to partial takeoff power.

A minute later, he announced to himself, "Runup checklist complete."

Aloud, he repeated a memorized ditty and touched each switch and lever assuring its proper position.

He flexed the flight controls and looked at the runway approach to ensure no other aircraft interfered.

The radio keyed open with a touch of the yoke's button. "Winchester Traffic. November 2668Z departing Three-Two left turn southbound."

Naturally, no one answered. No one was supposed to answer, and only a few on the same frequency might chance to hear the transmission. They would not care.

He resumed talking to himself. "Taxi into position and wait."

He did so and made a final check. Pushing in the throttle, the engine's roar broke the silence of the night.

At about twenty knots the tail lifted, and he eased the yoke forward. The wheels quickly broke free as the mountains, sky, and horizon disappeared into the murk. The lights of a few houses appeared below while a lone car drove toward DC on the freeway. He began a slow turn south and settled into the long climb.

The night hid the horizon for now, so he concentrated on his instrument panel.

He was about to key the radio, but then let the switch go. Habit almost had him call Flight Service. There was no need. His transponder automatically told them he climbed away from the metro area and that he was authorized.

Sort of. He smiled.

The night calmed him with smooth air and quiet radios. This was the euphoria he liked; this was the runner's high for pilots. Wes Teague had been right. He needed to be away from the office and Sylvia Flores's questioning stares. What did she believe? Could she actually think him capable of the spurious op-ed speculation appearing in the *Post* or the *Times*? Every journalist, no matter how senior or untried wanted an interview, or at least a sound bite.

But not here, and not now.

He forced Sylvia Flores out of his mind and crossed the valley with sleeping Luray, New Market, and Harrisonburg in the distance. The aircraft leveled at eight thousand, five hundred feet. He adjusted the power and set a manual heading bug. Navigation and piloting were up to him, just as he liked it. He did not own an autopilot.

After thirty minutes Roanoke appeared, only to flicker and disappear in the distance. Low clouds would burn off at sunrise. A common weather phenomenon this time of year. No worries.

He watched his instrument panel. Wings level, gauges in the green. And he was on course.

Other ground lights flickered ahead of him. Some blinked and then covered over, and some never revealed themselves.

He hadn't forgotten Angie's admonition. No weather and no chances. Of course, that was before the rest of the world, including his loyal wife, believed he had cheated on her with an employee who then ended up dead. Now rumors circulated she had been pregnant with his baby.

My God. How could it get worse?

His mind returned to the cockpit. Without Roanoke's lights, he switched over to a ground navigation station to check his progress. The off flag remained.

He tapped the instrument. Nothing. Old instruments. He needed to upgrade his cockpit. Maybe after the summer's convention. For now, he might need the money for other projects.

No matter. The satellite GPS on the government purchased iPad tracked his progress, and he was right on course.

But, better safe than sorry now that he was away from DC.

He dialed a frequency and keyed the mic. "Roanoke Approach, good morning. Cessna November 2668Z at eight point five looking for flight following."

Silence. He waited to give a sleepy controller time to put down his coffee cup.

A short minute passed. "Roanoke? Cessna N2668Z radio check."

Still no answer.

He changed to his second radio and dialed in Roanoke, again without any luck. He rotated the knobs to a new frequency. "Washington Center, November 2668Z, five miles north of Roanoke requesting flight following."

No answer.

He waited a few moments, checked the frequency, and tried again. When no one answered, he dialed up a nearby airport's UNICOM, knowing the likelihood of another pilot being on the air at this hour was slim.

He was right. No one responded.

He flipped the frequency to a continuously broadcasting weather station a few miles away in Bluefield. No audio on his navigation radio.

His stomach tightened, the first inkling he might have a problem. As he reset his transponder code from 1200 to 7600, the lost-communications squawk, he noticed the amber reply-light.

There was none. The LED was dark.

"I'll be damned."

He was certain the transponder worked an hour ago on climb-out. As if to confirm his recollection, he noticed several of his circuit breakers popped out. He pushed the alternator in, but it wouldn't stay.

He looked at his charging indicator pegged to the wrong side of the instrument.

Mystery solved. The alternator or maybe the voltage regulator had failed. Both were critical to the airplane's electrical system even though electricity was not needed to fly, only to talk and find one's way around. The deep night raised the system's failure to be important but not critical.

He ran through the emergency checklist by turning off electrical equipment and sending the cockpit into near blackness. Saving the battery was important now, and besides, he had a light. The iPad only pulled microamps with its supplemental internal power. He liked the comforting glow and left the plug in the airplane's auxiliary port. He looked at the screen. Right on course.

Thirty minutes to civil twilight or the first purple of the coming day.

He re-read the printed checklist using his penlight then sifted through all the stories and texts he had ready to come up with a solution.

Nothing.

The airplane ran strong while his mind continued the search. He dreaded hearing Angie's face-to-face admonition. He could work this out. He was about to run through the checklist again when the iPad's blinking low-battery alert indicator caught his attention.

"What the hell?"

He checked the cigarette lighter charging plug. The hot malleable plastic stung his fingertips.

"Damn it."

He gritted his teeth and pulled the insert loose. Too late. The damage was done. Somehow the airplane had sucked the iPad's power.

The screen blinked, then failed.

"Son of a bitch."

He reached down and flicked on the tiny flashlight hanging around his neck. The cockpit lit but the rest of the dark world's silhouettes disappeared in the Plexiglas reflection. He pulled out his old paper map and penciled in the time and his last known position.

The compass showed a drift off course of nearly thirty degrees. He corrected.

Having an electrical problem created an issue, not a crisis. He could simply wait for the sun to rise high enough to find himself on the map and follow mountain tops and roads to Andrews Murphy. Even if the mechanic could not fix the airplane over the long weekend, he could always rent a car and still be back in time.

The thought relaxed McHale. Bit by bit, he resumed enjoying the flight and the night. He tried to identify the occasional ground lights on his paper maps by keeping a close eye on heading and altitude. He grinned and wondered if the penlight battery would join his other failed technology, too.

The first rumble, deep in the little airplane's guts alerted him. His hand rested on the throttle, a plunger with a knob and a rod extending into the forward cowling. Experience taught him to see and feel the engine through his fingertips.

Ice in the carburetor wasn't unusual this time of year, especially at altitude. Nevertheless, he pulled the carburetor heat control. No change, no ice, just nerves. He rechecked the throttle wide open.

McHale sighed. "I have got to get out more often."

At the same moment, he smelled the first hint of smoke. "Oh, no. Don't do this."

The flashlight bounced gauge. Needles in the green.

He glanced up. The eastern horizon slept darkly.

He bent to sniff. Nothing. The engine ran smoothly, the controls felt unchanged. No sign of anything untoward around the engine cowls. The paper map showed hills, forests, and mountains for thirty miles in all directions.

He arched his neck to see any lights behind. Only the black horizon. He flicked off the flashlight. No glow outside around the engine.

He corrected the heading to get him back on course.

For several minutes, he wondered about the odd smell, deciding his imagination had run away. He fought to put the uneasiness behind him. This was probably not the smartest trip he had ever taken. He needed that instrument cockpit upgrade. Money was not a reason to delay if he planned flights over mountains.

The night stars reminded him that the ocean, flatlands, and cities were a simple turn east and toward the rising sun. The restricted areas in central Virginia were big enough that he might be intercepted by an Air Guard F-16 fighter jet. Especially, because he was without a working radio.

That would be embarrassing, and he would have even more questions to answer.

No way. He wanted to figure this one out rather than shame himself yet another time. The Cessna's fuel would take him far beyond the Andrews-Murphy airport, and if necessary, well into the daylight over central Tennessee, Georgia, or even Alabama. He could miss the restricted airspace, and no one would be the wiser.

Even Hal, his buddy, knew to cancel the reservation by noon if he didn't call.

Cell phone.

He patted his pockets. Even if they only rarely worked from the airplane, its battery would at least give him light.

But he already knew the answer. The phone was safely in his luggage and far behind him in compartment storage. He could never reach the phone before the pilotless airplane reacted to a change in center of gravity and lost control.

Twenty-six minutes to civil twilight on Hamilton's luminous dial. No light and no problem. He could do this.

Piece of cake.

Orion's belt slipped behind his wing as he scanned instruments and calculated a position on the map. Dead reckoning with time and estimated ground speed for the next thirty minutes would take him near enough to the Nantahala Mountain range where he could circle and wait for dawn.

The smell again.

He flipped off the mini-flashlight and suddenly knew exactly what was happening. A dim yellow orange flickered near his feet.

The illumination caught wisps of smoke swirling toward his face.

He pulled the throttle back to idle and closed the vents.

The comforting growl of the engine quieted. The glow remained under the instrument panel.

Engine fire would be a nightmare scenario.

Flashlight back into the mouth. He pulled the fuel-air mixture out and turned the fuel tanks off. The engine would die.

He worked from memory. No time to look up the book procedures. He pulled the nose up to seventy-six miles per hour. His descent slowed.

The engine stopped making power. The propeller spun without thrust. Only wind noise remained. That and his beating heart. He would try a restart hoping the fire would not rekindle.

The master electrical switch was already dead. He hit the switch anyway and twisted off the magneto ignition key.

The fire must die. Remove fuel, ignition, and air. Right? Find a place to sit down. Night black outside. Sacrifice the airplane to let the pilot live.

The flashlight beam scurried around the cockpit as his head turned. No need to save the battery now.

The orange glow and heat grew worse. He worked the fire extinguisher from its clip and gave two short blasts. A white cloud of vapor and particles filled the cockpit floor.

He stared. Orange flames escaped worse than before.

He jammed the nose down into the ocean of ink. The seat of his pants lifted off the airplane's padded leather frame. He needed to blow the flames out. Wind noise grew. Altimeter unwound. Eight thousand feet. Seventy-five hundred. His breath came in gulps. The airspeed needle rose into the yellow arc. Seven thousand feet. The nose fought to climb. He pressed forward until his forearms ached, then trimmed out the back pressure. The strain grew. Keep the speed up. Blow out the fire. Keep the speed up.

As suddenly as the fire had appeared, the flames were gone. The heat lessened. The glow subsided.

He took his first breath. Tiny shards of glass nerves pricked his hot skin. Nothing out the windscreen. The altimeter passed six thousand, then five-thousand-five hundred.

He gave an extra moment then pulled up with all the strength remaining in his arms. "G" forces pressed him down. The wings strained. A yell of exertion escaped as his back arched and a grunt escaped his maniacal grin.

His mind's eye waited for a mountain peak to crush him.

Wind buffeted as the airplane settled into level flight. His speed remained in the high yellow arc, so he climbed to five thousand. The airspeed needle moved into the green.

He took a calming breath too soon. As if having a mind of its own, the fire did not just return, a blowtorch reignited and torched his jeans threatening to roast him alive. He barely held in the scream as fire and heat attacked his feet and legs. Yellow orange reflected in every corner of the cockpit as smoke from the inside filled the windscreen.

McHale breathed openmouthed around the flashlight, fighting to remain calm. He pointed the extinguisher's nozzle at his leg and pushed a rudder to the stop. The fire ignored the dusting of white flakes as the out of balance skid sent the blaze to one side. He immediately lost the choicest aerodynamics and altitude and began a killing.

He must find the ground before it found him. The altimeter unwound with gut-clenching speed. A death race to a mountain top.

The rug beneath his canvas shoes smoldered. New waves of acrid fumes burned at his watery eyes. The stench choked him. Flaming plastic dripped from the instrument panel's guts. He gave a last blast of the extinguisher, and it was done.

The noxious air choked into an acrid poison.

He stamped his free foot, trying to kill the smoking fibers as the altimeter spun down. His pant leg burst into flames. A shadow passed to his left. He snapped his head up but saw nothing. The flashlight showed four thousand-three hundred feet. Low moans escaped the melting firewall. The fire demanded to come inside. He fought the pain in his burning legs.

Taunting flames ripped through the instrument panel, and it was over. Blistered hands beat at his jacket cuffs. The altitude unwound past four thousand feet.

You've got my attention, God. Now what?

A second shadow passed the windscreen. The airspeed dropped to sixty knots and the wings began to shudder. He evened up the rudders and pushed the nose over just as the first and tallest of the trees hit him. The trunk of another ripped off the left wing and slammed his face into the panel. The flashlight drove deep into his throat as the cabin twisted in a wild tumble. Sheet aluminum, seats, and plexiglass ripped and tore in a flaming plunge from hundred-foot pine tops to render his final judgement on a wandering moral compass.

McHale's pleading words fell on a silent forest. *Mi Angela. Te amo con todo mi corazon.*

Chapter 24

Adlai

By the time the two men tossed their gloves and goggles into the locker, the afternoon sun already touched the western hilltops.

"Jesus, Abel. Can't you hurry it up?"

The brothers, as different as any two unrelated men of the Appalachians, grew up inseparable. Abel stood taller but stooped after a lifetime of mocking. His dark hair and stringy matted with sweat. He had been cursed at birth with a long face and then managed to both mash and break his large nose. The family didn't have money, so when he fell hitting tree branches on the way down, nature healed the nose for him. The more charitable around the hollow referred to Abel as slow. The rest of the world would come to know him as mouth breathing and retarded. And, of course, the older brother to Adlai of jail and local fame.

Adlai and Abel shared the same deceased mother, but similarities stopped there. Younger by several years, Adlai, with heavy shoulders and a wide chest, stood shorter by a foot with disproportionately short legs. His perpetual smirk laughed at the wrong times and hid a mean, quick mind. He devised the get-rich plans that drove the slower-witted Abel. Even though few schemes ever bore fruit, Adlai's brain never slowed his penchant for notorious trouble and Saturday night jail.

Adlai stood outside of the locker room's toilet and banged with his fist. "Abel? Can you just wipe it off please, and let's go."

He gave the rusting metal door a last punch for good measure and opened his second can of beer.

A halting laugh from inside the stall. "I'm almost ready. Keep your shirt on. I think I broke my buckle again."

Abel stepped out grinning and yanking on his twisted hand-me-down leather belt. His long, muscled arms worked at a dirty blue-jean top.

Adlai waved a hand in the other's face. "Oh, good Christ. I guess you can't smell with your broken honker, but I think somethin' died in you."

Abel laughed, his cadence slow and deliberate. "Oh, I can smell okay. My honker works just fine."

Before predeceasing his wife's death by a month, their father worked the coalmines with a temper as dark as the tunnels. After a third of his own life passed and with a chronic cough and sniffles, he presented two younger sons and a middle sister to the same mining company.

But the mines were not for Abel and Adlai. The men pledged themselves to a life on a California beach eating oranges and avocados and working in the movies. Failing that, Adlai promised his older brother he could sell his sexual favors to the beautiful blond ocean worshipers. They had watched a movie about a cowboy and learned exactly what men did in the city.

The day after his sixteenth birthday, Adlai talked Abel into stealing their father's pickup truck for the drive to the West Coast. The truck blew a head gasket in St. Louis, stranding the pair. Each got twenty dollars for scrap value and a job working the barges before returning to the mountains. Their father beat both sons and told them to report to the mill office in the morning. He could not trust them to go back into the mines and besides, working the lumber yards paid nearly as much as chipping and loading coal. The two worked until their father had another truck, after which, he promptly died.

One the day they committed murder, the two drove the same truck back to the hollow. They stopped at the Piggly Wiggly for beer and meat sticks. An hour in the afternoon heat with windows open, the six-pack was gone, and the slanting sun closed their eyes.

The Mexican was invisible on the dirt road.

Thump.

The slow-witted Abel screamed. "Jesus, Adlai. I think you killed him. I hope he wasn't nobody we knowed."

The younger brother braked slowly to a stop and stared straight ahead. "He stepped in front of me, a ignorant bastard. He's just a Mex, and I only clipped him a little."

Abel turned his mouth down. "I know you saw him, so don't you tell me no different." Abel shook his brother's heavy shoulder. "You did see him, didn't you?"

Adlai had seen the drunk and intended to give him a start, have a laugh. Now, he wasn't so sure.

Adlai adjusted the rearview mirror. "I think maybe I killed him."

The two sat in the dented GMC and wondered what to do next.

Abel's voice quaked like a child. "We should just go on home. Leave him here, then no one'll know who done it."

Adlai already thought through such a scenario and rejected it. He watched police shows like *CSI*, and learned about paint transfers and DNA. He did not actually know how the science worked but the police always arrested the guilty man. He believed DNA must be a vapor of some kind unique to a person. Like a fingerprint, the police likely kept a DNA master file.

Adlai clinched his jaw. "No, big brother. We can't leave him, because we the only ones driving this road 'cept for old man Smith and the Cotton boys. If one of them see'm first and calls the sheriff, he'd bring the others, and they'll get us for sure."

Abel put his long face in big hands. "What are we going to do?"

Adlai angrily gripped and regripped the steering wheel. "Goddamn stupid Mex. We need to figure how to get the DNA vapors off the fender."

Abel looked up, confused. "What's a DNA vapor?"

"Shut the hell up and help me get him loaded. We gonna drop him in the hills."

Abel knew when not to question his brother. For the better part of his life, and certainly, since their father died, the younger brother made all the decisions for both of them.

Adlai shifted the grinding gears into reverse and backed up next to the body. Neither man got out of the truck. Both gazed at the unmoving form. Death came to everything in the hills, and both had killed animals since they were old enough to walk. This would be their first man.

Adlai heaved his wide chest. "Come on. We best check to make sure he's dead. This is not our lucky day. You heard me, get out."

Abel undid the door latch with halting fingers and stepped onto the packed dirt. Adlai slid out but remained on the far side of the truck, running a hand through dirty brown hair.

"Go on, Abel. Check him out."

Both watched blood trickle around the man's mouth and engorged throat.

"Goddamn it, Abel, you dumb bastard. Check him. Is he alive?"

Abel bent and pushed with a large hand. The man rolled onto his back. "Looky at his neck. Oh shit, oh dear, little brother. You broke it. This is so bad."

Adlai thought that did not make sense. He had aimed for the man's arm and hip, and he was a good driver. Everyone said so.

Crickets started in the darkening woods as a cool breeze rubbed branches together.

Adlai still had not moved. "Toss him in the back. Quick. Those Cotton boys will be coming any time, and they'll be drunk. Pick him up. I'll get the tailgate."

Abel did not want to touch the dead man. He has seen the same television shows as Adlai.

But his brother growled incessantly. "Get him in there, Abel, and then, you drive."

The answer came slowly. "Okay."

Abel bent to pick him up, then stood quickly up. He wrinkled his big, crooked nose. "He done been in a fire and it burned him up. We didn't do no fire."

Adlai took a few slow steps, not wanting his vapor to touch the dead man. His dumb brother could be right. The smell of burned flesh and clothing stopped him.

Abel worried, looking at the darkening sky for an answer. "He looks like hamburger. You really hit him hard."

Blood oozed from broken teeth and a ripped mouth.

The man moaned and threw up a frothy pink and red.

Both reared back.

Abel shrieked. "Oh, shit, oh dear. He's still alive. What we gonna do now?"

Adlai didn't know. "Shut up, for God's sake, just shut up."

Abel bounced around the prostrate man, rubbing his big hands together.

A voice spoke from behind "What you two got there?"

Chapter 25

Ada

Both jumped and turned to face a young woman. For the last few minutes, she'd watched her two bumbling brothers as they schemed and connived.

The hulking brother keened. "Oh Ada. We done killed this man."

Adlai skulked a step back and watched his sister. "He ain't dead."

She dressed in the same brass-button blue jeans as the boys. Her rough, callused hands worked the farm's few dairy cows, chickens, and goats. Since their parents and siblings died, she ran the house and the land.

And, her brothers.

Ada glanced between the two men and eased down the bucket of dying catfish. "What was you gonna do with him now, Adlai? Now that he *ain't dead*."

Abel bounced on his toes. "We thought we done killed him ... and we was gonna take him to the hills ... and then we saw he was alive and making this pitiful noise."

Adlai interrupted. "For God's sake, Abel."

Like the long generations of women before her, the plain-faced Ada hardened early in life. The loss of their parents only meant she stepped into her role earlier than usual. The two brothers who remained avoided as much work as possible, so little room remained in her heart for the superfluous.

She knelt to look closer as the chilling wind promised rain.

Abel looked to his sister. "Ada, what are we going *do*?"

"You two set him on fire before you run over him?" She pushed stringy blond hair from her pale eyes and looked up with a granite face.

Adlai answered. "What do you think? We just got off work. That's just stupid."

She stood up. "No, you're stupid. Stupid for hitting this Mex and not killing him. Stupid for stopping."

"We didn't actually hit him. He more like just sort of fell in front of us, like he's drunk."

She grew angry, his obstinacy a constant irritation. "He ain't drunk. He's been burned up. Hurt bad."

The prostrate man groaned as she nudged a boot toe into his side. "Must be them Cotton boys. They hate Mexicans and they're crazy mean. They musta beat him and set him afire."

Abel stood to one side saying nothing, trying to follow the conversation.

Adlai answered. "Well, he ain't no problem of ours, then. We need to just leave him here."

Ada considered as the first wet drops fell. "Shut up, Adlai. You don't know nothin'. If you just tapped him, he's probably not too broke up inside. If you jus' leave him here, they'll be sheriffs and such all over. We got to get him away from us and out of here."

The younger brother bristled. He'd thought of the same thing and couldn't afford to let his sister get too far ahead of him.

She shook the wide-eyed Abel by the sleeve. "Listen to me, big brother. This is like tag, you understand? The Cotton boys done tagged him. And he is *it*. He tagged you and Adlai and you're it. But then you runned over him. So, you is still *it*. Now we need to get him to tag someone else. You see?"

She looked up into Abel's long face. "You understand what I'm telling you? It's like a game, and we is all playing. Now, we're *it*, but we won't be *it* for long. 'Cause we got fish to eat tonight."

Tears rolled down Abel's gaunt cheeks. "We could nurse him then he could work the farm 'cause he's so happy being alive and all."

Both siblings looked at their older brother. The man rarely fostered an idea, no less an idea worth considering.

Adlai immediately warmed. "A field hand what can't ask for a wage, because he is beholding to us for saving his life."

Ada ignored Adlai and spoke with a gentleness only Abel ever heard. "He ain't no bird, big brother. He ain't got no broken wing or nothing. He got beat up and set a'fire by the Cotton boys, who's been a thorn in our asses since we was in school. Now, we are going to clean up their mess. Again."

She faced Adlai. "Even if'n you two boys didn't do nothing, it looks like you did. The sheriff is gunning for you, Adlai. You understand, right? So, we got to take care of this right now. We will load him up and take him to Beaner Town."

When she took the tone of their mother, disagreement was impossible. Adlai nodded. Abel shook with sobs.

Ada turned to the big Abel. "Are you understanding what I'm saying? Those Beaner folks can take care of him.

He is not our problem, but he will be if we don't get him off'n this here road."

Adlai didn't want to be bested by his sister. "I was thinkin' we just put him back up in the hills for the bears and coyotes. It don't matter what happen to him."

Her voice drew close to a line her brothers avoided crossing. "He'd just get up again and wander around and bring the law down on us. You understand? Just do what I told you. You got tagged last. We're going to Beaner Town and tag those folks."

Then, Adlai's face relaxed in understanding. "I know what you're talking about. You mean the DNA and the vapors. I done thought of all that already."

Ada learned early in life that to move an ox, one must use persuasion and not might.

She glanced up and patted Abel's meaty forearm. "Put him in the truck, big brother. I'm gonna go with you and make sure there's no funny business. The Cotton boys might be watching us right now and laughing their asses off."

"Okay." Abel sighed with relief. His sister solved problems, and he could smile again.

He hefted the man and slid him along the dirty metal of the truck's bed. Ada removed the man's wallet.

She deftly pocketed a half-inch-thick stack of bills. "You drive, Adlai. It'll be dark in a few minutes, so don't break no speeding law. Sit in the back, Abel, and keep an eye on him. Make sure he don't wake up and jump out or something."

She settled her pail of still fish on the floorboards and thumbed through the credit cards.

Adlai watched her. "He got any money?"

"Twenty dollars."

"That'd be mine."

"That'd be our Saturday money and maybe a new shirt or two. It also goes in my jar until then."

Adlai shifted and clutched, turned, and headed for the migrant labor camp.

After a minute, he glanced at his sister who watched the headlights. "I don't need no new shirt,"

Ada didn't answer. She was wondering how to turn the Cotton boys' mischief into her fortune.

Chapter 26

Camilla

Camilla woke when the baby stirred and whimpered. A noise in the yard outside. She looked across the dark room of their hovel and wished for the hundredth time Raoul would come home. For months now he'd been away from the little camp, and she worried.

The baby had been born in San Antonio the night of his first arrest. A policeman drove her to a shelter, and there she stayed until Raoul's release. A week later they were on the road, following work, staying in shelters that would accept them until finding refuge in the no-man's-land between North Carolina and Tennessee.

Six months ago, he left to find work on the oil rigs, and soon after, Camilla found out she was pregnant. The last she'd seen him was the morning he joined four other men heading down the mountain. Now, with a swollen belly and a tiny baby still suckling, her life dimmed to fantasies and hopes. The baby quieted and grew sleepy as she laid back on the pillow.

Gears clashed and the muffler chugged as a pickup came into the narrow stand of tiny houses. Everyone could identify the sound of their few vehicles and this one meant trouble.

No villagers emerged. None looked out. Tires crunched against the gravel, and the engine idled. Fear gripped Camilla's stomach recalling the difficulty before. Drunks from nearby towns sometimes came and threatened the men with a beating. The invaders usually left without causing real harm. The last time, the men of the camp lined up against them and several on both sides were injured. Because of their isolation, the police did nothing.

For a moment, she thought the federals might be staging another raid. US Immigration knew about them but only wrote in their notebooks when they came. No one was ever taken away. Nevertheless, with each federal visit, she took the baby and hid in the woods. She was simply too afraid to chance deportation or worse, to be forever separated from Raoul.

Outside a car door opened. So many times, she prayed a visitor might bring him back to her. She tossed the covers aside and crept to the door. The baby stirred as the tailgate slammed and the engine revved. She opened the thin curtain enough to watch watery white haze mix with the single overhead light as the truck retreated into the night. A figure slumped in the middle of the pockmarked mud. The man had no coat for such a cold night.

And he was not Raoul.

She waited to see if anyone else watched, but the quiet hamlet did not stir. When she could stand it no longer, Camilla pulled on her own coat and heavy boots. Rain hit the puddles, mixing with the penetrating chill of the Blue Ridge Mountains.

She knelt as the man coughed a bloody mist into the cold night air. Doctors avoided the migrants, but the village's patriarch knew some healing. She ran to Fernando's door, knocking until he joined her. They hiked the man over their supporting shoulders and walked him into Camilla's tiny cabin.

She lighted her kerosene lantern as Fernando pulled clothing back to examine him.

He spoke Spanish in a low whisper. "He has been burned. We must keep him warm until someone can take him to a hospital. I will bring you some of my wood."

The man lay unmoving eyes closed to the ceiling on her pallet. Camilla's blanket covered him.

She rose from dabbing water on his face. "How is a hospital possible? The only car is low on gas, and I cannot ask this of Marie. Just as I cannot have him here. What if Raoul comes home?"

Fernando watched the young woman's face, hardly more than a girl's really, and then told her to boil water. "I have poultice in my cabin, and I will bring more sticks for the stove. You saw his mouth and teeth?"

She nodded.

"Try to get him to swallow a little tea."

She put the pot on the white-gas stove, and sat. The feet of the injured man hung off the end of her bed. After the pot whistled, she tried to have him drink, but each sip met a bloody disgorgement. He blinked, opened his eyes for a moment, gazed at her face, then fell unconscious again.

She caught her breath and crossed herself just as Fernando returned and dropped kindling at the small stove.

"He cannot swallow, grandfather. His mouth is injured so. Who would do such a thing?"

The old man palpated the upper neck. "We should be thankful he still breathes. Drip only enough to wet his lips. Nothing more. We must keep him from coughing."

She glanced over as the baby began to stir and whimper.

The old man carefully removed more of the stranger's clothes. Nylon sleeves had melted into his hands, arms, and fingers.

He pulled the small jar from his pocket. "The burns are bad, Camilla. Mix this with water, and keep it applied. You will need help."

He nodded to her belly.

"Paloma is a good person. She can help you."

"Please, Grandfather. The man cannot stay here."

Fernando pressed his lips together and said nothing.

She cast her eyes down. "I know the talk in the village. My husband is either deported or gone but it is not true. He will come back for Pablo and me. It is not right for a married woman to have a strange man under her roof. Even if he is injured."

"It is what God and the Church would expect, and this is your duty to the Holy Mother. I will explain to Raoul."

At that moment, the stranger seemed to become lucid and glanced slowly around the tiny room. The old man and the young woman watched him. He finally settled on Camilla, and he tried to speak. Only gurgles passed the damaged lips.

The baby cried louder, and she rose.

Fernando gentled the man's shoulder. "Do not try to speak, my friend. We will get you help but you must rest."

When the other made no effort to acknowledge, Fernando repeated in Spanish.

The tall man blinked and nodded slowly. The blue eyes had thrown him off. He did not speak English but Spanish.

He glanced at Camilla's back as she fed the baby. "Hold your hands out. I will put medicine on them. Later, you can tell us what happened."

As the old man finished applying ointment, Camilla returned from Pablo's bed. She watched as the stranger slipped back into sleep.

She started to speak, but he held up a hand to move her away.

Fernando whispered. "I know. His eyes."

"What does it mean?"

He shook his head. "I do not know. Maybe Argentinean or Andorran? He is tall. The accent will tell us when he speaks. He does not seem to understand English."

Camilla watched the injured man's face, fascinated. Despite the burns and the swollen lips, he was familiar, and handsome. "His is Norte Americano, I think."

Fernando shrugged and gathered his kit. "It is possible, I suppose."

Chapter 27

Angie

The detective punched in the numbers and nodded to his partner, who picked up the extension.

McHale didn't answer. He had missed his Monday subcommittee meeting, too.

Angie spoke in a calm and measured voice. "Will you repeat your name, please?"

"Truax, ma'am. Jonathan Truax." A sonorous voice, deep and rumbling.

"I recall the name. You're the DC detective investigating Juliette's disappearance."

"Yes, ma'am. That's me. Ms. Pearson's case is closed. SFPD has it."

"Of course. Will you give me your badge number and your extension? I'll call you back once I verify your identity."

"Yes, ma'am. Would you like the station number, too?"

"Now that wouldn't make much sense, would it?"

He chuckled into the phone and glanced at his partner. "No ma'am. I guess it wouldn't."

Smythe sat across the desk, rolling his eyes, and offering his partner a hand-job gesture.

The big detective replaced the phone. "Polite to the end. She's going to check me out and call back. Smart lady."

Smythe's acne-scared face broke into a rueful smile. "I'll buy lunch if she calls you back by this weekend. You got played, bro. She's a politician, too."

"Oh, I don't know. She struck me as the standup type. Just trapped with a lying, cheating old man."

Truax nodded toward old photos of Juliette Pearson's glamour shots on a San Diego beach. "Is there any doubt that bastard McHale was doing his secretary?"

Smythe fingered a glossy. "The coroner's pics don't look so hot. Forty days in the water with no head and no hands."

Without DNA, SFPD would not have a clue, and they would have a perfect crime to solve.

Truax opened the file again and leaned back with his coffee. The squad room was noisy and active, but neither man noticed. They were used to the frenetic hubbub and cross-room conversation.

The phone rang. "Truax."

Her voice was pleasant. "Angie McHale, Detective. I'm returning your phone call. What can I do for you?"

Truax didn't miss a beat as he eyed Smythe who hit the illegal tape recorder on the extension. "Thank you for calling back, ma'am. I've been trying to reach your husband, but he isn't at your brownstone or in the Senate offices this morning. I'm wondering if you could tell me where he is."

He picked up a pencil and doodled in the silent pause.

"You went through proper channels this time, Detective?"

"Yes, ma'am. I spoke with the Whip's secretary this morning. Per procedure."

He heard the sigh over the phone. "I don't know where he is, Detective. Mrs. Sylvia Flores, his office manager, called me this morning."

"Is it unusual he hasn't called you?"

"Yes. We usually have a morning conversation, but I was on the road over the weekend for one of my groups. I spoke with him on Thursday. We haven't spoken since."

Truax took the plunge, knowing wives, like politicians, were hands-off to the DC police. "Can you tell me what you discussed with the senator?"

She didn't hesitate. "Well, no revelations there, detective. Husband-and-wife talk, mostly. Joy ... our daughter is having a challenge or two. We spoke about that."

Truax pictured the senator's lovely wife, then looked down at the photo of the headless body. "Did the topic of Juliette Pearson come up, ma'am?"

Now she hesitated. "We talked largely of private matters. Scott ... the senator was tired. He never fully recovered from the shock of Juliette's death. And, yes, as I recall we spoke of her, wondering what progress you've made in the case. You're aware he's still suffering the effects of his respiratory illness, and he won't stop working fifteen-hour days. I believe the stress of her awful death, and his lack of proper sleep, caught up with him."

"Thank you for being so forthright."

Even Smythe gave an approving shrug.

She continued. "You know Juliette was a part of our family and we all took it hard. Scott possibly hardest of all. He loved her like a daughter and worked hard to recover his equilibrium. Scott is a combat veteran and a former wounded cop. He's a pretty tough guy and this hit him hard. He's also key to several vital pieces of legislation, and he may speak at the national convention."

The choice of keynote speaker would be a closely held secret until the last minute.

"Sorry, Mrs. McHale. I don't follow politics much."

Truax scribbled a note and pushed it toward Smythe.

"Of course. My apologies. You might think of me as just the politician's wife, and you might be right. But I've thrown the red flag more than once to slow him down. This is not about me. I'd suggest you send a car to check the residence again. You might check with Paula Houston at the airport, and Twila Crawford in the House. They're both close friends of Scott's. And of course, call back and speak with Mrs. Flores."

"Was the senator planning to leave town?"

She paused. "No, why do you ask?"

"I'm sorry, ma'am. I didn't mean anything by that. I'm just wondering."

He saw Smythe hang up the phone and tune back in. The man's expression was pure anger.

She spoke again. "Scott said if he felt well enough, he'd take a United flight to Phoenix on Thursday after his floor speech to meet with Theo Haines, the Pima County sheriff. The construction of the next power plant is nearly done, and they'll throw the switch anytime now. You mentioned you don't pay attention to politics? Well, the Deer Park WCG ... the Western Central Grid ... is soon to become the major energy supplier for eleven western states and a big piece of Texas. This is landmark legislation, and something to live long after Scott leaves public life. After the trip, he was coming home to have dinner with me."

Truax couldn't recall a more forthright statement from a murder suspect's wife. She was either a great actress, or he was way off-base.

He saw Smythe biting his lip and wanted off the phone. "Could you have the senator contact me when he calls you?"

"Yes. I'll be happy to do that. Anything else?"

"No ma'am."

"Will you let *me* know if you hear anything?"

"Yes, ma'am."

"Then have a nice day, Detective."

The phone clicked in Truax's ear.

Smythe gave a sour twist to his mouth. "The lady at the airport wouldn't tell me if the plane's in the hangar. An invasion of a client's privacy. Wanted to know if I had a warrant."

The ferret face Smythe flicked the button on his pen, on-off, on-off. Truax said nothing and looked out the window.

Smythe continued. "She's a smart cookie. The law is pretty plain, of course. The guy has a lock on the hangar door. That means we need get a warrant on the property of the United States senator or get the FAA to cooperate. I'm sure those fly-guys would *love* to help us out."

Truax spun in his chair. "Let's track his credit cards and see where he's buying. Run a passenger manifest check on Dulles and Reagan National."

Smythe glanced at his watch. "I can get that started. It's almost two and the traffic leaving town's going to get rough soon."

Truax scratched on a yellow sticky note. "Here's his number. Why don't we have the lab guys run the phone and see if he's hitting any cell towers. I'll check out a unit, and we can take a face-to-face crack at Paula Houston. Maybe the LT will get a rookie to write the warrant for us."

Smythe grinned. "Fine. You are the charmer, after all."

Truax retrieved his service pistol from the side drawer. "Make the calls and let's go. Ten bucks says the airplane isn't in the hangar and hasn't been since Thursday. You already owe me one lunch. Let's get on the road. Cerise has a recital tonight and I can't miss it."

"Family man *and* a charmer. I am in *such* good company." Smythe typed off an email and hit send. He snagged his pistol as well and followed Truax out the door.

Chapter 28

Truax

In an hour, the two officers crawled in traffic joining Interstate 66. Smythe spoke with the phone wedged between his chin and shoulder, taking notes. He clicked off and said, "FAA doesn't keep local tapes for more than twenty-four hours. If he left Thursday or Friday, we're days too late. The guy said he'll search the database for the McHale's side number. Reagan Approach Control said they'd send an F-16 if he tries to sneak back. I guarantee even if the plane is in the hangar, he's in the wind."

"We should've been on this yesterday."

Smythe read his phone's email. "Yeah maybe. The cell phone's a bust, too. Techs say he ain't using it or the battery's dead."

Truax touched the accelerator to keep another car from merging and received a scowl in return. He picked his red emergency light off the seat and the other driver eased back into the slug line to wait his turn.

Smythe ignored the drama and read. "Techs also remind us that cell towers look out, not up. No service means no triangulation above a couple thousand feet. If he went someplace without service, the phone won't hit a tower and we're out of luck."

"So, he doesn't even have to pull the battery to hide."

"That lying bastard is running. SFPD needs to get the FBI involved and get a wiretap on the Missus."

Truax said nothing as they drove. After an hour, they turned in for the front range airport.

Grim-faced, Paula listened, and never stopped shaking her head. "This is private property like I already told you. Without a warrant, it's simple. You don't get in."

Truax explained a citizen's welfare check didn't need a warrant. "If his airplane is there, then he's okay as far as we know."

"How dumb do you think I am?"

"Please ma'am. All I'm asking is a quick look. You look, we'll just stand behind you. Way behind you. If the airplane is there, you close up it up and Detective Smythe and I go home."

She tapped her front teeth together and nodded. "You can look but you can't go in. I'll call the sheriff in a New York minute if you do."

"It's all I ask."

Truax glanced at Smythe and mouthed *Lunch*.

Smythe scowled in return.

The small metal T-shaped sheds lined both sides of a long strip of black asphalt.

Truax stepped to the door as Paula rolled the combination. "We appreciate it. You're saving a lot of time and Mrs. McHale is pretty worried."

Paula clenched her jaw. "Don't bullshit the bullshitter. If you were really concerned, a deputy from the sheriff's department would've been here after your partner called."

With a shove, the door slid open.

The senator's blue Buick sat where the airplane should have been. Smythe stepped around Paula and glanced around inside. A double-door wall locker caught his eye.

She spoke quickly. "That's private. And I will goddamn call the deputies if you touch it."

Truax ignored her. A warrant would be no problem. "We're going to go. I'm going to send an evidence recovery team. Don't let anyone inside. This is now a crime scene."

Ten minutes later, he pulled a roll of yellow tape across the entrance as she locked the door.

Truax turned to her. "Sorry, Mrs. Houston."

Her features clouded. "Yeah, right. I was hoping the Cessna would be there. That's the only reason you got to see inside."

"Yes, ma'am."

"Make sure your evidence team brings the warrant."

"Yes, ma'am."

They stood at the cruiser's door. Truax held the microphone as the evidence team request was denied.

The detective's lieutenant over modulated the car's speaker. "The answer is no, god damnit. You clear that scene now. You and Smythe are to be in the chief's office at 0800 sharp to explain why you'd place a trap and trace on a US Senator's phone, make a call for cooperation to the FAA with a public airplane side number, and then galivant off into a public arena demanding other detectives write up warrants that you should be writing up. I'm not going to cover you two clowns this time. I'm done. Have fun explaining to the chief why you two can't seem to listen to instructions."

The next morning, both men stood in front of a livid chief of police.

"I've got six months to go before I retire, and you two jerkoffs are not going to cost me my job."

Two unsigned letters of reprimand sat on his desk.

"I'm holding on to both of these in case you decide to go freelancing again. I'm not taking any more phone calls from the United States goddamn Senate, and I swear to God, I'll have you fired if you do. That includes any loose talk about McHale. You got me, dickweeds?"

Both understood, but only Truax answered with "Yes, sir."

Later that day, the Senate minority leader released a statement McHale had a relapse and was recovering from a severe respiratory illness in an undisclosed location. The *Washington Post* reported Twila Crawford's name appeared in his place on the list of speakers at the national convention in Miami.

Three weeks later, an NBC investigative reporter broke the story Senator McHale had disappeared. She refused to name her sources. The senate leadership issued a statement they had been misled by the senator's office did not know McHale's whereabouts. Reporters conjoined the story of the senator's missing aide. The opposition party's senate judiciary committee chairman called for immediate hearings. The outcry deafened all other news as each day, the public awoke to another lurid story of speculation and innuendo.

Angie maintained her poise under questions and the committee hearings, admitting that for nearly a week she had searched privately for her husband. When she confirmed the DC police had contacted her and discovered his airplane was missing, the police chief took an early retirement. Like hounds after the rabbit, journalists who exposed the misdirection finally had their story.

Detectives Truax and Smythe went on a tour of national television and laid before the nation a story of alleged perversion, avarice, and lust. The FBI's Washington field office drew the Office of Origin assignment, and immediately sent leads assigning agents in the other one-hundred and nineteen FBI national and international offices.

The hunt was on.

Chapter 29

Angie

Ken Litton glanced without surprise at the image in the security monitor. As the new Los Angeles Assistant Director in Charge, he rated a second level of security. Litton didn't like the idea of an armed agent sitting around with nothing to do except guard his office door and play on his cellphone. He kept his secretary behind bulletproof glass and the security cameras in the reception area. The agent went to the cyber squad to chase down criminals.

Angie paced on the screen. She looked tired and drawn. When he opened his office door, she went to him, and they held one another close.

"Thank God you're here, Ken. I don't know what I'd have done if you weren't." Her face lost its impeccable public demeanor.

"Come in, Angie."

Her question came like a shot. "Do you know anything more?"

"One moment."

He turned to the serious-faced woman staring from behind her desk. "No calls, Mrs. Peoples, please."

He closed the door. "Nothing new. Washington field office handles all the data. We're working leads here in LA, and I've assigned one of our best agents. We stood up a task force, but so far, nothing."

"I just can't find him, Ken. It's been fifteen days now, my God. I'm going crazy. How does someone drop off the face of the earth for that long? At least I'm done with committee hearings."

Angie sat, pulling a wadded tissue from her pocket, and taking a calming breath.

"Committee meetings couldn't have been easy."

She looked up. "No, it wasn't. The congress is a shark tank. I couldn't tell them much. Scott and I have meeting places, you know, in case of earthquake or disasters. We have some here and in DC. His brothers are watching in California. The investigation firm—"

"I know them. They're ex-agents and we've been talking. Unofficially, of course."

Her eyes steady and dry held him. "Thank you, Ken. The papers, the news shows. They all think he's running."

Litton nodded. "Not as much as their mouths. I've got a friend who's telling me what the high-level people are saying. A lot of them call for calm and understanding in sound bites, then excoriate him in private."

"Typical DC. Do *you* think he's on the run?"

Litton sat next to her. "Absolutely not. Scott doesn't run from trouble. He's the first guy there with a fire hose. Even if it is his pants on fire."

She smiled weakly and wiped her nose. "Maybe once, but now I'm not so sure. Politics made him gun-shy. At least, our story is under the fold now."

She had come straight from the airport and worked her hair into a ponytail on the cab ride. She pulled a pack of cigarettes from her wrinkled business suit's jacket pocket.

"Sorry, Angie. We can go outside if you want."

She offered a short laugh. "That's all I'd need. A *Times* reporter will have a picture of me and you talking. Scott won't need a trial then. They'll just string him up."

"Have patience. We'll find him but you need to keep it together."

A fleeting, awkward look passed over her face. "I need to talk to you confidentially."

"I'm an FBI agent, Angie. There's no confidentiality when it comes to the law. You either trust me or you don't."

She rose and walked to the wide window. "Okay, then I'm going to trust your discretion. I've got no one else to talk to."

He looked at the pack of Winston and pulled an ashtray from his bottom drawer, rose and rotated the handle to open his casement. "Sit here."

She let out her breath and sat next to the jalousie. "Thank you. I'm glad we can still count on you being in our corner."

"Always. But you know things sort of changed between Scott and me when I warned him off Jim Dearborn. That was a long time ago, but I still think it was good advice. We're not as close as we once were."

She touched the cigarette's end with a small gold lighter. "I know all about that. He told me. He thought more of you because you'd risk your friendship to tell him what you believed."

Litton said nothing.

"You know he broke, right? I could see it, but I didn't know how to fix him."

"He called me a couple times. Wanted to get together, but I just couldn't." He let out a ragged breath. "I should have made the time."

She glanced down at busy Wilshire Boulevard. "Not your fault. He spent too long in the office, seven days a week, working deals, trying to fix our unfixable government. Sometimes the day-to-day work wouldn't get done, so he'd spend nights sleeping on the couch, trying to get everything right. Mr. Perfect."

"It happens when a person serves two masters."

She turned as if she'd been slapped. "What do you mean?"

"Disabuse me, Angie. Help me believe my best friend wasn't torn between Big Jim Dearborn and his responsibility to the American people."

She crushed the cigarette to smoldering ruins. "Maybe in the beginning he balanced Big Jim and everything else, but not in the last few years. You know about the bad blood, right?"

"Sort of. Big Jim kept forgetting his place. Things wouldn't go the man's way, and he'd pounce on Scott."

"That's one way of putting it. Scott left Big Jim behind. Outgrew him. He became a man for the nation, not just California. He had his shortcomings and who doesn't? I'm not excusing him. I'm explaining. Scott believed Big Jim should be content as king frog in a little pond."

"Did Big Jim stay in the water?"

She puffed air. "Not even close. He sent Wes Teague and then Juliette Pearson."

She watched Litton's wide, unreadable face.

Angie made a decision. "I want to tell you something that might hurt Scott when he comes back. It's better if it stays between us."

"I already explained, but I'll try, okay?"

"Okay. Juliette started as Big Jim's spy. Just like Wes Teague. Scott knew Teague would never change, so he set his sights on Juliette because she was ambitious and smart. He told me this, later of course, after his heart attack. He brought her into his confidence, carefully, but the relationship grew too close. She became more confidante than admin assistant. She ... became important to him." Tears rimmed tired eyes but did not fall. "Maybe too important. Maybe a little bit like me. He promised they never slept together."

"And you believe him?"

"Yes. He told me she left DC after he refused her. He tried to explain but she showed up on Big Jim's doorstep, anyway. I guess that didn't work out either."

Litton said nothing.

"I think her realization was the Bay Area hotel. I don't know everything that happened when she finally gave up. It must have been awful for her...and Scott. Do you know about that night?"

"Witness and police reports in a warrant to a federal judge."

Angie tapped another cigarette against the lip of the ashtray. "Juliette was an adept politician and learned quickly. She had a brilliant future, but she was in training. I believe she saw Scott as her mentor, a ticket to the future. Big Jim probably didn't offer her those kinds of opportunities. I've always thought of him more in misogynistic terms, a user of women. Like Lora Lu and maybe even me."

Angie paused, studying the wide sky.

"When Juliette shifted her loyalty from Big Jim to Scott, she did it with cold calculation. She sent good reports back to Big Jim and in return, Scott took her to charity functions, dinners, and DC events, whenever I wasn't there. I think some of those glowing reports didn't jive with what Big Jim was seeing. She might have taken heat for Scott, but she'd already pushed all her chips in and there was no going back.

"Do you see what I saying, Ken? She gambled on Scott and lost. Maybe she saw him as a shortcut to a political office. She was his researcher and knew everything about his ideas and legislation. Scott said he rebuffed her advances, so she must have realized just how badly she'd miscalculated. All the work gone."

Litton rolled a pen between his fingers. "I know Juliette was smart. I saw it firsthand many times. What doesn't make sense to me is why she didn't just rebuild those bridges. Why quit ten years' worth of work and move to the South Bay? I wonder if there's something else."

"You're avoiding the rumor she was pregnant."

He remained as unreadable as a stone.

"I believe in Scott. Juliette was always a friend and an aide. Bright, cheerful, and of course lovely. He had thoughts, he told me. Actions? He promised me, Ken. I don't believe she ever became 'the other woman.' I can't blame your investigators for thinking Scott's a person of interest. How could they not? They were so close and at the moment, he's not around to protect or explain himself. That's my job now."

Litton watched her as the cigarette smoke drifted over the world fifteen stories below. The report on his desk said California state crime labs shipped body-tissue samples to the FBI lab in Quantico. The Bureau would try to extract DNA from those to find a clue to the father's identity. The experimental process wouldn't hold up in a court of law. For the time being, he saw no reason to tell Angie.

She offered him a smile. "You know, I figured his story was about ninety percent accurate. We all see the truth in our own light. I don't truly know if he had sex with her."

"He wouldn't cheat, Angie. He's loyal to a fault."

"You boys do stick together, don't you."

He shook his head. "Not in this case. I grant you, there's something about politics that drowns lesser men. Scott's an exception. I'd stake my life on it. He might flirt with temptation. Even think about it, but he would not have killed Juliette. No way, no how."

This time, a tiny tear formed. She swiped it away. "Thank you. I'm glad you feel that way because I do, too. I haven't given the police a statement. I wanted to give it to you."

Litton looked at his desk blotter calendar. He counted the days since McHale's disappearance. days

Her eyes followed his. "I know. *Why did I wait this long?*"

"It'll be the case agent's first question."

"I wanted the chance to find him myself. Then, I wanted you to know it from me, instead of reading a report, and of course, the committee hearings kept me from...." She trailed off, deciding to drag on the cigarette rather than find one more terrible excuse.

He picked up the desk's phone. "Mrs. Peoples? Please find Orlando Gutierrez and have him report to my office."

He hung up. "Before we start, you know everything will be shared, right?"

"Yes, of course. You're the one Scott and I trust. That will extend to Agent Gutierrez."

Chapter 30

Scott

An indifferent rain cooled the day as Camilla watched day pass out the window. A slow procession of villagers jumped from the truck's bed after a day of work. Brown water pooled in mud depressions and broke into ripples as the men and women splashed to their homes. She wondered about her own man, where he was and what he was doing. Did he labor warm under the sun, or was he as desperate as those she watched now? Deep inside her, the baby shuddered, and her stomach growled for dinner.

The stranger with the blue eyes stared into the open flame of the corner woodstove. He had slept away the day after a night of pacing on pained limbs.

"Good afternoon, sir." Her Spanish was a second language to her native P'urhepecha.

The stranger looked up and nodded offering the barest hint of a smile. Healing came, but slowly. His beard thickened in gray with brown streaks and covered the misshapen throat. He ate little and only the gruel Fernando recommended. Fat and muscle vanished, and his body grew gaunt.

She moved into the area that served as a kitchen and took a battered aluminum coffeepot from the counter.

Using hesitant English, she whispered. "Would you like coffee?" He looked without responding. She repeated in Spanish, and he nodded.

"*Por favor.*" His mouth moved but no sound came out. In the weeks since he had arrived, the stranger never spoke, and only mouthed brief words in Spanish.

The door gave a soft rap, then opened. Fernando doffed his cap and unbuttoned his rubber slicker.

"I've come to see you and our guest."

She glanced at the stranger. "In Spanish, grandfather. It is impolite to speak a language he does not understand. I think he heals, but he still doesn't eat enough."

Fernando switched to Spanish. "How are you, sir?"

The stranger nodded slightly.

"And can you speak at all?"

The man shook his head and blinked tired eyes. With a slow and deliberate movement of a hand, he cautiously touched his neck. His head lolled to one side as the damp wood crackled in the potbelly stove. Fernando examined the burns and ragged flesh. Small white pustules had grown scarlet over the last few days.

"These are healing, although not so very well. You need a hospital and antibiotics."

The man shook his head slowly.

Camilla witnessed this exchange daily. "I am going to make coffee. Do you think it is permissible for him?"

"Clear soup is better, no meat or vegetables yet."

The baby cooed from his bassinet and Fernando smiled.

Soon she would call him Paul in honor of his new country. The infant listened to the adults, alert eyes shifting back and forth.

She used her halting English. "What a good baby you are."

Fernando addressed her in English. "Can you continue to do all this? Care for a stranger and a baby? You have so little."

"Yes, of course. Raoul will be back soon. We will have much money then." Camilla watched her baby's face smiling back at her, preferring her own reality to Fernando's.

The older man dropped his gaze and said no more. Her man probably resided in the custody of the Americans or the Mexicans, neither of whom wanted Guatemalan natives in their country. Or even more likely, he could be dead. Bandits and criminals on both sides of the border preyed upon the thousands who came north.

Fernando did not give life to the idea her man could have deserted her and the small family. "I have a little money. Tell me what you need, and I will buy it."

Camilla bit her lip knowing she had little choice.

"Your needs are so small, Camilla. It is nothing. So please, tell me."

Chapter 31

Scott

Camilla slipped back and forth from her own broken Spanish and English, but this didn't matter to the injured man.

McHale understood both sides of the conversation. Understood yes but as yet, unwilling to admit it to them. At first, his addled brain thought he survived the plane crash only to be murdered by men waiting on the ground. When thoughts began to jell, he understood that Providence had saved him. Somehow, he had been deposited him among migrants willing to take in a stranger, obviously not one of their own.

The talk of his blue eyes did not escape his hearing.

He felt badly about this deception but only because of Camilla and Fernando's kindness, and of course Angie and Joy. His desire to call his wife might do nothing more than put the target on her, too. He would not do that to his daughter or his wife. For the time being, he needed to hide. The vultures of DC politics hired guns, sensational media, and law enforcement bided their time waiting. A confluence of circumstantial happenstance would exploit him for their own gain and end his freedom. He had no doubt his hiatus in the mountain camp would end soon.

McHale knew the facts of his case better than most and believed when he was arrested, exoneration in the courts would be only a matter of time. And yet, rumors of matching DNA and convenient testimony gave him pause. To be naïve and incarcerated would leave him a husk of his former self, especially after revelations of a tryst that never was.

Angie was right, of course. His dishonorable treatment of Juliette made him no better than any number of American political philanderers. He would not survive and was unwilling to give up all that he'd worked for without a fight.

McHale wanted to remain outside the grasp of his killers for now. Weeks of little sleep and incessant analysis of the incident in San Raphael, the aftermath, Juliette missing, and then the flight into a mountainside convinced him the crash was an assassination attempt.

But by whom? He was an outspoken hawk willing to bomb the Taliban and ISIS into the dark ages. He fought the Communist Chinese-backed cartels for the streets and made enemies on the way to the Senate. The cops and the public had always been on his side. Rumors of a shadow government mocked him, but he never experienced anything close to such a thing. His friend Ken Litton warned about a minority reaching for the brass ring but how is that possible in today's America?

McHale was the first to admit, his cognitive abilities needed to heal along with his body. The time in the camp was a godsend and he didn't want to squander the gift.

The hovel quieted and the house fell still in the night. Even the baby breathed softly in his crib. McHale rose and pulled the blanket from his pallet and sat at the small kitchen table. Sleep came in fitful half hour shards. In his mind's eye he saw the trouble he brought to Camilla and Fernando and perhaps the entire village. He heard no news, watched no television, read no newspapers. The people here cared little for the outside world. They had troubles of their own. The FBI and the US Marshals would never stop hunting if he'd been indicted and of course, there were his neglected senatorial responsibilities. He tried to smile at the irony, but the skin around his mouth and ears screamed in pain with any change of expression.

He needed to take some action. His wallet was gone along with about four hundred dollars in cash, all his credit cards, and his identification. If anyone in the village used the credit cards, the national system would alert. The authorities would not be far behind, and the trail would lead to him.

Several nights ago, Camilla returned the heat-deformed gasoline credit card he used for airplane fuel. He'd forgotten and slipped the plastic into his shirt pocket at Front Royal. Maybe she didn't read his name or didn't understand. More likely she did and chose to say nothing.

Yet.

In the short time he had been in the village, McHale worked out several facts. His Cessna did not just catch fire by itself. These sorts of blast furnace blazes happened in the movies, not in real life airplanes. Timed or proximity sabotage brought the aircraft down above a national forest the size of Delaware. With peaks over five thousand feet and wilderness thick as any in North America, he should have been killed. That must have been the plan. He recalled a haze, perhaps a walk in the daylight, then another at night before stumbling upon a dirt road. He could have been dead and lost for years before anyone ever discovered the wreckage. Some aircraft thought to have been lost in the Nantahala mountains have never been found. Certainly, enough time had elapsed for the assassin to cover his tracks without Scott McHale interfering.

He also knew the police considered him their only suspect in Juliette's disappearance. His life and political career disappeared like liquid quicksilver through slippery fingers. Every talking head, blogger, and radio announcer must have found him guilty after the investigation went public. Now, there could be nothing left.

One of Dearborn's last phone calls had warned him about a failed search warrant in California. Only a judge who owed the Kingmaker delayed the inevitable. Like Aaron Burr two hundred years before, a missing United States senator who murdered an aide would cause a hysterical manhunt unprecedented in the country's history.

Angie had likely enlisted Litton by now. What would his best friend believe, especially with the FBI's statutory mandate? He wondered why he hadn't heard a search plane. The mountains should have been gridded and sectioned with planes and helicopters combing for signs of broken treetops and gleaming aluminum. He guessed that would change soon enough.

McHale wanted to face his accusers, and yet knew knew little could be done sitting inside a jail. Where should he go? Home was the logical choice for him as well as for the police. Camilla, Fernando, and the others stayed silent now, but for how much longer. The migrant camp would be the real losers if the authorities or his assassins thought he might be hiding there.

Every day, he tested his body, walking more, insisting on chopping the kindling, gathering the season's early berries.

One morning when a boss honked his horn, McHale pulled a borrowed cap low and sat in the pickup truck's steel bed. For an hour, he tended grape vines, kale, and new greens, then slipped away to hitchhike into town.

Even though few gave him a second look, he kept his ball cap pulled low. After the librarian's help, he logged into the local ISP and set up an email account. He typed Angie's address from memory and wrote quickly. He hit the send button, erased his history, and walked for the rear fire exit. He pushed the door bar, set off the alarm and headed into a suburban neighborhood. In twenty minutes, he switched his undershirt with his pullover and walked unconcernedly down the city's sidewalk. The next day he walked the six miles to a different town and a different library. He logged in and read that Angie's account accepted no unknown emails.

Of course. Stupid mistake. Any expectation of privacy would be compromised by media scoundrels and the police.

He needed a different approach and waited for the work truck the next morning.

Two nights later in the hilly approach to the camp, the beat of rotor blades mixed with the sounds of nocturnal animals. The first helicopter pulled into a hover twenty feet over the mud courtyard and its single light. Heavy ropes flew outward with men sliding to the ground below. MP10 submachine guns snapped into hands the moment feet touched down. Two Chevy Suburban SUVs rounded the corner skidding and roaring as black clad men set a perimeter. Weapons pointed, fingers rested on triggers, safeties off.

All wore vests marked "Police."

Chapter 32

Scott

Thirty miles west of Crossville, Tennessee, a tractor-trailer rig shifted to climb the ramp on Interstate 40. A hitchhiker startled the driver by stepping onto the right shoulder. He stared blankly at the oncoming traffic. Surprised, the driver braked short of the man and revved the big diesel engine. The big rig with its fifty-thrree foot trailer shook to a stop.

The hitchhiker trotted with an obvious limp to the driver's door. He held a piece of paper high at the closed window. Windshield wipers cleared a spotting mist every few seconds as the driver made a decision. Talk of increased big rigs highnacking often filled driver's lounges. The figure was not exactly welcoming with an unshaven face and fire wrinkled skin.

The driver sent the wind down a few inches.

"You should be at the truck stop, dude. It's damn near impossible to stop a big rig on an interstate ramp."

McHale nodded his head and handed the man a note reaching well over his head.

"What this?"

He read. "Shit, can't you talk. Oh, geez. Sorry. I didn't mean anything by that. So, where you headed?"

Another wet note.

The ink ran together. "I ain't going that far. I can only take you to the Lebanon exit and I'm due in a couple hours. They won't look kindly if I hold up the load. After that, I'm headed home to Holloway for days off."

The hitchhiker started on the pad again, but the driver shook his head. "Nah, nah. Come on and get out of the rain. At least I'll get you a little further down the road. Maybe it ain't raining there."

McHale ran through the headlights and climbed at the passenger's door. The warmth hit closing his eyes. He breathed relief to be out of the cold drizzle.

The truck shifted and moved slowly back onto the deserted ramp. "If it's too hot let me know. I like driving in short pants. All kinds of weather. Don't bother me none. Kinda my brand."

He grinned to the hitchhiker. "Maybe that's why the wife left. Ha. We drove together for a while then she booked it. Lives in Miami now."

He shook his head and sighed a deep breath.

"We've been divorced for a couple years now, and I appreciate the company on nasty nights. Sorry if I'm talking your ear off. She's waiting tables and living with a couple other road refuges she met driving."

Another laugh.

"Different strokes. We still talk. Shit. She owns half of this rig. Maybe one day... You never know."

Another note. The driver read. "Hey, no problem. Relax and get warm. It's about four hours to my turn-off."

He glanced at the fire-damaged side of McHale's face.

The hitchhiker wrote. "Kind of you. Must be Memphis two days."

The driver lifted a cell phone off the console before McHale could stop him. "Oh, hell. I might be able to get you part of the way."

The call was answered. "Hey, Jenny. Yeah, it's me."

He listened. "About five hours out. You got Billie Westfall going to Fort Smith this morning?"

Pause. "Uh-huh. Can you check? I got a buddy who needs to get a drop in Grind City."

He looked over and winked. "Nah, he's cool. She'll like him, except he don't talk much."

He listened again. "I'll hold for you anytime, darlin'."

The driver shifted downhill and balanced the mobile phone between cheek and shoulder. "I'm here."

Pause. "That's great. You're a doll."

He clicked the off button and tossed the phone on the dash. "Got you covered at least part of the way. A friend of mine is just as sweet as sugar. She'll drop in Oakville at the Love's. She'll meet you at the Lebanon Pilot on 231 and wait. Too damn cold and wet to be out there tonight, anyway. She's on a tight turnaround so if you're not there, you'll walk."

McHale mouthed, "Thanks."

• • • •

Three days later, he stood at another Love's Truck Stop but in Lee, Florida. The decision to move in the opposite direction was hardly random. Until he could put together a plan, he chose misdirection and accepted the fact not everyone would be pleased to meet him. The lady driver dropped him at a Love's Truck Stop short of Nashville. This time he wrote notes in the parking lot and snagged a ride heading south.

McHale walked the mile from the glitzy, big-box truck stop to a mom-and-pop convenience store and gas station. The highways intersected another mile east. He'd try his luck for a ride there.

The aviation fuel credit card worked well to buy the second-hand notebook computer in Nashville, but now the card was in play, and he needed to move. A few customers came in and out until finally, a Mustang stopped. Eight years old and ridden hard, the car had a broken windshield and tricolored fenders.

One boy paid for the gas inside, while the driver knelt on one knee to fill a tire.

A third boy ate a hotdog from the store's grill. "I'm tired, dude. Let's go if we're going. Your old lady's not going to be pissed we show up unannounced, right?"

The kneeling boy wore a ripped pink t-shirt with a smudge over Prince. "You could've done this while I took a piss, you know."

He wiped his mouth and took the filler nozzle. "Only three beers, and you piss like a little girl. Your dog's on the dashboard by the way. Mustard and onions."

McHale shuffled up to the pair and rapped his scabbing knuckles on the fender. He smelled his own neglected body and stopped short.

He handed one of the boys a scrap of paper. "Need ride to St Augustine."

The boy looked at McHale. "Dude, what happened to you?" A month of growth on his face didn't cover the healing red skin and scabs. He'd beaten the staph infection, but scars would forever mar the face once destined for the White House.

The boy shook his head and handed the note back. "No hitchhikers, dude. Sorry."

The boy grimaced at his friend. McHale hurriedly scribbled and tapped the fender again. "I'll buy the gas."

The boy read and whistled softly. "Now, he says he'll buy the gas. What'd ya think?"

"We already ..."

The third boy joined the conversation. He eyed the bum. "Whoa, whoa. Let's think about this. A few extra dead presidents can't hurt. Know what I'm saying?"

McHale smiled, nodding. His broken front teeth were evident.

The kneeling boy straightened and tossed the air hose back. "I don't care. He could be a Mexican serial killer. Like a Taco Jason, dude."

He reached in and grabbed his hot dog.

"If he's a serial killer, I'm Santa fucking Claus. We can use the money."

They thought this funny and turned to McHale. "Okay, dude. You got twenty bucks? No, make it forty."

McHale shook his head.

The other boy laughed with his mouth full. "Oh, yeah. '*I buy you gas,* meester.' Dude, you are so fucking dumb."

The third boy spit on the wet pavement. "Shit, dude."

McHale held out the credit card with a finger covering his name.

The boy looked at the plastic. "Whoa, dude. Is this good?"

McHale nodded and smiled.

"Well, you see, we already—"

"Goddamn it, Ben. Just take the card and see if it's good."

McHale pointed toward the store clerk and handed the boy his card. He wrote quickly, "Get us beer. Back in 5." He turned and headed inside to the men's room. He hoped his guess was right. From the door, he watched the driver buy a case of beer.

Five minutes later, he emerged drying his hands. The store was empty. So were the pumps. No Mustang and no boys.

McHale exhaled relief and avoided the clerk's stare as he walked out. Another all-night gas station sat a half-mile away. He needed the cops to believe he was headed to the convention in Miami in some sort of crazed mental state. The boys would be under arrest after they filled the tank for the last time. He hoped they at least got some more hot dogs before the NSA tracked them down.

• • • •

The following week, Twila Crawford gave a brilliant keynote speech in Miami, the same speech McHale had rejected. Her husband Tom joined her on stage. On the fifth ballot, she led the California rally by endorsing Freeman Swanson, calling him the nation's mayor and a Washington outsider. New York rallied behind their favorite son. New Jersey and Pennsylvania claimed him, too, and fell in line. When Swanson garnered nearly enough delegates, he chose Twila Crawford as his running mate and blew the convention wide open. The acclamation was unanimous, and everyone headed to the bar or a bed.

Chapter 33

Angie

Angie remained popular and available for interviews. She proved to be completely comfortable in front of a television camera or a cell phone. She avoided answers that could be misinterpreted and redirected using charm and finesse. Days of charity and volunteer connections served her well, especially when she refused Scott's political opponents' calls for her resignation. His reelection war chest funded economy class airline tickets and modest hotels as she redoubled appearances in his place. Even after the terrible publicity of Scott's disappearance and the wild conjecture surrounding Juliette, Angie was seen as more than just a *stand-by your man* figure. Groups diverse as Second Amendment Advocates and National Teacher's Unions found in her a thread both thought they could exploit. Angie bested them all in keeping Scott's name on top and her appearances apology-free.

When friends or foes launched difficult questions, she addressed straight with no prevarication or evasion. In fact, snippets and sound bites drove Angie's popularity into becoming a YouTube and podcast heroine. Money from internet crusades soon exceeded Scott's flagging campaign fund. She smiled at the most demeaning interviews, never flustered, and answered every question.

Scott's admonition that she should have run in his first congressional race often came back to her.

A month after convention night had passed, news outlets and podcasts clamored to book her. When the chair for the national committee to elect Freeman Swanson and Twila Crawford asked that she address California's assembly of state civil workers, Angie knew she's crested the tsunami. Now she must ride and not fall. She agreed and stirred the stodgy and suspicious bureaucrats into several standing ovations.

Angie captured the nation's imagination.

A few days after the Sacramento speech, she visited the Los Angeles FBI office. Men and women stood and nodded. A small group broke into muted applause. She waved modestly until finally escorted into the office of the Assistant Director in Charge.

She collapsed on the leather couch. "Impressive crop of agents out there, Ken. I'm glad they're on my side."

Ken Litton dropped into a chair across from her. "People love you, Angie. We love you but we hate what has happened. Is it true the governor is about to offer you Twila Crawford's place in Congress? Why would he do that when the general election is only a few weeks away?"

Angie touched a small gold cross at her neck, an attractive contrast to her cream tan skin. "He can't get the ballot changed this quickly. He needs a month. Maybe two. He's going to claim this is an administrative issue and announce a special election next January. In the meantime, I'll sit in her seat."

Litton rocked back. "If you're going to be a lyin' cheatin' politician, Angie, you're gonna have slow down with the shock factor."

She didn't smile.

He held up his large meaty hand. "Hey, I loved Scott, too, but I never wore rose glasses, so I'm going to be as apolitical as I know how. People are going to ask. You need an answer. I don't know I'd go with his so called: 'Not enough time.' What possible motivation would the governor have for you to sit in the seat and cost the state a special election? You're a great choice, of course, but he's got a boatload of political hacks out there with none of the baggage you're lugging around."

"The decision was his alone, and my baggage won't be a problem, at least for a while. In the meantime, we've rented an apartment in Arcata. It's nice. On the ocean. Bring the family for a visit."

His jaw worked at the blasé attitude. "I've got an ocean, but thanks. I grant you Scott's not a national story for the moment, but the governor could avoid all the second guessing by picking someone from the state assembly. Both he and I know you're not going to pay him back. Nobody is ever going to tell you what to do. So, this has got to be a steppingstone. Would someone else have their fingers on the scale?"

"It's demographics, Ken. There's not going to be enough time to get both major parties on the ballot by the general election. Its not just me. A dozen others will be vying for a party spot. Try to rush it and law suits will take years to settle and California might lose their seat with the new headcount of illegal immigrants. Forgoing the seat is not out of the realm of possibility if we screw around. Elections take time and a primary. Consider that the lead contender, Lora Lu

Chow hates the governor, and she is a lawyer with a staff. The law suit is probably sitting finished on her desk already. The governor knows I can beat her in a special in my own right and not just as the grieving widow. It's that simple."

"Congratulations." His words lacked enthusiasm.

"Please understand. I'm not trying to usurp Scott, but I know Lu. She isn't a team player. Never has been. She hates criticism and can be vicious when trifled with. I always thought Juliette would have been a better choice for the seat. Scott thought so too even though Lu is an Asian. Lovely and equally as smart as Juliette, it's all a matter of timing. The Bay Area has a big minority, but right now, the governor doesn't need Lu. He needs me. The illegals welcomed over our border a decade ago are now citizens and voters and for the most part, they will vote for me. With millions more using the temporary green cards and backfilling the vacated entry jobs, it is only a matter of time before whites, blacks, and browns are eased out. It's been happening this way since Adam had to relocate with Eve."

He said nothing.

"*I* need this, Ken. I'll have my paperwork submitted tomorrow. Just like when Scott started out, I'll have a little time in the seat, but not enough to make big mistakes and get outed."

"I see Jim Dearborn's fingerprints all over this."

Her jaw worked. "I'm the best candidate hands down. Woman, Latina, and known. I'm either up or I'm out, Ken. Then, I just become a footnote. You disagree?"

"Of course not. You know me better. I'm not political. I'm just getting used to the idea that's all. I think you'd be great."

She considered him for a moment, needing this alliance personally and professionally. She worded her response carefully.

"I do know you, Ken, but others do not. You and I both know there's a rivalry in this country. Black versus brown. This state will be the face of that challenge until race baiters finally give up. Big Tech, corporations, and Hollywood drive the campaign rhetoric in the Golden State. For now, I have the support of all three. Soon enough, that goes away, and this becomes a competition of ideas with ethnicity slipping to tenth place where it should have been all along. The fact is my Latino minority votes. Neither yours nor the WASPs vote enough. We vote in a block. Blacks vote for their favorite sons. Asians know the facts, but they lack cohesion. This year. Maybe not in two years. This might be my only shot and like I said, the governor is hedging his bets."

Ken leaned back and tented his fingers. "The time is coming where we all need to think and vote with one color. Red, white, and blue. Not in shades of pink, black, and brown."

She smiled. "Your nativity is one of the things I admire most about you, Ken. And, I agree, but that's only going to happen somewhere down the road. I need to stake my claim now, while I'm still a commodity. Our leaders have got to be the talented ones, like you. Not me. Politicians don't lead, they exploit. Let me do this for the right reasons."

He leaned back and exhaled a chest full of air.

Maybe she'd gone too far. Too much honesty.

He said nothing.

She tried once more. "Scott believed too and yet he set us back more than an election cycle with all the questions he left behind. The governor is gambling I can make up the difference."

Ken rocked forward. "Okay. I agree."

She relaxed and now needed to move him along. "Great and thanks. What's happening with the search?"

His lips pressed together, as if he wanted to ask more questions. "This is the last week for the Civil Air Patrol, I'm afraid. It's been a couple months. They haven't be in the rescue mode as much as the recovery."

"Does that mean the search is off?"

"No, just facing reality. Did you know an F86 crashed in those mountains in 1955 and wasn't found until 2001? There's no more remote and isolated wooded mountain range in the lower forty-eight."

"Ground searchers?"

"From three states. They have dog teams, infrared, listening devices. As long as the feds fund them, they continue. The Bureau shipped the best technology to whoever took up the search. All the park rangers are briefing hikers. They're doing everything anyone can think of. ICE raided a little migrant camp, but they didn't find anything. One woman said she gave a dinner and a bed to a tramp, but he'd moved on the next day."

Her gaze shifted from his face to another time, another world.

Ken continued. "The NSA intercepted an email sent to your Hotmail address."

Angie knew the question was coming. "That was weeks ago. Why are you asking me now?"

He ground his teeth. "Because I didn't know. Someone at HQ decided I wasn't to be trusted. *'You're too close, Ken.'* That's a quote from my friend on the seventh floor."

"You know the email went to a bulk account that only my aide opens. I thought the account was closed."

He nodded. "I read the report."

"We closed it a couple months ago. I don't know how people got the address."

"Gaslighting on the Dark Web."

"Unbelievable hate mail, Ken. People can be so... mean."

He shoved the legal pad to one side. "You gotta believe he's okay, Angie."

"I believe. I just don't understand."

"When is the governor going to announce Twila's Congressional seat?"

She puffed out her breath. "Today or tomorrow."

He moved to stand, but Angie didn't stir. "What aren't you telling me?"

"The state's going to declare him dead after the special election."

His face clouded. "I see where this is going."

"Politics makes it pretty obvious, doesn't it?"

"Should I assume you then fleet up to the Senate by election time and Lora Lu is free to float for your congressional seat?"

She said nothing.

"Pretty slick. You run against a temporary hack holding the senate seat, then everybody sits in their nice little places. All the while, the electorate thinks their vote counts."

"Ken, please understand–"

He silently shook his head. "Full disclosure. In the coming month, San Francisco field office will declare Scott a material witness in the deaths of Juliette Pearson and the unborn baby. They'll reopen their original case and he'll be detained when found."

Angie hadn't heard. Teague should have told her.

She barely whispered her question. "DNA of a baby?"

"More closely guarded than Fort Knox."

She slumped in the chair and fumbled for a cigarette.

Ken pulled the ashtray from the top drawer. "If the worst happens, headquarters puts out different orders, and Scott's options will change. The attorney general's office can step in and declare Juliette's death a murder under federal statutes. They might put him on the Ten Most Wanted list."

He considered the wife of his stalwart friend. "Did Dearborn tell you who'll be the temporary appointment to the senatorial seat?"

Her eyebrows furrowed and her voice had an edge. "What makes you think I'm talking to him?"

"No one make a political move in California without Big Jim."

"I've got friends talking to me about lots of things, because they're friends. Like you."

For a moment, they held one another's gaze.

He spoke. "I just needed to know."

"That's okay. Now you do." She said the words, but knew the tiniest rift just opened between them.

"What else can I do for you, Angie?"

"Twila would've been the perfect appointee, and of course she was his hero for the heart attack. Now, she's the vice-presidential running mate with Freeman Swanson. There's a vacuum that needs filling. I'm the right person."

"I've never cared for Crawford or Dearborn. As far as I'm concerned, the only person worth saving is Scott McHale. And, you."

Lovely brown eyes watched her friend's.

"Watch your back, Angie."

She reached into her purse and turned her cell phone back on. "I've got to go. But you can see Scott's seat is a good move for me, right?"

"Yes, because I know you'll be great. Others will see it as a neat little package. Congresswoman this year, senator in two."

She shouldn't have been surprised. "You're right, I benefit. Ergo, I should be under suspicion."

He rolled a shoulder. "Everybody seems to be taken care of. The problem is Scott doesn't get a chair when the music stops. He'll be hunted down and sent off to prison for something he didn't do. Or, he's..."

Litton stopped.

She smiled. "Thank you for being such a loyal friend."

He leaned toward her. "That's not loyalty. That's reality. We'll find him, one way or another. Not because I've got faith in him but because it's what we do. People don't disappear unless they've been planning and plotting for a long time. He wasn't doing that. I know it in my gut. Whatever happened: he was just as surprised as everyone else."

He accepted her sullied ashtray. "I don't control the cops or agents' search, Angie. My part in this will be to make certain he's treated fairly. Your challenges will be far greater than mine."

He stood and kissed her offered cheek.

As she walked out of the office, Angie wondered why he hadn't mentioned the three Florida hooligans and the credit card. Ken would remain her friend, but now she must win back his loyalty.

. . . .

She took the elevator to the lobby and walked across the street. In an hour, she stood in front of a sea of faces in open conversation smiling, cajoling, and talking of dreams and realities. Thirty minutes after the last handshake, her car pulled into the Westwood Mall's parking lot and drove to the second level, northwest corner. She lit a cigarette and leaned against the fender. The breeze and the sun felt good. Anticipation churned her stomach, but no longer from indecision.

A black Tahoe pulled up and parked. She crushed the cigarette under a high heel and stepped into the car. Wes Teague closed the door after her and moved to stand at the front bumper.

Her mouth was set and grim. "It's done, so you'd better not be bullshitting me."

"It's no bullshit, Angie baby."

Big Jim Dearborn grinned behind artificially bright eyes. "We're off and running, so hold onto your hat. There's not much time left and no turning back now."

• • • •

The first rolling blackout hit the southern states from Atlanta to Houston on the Monday after Thanksgiving. The following day critical substations failed, throwing Chicago and the Great Lakes into darkness. Sixty-eight people died the week before the new administration's inaugural. When the Seattle-to-San Francisco grid failed, backup mini-nuclear power stations took over and supplied emergency power to run nearly all the major West Coast cities. Much of the nation cried foul.

Angie sat in her DC office and watched vice president-elect, Twila Crawford, speak from her front porch in Eureka, California.

"... I'll end my remarks with an observation. The last coal-fired electrical plant in our country closed on January 31, last year. The current administration's EPA looked on and they were happy. Not only was coal dead, but they successfully prevented nearly every other attempt to find clean fossil fuels or alternate fuel sources that made sense. Their solution: Electricity. Fine, but explain the gap between production and demand. The administration refused to invest in our safety and wellbeing and now, the failure of our grids has resulted in the near collapse of our nation's vital power infrastructure. We must fix our shortfalls but know this well: California and the west's mini-nuclear program cannot supply the rest of the nation, and even now cities are struggling to keep up with the eleven western states. This morning, President-elect Swanson and I pledge to properly fund Deer Creek's Western Central Grid ..."

The documents spread out on Angie's conference table showed McHale's firm support, and with special earmark funding to install the mini-nuke system. He never spoke about these things, and she wondered why something so important had been left out of their pillow talk. She burned to ask him about these sweetheart deals, just as she ached with his loss.

Before the day was out, the Speaker of the House formed a committee and ordered an investigation. Angie received her call at one in the afternoon and accepted twin appointments as a majority member and the legal advisor to the committee. Two weeks later, sitting next to the Speaker of the House, Representative-elect Angie Molina-McHale appeared competent, beautiful, and informed. She pulled no punches, captivating much of the nation on primetime television with hard-hitting questions.

Three weeks later, the new Executive Branch took their oath to protect and defend a nation on the brink of uncertainty and economic chaos.

Chapter 34

Scott

In the late spring at a mission on the Wilmington, Delaware waterfront, McHale slopped soapy water on the floor. Thirty or so men had eaten the spartan fare, some so stricken with finger shakes that scrambled eggs and Cream of Wheat dripped from the plastic tabletops. The night before, the minister turned him down for a job at the shelter saying there was no money for hired help. The reverend was obviously sick and hadn't shown up to work breakfast the next morning. McHale stepped in. He'd snatched up a rag and spray bottle to clean, and later found the mop and bucket.

No one questioned him.

The shelter closed after breakfast and wouldn't open until just before the evening meal. McHale closed his laptop and went in search of more free Wi-Fi signal. The search for the missing US Senator barely rated a mention anymore. Occasionally, a journalist with slipping ratings came up with a new theory and blogged or appeared on a Podcast. The latest conjecture had him disappear just as the Virginia coastal marshes experienced a resurgence of UFO sighting.

McHale chuckled at that one.

Angie and Twila began to appear more routinely in several national news and video pieces. He was proud of both, especially the way they often shared at the podium in public events especially when discussing the nation's aged power grid.

He pulled up the local Muroc County weekly's news which he thought was most likely monitored and tracked. He routinely prepared an escape route. This time he sat nearest the Starbuck's rear door. Big Jim Dearborn was in play, too, but of course, from behind the scenes. The governors of western states were fearful about declining revenues, brown and blackouts, and worse, that their popularity might slip. Several redirected federal educational funds to supplement purchases for their unreliable power grid. Lots of hue and cry from the teacher's unions but not so many from parent organizations. Rolling brownouts and the occasional total loss of power had become the norm in many regions of the west. The no-bid contracts seemed to fall to friends of Dearborn. The blame rested on aged and outmoded equipment. McHale knew better. He'd been a part of the planning but now wondered where it had all gone so wrong. What were they trying to do?

He changed coffee shops and signed signed into an underground deep-web site. After several moments, a second site verified his computer, and he found two messages waiting. He knew skulking NSA operators often baited their traps with interesting titled emails, so he was cautious. In this case, both showed no subject and the addresses of an underground blogger he had come to know as Patriot Flame.

Probably safe.

For the last few days, the blogger called on other dissidents to join local cells. He said the time may come to resist an ineffective and arrogant government. It was time to prepare. Private citizen groups began to challenge gangs and criminals in open combat in Los Angeles and San Diego.

Police departments called for calm and an end to vigilantism. The fights were generally quick ambushes by home and store owners and ended long before the police could arrive. Second Amendment advocates stood on the sideline and watched and called for effective law enforcement.

The streets became no safer according to the bloggers. Others disagreed and credited veteran's groups. Governors threatened to call up the National Guard. Locales simmered while many stayed in their homes.

After five quick minutes of scanning and reading, he closed the computer and left through the back. For several hours he wandered the streets, doubling back and watching for lookers in store front glass. When the chime in the public square finally sounded four, he queued up for a bed. Dinner was served at five. The regular minister was replaced with a substitute preacher speaking until seven. By nine, he slept with the computer clutched to his chest as it recharged. His sleep was never restful, but nevertheless, he began the day early by unstacking chairs and wiping down the kitchen.

The preacher touched his arm. "Say listen, friend. I appreciate you cleaning up around here, but I can't offer anybody a job. If I did, there'd be no money in the till."

McHale nodded and said nothing.

The man glanced at the gauze around his throat. "You're the one who can't talk, right? What's your name?"

He wrote on a small spiral pad. "Tony."

"Okay, Tony. Did you hear what I was saying? No work, because I can't pay you."

McHale wrote. "No pay. Just thankful."

The preacher was still pale from his bout of illness. "Well, God bless you, then. I got to get some aspirin."

McHale continued to man the serving line and clean the tables between patrons. Most homeless didn't look up as they shuffled through the line. After the last man, he ate in silence then began kitchen cleanup. His day followed much as it had the day before although he never sat in the same store front twice.

The preacher returned for the evening prayers and found McHale before lights out.

"You need to be gone in the morning, Tony. Understand? *Gone by six*."

The preacher sighed as he stuck in hands in baggy pockets. "It's a funny life, and I know there's a lot of things I just don't understand. Tomorrow, I'm going to make the call. I'm sorry but there're lots more men in here who need help just as much as you. I can't afford to get shut down. Do you understand what I'm saying?"

McHale nodded. The reward for information leading to his apprehension was a hundred thousand dollars.

"Okay, then. Get some sleep now but be gone in the morning."

He waited until the man began the locking up routine, then slipped out the kitchen door and into the night.

Chapter 35

Angie

Angie sat in Twila's former office with her new laptop. Joy's email from earlier in the morning needed an answer. She didn't have any more information. In fact, she hadn't thought about the hole in her life since four that morning when she went to the gym. It seemed her duties filled the void in spite of herself. She would not share Dearborn's opinion with Joy. He simply wrote her husband off and believed McHale had perished in some forgotten canyon or creek. Or, that he hid in South America.

The thought twisted her gut in pain.

Angie believed differently but as time went by, the priority to find her husband waned with the crushing work of serving as a member of three charity board of directors and a US Representative.

She could not keep the candle lit in the window forever.

Civil unrest rocked the nation as power grids degraded and vigilantism encouraged sympathetic uprisings. People were dying. A few by the hands of authorities but many random murders and even revenge killings as gangs vied for dominance. By latest counts, two dozen major American cities joined the two in California. Blocks smoldered from alternating rioting and looting. The fascists of social upheaval found common ground with socialists and communists in spite of their many differences.

Terrorists stoked both fires.

Armed National Guard patrols posted forces largely on the East Coast. As the lights went out, Midwest cities like Chicago, St. Louis, and Kansas City joined in. Street gangs roamed Philadelphia, Baltimore, and New York City. Food supplies plummeted and crowds took to the streets demanding government action. In the west, Dearborn's mini-nukes prevented grid failures from imploding society. Los Angeles, Seattle, and Portland's Antifa and BLM rioted for rioting's sake.

Just as it seemed experts brought generating stations back on line, hackers concentrated raids from the Gulf Coast to the Great Lakes. Reports of snipers shooting police, firefighters, and the Guard shocked a nation in turmoil. Anti-Second Amendment groups demanded the confiscation of guns, magazines, and ammunition. Businesses shut down and the middle class took to the streets.

Beleaguered public officials thought a corner had been turned when six weeks earlier the Western Central Grid brought a reactor on-line. Hackers immediately attacked the facility. Only backup processes and software coupled with the quick thinking of a lone night manager managed to save the facility from a catastrophic implosion.

Angie found the remote as NBC flashed a "Breaking News" scroll on one of her four wall-screens. A bright-eyed redhead with flawless features and cherry lipstick spoke. She recognized the woman who'd covered her husband's story in the Bethesda hospital.

"The President's office announced he will address the nation at nine pm Eastern this evening. An advanced copy of the president's speech confirmed unknown hackers successfully shut down two of the four main US power grids over the last ninety-six hours. Beta power-tests from the multiple nuclear reactor site, the Western Central Grid, were curtailed this afternoon when a hacker succeeded in breaching network security.

"Rolling blackouts struck the eastern seaboard as emergency power quickly ran low on scarce fossil fuels. Local officials prioritized hospitals and other key services leaving homes and businesses without lights. The Canadian Prime Minister today again refused to release its strategic oil reserves. In a move designed to placate hackers, a moratorium was declared ceasing any further assistance to the American grid."

The news anchor turned an unread page as the screen switched to black clad protesters facing a line of police officers.

"A usually mild March in the South was counterbalanced by a late-season blizzard across North Central states. White House officials said the storm was evidence of climate change and accused deniers of blocking proper preparation. The death toll stands at ninety-six and is expected to go higher. National Guard troops in the affected areas evacuated citizens at risk and supplemented depleted police departments. Smaller cities and towns appealed to FEMA for relief as the lights stayed off. Heating oil reserves once again ran low as trucks were unable to move and pipelines remained shut down. Several members of Congress brought a declaration of war to the floor for a vote in this latest cyberattack. The Speaker of the House shelved the move until the FBI and NSA could confirmed the point of origin. Several sources pointed to Russia's traditional role in hacker attacks with unverified claims. The Kremlin denied any involvement.

"Alone in the nation's chaos are the eleven western US states and part of west Texas. The yet-to-be-certified WCG and the prepositioned standby mini-nuclear reactors overcame the latest shortfall but left the eastern grids lacking. Even though environmental groups protested, the small generating facilities were 'awakened' and now provide power to every major western city including those where riots are occurring.

"Many municipalities in California, Oregon, Washington, and Nevada unveiled their own mini nukes, giving widespread credit to the forward-thinking environmentalist and the newly inaugurated vice president, Twila Crawford. As you may know, Crawford joined President Swanson's ticket on the final ballot following the outcry over then-President Timothy Pruitt's failure to protect the nation's grid system. An interesting historical sidenote is six weeks before the convention, then Congressman Crawford was tapped to fill the missing and presumed dead Scott McHale's vacated senatorial seat. The missing McHale's rescue mission became a nationwide manhunt after authorities declared him a person of interest in the death of his aide and unborn child. The ex-senator remains unaccounted for and has since been declared dead by the State of California."

Angie touched the off button fighting anger and grief. Scott had lied to her face. And she'd believed him. She'd supported him. Even though the comparative technique used in the DNA analysis is considered experimental and largely unproved in court, the California lab results gave McHale a ninety-nine percent match to the thumb-sized fetus.

"You're a bastard, Scott McHale."

Her words came out aloud and yet the empty office said nothing.

She tapped a quick reply to Joy and closed the screen. A knock sounded and she glanced at the security camera. She rose and unlocked the door.

"Good evening, Madam Vice President. I was just listening to NBC worship at your altar."

Twila rolled her eyes. "Oh, please." She turned to her security detail. "You guys wait out here. I won't be long."

"Yes, ma'am." They stepped back into the unlighted hallway and took defensive positions.

Angie shut the door. "How are you handling the armed entourage?"

Twila smiled. "You'll know soon enough."

Angie hit a remote to close the drapes. "Really?"

Twila waited until the world was shut out, and then walked into the room. "Really. Not long now."

Angie held out a bottle of scotch. "This is all still just a little heady."

Twila nodded and lifted two glasses from the serving tray. "I feel the same way sometimes. And then the next minute, I want Jimmy to kick ass and get the show on the road."

Angie handed over a tumbler. "I find it hard to believe he's getting this done. The guy's amazing."

Twila swirled the amber liquid for a moment's reflection. "Amazing and treacherous. Probably about as dangerous as they get."

Scott had told her the same thing many times. "I remember."

They touched glasses as Twila turned serious. "Let's not underestimate ourselves, Angie. Together, you and I are a formidable team, and this is our time."

Twila took a place on the leather sofa. "I always liked this office. Took a while to get it because it's a corner suite."

"I like it, too. I know you had to pull strings." She sipped. "Have you seen the city at night recently? Army Humvees roving the streets. Gangs breaking curfew. I can hear gunfire sometimes. It's pretty scary out there."

Twila sipped her whiskey. "Most of the heat's coming down on the National Guard right now. Jimmy anticipated that. The president's getting pressure to send in military troops. Active-duty troops. I'm on the record, private record of course, opposing that move but you know Swanson."

They were both aware active military troops in American streets was strictly prohibited unless the country experienced an extreme emergency. The President had not yet hit that switch.

"Actually, I don't. I've only talked to him once or twice when he was the mayor in NYC."

"He's a bullheaded old socialist. A lot like Jimmy, I suppose. Just not as scary. No national government experience and he hates his cabinet. Sometimes I think he hates America, and only tolerates the rest of the country because New York's got to be somewhere in the world. Mark my words, in the coming months, he's going to order troops in. An undeclared martial law will come under big-time scrutiny. Congress will raise the roof. The Supreme Court may have to work quickly, something they rarely do. It's what Jimmy's counting on."

Angie blinked her concern. "Then, I'm supposed to rally the opposition and challenge him on the House floor and in Federal Court. You'll keep your head down and be ready."

Twila stood and walked to the closed drapes. "It's all going to happen without us doing a thing. The toughest part will be to file a leak-proof lawsuit with Judge Nieto."

Angie hadn't heard about the judge being involved. "He's in the know, too?"

"Only a little piece because he doesn't want to know much. Wes Teague will help you with the suit in Acadia. Both briefs are already written, waiting on Swanson to spin out of control. We'll just fill in the names, and the administration's stupidity will be declared unconstitutional by the Ninth Circuit. The government will appeal, of course, and the Supreme Court will then get the case. Swanson will violate *posse comitatus*, so it's a slam-dunk. I'll be on record as opposing, so the president takes a major black eye all alone. He won't resign, of course, but there'll be a movement to invoke the twenty-fifth amendment. You and I will be on the sidelines wearing the red, white, and blue capes."

Angie said nothing, her mind spinning every time she heard the plan.

Twila tipped up her glass. "Swanson will eventually quit to save his legacy. I guarantee it. Or actually, Jimmy will. And if the need ever arises, the impeachment papers are locked in my safe."

Angie nodded. "And you'll become president."

Twila gave a sharp nod. "You can thank Scott's penis, honey. This was his slot all along, but he blew it."

Angie tip more into Twila's glass. "I'll tell you again. You were the person we wanted from the beginning. I was always slated to stay in California, but not Scott and not you. The minute Jimmy and I saw you two on the campaign trail, we knew it was Camelot all over again. But it was the wife of the candidate who should've been our first pick. You've got to understand. At the time, he was Latino and acceptable. And male, of course. The demographics were perfect for him. That was then, not now. At the time, you would've been too controversial: activist lawyer, granddaughter of a field hand, and movie-star beautiful. But, hey. It all worked out."

Twila sat and tossed an arm over the sofa. "Talk about all the right pieces falling into place. You're our good luck charm, girl."

Angie gripped her glass and fought a stomach in turmoil. "There's still a lot of those little pieces bouncing around. Besides, Big Jim says we make our own luck."

"I approve the quote, but don't get too wedded to that guy. He's one tough son of a bitch, and he'll toss your ass under the bus the first time you cross him. Just look at Scott."

Twila held out a quick hand.

"I didn't mean it like that. Scott just had some rotten luck. What I meant was we've got to toe the line for now.

A maverick will cause trouble we don't need. Besides, everything is rolling along. Pretty soon, we won't need Jimmy at all."

Angie set her tumbler down. "You've thought through your end game, then."

"I had to. We just need to be careful what we say and do. Nothing can raise suspicion. We have to keep each other in the know. Watch each other's back. No one else will do it for us."

Twila glanced toward the door and leaned closer to Angie. "You know those two gorillas out there aren't Secret Service, right?"

Angie shook her head.

"Didn't want that. Jimmy had a cow. He's got fingers everywhere and can keep tabs on me. But not with those guys. The blond crew-cut is Hugh, a special friend from my Cal Northern days. He dropped out to become a SEAL, then got the GI Bill, graduated and joined LAPD. Strictly hardcore all the way. He only came back because he loves me and will do anything I say."

Her blue eyes were merry for a minute. "The other guy is his SEAL buddy, and they're tight. I'm surer of them than any government guys."

Angie watched Twila for a moment, a concern working her mind. "You're pretty high profile now. Is this going to be a problem for us?"

Twila answered quickly. "No. Our time is coming like a freight train in the night. No stopping now."

Angie laughed and took up her glass. "To night trains and our time, then."

Twila laughed and clinked. "Our time."

For the next hour, the two women went over the details of the schism, the re-alliance, and the constitutional amendments they needed in place. The plan was Dearborn's molded in their own image.

After Twila left, Angie slipped off her blouse and skirt and pulled on one of Scott's old t-shirts. She inhaled the cloth to see if he was still there. But no, only Tide.

She made up the couch with sheets and a blanket, and lay down, tired and troubled. Long days dealing with California issues left her weary, and now long nights strategizing for the special summer gubernatorial campaign gave her no rest, no time to recover. Tomorrow, she would fly to Sacramento and begin a nineteen-day tour of industrial and commercial centers, then begin a second trip to meet the influential in all the western states.

Not by random chance, each location would be eventually serviced by the Western Central Grid when the system finally came online. From her reading, she also knew the mini nukes would be "idled for maintenance" as the plant managers received the nod. So far, Federal inspectors have continued to fail the WCG's system at Dearborn's direction. The Kingmaker wanted the crisis to tip desperately at the edge before his next move.

As she reached to turn off the lamp, her private cell phone rang. She read the number. A 505-area code. Albuquerque or New Mexico. She refused the call as her head touched the pillow.

• • • •

Twila stopped on the darkened street below and looked up at the window with its closed curtains. The same number vibrated her cell phone. She looked at Hugh, who punched in the trace with a private detective agency. On the third ring, the shadowed call terminated.

He grimaced. "Sorry, Twila. She hung up without answering."

The bastard was still on the loose.

She smiled at her bodyguard. "Probably just a staffer. Check Angie's calls against the number. Get me the NSA update to make sure I'm still tracking Angie and Dearborn's incoming calls."

"Yes, ma'am."

The former SEAL held open the limo's door as two additional Chevy Suburban's with came alive in the night. Red and blue flashers cut through the dark city street.

Chapter 36

Scott

The ramshackle middle school closed years before. The talk of turning the red brick building into a civic center turned out to be just that, talk. In the town a five thousand and dependent on timber, tax money remained scarce. Only the gymnasium with a concrete floor remained partially serviceable. Thieves made off with the oak basketball floor and all the copper pipes. An enterprising charity repainted the lines for neighborhood games and opened nightly meal line.

McHale dipped bread into thick congealing brown gravy and chewed. Even after eighteen months on the road, forcing food beyond the scar tissue left him in pain. As he swallowed, the man he had been waiting to see walked through the doors.

Bulky with wide shoulders and a heavy winter coat, Brian Peterson scanned the room. He let his eyes drift over the homeless then then accept a bowl of stew. He sat with a half-dozen others, eating silently. His short blond hair and powerful frame made a remarkable contrast to the lost souls of the night.

McHale sat near a side exit just in case the reward for his capture proved too tempting. He prayed he hadn't been stupid to leave a messages for a man he hadn't talked to in a decade.

When the others at his table left, McHale moved to the room's lone occupant.

Brian looked up. "I wasn't sure it was you, Scott. You've changed. How are you doing?"

McHale had regained all the voice he would ever have. He rasped a reply. "I'm good. How's the family? How's Peterson Construction?"

"We're okay. Went public a few years ago."

McHale nodded. "I know. I bought it. Smart money."

Brian's eyes squinted as he scanned the other man's tired and lined face.

McHale saw the stare. "Family okay?"

"Yeah, yeah. We're all good. Jesus, Scott. I feel like I'm seeing a ghost. What the hell happened to you?"

McHale eyed his old friend and business partner. "Got banged up. Been spending a lot of time on the road running away."

"Yeah, no shit. The Feds upped the ante on your reward again. They don't agree with California that you're dead. Clever move my home state. They get a new senator right away, and still get to chase the old one."

"Yeah. Clever."

Peterson scrunched his forehead. "I'd never have recognized you on the street. I wasn't even sure it was you when I sat down. The beard, the gray hair. How much weight have you lost anyway?"

McHale shrugged. "Some, I suppose."

"A lot you mean. You're plain skinny, for Christ's sake."

Brian pushed a meaty hand under his ball cap and glanced around the room. "Are we just going to talk or what?"

McHale smiled inwardly. His friend would never change. No social filters, straight to the point.

"Look, Brian. I need help—"

"And you chose me because I owe you, right?"

McHale tempered his words. "You don't owe me a thing. I needed someone I could trust."

"What about your FBI friend?"

"He'd have to turn me in. He wouldn't have a choice."

Brian snorted. "What makes you think I won't? A quarter of a million would look good in my bank account."

McHale grinned. "Where would you spend it? The country's crumbling fast."

Brian searched his friend's scarred face. "There's a lot of shit going down I don't understand. Let's get out of here."

"You go ahead. I'll meet you in the parking lot."

The moment of truth. Blue eyes to blue eyes.

A kitchen man stepped in and began to wipe tables at the furthest table.

Brian pulled back a coat revealing the pistol in his waistband. "You know I can take you anytime I want you. And you contacted me, remember? Something about needing a friend. Said you knew there were others out there but didn't know how to find them."

"Right, I know—"

Brian interrupted. "You wanted me to stick out my neck. Now I'm supposed to stand in the parking lot with my dick in my hand, while you make sure I'm not the enemy? No way. I'm the one hanging in the wind, here. We can either walk out together, or I go the hell home."

McHale pressed his lips into a single line. "You're right. Sorry. I'm a little jaded after so much time. Just didn't have anyone else I could trust. You see, I know what's going to happen. I just don't know how to stop it yet."

"Yeah, well. I suppose having a crystal ball is a wonderful thing, but I don't have a clue what the hell you're talking about. Come on. We can't talk here."

They walked into the clear cold night.

Brian pointed at a white Ford sitting high on its springs. "That's mine. You tell me what you know, then I'll decide if I'm going get involved."

For the next thirty minutes, McHale explained to his old blocking back what he'd gleaned from his research and travels across the country. Much of the best information had come from the street and outlaw blogs willing to taunt the tiger.

McHale's voice grew weak with overuse. "I'm not exactly sure how they intend to pull it off, or where Angie fits into all this. All I know we are not far from a catastrophe."

Brian watched the gravel at his feet. "You're right about the country crumbling around our ears. You're the one who gave speeches *warning* us about the electrical grid. Well, you were right. Now you're acting all surprised. Why's that?"

McHale massaged his distended throat. "Right, yeah. But we should've never come to this. The grids aren't separate. They're all interconnected. The system might've been invented by Edison, but there's been a lot of smart people since. No hacker nation could do this so completely from the outside."

Determination won over the pain in his throat. "Conspiracy theorists are only nuts before they come true. Then, everybody asks why no one listened. Listen, Brian. This is too cataclysmic of a collapse. Insiders high up are involved. They must be stopped."

Brian watched him for a moment. "There's a lot of people saying it's you."

McHale watched the night-black desert for a moment. "Yeah, I know. I hear it on late night radio, but it isn't me. It's never been me."

"You're the one who got the money for the mini-nukes, dude. I've read all about it. Earmarking and horse-trading. Then you pushed for the West Central Grid. A lotta shady crap, you ask me. You helped bring down the dams, and never once said a word about the wind-and-water whackos. It seemed like you're kept a low profile and all the while you were right in the middle of this thing. Now you're saying it's somebody else. Help me understand."

McHale had read the same editorials, the articles, the blogs building a case against him. He'd lost his one and only ally and didn't have anything else.

"I know what they say, but it's not true. I didn't have any part of this thing."

Brian rolled his shoulders and blew air to stars. "Well, I, for one, believe you."

McHale snapped his head up. "You do? Thank you."

"Shit yeah. You're ain't that smart." He grinned wide. "I got to make a phone call. You wait here."

McHale fought the wariness that had become his nature as Brian took out his mobile and stepped away.

Brian hesitated. "Don't you want to ask who I'm calling?"

McHale shook his head.

A big trademark grin. "About fricking you started trusting me."

A minute later, he climbed back in. "You ready? We got a drive ahead of us."

"Where're we going?"

His old friend smiled. "You relax. I'll drive."

• • • •

After three hours and a double thermos of coffee, the Ford pickup pulled into a closed gas station. High in the barren hills near Bishop, California, the dash clock clicked past midnight.

McHale woke and looked around. "Sorry. Didn't mean to fall asleep on you."

A Winnebago idled nearby. Vapor puffed from the tailpipe.

Brian's face reflected the truck's lighting. "I think you needed it. We'll catch-up a different time. The RV is your ride. Don't bother asking me because I don't have a clue where you're headed. If I'm caught, I can't tell them anything."

Brian held out a hand. "I believe in you, Scott, I always have. Don't let another ten years go by without coming by for dinner. I definitely won't recognize you then."

McHale slapped the other man's hand away and pulled him into a hug.

Brian's voice choked. "Safe travels. You're going to find out soon, but it's all pretty much up to you."

• • • •

The van's driver held her brown hair in a ponytail with a pink scrunchie. "We've got better than a day's drive, so you'd better make yourself comfortable."

He started to sit next to her, but she jerked a thumb. "Not there. In the back."

"Sure. Where are we heading?"

She said nothing and accelerated into the dark. He got the best six hours of sleep he'd had since leaving Camilla in North Carolina.

The young woman shook him by the shoulder holding a black bag. They idled on a broken asphalt road; headlights pointed into the night.

"You've got to wear this but I'm going to tell you when, all right? No need to tie it but put it on when I say so."

Her steel eyes dared him to protest.

McHale accepted the bag. "I can do that."

"Good. We still have a good way to go. Just stay back here."

This time he did not sleep. The occasional headlight filled the RV's cabin as the engine droned on.

When a blue haze filled the horizon, she called to the back. "It's time, Senator. Put the bag over your head. Leave it there."

He did without protest so surprised he was to be referred to as Senator. They soon left the blacktop and crunched on a gravel road. Rocks clacked against the undercarriage.

McHale could feel the sunlight as it rose through the RV's thin curtains. He did not try to look and instead filled his mind sorting facts. He invariably reached the same conclusion every time he did this mental exercise.

When the side door finally opened, chilled air braced his body. He felt hands guide him down the metal steps, up onto concrete, and then down several more steps. The smell of earth and vegetables permeated. He could feel others nearby.

The lady driver's voice. "Take the bag off."

He did and found himself facing a dozen shadowed men and women. Some sat, others stood. All gathered in the dank air of a root cellar. A single light bulb shone overhead.

A tall man stepped to the edge of the dark. His face remained invisible. "Have a seat, Senator. You need to tell us what's going on."

A single straight-back chair waited under the light.

McHale sat. "Can I assume you want to hear my side of the story?"

"Yep, and we've got some questions, too." The large man wore dark trousers and a blue shirt. A jacket lay over the chair. McHale saw the six-pointed star as well as the alert eyes of a Belgian Malinois near his feet.

McHale nodded toward the dog. "Your BS detector?"

"That would be all of us, sir. Please proceed."

McHale gathered a breath and started at the beginning. He retraced his time in Congress by pointing to legislation that came from sponsors. He described support for dam removal and agreed the result was a thinning of the electrical grid. He explained how he'd been brought into the mini-nuke powerplant program late in the game. McHale talked openly about the night in San Rafael and the last time he'd seen Juliette. Finally, he offered a summation of his open and closed source online research and the conclusions he'd reached. He did not prevaricate.

"My latest adventure was a day long trip in a Winnebago, but you know all about that. Now, it's your turn. Ask away."

For another hour, he explained in more detail his relationship to James Dearborn, Twila Crawford, and Juliette Pearson. He hid nothing, admitted his mistakes, and let the chips fall where they may. Several people asked probing questions about his legislation.

Very good questions, McHale thought, regretting he hadn't asked the same one's years before when Dearborn had been calling the shots.

A woman at the back wall stepped into the light. "These mini-nukes weren't a big surprise to you, then. Right?"

"No, ma'am, they weren't. I've been earmarking and approving funds to replace the West Coast's hydroelectric capabilities for a long time. This was legislation directed by my sponsors through Jim Dearborn, but I hadn't known about the replacement equipment until later. I wrote a piece of legislation to form a commercial partnership—"

The woman interrupted. "For the Western Central Grid, we know. The was nine years ago when you were still in the House."

"Yes. This was to be a commercial venture with the government and private industry modeled after the Tennessee Valley Authority."

She stepped back.

He continued. "The legislation had plans for electric service interruptions. The mini nukes were a part of the network but not the only ones. Existing plants would be converted from dirty coal to clean natural gas. The Bonneville Dam complex would accept nuclear power from a rebuilt Hanford facility. I recall dozens and dozens of confidential meetings having to do with national security. The mini-nukes were only designed to supplement the grid. Never to take over and act independently. I'm not sure how they're being used today but I've read some underground blogs claiming the ones around LA are producing at less than forty percent—"

"Fifty-five is more like it." A voice from the dark.

McHale conceded holding up an open hand. "I don't have the inside information anymore, only what I've read. If it's fifty-five, then why aren't we using the other forty-five for the rest of the country? We're not alone in this crisis. People are hurting out there."

McHale described the state of the nation from the point of view of a homeless transient. He talked about migrant camps and the small day jobs he took, the months on the road hitching rides with truckers and sleeping under bridges. He told stories about spending time in soup kitchens and warehouse dormitories and held the hidden eyes of his small audience as he described the misery of a nation balanced on the edge.

A new voice. "What about Angie? What does she say about all this?"

McHale sighed. "I haven't been in contact with her. I've tested the NSA and probably the FBI counterintelligence gathering techniques by using burner phones a couple of times. I've never gotten through within the thirty-second limit—"

"What limit?"

McHale answered with more hesitancy than before. "I'm not completely sure of my information. The Internet made a big deal about Snowden's interviews. In one of them, he talked about their electronic gear using the first thirty seconds of a conversation to establish the monitoring protocol, keyword meta-mining. I'm not sure what specific data they'd gather in thirty seconds except it took me a week of washing dishes to buy a forty-dollar prepaid phone. If Angie didn't pick up within the first twenty seconds, I disconnected and destroyed the phone.

"One note here. I knew if I ever did make contact, she'd be caught up in my screwed-up life right along with me. I didn't want that. Not yet anyway. As much as I wanted to talk with her, and I was weak, I admit it, she needed to be set free to put things right. I trust her."

The basement shadows revealed a man in the business suit. "You might but I don't understand her relationship to James Dearborn. Lately, she's been meeting with the western governors. I think they're the reasons for all of that. California is squeezing every penny from the other grids when they do sell power. Seems to me your wife's right in there with them."

A man with a green John Deere ball cap sat next to him. "That's right. It's the Californians running the Western Central Grid at ten percent capacity. They're holding back energy from the rest of the country."

The RV driver spoke up. "We all got that, guys, but right now we're talking to the senator about things he might not know."

"It's all part of it, Marilyn. One hand is washing the other."

A voice from the back. "His wife only got there because she was married to this guy and knows the governor. Dearborn had something to do with getting her to congress. Mark my words. If there's a debt there, it's going to be paid one day."

McHale interrupted. "She knows Big Jim. I've already told you about my relationship."

Marilyn stepped back in. "We're not here to debate this guy. I think everyone's got the picture. Anyone else have a question?"

The green John Deere cap stood up. "Isn't it true your wife is working against this country?"

McHale barely kept his anger in check. "Absolutely not. She's a good person. A great person. She would never do—"

A woman with a faded Carhartt leaned into the conversation. "Sit down, George. That's uncalled for. Sorry Senator, but we both know there's lots of those types in DC. Wave the flag until it comes time to put up or shut up. Then suddenly, it's me first, country second. So, we need to know where she stands, just like we need to know where you stand. You just told us you haven't spoken to her, but you trust her. How? Why?"

The tall, uniformed man joined in. "The evidence doesn't agree with you, Senator. She's been on tours talking energy supplies to the western states' governors. She's not talking to the other thirty-eight. We know what's she's saying. There are rumors she'll be on the ballot for California Governor seat in the fall. It seems like these fancy trips between the western states are ally building. We just don't know for what. I'm not into conspiracy theories, but this all looks pretty suspicious to me."

McHale kept control. "Look. I've known Angie for the better part of three decades. She's smart, hardworking, and dedicated. She is *not* a conspirator."

The man did not back down. "There might come to a time when you need to make a different decision, Senator. Are you open to new information?"

The John Deere hat stepped up. "Come on, Bill. What's he supposed to say to that. A better question might be to explain why a freshman to the US Congress appoints herself ambassador in a national crisis?"

McHale knew independent blogs and podcasts did not treat her kindly. The national media split between party lines.

"Look, folks. I'm living proof evidence can be manipulated. I did not hurt my legislative aide, and the child who died inside her was not mine. I don't care what some lab says. I believe in Angie. She believes ... believed in me. That's the bottom line. She's doing what she can do to keep this country together. If she's going all over the west talking to important people, then you should be in her corner until the truth shows otherwise."

Silence enveloped the group until the cop slipped on his jacket. "I'm due at work. We need to talk a minute without you, Senator. Please go with Marilyn."

The driver stood. "We've got some dinner in the cabin."

The officer snapped two fingers and the dog rose. "Chester will wait with you while we talk."

McHale walked to the man with an outstretched hand. "Oregon State Police, right? We have history together."

"Yes, sir, we do. I know your history."

McHale shook his hand and paused at the door. "I'm not sure what this group represents, but I swore an oath to protect and defend the Constitution of the United States from all enemies foreign or domestic. It doesn't matter if I took that oath as a senator, a soldier, a cop, or a citizen. It doesn't even matter that I'm on the run. The oath is the same, just like the promise in the Pledge of Allegiance. I don't take either lightly."

He looked around the dark room with its hidden faces. "The oath binding me binds my wife. She feels the same way. If our sort of patriotism doesn't sit well with this group, then you've wasted an evening. God knows I've made mistakes but trusting Angela Molina-McHale is not one of them."

Chapter 37

Big Jim

"Aren't you taking a chance going to Las Vegas, Mr. Dearborn?"

The kingmaker looked up from his iPad and touched the screen. "They won't even notice me. Just the way I like it." He lifted his cigar from the armrest tray table as city lights disappeared under the Hawker 4000's wings. "So, when will our boy be on the FBI's Most Wanted list?"

Teague waved the steward back as his jaw worked in a rare show of emotion.

Dearborn rolled the cigar in moist lips, watching his number two. "That's okay, Wes. You did what I asked. It's not your fault he lived through it. I'm still laughing about the hillbillies, though." He looked at the aircraft's curved upholstered ceiling. "He lives through an airplane crash *and* getting run over. The guy is charmed."

"I should've had the chance to finish the job. Personally."

Dearborn shook his large head. "Nah. He's just meat on the hoof now. Besides, I've got a pair of numb-nuts following him." He blew smoke to the cabin's top and offered a humorless laugh. "They're actually not half-bad trackers if you give'm a little help. When I'm ready, you can have him."

Teague said nothing.

He tipped the ash into plate. "I gotta say for a pansy politician, McHale's got some skills."

Teague worked his face back into a mask.

Dearborn waved his hand, dismissing the other's worry. "I need to see who he's talking to, Wes. I got to know so when the time comes, there no surprises. You would've just pinched his head off, for Christ's sake. For now, I need you concentrating on getting this right."

"We don't tolerate failure in others, sir, and it shouldn't be tolerated in me."

Dearborn soothed his tiger. "And I appreciate that, Wes. I really do. But it's high time you knew some details about our Mr. McHale. He's nothing but a small thorn. We'll remove it when it suits us. You agree?"

No hesitation. "Yes, sir."

"Good."

Dearborn waved the steward forward and pointed to the dinner plates. "Scotch. Two." He looked at Teague. "You and I need to talk."

The steward poured and moved to the business jet's rear seat.

"You've done a good job, Wes. We only need a few more months. The momentum's building, and pretty soon, we're going to be unstoppable."

Hundreds of people in dozens of locations moved money buying influence, loyalty, and cooperation. Government regulators dropped the roadblocks, making milestones easier to meet. If someone balked or came up short, Teague practiced his personal dark arts. The rumor got around, and people fell in line.

Scotch running to the back of Dearborn's gullet drew a satisfied grunt. drank. "I'm planning to let Angie take the lead for a while. Meanwhile, I need you to watch the Vegas and Reno operation and keep those yahoos focused. Once we start to roll, you'll follow her back to California and keep a thumb on your own crews. I'll be busy with other things. Even with people everywhere, you're the only one I trust. This is critical."

Teague's glass remained untouched. "Angie's a good choice, sir."

"I'm glad you agree." He tipped his glass. "To you, controlling her."

They both drank.

Dearborn set the tumbler on the seat tray. "Right now, she's charming the old fat cats into thinking we're building a western coalition. We're doing just that, and she'll be a hero. It'll be too late when she realizes we're building a whole new goddamn country. You've got to stay close, stroke her if you must, but control her. She's our public face and we need to keep her from balking. By the time we pull the curtain back, you'll have the organization to put her into office. Or take her out if I say so."

Teague nodded. "Yes, sir. I assume the last couple of weeks with my computer guys was a test."

Dearborn smiled. "You assume right."

"We did well, sir. The grid is still vulnerable, and we proved it. Social media is child's play. NSA can't break TikTok's commercial encryption. We can. With the consolidation of the Internet into four or five major ISPs, we'll control nearly ninety percent of the public's access."

"Almost like having an A-Bomb, isn't it?"

"Better, sir. This weapon does its job, and nobody's the wiser. When the FBI and Homeland Defense figure it out, they'll be too late."

Teague spoke again. "I wouldn't mind knowing how President Swanson will be handled."

Dearborn rarely confided his plan to others. "He's oblivious, Wes. Power does that to people. Makes them blind, and they believe their own press."

"And Twila?"

Dearborn chuckled. "Ready as hell and chomping at the bit. She'll feed us whatever we need. Swanson's on record fiddling with Homeland Defense to get Second Amendment guns. Twila opposed it. Both stories will be leaked to the media when I decide it's time. You took good care of Judge Nieto. He'll declare Swanson's initiative unconstitutional when the White House makes its moves. SCOTUS will take its sweet time, but the guns will be idling in a warehouse. Once the decision goes against him, Swanson will resign instead of being impeached or having the twenty-fifth invoked. We'll throw the switch at Twila's swearing-in. She'll be a hero, and Swanson will go home to New York with his tail between his legs."

Dearborn rolled the cigar's soggy, mashed end, and leaned toward Teague in a rare moment of comradeship. "McHale would've been easier, but the guy just wouldn't listen. I'm sorry about Juliette. I know she was a friend of yours, but you can't let his bullshit eat you up."

"Nothing eats me up, sir."

Dearborn decided Teague needed to continue in the dark about those details. "It'll all come together pretty soon. Then? Scotty's yours."

"Yes, sir. I think you'll like the operations in the desert."

Smoke curled around the ceiling. "Your guys are doing good work. When Nevada declares independence, shit's gonna collapse left and right. We can control Vegas, Reno, and El Gordo. We have the idiot governor over a barrel. The feds will be out of the picture, and the state gaming commission will leave because I'll make them a better deal. Meanwhile, everyone will be happy because the power stays on as long as I'm happy."

Teague stared silently out the dark glass. A rare breach of emotion in the man.

Dearborn considered how much more he could tell the man. "I'm sure the media will be screaming their asses off, but Swanson's not sending in the Marines. And Twila sure as hell ain't. And for who? There's no enemy. They're all in DC, because you and I will see to it. When Colorado and Wyoming drop into place, we'll close off the highways. I'd love to be a fly on Swanson's wall when *that* shit hits the fan. California and Nevada will declare themselves in the Federated States of America and then, not even New York will want Swanson back. Can you see why holding Twila and Angie's hand is the key?"

Teague said nothing.

The man's silence was one of the things Dearborn like most about the guy. "Good. Once Twila's sworn in, you come home and bring Angie. I don't give a shit about the rest of the House or the Senate. An NSA-free line to Twila will be in place, and you'll open the Western Central Grid floodgates. The east will get bailed out, and they won't squawk at losing a troublesome piece of real estate like California. Twila will crack down on the violence, but most of the guns will be in furnaces by then. Only the cops and crooks will be armed, and frankly, it doesn't matter to me who wins as long as Angie and Twila are there to pick up the pieces. We'll impose martial law and get away with the same crap Swanson gets fried for."

Dearborn laughed. "Most people will be waiting on their EBT cards and won't give a shit what's happening to the country."

"Timeline, sir?"

"One more year and then on April 19: American hater day. The day Timothy McVeigh dropped the Murrah Federal building, and the day the Waco siege ended. The day before the Columbine school murders and Adolph Hitler's birthday. April 19th will also be the day the western states declare allegiance to the Federated States of America, and we get our own damn country without us firing a shot."

The aircraft banked and lost altitude in preparation for the North Las Vegas airport. Lights in the distance welcomed.

Dearborn leaned toward his protégée. "This is our time, Wes. Consider that more than thirty percent of the US's arsenal storage is in California, Oregon, and Nevada. Sixty percent of the National Guard soldiers are in western states. Hell, we'll even have our own air force if it really came down to protecting ourselves."

Teague knew all this. "What about the missiles and the nuclear bombs? The Air Force isn't going to pack up and leave because we tell them to."

Dearborn agreed. "We don't want 'em to leave. All the soldier boys will stay inside their bases because Commander in Chief Twila Crawford will order them to. The USA and Federated States of America will sign an accord. Hell, it's already written, and why not? We control both halves of the deal. It ain't a negotiation when everybody's in on the win."

Teague fixed his eyes on the forward bulkhead. "This is a good plan, sir."

"A great one, actually, and thirty years in the making. Oh, our new republic might be at risk for a bit while the key players line up, but sometimes you just gotta roll the dice. We'll gamble one country and win two. Electricity's the key. Whoever controls the flow, controls the show."

"You're not worried about McHale still running around out there?"

Dearborn eyed Teague, lines deepening with the question. "No, I'm not, and neither should you. He was nothing before I found him, and he's nothing now. You're going to put a bullet in his head when it comes time. Yours might be the only shot fired in this entire fucking coup d'état."

. . . .

Dearborn often kept secrets from him. Or tried to. The black ops world may have shifting loyalties, but money remained the single, common truth throughout. The big man often used services like the Atlanta's Cornerstone Detective

Agency without telling him. He thought he was smart and at first, the two hillbillies obviously confused him.

Not Teague.

The boss loved his little secrets. He tended to forget Wes Teague eventually executed those secrets. Just like now.

As lights appeared in the desert night, the sleek Hawker Jet slowed for the descent. Deep in his gut, Teague ached for the chance at happiness that Juliette could have given him.

Then, of course, Scott McHale had stolen her. Wasteful and misogynistic, the smooth talking, fancy man. The man the world only thought they knew. The dead man who walked the earth.

One day soon, Teague would drain McHale's evil lifeblood into the dirt. Nothing and no one could stop Teague from fulfilling McHale's destiny. That included Big Jim Dearborn.

Chapter 38

Scott

Even though the calendar said early spring, the cold breeze chilled the frozen iron bench outside Salt Lake City's library. The last of the day's warmth escaped in the arid sky as McHale fought a chill and pulled his thin jacket closer. The Wi-Fi was better the inside building, but he needed to avoid the security cameras. Besides, his latest thrift store purchase gathered enough errant signal to make his efforts worthwhile.

The *Phoenix Daily Sun* reported WCG's daily output and had become a cult following. Anxious businesses and homeowners watched the effect of their cousins in the east suffer rolling brown and often complete blackouts. A fourth reactor coming on line actually made the both the print and cyber services when management claimed the successful thwarting of hacker attacks. Little of Number 4's energy would make it to the eastern grid but hope nationwide proved a powerful tonic.

McHale knew why.

Eighty percent of the power in the western states hummed unimpeded across a web of high-voltage overhead lines. From valley floors and across wide spans of arid land, power flowed. None crossed into the eastern grid except for a modest six percent. Cities like Houston and Dallas and a few others in Texas benefited. When the Perry nuclear facility shut down on schedule the week before, patience wore thin.

CBSN talked about mobs looting the few remaining downtown stores in Cincinnati and Cleveland.

Hacker attacks became a way of life.

McHale scanned F Street, but few people noticed a street bum, even one who was head-down in a computer tablet. He pulled up the *Atlanta Journal-Constitution.* Georgia National Guard positioned themselves in the affluent suburb of Buckhead. The St. Louis Post-Dispatch reported gun owners refusing to comply with America's new Australian-style gun buyback. Agents on search and seizure teams found hundreds of neighbors blocking their way and were sent packing. Clashes with more aggressive local police sent dozens to the hospital. One death was reported. Angry citizens barricaded the homes of judges to stymie local enforcement of the Patriot Act. Requests for weapons search warrants dried up. The Municipal governments of Richmond and Charlotte slow-rolled new gun registration, preventing deliveries while guns awaiting hearings and other legal procedures were quietly melted in government furnaces.

McHale believed the attacks on the country and her institutions came from Big Jim Dearborn, even if he didn't know why. Too many clues dropped over the years led him to forming a theory...a conspiracy theory.

He grinned in the cold evening considering the irony of becoming one of the unwashed accusing the federals of overreach and illegal surreptitious gathering of information. He couldn't prove his case or find enough hard data to convince others. Yet. Small groups like the one in Oregon listened when he spoke, Distrust remained high and he rarely received a second invitation.

He continued to plug along. One man flailing in the forest of an overwhelming juggernaut of apathy.

McHale pocketed the thumb drive and slipped another into the slot. He was certain this national malaise would not continue for much longer. So much now made sense to him about Dearborn's apoplectic anger over his career of senate quips and ad-libbed remarks. His travels took him to sites where old power sources had been dismantled. He walked the hills with subcontractors picking up windblown trash during the construction of joint wind and thermal sites.

And of course, he followed Twila's behind-the-scenes agitation and arm-twisting. Information that excoriated the government died on the Internet as fast as it was published. The major tech companies in upstate New York, California, and even Texas fell into line. Few noticed or cared. Lately, the censorship of human sheep became secondary to the next shipment east of Midwest or Ukrainian grain.

The scarred and dented Dell surfed the Internet under his fingers, stopping once more at the Salt Lake City blog. The author, Joshua Harrison, warned about the perils of social media and the government's collective half-truths. As Stake President in a middle-class suburb, he openly questioned the LDS church and state government's acquiescence. He regularly decried the erosion of power from the people to the government. His bio listed him as a teacher and builder, as well as an influential volunteer in the church's community.

McHale shut down the tablet's power and hefted his backpack. The clatter and airbrakes of the natural gas city bus approached. Headlights picked him out of the small crowd waiting to go home. He was last to board. He did so slowly gripping the chrome hand rails. The driver smiled patiently. McHale nodded in reply. Tonight, he would roll the dice once more.

• • • •

"That's quite a tale. What makes you think I won't call the Holladay Police as soon as you walk out of here? I saw you're on foot, and that makes you easy to catch."

Joshua Harrison, a tall balding man in his sixties, relaxed with the grace of someone accustomed to hard work, confrontations, and challenge. They sat around the dining table in the neat home of someone comfortable in simplicity. The man's gaze held the visitor with a grim and set mouth waiting for an answer.

This was the often-asked question. "I can't stop you, Mr. Harrison, but since my troubles, I've taken this message to whoever would listen. Some do and some don't. I openly admit my complicity. I took orders. Too late in the game, I started asking questions. My fall from grace makes sense to me. Now, of course. Not then. In those days, I wanted to be President. I wanted it so much; I sold my soul. By that time, no one was buying. Now I'll talk to anyone that'll listen. I hoped one of them would be you."

The man started a slow nod. "I'll hear what you have to say. For now. Doesn't mean you might not end up in jail tonight. I still don't know what you expect of me."

McHale had already judged the distance to the front door. He'd run before.

He didn't relax, but he did allow himself hope. "Fair enough. I'm a fugitive, but I haven't broken any laws, man's or God's. I promise you I've made plenty of mistakes and a lot of compromises. Things that make me cringe now, but I never hurt Juliette Pearson. I'm not a murderer. I spent my career looking the other way, carrying out orders. By the time I started to ask questions, it was way too late. I haven't any excuses, Mr. Harrison. What I'm trying to say is the scales have fallen from my eyes. I understand. I know what's happening."

The Bible verse did not change the other man's expression. "Call me Josh. I looked you up after I got your email. The state declared you dead, so you've obviously beat that rap. Too bad for you but the Feds don't think so. They're the ones with a lot of money and I think people still want you behind bars. The girl's family for one."

McHale knew saying too much hurt his case. "I'm the girl's family, Josh. She's been with my wife and daughter, and me for years. Since the first election decades ago. I did not hurt Juliette."

"I followed the story. I never understood why you weren't arrested outright."

McHale shifted his backpack to the floor, deciding he would not argue his innocence again. Listeners either believed him or did not. Now, he only wanted to head off what seemed to be their shared destiny.

The small home had memories on the walls and propped on tables. Family photos with uniformed men and children in happier times. Some yellowed with age. Many not. All stared into the silent room judging him.

Maybe he'd made a mistake, and his journey ended here. Once arrested, he would not survive an arraignment. He almost welcomed the end. He would be killed in prison, and what's worse, no one would morn him. He was convicted and simply not yet sentenced.

He also would not give up. Could not give up. Sometimes, he forgot why.

"Believe what you want, Josh, but I'm telling you the truth. Her death was part of wider scheme I still cannot explain. I did not hurt her."

Josh didn't flinch. "And I didn't call the cops. If Hannah was still alive, someone would've been here waiting to put handcuffs on you the minute you crossed my threshold."

"She was probably a wonderful woman, In this case, she would've been wrong."

McHale knew the widowed man's history. Google watched everyone.

McHale leaned over the dining room table. "I'm not worried about me, but the country. I need to keep moving. I need to keep trying. Talking."

Josh worked his jaw, then stood and retrieved the old dented percolator. "Your email mentioned the article I wrote. Why?"

He poured coffee into two mugs.

"Because you were close to the truth, but you stopped."

"No facts to back it up."

"I can give you the facts. I can tell you why there's rolling blackouts in some places, none in others. You said Iran,

Russia, and North Korea weren't behind the hacking. You're right, but how did you know?"

"I read. I don't find my facts filtered through talking heads. There's a nice library 'cross town—"

"I'm familiar with it."

"Then you ought to know most everything we need is right there. If you look for it."

McHale pressed. "What about the WCG? Why is the plant working at twenty percent capacity? They could be sending power to the rest of the country, but they don't."

Harrison lifted his cup and sipped. "I wrote about this. The Western Central Grid is private business. Yes, they have an MOU with the government, but they sell power to the highest bidder. They make a profit. Right now, it's the west, America be damned. That the capitalist way. Memorandum of Understanding or not, we've traded integrity for comfort."

McHale tasted his own cup. "Well, you're right about one thing. The facility is designed to power more than just its neighbors. At eighty percent capacity, the WCG can theoretically supply enough power at non-peak hours for the much of the United States and western Canada and never break a sweat. I know. As a junior congressman in the House, I co-sponsored the funding legislation. I'm an engineer. I did my own study."

"Then why have we got a crisis in this country?"

If Josh was going to ask the right questions, McHale owed him the truth. "We shouldn't. Those thousands of acres in Northern Arizona should be operating ten or twelve super nuclear reactors, not four or five. The money to fund the plants is there. Just look at what marginal production is doing. But that's not happening. Why? We have are barricades and pissed-off people, and I don't blame them. We need someone to call a spade a spade. We need a savior."

"You?"

McHale rocked his head to one side. "God, no. You're not listening. I had my chance and blew it. People have died because of me. That's something I'll have to live with for the rest of my life. We need leaders."

Josh sighed noisily setting his mug on the polished wood. "To do what? Stop a conspiracy. Come on, McHale. You can do better than that."

"Conspiracies look a lot different from the inside when you're one of the conspirators. For better or worse, my entire career was a setup. I was supposed to be a good monkey and dance when the organ grinder played. And frankly, I was good at it. For a while. Maybe the best thing that ever happened to me was my plane crash."

Josh's jaw worked. "Early on, it seemed like you had a real future, you and your wife."

McHale felt the arrow go deep and silent into his gut.

Josh watched closely. "Maybe you *were* too full of yourself and getting taken down a notch didn't sit well. I can quote scripture, too. 'The sluggard is wiser in his own eyes than seven men who can answer sensibly.' Proverbs 26:16."

McHale stared at the floor. "You know, Josh. Humility's the first thing that dies in Washington. The ethical compass comes next. Depending on the outcome of this evening's conversation, I'm going to Tucson to see a friend of mine.

You remind me a lot of him. I don't know if he will arrest me, or believe me, but I'd like you to come along."

Josh's gaze looked over the other man's shoulder to the picture of a lovely woman. "Now why would you want me to do that?"

"Because this country is in desperate need of patriots and leaders. I don't know exactly what's coming but when is does, people like you need to be at the epicenter."

Harrison raised an eyebrow. "Not you?"

McHale offered a rueful smile. "No. I don't have a car. You do."

Josh chuckled for the first time that evening.

Fourteen hours later, Josh and McHale pulled into a windblown Central K gas station north of Tucson's city limit.

Chapter 39

Scott

Sheriff Theo Haines walked the shadows across dark Forgeus Avenue. The man who had introduced himself as Josh Harrison stood in a shadow cast by a dimmed streetlight, waiting. Most cities went dark when the sun set. Sherriff Haines's hand gripped a Chief's Special .38 revolver inside his jacket pocket. Death threats had become commonplace in Pima County when the authorities threatened to take the guns. Three white-and-green patrol cars waited in the parking lot while the Tucson police handled a small demonstration in the city.

Haines stepped up and growled out a warning. "This'd better not be crap, because I committed the sheriff's department to help the city cops out tonight. I need to be on the street with them."

The heat from the day tried but could not win against the cool of the evening desert.

Harrison stood very still. "I understand, Sheriff, and I appreciate you believing me. I've spent the last couple of days with him driving here, and I believe he's telling me the truth, at least as he sees it."

Haines looked around the empty sidewalk. "So, where the hell is he?"

"I'll take you to him."

Haines shrugged. "Let's go."

The two men crossed into the municipal athletic field.

Josh broke the silence as they walked. "McHale's come to know things living underground that make sense if you can believe his story. You have secrets he can't get, so you can decide if he's crazy, or if we have a revolution on our hands."

"I'll ask again, what are you doing with him?"

Haines did not reply.

They stepped through a break in the fence and onto the track.

Josh pointed at the far fences. "He came to my house. I write a blog. Apparently, my articles agree with his ideas. But what he really wanted was to talk to you. I just had a car."

They reached mid field. Haines looked around. "Is he coming or not?"

McHale stepped from the corner of the dugout. "I'm here, Theo."

Both men turned. McHale's formed bent at the waist. His shoulders were uncharacteristically rounded as if he was about to crumble.

Haines covered the distance in a half dozen giant steps "Goddamn it, Scott. Where in the hell have you been?"

"I'm sorry to put you in a trick bag, Theo..."

McHale was muffled by Haines' duty jacket as he was pulled into a bear hug. "Ah, Jesus, man. You're all skin and bones."

Hanes' voice broke as he released his grip. "*That* was your old friend talking. Now, the sheriff is back in town. Start talking, goddamn it."

McHale took a deep breath. "I don't have the whole story. Someone sabotaged my airplane and tried to kill me. I didn't hurt Juliette. The nation is coming apart and I've been on the run for what seems like my whole life. Maybe you can tell me what's going on."

"Why me? Why don't you think I'd just drag your sorry ass in?"

"Because I know you trust the law as much as you trust the truth. And I'll promise to go with you if you decide I'm full of shit."

Josh cleared his throat and looked from man to man. "You guys want to do this without me?"

McHale shook his head. "No, not unless you'd rather go."

Josh glanced at Haines. "Then it's up to you, Sheriff. Do I stay or go?"

Haines puffed out a breath. "You stay. I might need to arrest you, too."

Josh held out a hand. "McHale told me about you. I'm First Battalion, 9th Marines Vietnam and Second of the Eighth, Twenty-Second Amphibious in Grenada. Semper Fi."

Haines took the hand. "Thought I recognized you. First Battalion, Eighth Marines, Fallujah."

McHale rolled his eyes. "You Marines. Geezus. Get over yourselves, would you?"

All three only smiled because laughing was just a memory. The men spoke in low tones for nearly an hour.

Josh finally turned to Haines. "Sheriff? Can I assume you conditionally agree with McHale?"

"More than agree. I've been mulling this thing around in my thick skull for a while. One of the fellas I drank some beer with at the Academy is a supervisor at the Defense

Intelligence Agency. We've been talking, but he can't say much because frankly, a lot is classified, and big ears listen. Maybe I need to take Missy to see the DC museums."

McHale scrunched eyebrows. "Not a good time for big cities back east, Theo. We might need to think of something else."

Haines pondered an idea and turned to Josh. "You're an elder in the LDS, right? Can you get me access to a phone landline inside the church? The feds can't monitor without FISA warrants, at least not yet. And there ain't no terrorism inside the Mormon Church as far as I know."

Josh considered his answer. "Yes, I can get you a phone line. Can I ask why?"

"Because we need to start bringing together some of these groups McHale's talking about. We're going to need some organization. Can't use cell phones. Those damn things are worse than sieves. Churches are much tougher to monitor."

Josh understood. "I can do it. But we can't put the entire fourteen million church members in the middle of some very unwelcome light. The wrong turn here, and a lot of innocent people will have big problems. A couple Catholic churches had the weight of the Federal government come down on them not too long ago."

McHale set his jaw. "Josh? I'm afraid your church is already involved. Lots of folks are making plans for the collapse of the federal government. Like I said before, the states are going to be left on their own, or maybe re-formed into some sort of a coalition as the east coast just tries to survive."

He looked at the two men, one an old friend, one new, and cast his final thought upon the waters of trust.

"I've thought about this day and night since I've been on the run. Somebody's looking at the chaos and believes there's a chance to be king. I don't know all the moving parts, but I do know while we're fiddling, fires burn in Rome."

• • • •

McHale was partially right. The big party began six weeks later when Las Vegas declared its independence. Hollywood stars, wild publicity, fireworks, and free booze for a million people accompanied the playful announcement. A thousand US dollars exchanged for two thousand Vegas dollars. Giant roulette wheels gave hourly packages of a hundred-thousand Vegas dollars. Lotteries up and down the strip gave away brand-new cars. Blogs and social media with a half-billion hits in twenty-four hours guaranteed only the most unconnected didn't know about the biggest party in human memory. Happy people cancelled their plans and drove, flew, or bused their way to celebrate a festivity previously unknown to humankind. The airlinAes put on more flights to handle travelers. Amtrak added train cars and engines. The major car rental companies offered vouchers for free cars redeemable on the Vegas strip. Even the mayor of the tongue-in-cheek Conch Republic of Key West, Florida extended "diplomatic relations" to the new country of Las Vegas.

The party rolled on for weeks. No records were kept, and no funds were withheld against a future bill. Thousands of partygoers became winners, and the government collected no taxes. In fact, the government disappeared. When the IRS on North City Parkway informed the Department of the Treasury that revenue payments had stopped, the United States Attorney General ordered an immediate audit. Agents from all over the country boarded government aircraft because no airline seats were available. The first to arrive were denied landing rights at Harry Reid and even North Las Vegas airports. The flights were redirected to Nellis Air Force Base where the military had quarantined themselves. When Federal agents attempted to leave, their vehicles were stopped by uniform policemen and told to return to base or be arrested.

When the Nevada governor was informed, all seven Army National Guard units were ordered to early annual training at the remote Tonopah preparation facility. For weeks, the guardsmen and women were confined to base until supplies and leadership ran low. Soon enough, and in spite of frenetic orders, the four thousand who gathered returned home and abandoned the facility.

Not far away, the Predator unmanned surveillance unit at Creech Air Force base north of Las Vegas received orders to return international patrol and fly missions over Arizona, Oregon, and Utah. California and Nevada remained drone free.

The government standstill soon ceased and replaced as lights in the remaining eastern thirty-nine states blinked off. What began as an annoying power loss along the Gulf of Mexico Coast, brown then blackout made their way north until finally blinking the major east coast blind. Chaos and violence followed the loss of electricity as major cities lost services, supplies, and organization.

Missile Command in Colorado went on high alert, and America held her breath.

Chapter 40

Scott

In the two months since his meeting on the dark Tucson track, McHale's beard thickened even more gray. His skin grew dark and lined from the sun. Contact lenses hid his trademark blue eyes, and he limped in thrift store hand-me-downs. Like many other thousands, McHale remained the invisible man living the streets in America's underbelly. Yes, even this disguise did not prevent Angie from picking him out in the crowd.

She addressed several hundred well-wishers at the El Paso Airport. Television crews from local stations videotaped her remarks as she accepted accolades from the Fort Bliss base commander and the mayor's office. West Texas experienced far fewer interruptions than the rest of the state, but many feared the anarchy of the east and the madness of Las Vegas drew too close.

McHale stood on the far side of the passenger lobby and saw the hesitation as their eyes met. As he had several times before, he waited behind the crowd to see if she'd give him a signal. None came. None had ever come.

Two men surprised him near the exit door.

The bigger of the two held out a hand to stop him. "Let me see some ID, friend."

McHale eyed both men.

He tried to side step them. "Why? I'm not doing anything."

The other man blocked his way. A hooked thumb over his leather belt kept his hand close to a holstered pistol. "Can you just do it, please? This is routine. We're security for Congresswoman Molina-McHale."

McHale shrugged. "Hey, come on. I only stopped for a second. Just flew in from Dallas. I don't want any trouble."

"Can I see your ticket? That'll be okay, right." The man sounded reasonable.

"I don't keep tickets. I wanted to hear her speech, so I hung around. Is that a crime? My bag is in a locker."

He held up a key to an orange airport locker. "And besides, I'm not breaking any laws. You're harassing me."

The security man's patience slipped. "I'm not harassing you, friend. I'm simply asking you to do something very reasonable. You're a conscientious citizen, right? So am I. You're in a secure airport facility. I can call the airport police because you look very suspicious to me and that's my right as a citizen."

McHale responded with the same reasonable tone. "Call them. Otherwise, stand aside and let me pass. I don't have to wait here while you make an ass out of yourself."

When McHale stepped to one side, the younger man lost patience and grabbed his arm. McHale wheeled and barely stopped from striking out. Instinct of street life.

He shook the man's hand free. "Do that again and I'll be the one calling the cops. Now get away from me. What's wrong with you people? What's happened to freedom in America? You folks see these thugs?"

His voice rose, and travelers stopped to watch. A grumble from the group, and the security men reluctantly stepped back.

McHale hurried to the locker area, listening for footsteps, and using shop glass to watch behind. He rounded the corner and waited. After a moment, he saw both men enter Starbucks. He angled to a corner and saw Angie speaking to a handful of people.

Must be donors. He walked quickly on.

Twenty minutes later the group left the shop, and a uniformed guard rolled a "closed for cleaning" sign in front of the glass door. Angie sat alone. He two security men were not in sight.

McHale approached the cafe. An older man glanced at him and pulled the door open.

She looked up from her reading and watched him limp across the room, He slid into the booth.

Dark eyes, scarecrow scarred face, gray beard. "Hi, Angie."

She set her jaw. "Scott. Jesus. I wasn't completely sure. Where've you been?"

His breaths did not come easy. "Wandering. Trying to understand. I wanted to call you ... I just never could."

"And, why is that?" Her words, while not exactly harsh, carried little understanding or sympathy.

"A thousand reasons I can't remember now. I've been to a couple of your rallies."

"I thought I saw you."

"I'm really sorry, Angie."

Her head popped back. "You're sorry?"

He swallowed and grimaced, almost a reflex after so much time. "Yes. At first, all I wanted to do was get to you. Then, the more I stayed away–"

"The harder it became?" She finished his statement.

He looked up and held her gaze. "Yes. I ran because they tried to kill me. What would stop them from killing you, or Joy?"

An edge of sarcasm answered him. "You were protecting us, then."

He sucked in a breath and leaned back. The waiter set coffee on the table. He watched the man go. His fingers shook as the cup shed heat "In a manner of speaking, I suppose. They were after me. I had to keep moving. Then, California declared me dead. The political machine churned along fine without me. I went from missing to running. Someone held a grand jury–

"California."

"Yes. After a few months, I couldn't go back. Not when I found out what they were doing."

"What was who doing?"

She held up a hand. "No, wait. You were hiding out. It's that simple."

"Not really."

"Yes. I would've never thought that of you, Scott. You ran away."

He let the cup loop on the saucer. "Not at first. They sabotaged the Cessna. I was hurt but I got better. I tried to contact you. Then? It became a habit. That was before the world started coming apart."

"Ken and I couldn't be sure why you were running. Why did you disappear into the mountains and then hide out? For God's sakes, you were a United States senator."

"I didn't hide out as much as I hid from my attackers. God, Angie. I loved you so much."

"Stop that and talk to me. What happened to your voice? You said sabotaged. Were you injured?"

"Yes. Burned mostly. But I'll probably always sound like a three-pack-a-day smoker."

She leaned forward. "The DNA was yours, Scott. Juliette's baby was your baby. You lied."

He shook his head. "I didn't. We never had sex, no matter how you want to define it. On that morning in our DC place, I told you the absolute truth. I may have screwed up but that's all."

She sipped and replaced her cup. "You know, maybe once I would have accepted that, but not now. Too much time has gone by and too much has happened."

"Yeah, I know. You're on a goddamn rocket ship. I know what it takes to get as far as you've gotten in so short—"

"Don't you of all people accuse me of anything other than working my ass off, Scott McHale."

He words sharp and passionate shock both of them.

They stared at one another until his tired face broke with a smile. "I miss that fire."

"Such charming bullshit. Explain to me how your DNA got into Juliette's baby if it wasn't you. I want to hear this fairytale."

"I don't know. Somebody could have swapped my records or stolen my DNA. When I was in the hospital, lots of blood was drawn, lots of sheets were changed, and lots of plastic spoons and forks were thrown away. I can't say how it was done, Angie. Only that it was."

"A few years ago, I wanted to believe you."

"But not now? What changed? Certainly not the truth."

She looked beyond the café's grayed plate glass. "I've moved on, Scott. It doesn't matter whether you slept with her or not. I don't like being lied to, but I also don't believe you killed her. The world doesn't care about you anymore. I don't know what your game is now, but you need to go back to where you came from. There's a lot going on that you just don't understand."

"Help me understand it. I'm on the road everyday talking with people. I'm asked all the time about if you're on the level or working against America. I will never let them get away with that crap, I promise. But everyone knows there's a reckoning coming. Is it Jimmy Dearborn? Does he have his claws into you? What's going to happen?"

She said nothing, instead only watching him.

"I'm afraid for you, Angie. Please let me help you."

She leaned back and slowly shook her head "You almost had me, you bastard. I wanted you to come forward for a long time and fight. I would've stood beside you no matter what. But Dearborn was right. You're a coward with big game-talk and no guts."

McHale swallowed hard. "Okay, you've moved on, but you don't know everything. Nothing I've told you is a lie, but it really doesn't matter anymore, does it? Just like you said, I don't matter. You need to protect yourself. And you need my help. Dearborn and Wesley Teague will lie to you, then throw you away, just like me. If you won't trust me, find friends, real friends, and trust them."

She shook her head. "You're pathetic. Maybe even deranged."

"I can't disagree I'm pathetic, but I've never been surer of myself than now. You've got to believe me. There's something coming. You may even know what it is."

"You need professional help, Scott."

"Okay, but before they lock me up, let me help you."

"No. You stay the hell away from me."

"I'm only trying to protect you."

"You sanctimonious bastard. You got caught, and a wonderful girl ... girls are dead. You either leave me alone or I'll help them lock you up."

She pushed back to stand.

"Okay, okay. I'll stay away but please listen for just one more minute. In my backpack is a burner phone. It's all going to come to a head soon and I'll warn you if I can. You can take the phone anywhere. Have it activated at a store not the internet.

Her voice barely contained the depths of her fury. "Absolutely not. This is the first and last time we talk. You try to contact me again, and they'll be taking you away in handcuffs."

She stood up. "What do you know? What's coming?"

He marveled at her lovely features, fine skin and dark hair. This beautiful woman had once loved him.

His "A friend from Salt Lake, others, they're in contact with small groups all over the country trying to find an answer. They disagree on the reasons, but they're sure of one thing. They will fight to keep the country together and arrest whoever's doing this. They're pretty sure you're right in the middle of this, Angie."

"I'm helping Twila Crawford. No one knows what the Vegas publicity stunt means, and she's concerned, that's all."

Unsteadily, he rose to his feet. "You know its bigger than that. I can see it in your face. Please, get away from this."

"Go somewhere, Scott. Get some help."

She signaled to her security.

He turned to the man approaching. "Give us one more minute."

The man looked at Angie. She nodded. "One minute."

"You don't need to love me, Angie. I'm not going to stop loving you, but you need my intelligence. I know what's going on in the America you can't see. Take the phone. Use what I tell you. I hope it'll be to save our country, but I'll leave that choice up to you."

She watched him for a long moment then walked out.

Chapter 41

Abel

Slope shouldered and hulking, Abel sat behind the wheel of the old pickup truck while younger brother Adlai snored out the open window. A plastic bag filled with dirty wind drifted across the Wal-Mart parking lot and caught in the far fence.

A hundred miles of open, arid Texas lay beyond. He wondered where the bag would have stopped had Wal-Mart not been in the way.

But only for a moment as the thought quickly slipped away.

An early morning turkey vulture caught his attention as it pulled flesh from a flattened jackrabbit. Each time a car or truck drove into the morning twilight, the scavenger rose with lazy wings and circled. The size and heft of a large steamer trunk, the bird would block the sky only to land again and eat. Over and over as the sun rose and chased the night chill away, the buzzard ate its prize one cautious bite at a time. Occasionally, a crow tried to grab a meal, but the forager's sheer size discouraged these interlopers.

Abel thought his prize was here, too. Forgotten by the world, but here, waiting to be eaten like the flat rabbit. For an instant, the thought connected across the chaotic synapses of his brain. Like every other time, he soon became lost in his own confusion.

Was he the buzzard or the jackrabbit? He would have to ask Adlai when his brother woke.

Ada knew the Mex's secret though. She told her brothers the migrant woman received phone calls from the man they chased. He was sweet on her. Ada also told them the Mex was wanted for murdering another woman and had a fifty-thousand-dollar reward.

But she wouldn't let them grab him. Instead, she said to watch him. The reward would grow and then they could cash in. For so many months now, they trailed around, sometimes spotting the man in a work gang, sometimes not seeing him for long stretches at a time. Yet, Ada never seemed to run out of Western Union money to keep them moving. The brothers didn't know about the big Yankee man with a badge who fed her information and financed their miles.

The months turned into a year, and then more.

Until yesterday. The big Yankee man finally called sister Ada.

"Listen to what I'm telling you. Don't stay in El Paso. Go to Childress, Texas. Wait at the Wal-Mart for a Silverado. Then, grab him. Alive. It'll be easy."

Adlai and Abel listened together saying nothing.

"You can hurt him a little. That'd be okay. But then, he's got to come home to the mountains. All the way. So don't hurt too bad otherwise he'll be moaning the whole trip. Drive through the night. I'll see you in a couple days."

Abel thought about the phone call. Hurt him a little was good. Fifty thousand dollars? He tried to imagine what all that money would look like.

The vulture flew as more cars drove into the parking lot.

Abel laughed. "I'm gonna get you, little jackrabbit."

"Huh, what?" Adlai came awake with a start.

Abel screwed up his forehead. "I didn't say nothin'."

Adlai shifted irritably. "Yeah, you did. You saw a rabbit?"

Abel licked his lips and pointed to the flattened, putrefying animal. "He's right there. Ain't moved."

He laughed.

His brother scowled. "Yeah, yeah. So, you see the Silverado, yet?"

Abel shook his head and let a moment pass. "I don't know what that is, Adlai."

"A Chevy pickup truck, you ninny. Gawd, you're so stupid sometimes. Shut up and let me sleep."

"Yeah, okay." He waited, then said, "Adlai?"

The brother opened his eyes. "Geezus, what? I gotta sleep 'cause we're gonna have to drive all night to get home."

"You mean it's a silver Chevy, right?"

"No. Silverado is a Chevy. Ada would of told us if she knowed the color."

Abel's hand worked on his forehead. "I mean a Silver ... ado can be another color?"

He followed his brother's eyes to the vehicles filling the lot. "Silver ... Oh, shit, Abel. Did you see the pickup truck already? Shit, shit. A Silverado ain't always silver."

The *shits* usually came with his brother's fists. "Is that one of them there?"

A tan-and-dark brown pickup sat beside a behemoth eighteen-wheel rig chuffing dark exhaust. The truck's passenger door stood wide as a gaunt man waved from the pavement. A moment later, he sat in the brown pickup.

"Go, Abel. That's him. That there is our jackrabbit."

Their old pickup's engine started with the first twist of the key, and the two brothers trailed behind the Silverado.

Chapter 42

Scott

A sliver of the moon lay low in the west as the night turned cold. All the cars and other pickups left earlier. Only the brown and tan Silverado sat in the driveway.

Abel rubbed his hands together for warmth. "We should of just run up and snatched him, Adlai."

His brother scowled. "I told you a hundred times. There's too many of them. Ada told us to grab him, not fight a whole, big bunch of folks. Now just go back to sleep."

"I'm too cold to sleep." But soon, his chin dropped.

An hour later, a single light showed through the front room's curtains.

Adlai hit his older brother's arm. "Someone's looking outside. Get ready."

A man stepped out on the porch and hefted a backpack. A few quick words with someone inside and the door closed to the cold night.

Adlai whispered excitedly. "That'd be him,"

The shadowed man glanced up and down the quiet neighborhood then walked quickly into the street.

Adlai shook his head when Abel reached for the key. "No. We gotta let him get away from the house. It'd be too obvious."

"I can hit him with the truck like you done."

The younger brother lost patience. "You're not going to hit him, for Christ's sake. Ada said not to kill him. Besides, too many houses. Just pull up beside him, real slow. But when I tell you."

They waited. Minutes passed. The figure reached the end of the block.

Adlai finally nodded. "Okay. Now real slow, Abel. You understand, slow?"

"Uh-huh."

The man with a limp moved closer to the grass as the sound of the engine approached.

Adlai leaned out the passenger door window. "Hey, there. You need a ride?"

Predators preying on the homeless were common.

A gravel voice answered. "Thanks, but it isn't far. I can walk." McHale edged onto the grass strip and judged the distance to the houses for a full out run. The limp had become permanent and painful.

Adlai spoke with folksy good humor. "Oh, it ain't no bother. We was just heading up to the Wal-Mart 'cause we is going fishing."

"Fishing?"

The man grinned with yellow teeth. "Yeah, Fishing for you."

Twin dark barrels eased out the window.

"Now drop that pack and get your hands up. Don't move or I'll fill you full of birdshot."

McHale looked at the old shotgun and the cracked lips of the grinning man. He eased his pack to the ground when the lumbering driver ran around the front. Duct tape quickly bound both wrists.

As the big man tore off the tape, his voice tittered in a high-pitched keen. "Got you little jackrabbit 'cause I'm the buzzard."

McHale glanced between the two men. "I don't know who you think I am, but you got the wrong guy."

The slack-jaw grin on the big man hesitated. "What?"

"I'm Barney Thompson. Why would you guys be looking for me? I'm just going to pick up my big rig at the warehouse."

Abel turned to his brother. "Oh, shit, Adlai. I thought you said this was him."

"It is him, you dumb shit. We been lookin' at him forever. He's lying, look at his neck."

Abel pulled at McHale's coat and shirt collar. Roiled skin above the collar line disappeared into the dark gray beard.

"Oh, yeah. This is him. See that?"

Adlai wearily shook his head. "Of course, it's him, you dimwit. What's wrong with you?"

Abel dropped the man's bound hands accusingly. "You lied."

McHale shrugged. "No, I didn't. That burn happened when I was kid. You're making a huge mistake."

Adlai stepped out and poked out with the shotgun's barrel. "Just shut up and get in the truck. You can live or die. Makes me no never-mind."

Abel was about to remind Adlai what Ada had said. A quick wink stopped him.

Abel laughed and ran around to the driver's side. "Jack rabbit, jack rabbit."

McHale squeezed next to the floor shifter. "You guys have got this whole thing wrong. I'm telling you."

Abel turned the key.

McHale repeated his plea.

"Make him be quiet, Adlai. He's confusing me."

The smaller brother squared himself McHale. "You either shut up, or I use a piece of this tape on your yap. We got a long drive, and you might get hungry. Which is it gonna be?"

McHale nodded and said nothing more. The moment had finally come but not the way he'd imagined. These two weren't cops, but bounty hunters. In a way, he thought someone looking for a reward was a better trade than being caught by Juliette's killers. He would probably survive the night and be dropped at the town's police or sheriff's office.

Others would carry on. Josh and Theo Haines. The tall state police officer in Oregon. Marilyn. A hundred Marilyn's. They must carry on.

McHale leaned back and watched his backpack disappear in the side-view mirror. All his worldly possessions left behind. The battered laptop, the gift of a toothbrush from a soup kitchen in Jackson, Mississippi. The streets were quiet. Only a few lights showed behind closed curtains and drapes. Other early risers. His heart swelled with the love of an America passed.

Abel stopped at the red sign on Seventh Street.

Adlai glanced down the block at the blinking red light. "Go right there. Left on 287. We'll turn at 83 and catch the freeway home. Gimme the phone. I'll let Ada know we is coming."

Adlai took the mobile and punched in the number. "We got him. Smooth as a baby's ass. Just drove right up and snatched him off the sidewalk. Nobody see'd nothing."

He listened a minute, grinning at Abel who grinned back. "It's ..." He looked at the dashboard clock. "Four o'clock. Not a soul around."

He listened then laughed. "Hell. No trouble at all. So, when do you get the fifty thousand dollars?"

Abel bounced in his seat like an excited child and signaled right at the sign for Highway 83.

McHale puffed air at the truck's roof. "Fifty thousand? You guys are getting scammed. The reward was *two hundred and fifty* thousand dollars over a month ago."

Abel turned to look. "Huh?"

Adlai shut the phone. "What'd I tell you about talking?"

Abel's voice whined in the early dark. "Brother? He done said the reward was two hundred and fifty. That's a lot more money."

Adlai shook his head. "Ada just told me, 'Bring him home, and I'll collect fifty for the three of us.' Ain't no two hundred and fifty."

Minutes passed. Both brothers stared out the windshield. The truck slowed. The freeway approached in the distance.

McHale laughed good naturedly. "Oh, it's two hundred and fifty, all right. Why would I lie to you? It isn't my money."

Abel whispered. "Oh shit, oh dear. I think Ada done told us a fib."

Adlai reached angrily across the cab. "Gimme that phone."

As Abel handed the phone over, McHale gripped the steering wheel and pulled hard right. At the same time, he mashed his left foot on the accelerator pedal. The old truck lurched and with a roar hit the curb. Abel's big hands yanked the wheel hard left, and McHale helped him overcorrect. The truck groaned, crossed the residential street with a roar, and clipped a fire hydrant. The old suspension wasn't up to the rough handling and rolled once, then twice, ending with a long rending scrape on its top.

McHale braced sideways as the first roll came, wedging two taped hands against the gearshift lever and a foot on the gas. Neither abductor bothered with seatbelts as both ended upside down on the roof with the engine screaming.

A dog barked in the distance. A second animal picked up the cadence with a howl. McHale head swam as he wriggled past a moaning and bloodied Adlai. The window was still open. They did not try to stop him.

A porch light came on, then another. A man left his home and ran to the wreck. A phone light came on as he videoed the scene. Another voice called out. McHale stumbled away unseen between houses and disappeared into the growing morning din.

Chapter 43

Ken

With the time change and late arrival in Los Angeles, Ken Litton let the FISA warrant sit on his desk. By midnight he'd have to answer for his inaction, so he still had time.

Time, he thought and looked at the antique Seth Thomas on his wall. The one-hundred-year-old clock, a present from Scott and Angie, had for the last twenty years replaced every generic government-issue timekeeping instrument in each of his many offices. He loved the clock and its meaning to his soul. Earlier in the morning, he'd watched a news clip on television of Angie arriving in Cheyenne, Wyoming. She stepped from a USAF blue and white G-5 jet after a stopover in Denver. Her travels reminded him of shuttle diplomacy, charging from one state's capital to another, working a deal, stroking anxious governors.

He wondered if that was what we'd come to.

A powerful tool against terrorists trying to take advantage of the chaos, this FISA warrant had a familiar signature. He knew the Associate FBI Director's home phone. They were friends and former new-agent classmates from Quantico. Still, he hesitated, needing to think this through. A Foreign Intelligence Surveillance Court warrant for Angie Molina-McHale sounded like political use of the Bureau. A huge red flag and clearly illegal. A tap on Angie's phone would reveal dozens of calls to and from him, many from the phone in his own office. He couldn't tell her to stop calling him or reveal the warrant without reprisals from his own internal Bureau watchdogs.

Litton hoped there might be another way. He dialed his supervisor's home phone in Annandale.

"Pappano."

"Litton."

A guarded reply. "Hey, Ken. You in town?"

"Don't bullshit me, Mark. You know I'm not. You waited to transmit this FISA shtick thinking I wouldn't get it till the morning."

Relieved laughter on the other end. "Hey, you're a field guy. I should've known you don't have a family life."

"Gee, thanks. How's Janice and those wonderful girls from her first marriage?"

Pappano laughed again. "Still an asshole, huh? You'd think I could get some respect considering I'm your boss now."

Litton dropped the jokes. "I have to ask you, Mark. Is this FISA thing for real? I'm not going to talk any details over the unsecure line, but I really don't understand."

The Associate Director's voice lost joviality, too. "It's real, buddy. And scary. I know you don't have the affidavits but check with your legal guy in the morning. He'll have everything."

"Yeah, I'll do that." Litton sounded gruffer than he'd intended.

"Hey, come on, don't bite my head off. I'm just the guy who signed the damn thing. I know you're close to Angie. I met Scott McHale and liked him. You know I can't stand politicians, but that guy seemed ... genuine. Like we could be friends."

"He is, was a friend."

"I got it. I really do. But this is different. This is for his wife, a US congresswoman. And that is no bullshit. Can you imagine the hoops the agents had to jump through and what the affidavit looked like? And this judge is no pushover. You might know him. Nieto out of the Ninth District."

"Right. And when did the pen register go up?"

The silence stretched at the other end as Pappano sighed. "Two weeks ago, and before you say it, every time you called, the agent made damn certain the voice monitor stayed off. Look. I knew you were going to be pissed."

"You got that right. Not even a heads-up to let me know you're listening?"

"We weren't listening, goddamn it. It was a pen register. It's your private number. What can I say?"

Litton knew he'd get no further. "Okay. But why FISA? There's nothing foreign about Angie. She's the target, so where's the terrorist connection?"

Pappano let a few seconds go by. "You're asking me a lot."

Litton pushed, relentless. "I know you outrank me now, but we go back to the Academy. I'm an Assistant Director, too, and we're talking about the wife of a guy who took a bullet on the job so people can sleep at night."

"He's a fugitive, if he's still alive. We owed *him* back then, not his wife."

Litton gripped the phone hard enough to crack the plastic.

Pappano spoke again. "I'll get my ass in a sling for this, but here goes. Angie McHale snuck away from her private security detail in El Paso to make a meeting. We've got CI info—"

"She's in my division, damn it. How can you open an informant without going through the LA office?"

"Because I'm the goddamn acting Associate Director of the FBI, Ken. That's how. Now can you shut up and let me finish?"

"Sorry, boss."

The man emptied his lungs. "Nah, I'm sorry. I didn't like this any more than you. I hate politics and if it were up to me, I'd move FBIHQ to Butte, Montana."

Litton chuckled. "Do it, and ninety percent of the HQ staff would build you a statue and anoint you the messiah."

Pappano roared with laughter. "If only we could and get back to American's real work without all the DC crap. So anyway, Angie ordered her security detail stop some guy at a rally in El Paso. He turned out to be a major asshole. Caused a scene so her guys had to backed off. Then, she sends the security detail on a break and meets the guy at a coffee shop. Figure that one out. Our CI doubles back and watches from a distance."

He stopped realizing his mistake. "Shit, Ken. Don't say anything alright? He's Angie's chief of security. You'd figure that out anyway but keep it to yourself."

Litton flexed his meaty right fist. "Okay. So, what's this unknown guy look like?"

"Possible middle eastern, well-spoken, no accent. About six feet and a hundred seventy pounds, dark complected, dark hair, dark eyes, full beard, brown and gray. Walks with pronounced limp. The informant said the guy was very familiar with Molina-McHale. At one point, he reached over and touched her hand. Then, the informant saw them in a heated discussion. He got one of the employees to talk. Said she overheard something about secret groups meeting. We got some photos but all from the side or the back. The El Paso office is following up with airport cameras."

"That's enough for a FISA judge? A terrorist connection without even reasonable suspicion?

"Jesus, Ken. Do you read the papers? This country is on fire. The administration's laying all this at the feet of Islamic terrorists and North Korean hackers."

Litton was incredulous. "You're thinking Angie's in the middle?"

"No, but we're looking for something, anything. The East Coast is holding nightly riots like block parties. The lights haven't been on in nearly ten days in some places, and people are shooting each other. Road rage is crazy. It's a good thing we're running out of gasoline. When they do manage to get lights back on, hackers fiddle with everything from pipeline pumping stations to the US Southern Command in Tampa. Hell, we'll save more secrets by keeping the juice off. This morning the Pentagon inadvertently released, read this as *hackers,* gaslighting, the personally identifiable information on all the military's high-ranking officers. Oh, boy did the shit hit the fan then. For Christ's sake, we even had a recruiting station attacked by a jihadist before noon. You do know who's responsible for statutory enforcement of cybersecurity in this country? And it ain't the NSA."

Pappano's words grew in volume, so Litton kept his own mild. "I know all this, I read the morning briefings—"

"But you're not understanding what I'm telling you. The cops are overwhelmed and the National Guard in thirty-five states are farmers and factory workers in uniform. What the hell are they going to do? Over the weekend, the Russians vaulted the border and seized Georgia and the rest of the Ukraine without so much as a how-do-you-do to NATO. That's not in the news yet, so keep it to yourself. The Iraqi government is fighting for its life from the Taliban and ISIS-K, and the royal family in Saudi Arabia is under attack. They're headed for Argentina if we can't help them, and the DOD says the whole shit-show might fold any time. Yemen is fricking gone as of eight this morning, and things are coming apart at the seams because the world doesn't have us as a benign hegemony anymore. China's licking its lips, and we're toast if we don't get a break."

Litton didn't know about Russia, or that suddenly the nation's oil supply in the Middle East was under attack again.

"Look, I'm sorry—"

Pappano wasn't finished. "NATO's demanding action, while America does a pole dance. You know the treaty: an attack on one is an attack on all. We ... frankly, Ken, we can't help. We're getting our butts kicked right here at home. Do you know how bad it looks that somebody took Las Vegas off the board? If someone actually knew how badly we've been hurt by hacking our electric grids, they might just drop a Nuke and finish us off. As it is, they're slicing off easy pieces and we can't stop'm. There's a lot of countries going to jump ship on us if we're not careful. We're way past close to the end and I don't know if we're already too far gone to find our way back. My take? History will note the turning point was the day Las Vegas threw a big goddamn party, and this administration ordered the federal government to stand down."

Litton could say little to this, insulated in LA and unaware of just how far the Federal government had sunk.

Pappano continued. "The House will probably file articles of impeachment in a couple of weeks. Keep that under your hat, too. Swanson will resign with a deal from the Veep, like Nixon did."

Litton heard a long exhalation.

"Good buddy? I don't like quoting Bogie, but your personal problem over getting your phone identified on a Pen register doesn't amount to a hill of beans. You and I have bigger stuff to deal with. Keep your nose the hell out of Angie McHale's FISA warrant and find a place for my family to sleep west of the Mississippi River. At least get ready to pick up the pieces when we collapse back here. You might be on your own out there in LA for a long time. You may have to take over the FBI."

"Jesus, Mark."

But the line was already dead. Litton replaced the receiver and rocked back in his chair. Without realizing it, he tapped his right hip for the gun always there.

Chapter 44

Twila

Twila sat cross-legged on the round sofa left behind from Pence administration. She dressed in blue jeans and an old sweater against the October chill and the Naval Observatory's notorious furnace. No US vice president had actually used the grand building as a residence, until Walter Mondale in 1977. He couldn't afford the exorbitant housing prices in DC and chose instead the government subsidy. Since then and until this day, the VPs lived, entertained, and held news conferences in the building that dated from 1893. The coffee table in front of her held files and a small stack of documents for signature, an iPad, her laptop, and of course, her coffee cup. Tom, husband of nearly twenty years, wore a cardigan and necktie, and propped his stocking feet on the table's edge.

She dropped her pen and leaned back. "Have I ever mentioned you look like a British college professor?"

He grinned at their old joke. "I am a Brit, and I am a college professor. Ergo ..."

"You only married me because you couldn't pass the citizenship test."

He folded his tablet. "Ah, so true. I don't really want to go back, Twila. This semester is killing me. And having Secret Service agents, not one, but two outside my door day and night, sitting in my classroom, following me to the loo for God's sake."

He shook a mane of collar-length hair, long out of fashion except on college campuses. "It's positively boring."

She held up her index finger. "And necessary, Tom, don't forget."

"And, I won't. Planning on bed soon? There are so many pretty girls on campus these days ..."

"What coed would want a neutered Brit?"

He laughed and slipped the tablet into his briefcase. "Don't be too long, love. I'm going to shower and make a few calls. Three hours' time change on the West Coast has its advantages."

She touched his hand as he walked out, but soon turned to the next page, scribbled, and flipped the document over. She liked paper and used her tablet only sparingly. A light knock at the French doors brought her head up.

"Madam Vice President. There's a courier at the door with a parcel from the governor in Sacramento."

Procedure prohibited any parcels from entering the residence before screening, testing, and opening. Twila insisted upon this one exception.

"It's okay, Agent. Please take it. Scan only, then bring it to me."

She kept Secret Service protection at the Observatory, giving her personal guards a chance to relax. Besides, this new one was bright and handsome.

"Done, ma'am."

Ma'am, she thought dryly. Oh, brother.

In five minutes, the envelope was x-rayed, tested for key chemicals, and scanned under powerful UV lights.

He handed the package to her. "Tests were negative, ma'am." His eyes lingered a moment too long.

"Thank you, Agent. Would you mind closing the doors on your way out?" She offered back the same smile.

"Yes, ma'am."

She didn't miss his glance. Younger men, like her private detail, excited her, and she probably could have shoehorned in a little time. Just now, however, events have reached a critical juncture and distractions could prove fatal. The closing clicks of the door sounded before she broke the seal. Two sheets of scribbles stapled to a photocopied official document brought her eyes to the wall clock.

She picked up the intercom and dialed the bedroom suite. "Tom, darling—"

"Oh, don't say it. You got a better offer."

"What I have is a conference call in thirty minutes that shouldn't last more than an hour. I'm really sorry, but there's no way you're escaping back to Humboldt State without me wringing you out."

"Oh, my. How I love it when you talk dirty."

She smiled. "If you liked, I can wake you up in a couple of hours."

She hung up and dropped the smile. Dialing again, she talked for a moment and replaced the phone. Angie would be here within the hour, and she needed to prepare.

• • • •

The knock came a little past midnight. Another agent escorted her back in the VP's residence.

"Hi, Angie. Sorry it's so late."

"It's me that's sorry, Madam Vice President."

The Secret Service agent closed the door.

"Madam? You make me sound like I run New York hookers."

Angie laughed and slipped off her coat. "We circled for an hour, and they talked about landing in Pittsburgh, but the weather cleared enough. I'm a night owl anyway."

The fireplace's log crackled, and she warmed herself. "Makes me appreciate the San Joaquin Valley even more."

Twila inclined her head. "You might not have to suffer Washington weather much longer according to Dearborn."

Angie arched eyebrows. "Oh? I didn't get the chance to see him on this last trip."

Twila worked her jaw. "You and I probably won't see him again for a long, very long time."

Angie said nothing but stopped rubbing her hands together.

"You're ahead in the polls, I read."

Angie sat. "Yes. I'm pretty confident at this point. Two weeks to go, and up by twelve."

"How's Rossi taking it?" Twila referred to the state's lieutenant governor and at one time, the favored candidate in the California special election.

Angie took out her cigarettes. "Do you mind?"

"Only if you don't offer me one. This is, after all, my smoking porch."

Angie smiled. "I wonder what Mike Pence would say if he saw us smoking on his couch."

Angie held the lighter for both of them and watched blue smoke curl above them. She spoke first. "It's a weird

House rule letting me run for state election and still holding a federal seat. Rossi's been trying to make a big deal out of it, but I don't think he's getting much traction."

Twila scoffed. "He's a titty-baby. Always has been. The only reason he ever got elected to a second seat was the voters not completely trusting Martinez. Finally, a Hispanic we can control in the governor's mansion, and then he dies of a heart attack. So, they got this lily-white old guy with zero ideas, except to chase his secretaries around the office. But with two years and a month left in Martinez's term, they had to have a special election. Voila, you're going to be the second Hispanic and the first woman governor. In six months, you'll be the first—"

"I'll resign next week, right before voting day."

Angie didn't want Twila to say it out loud yet. The idea of a separate country, a federated group of seceded states, scared and excited her. After Dearborn laid out the plan the first time, she excused herself and threw up in the toilet. But he'd been right. Right all along. Civil order crumbled in the aftermath of Las Vegas, and Swanson did nothing. Now Reno had announced its intent to follow in her big brother's image with the remainder of Nevada, voting in a referendum to be annexed to California. Fixed, of course. Dearborn had seen to it. Angie wondered about Martinez's heart attack.

Twila said nothing but watched her. "Scared, right?"

Angie looked around. "Yeah. I know this west coast thing was going to be yours before Scott died." The lie rolled so easily off her tongue. "All along you were going to be the president of ... why does Dearborn call it that, anyway?"

"The Federated States of America?"

"I've always hated that name. It sounds like the Confederate States of America to me. That a bad connotation, and no one is going to die in this civil war."

She looked at Twila. "Are they?"

"No good people have to die, Angie. Only the criminals and the outlaws. That's the beauty of this plan. Secession by mutual agreement for the good of everyone, with instant mutual protection and free-trade agreements, minimal border-crossing requirements, and for now at least, the same body of laws protecting all citizens. Barely a speedbump in history, especially with Madison Avenue paid millions dollars a week pumping out the *good news*."

Angie inhaled her cigarette and watched the fire in silence.

Twila knew she needed to shore up the other woman, especially when Angie realized her role in dividing the country.

"All our agreements stay in place, Angie. Look at the advantages you'll have. A readymade constitution with just a name change. You appoint your own Supreme Court. Your House and Senate are ready to go. Mutual economic and infrastructure aid, especially in the form of the Western Central Grid—all the power two nations can eat. Canada can go screw itself. The USA won't even remove its military from the west. When you can, the forces will switch to the FSA by mutual agreement. All the strategic weapons, like the ICBMs, will remain with me, but we'll have nonaggression and mutual aid in place by then. I'll even throw in a few international interventions just to make sure the world knows America is back."

Angie looked up. "East America, you mean."

Twila grinned. "Yep."

"And I'm West America."

Twila saw the hitch in the other woman's demeanor and thought she might need to work on her poker face.

"Angie? The bad guys of the world will think twice about getting a step on us. Twice the economic power. Think of having an entire elected congress ready to form a new nation in Carson City, the new capital of...?"

"The United Republics of America? Did I say I hated Dearborn's crappy 'Federated' name?"

"United Republics. Much better." Twila smiled and tucked a blond strand behind her ear. "Liberal Hollywood will love you. They'll find ways of bending over backward for another celebrity. I might not have been able to pull it off, you know. The stars and I have differences. You? They love you. They'll also love a flat fifteen-percent tax and a doubling of the minimum wage."

Angie downed her wine. "All this, without war or killing. As long as you keep pumping dollars over the border, of course. Are you going to tell Dearborn, or am I?"

Twila lifted her own glass. "He'll find out like everyone else after California annexes Nevada. I'll tell him Madison Avenue did a survey and gave us the new name. Dearborn won't mind. He'll be the king of both countries."

Angie looked up, surprised. "Really?"

Twila's eyes sparkled in the firelight. "Not a fucking chance in hell."

They raised their glasses in mock salute to one another.

A Faustian darkness crept into the room.

Chapter 45

Angie

Angie spent the following week walking the halls of the House. She concentrated on the members from the eleven western states and West Texas, just as she'd done in her face-to-face western tour with key state legislators. Only a couple dismissed Angie as possibly unbalanced, while most listened and considered their own futures.

The entire nation watched the economic disintegration of the world's greatest super power gain speed as power browned out to permanent black. Industries slowed, and financial empires crumbled. Corporations bailed out every day, moving headquarters to other countries and making plans to rebuild plants with cheap foreign labor and guaranteed electricity.

Only the western states lingered, somewhat immune and without strife.

Twila Crawford remained quiet during these times, as one might expect from the VP serving a president making grave errors in judgment. The news media had quit protecting President Swanson weeks ago and let his gaffs and missteps speak for themselves.

Congresswoman Molina-McHale resigned from the House on the Friday before the Tuesday election. The current Lieutenant Governor, Geraldo Rossi conceded defeat three hours after the polling stations closed. The election-night party lasted until midnight, although Angie left soon after her acceptance speech to make and take phone calls from around the western region. Governor Wilford Brewster of Nevada phoned his congratulations, and proposed what Angie knew was coming: the merger of two states.

Brewster ended the call by saying, "Thank you, Madam President."

The clock read five a.m. when she reached for the ringing phone. Wesley Teague had been up for hours.

"Is this line secure, Governor?"

"Of course." She eyed the pack of cigarettes on the table and instead fluffed her pillow and retrieved a notebook.

He cleared his throat. "The first cyberattack has taken down the national emergency response system. The federal government is unable to stop it, and they're quietly predicting the permanent collapse of two Eastern US grids by noon. This time the power failure will be complete. The Canadians will get taken down, too."

"Have you spoken to the vice president, yet?"

"Yes, ma'am. She was my first call. It's eight o' clock there, and they've been monitoring for a while now. The WCG also went down, so there's no backup except for individual power generation. The west is, of course, covered with its mini-nukes."

"What else?"

"Reno will confirm its disunion. I believe Governor Brewster from Nevada might have already contacted you. A letter will be delivered to the California governor's office just before your inauguration, asking Lieutenant Governor Rossi for asylum of all its citizens, and alliance with the state. Rossi won't sign it of course and will leave it up to you."

"And are the two cities going to rejoin the new superstate?"

"Dearborn still says no. He understands your reluctance. Reno will hold a referendum, but he hasn't told me yet if the results will bring it back or not. Vegas will not come back as per our agreement with the cartel and will remain the focal point as the east tries to stay afloat. In case things go wrong, and they won't, Las Vegas's recalcitrance will give us some time. Swanson's advisors are smart. They know how to keep their jobs and their heads, even if he's an idiot."

She listened to his silence. "Does Dearborn think the advisors will be trouble?"

Teague spoke after a moment. "Trouble, yes. There'll be some who will overreact. Some will say good riddance. Dearborn thinks you need distance from both groups."

"Fine."

"The Speaker will present the Articles of Impeachment in short order. Barring a visit from Jesus himself, Swanson's screwed. The House vote is a foregone conclusion. The Senate is close, but we're going to have a half dozen cross the aisle. Twila will promise Swanson amnesty in return for a quiet retirement. He'll resign by the week's end and head home to New York City where he should've stayed."

"Wes? I don't think I've ever heard you express so many opinions before."

"Sorry, Madam Governor. I'm excited."

Angie forced her reply. "Good, Wes. You should do that more often."

"Congratulations, by the way. I understand we changed the name."

If Wesley Teague knew about the name change, he might also know she and Twila intended to cut Dearborn out.

Angie answered with caution. "We have many things to discuss. Are you okay?"

"Yes, ma'am. I'm fine."

The burner phone in her purse buzzed. "Wes, I'm sorry but I've got another call holding. Will you circle back later this morning? I'd like to stay on top of Swanson's response to the blackout."

"Of course, ma'am."

She hung up and picked up the little flip burner, squinted, and freed her new reading glasses. The phone only accepted texts.

"Meet. Your book signing. Caution cameras."

She closed the phone wondering if the FISA warrant also included her secret phone. She snapped the phone in half and dropped the battery in the waste basket. As per instructions.

· · · ·

McHale never met in the same place twice. Her ghostwritten volume, *Freedom's Ring*, had been a Dearborn idea. He'd commissioned the book for Scott and okayed the changes to reflect her rise to prominence.

She spent a busy morning making thirty-second phone calls and thanking supporters. A staff lined up the calls and wrote the names, spouses, and kids on an electronic whiteboard. The operator broke in if the call went beyond forty-five seconds. At twelve-thirty a sandwich appeared in her hand, and they loaded into one of two black Chevy Tahoes heading for the Arden Fair Mall.

An hour into smiles and signatures, a woman dressed in slacks and a blue down jacket stepped up.

The woman handed over a copy of her book. "Will you sign it to Joy?"

Angie looked up. "Why that's my daughter's name, too."

The woman didn't smile back. "I know. Can you sign on the first page instead of the flyleaf?"

"Certainly."

She flipped the page and saw the note: "Second floor ladies' room 1:50."

She scribbled over the top and handed the book back. "I hope you enjoy it."

The woman nodded and walked away.

At a quarter to two, Angie set her pen to one side. The line showed no signs of shortening.

She signaled at the two state police officers. "I need to take a break."

Other business had taken Teague to Seattle.

Angie breathed easier and called over the crowd. "I'm so sorry. I'll be back in just a few minutes. If you can't wait, please leave your book and your address with Lonnie. I'll sign and mail it to you. I know you'll appreciate me more if I'm not wiggling in my chair."

Laughter and applause followed as she waved.

A janitor swabbed the floor tiles outside the ladies' room.

One of the agents jogged ahead and called to the bent old man, "While the governor is here, the area will be closed."

The man shrugged and put out two more signs while he wheeled his bucket into the closet. The officers intercepted three laughing young women, directing them to another facility.

As Angie approached, the man stepped back into the hallway. "It's okay, Governor."

Angie walked into the empty room. She washed her hands and glanced up at the same moment the janitor opened the stall door.

"Oh, Scott. You take so many chances."

He stretched out his back. "I needed to see you. There's a lot going on."

He stepped over and twisted the lock. Hollows in bearded cheeks accented the dark contact lens.

She touched his face then dropped her hand. "You're so thin."

They had met only once since El Paso and been frightened off once more when a grocery store clerk recognized her. After that, they texted using a different burner phone each time.

"Congratulations on the win, Angie. You'll be a great governor."

She pressed her lips together. "I don't fool myself. This was your consolation prize in case the presidency fell through."

He pushed the ball cap back on dyed hair. "I chose the wrong friends. You'll do better—"

She waved him away. "It's happening, Scott. You warned me, and now it's here."

He was silent for a moment, then pulled a new phone from his overalls. "Tell me quickly. Use the burner for the details."

Angie took a deep breath. "California will annex Nevada. I'll use Brewster as an advisor, until he runs for lieutenant governor."

"The other eleven states going to join you?"

"How'd you know?"

"It's not rocket science, Angie. They still have electricity, and hardly anything has changed. I know Rossi and Martinez received double the number of trade delegations from the Pacific Rim."

She stood silent, gripping and relaxing her fingers on the new phone as he spoke.

He turned to the sink and turned on the water. "You campaigned for corporate taxes being half of what they are now, and a reduction in personal income taxes. If people aren't banging on your door today, they will be tomorrow. Are you going to tell me California isn't the keystone for a new country of twelve former states?"

Angie nodded.

"That's what I thought. Are you the new ... leader?"

Eyes still on the floor. "Yes."

He shook his head. "I wonder how deep you're in. My guess is Twila's going to back your play, do something with all the military bases, and give you room to maneuver. She probably already has legislation waiting in the Speaker's top drawer."

Scott laughed without humor, "I wouldn't give you a nickel for Swanson's legacy. I'll bet the impeachment is already underway."

She looked up, watching him closely. "It's like you're a fly on the wall, Scott. Do you have someone inside feeding you information?"

"No, but I talk to people. Some are close to me, like Theo and a retired teacher from Utah. Others are trouble. We have a disjointed and fractious subculture and frankly, they scare the hell out of me. Most people just want the country back, warts and all. But God forbid, we've got dis-solutionists out there who want to grab a gun and secede. Neither side trusts me all that much, and before you say it, the vast majority of these groups are not survivalists or nut-jobs. They're just regular citizens, men and women like bankers, cops, and business types. Lots of people are putting loyalty to their oath and pledge of allegiance before ambition and money."

His words stung her until she recalled his own treachery.

But he'd heard his own hypocrisy, too. "Sorry, Angie. Dearborn knows all about our groups. He's just waiting to stop them and me."

Angie looked up, surprised. She had not known. "What do you mean? He's never talked to me about your groups."

"That's because he's keeping you focused. You're the prize. You make his dreams come true. This is a money-and-power grab. Pure and simple, and amazing it's gotten this far without America squashing him like a bug."

Her face hardened. "Did you ever consider you might be the one who needs to be stepped on?"

"Every damn day, and I don't disagree. The difference is I'm not shooting people in the streets. This is James Dearborn. I've no idea how he got his fingers around the throat of the power grid in this country, but he did. Juliette was murdered, and a little airplane sabotage got me out of the way. For a while, anyway. People probably died in Las Vegas and Reno, too, but we just don't know it yet. The group I'm dealing with has a list of over a thousand missing people. We have cyber chat lines with others trying to find loved ones. If you're interested, I'll send you a link. Maybe you should think about sharing it with Ken."

Her eyes held, then looked silently away.

"There's a lot at stake, Angie, and in the end, people won't think twice about killing a politician. Even a popular one."

"You speak from personal experience, of course."

She sounded harsh to herself and wondered if she had lost all that once had been important to her. They lingered on the cusp of perhaps the greatest coup of all time. She might soon be the leader of a new country. Maybe Scott was right, and she was already in too deep to stop.

He reached for her, but she stepped back. "Don't."

"Sorry, sorry. Didn't mean to be crass. You do realize I'm the poster child for screwing up, don't you? But I'm nothing in this struggle. Look at you. A beautiful lawyer overcoming a disgraced philandering...alleged...husband, elected in a landslide never seen in California. How could you miss?"

"If you're saying what I think you're saying, then screw you. I've got brains and the ability to run a state. Or, if it came to it, a county."

He hurried; aware the conversation had come to an end. "I know you do, and I'd be the first in line to vote for you. Jesus, Angie. You're probably the most important person in this country right now. The lives and fortunes of three hundred and fifty million people are at stake. Not everyone's going to agree splitting the United States is a good idea, but we've got to avoid hurting one another. Some wacko is going to fire a first shot, and we've got to stop it."

"So, say you."

Two former lovers, former husband and wife and former allies, stared at one another. Without another word, Angie snapped the lock and pulled the door open. McHale stood alone amidst the washbasins and toilet stalls and watched the tile floor.

Chapter 46

Scott McHale stretched and yawned, then eased forward from the back bunk. He had slipped into the tractor's cab late last night before the new driver took over.

He extended his hand to the woman who held the big rig's wheel. "Hi, I'm Sam."

"That'll be easy to remember. I'm Sam, too. Suzanne, really, but I like Sam." Her smile engaged him right away.

"Is this your normal run?"

"Yes, sir." She wore a heavy, red-plaid flannel shirt against the late fall chill and tied long brown hair in a ponytail. "Pocatello, then south and on to Logan. We should be at your exit in about two hours."

"That's great."

"You're going to catch a ride from there?" He didn't answer. "Oops. I forgot. Time to shut up, Sam."

McHale eased into the front with a laugh. "It's just better no one knows everything." "The way I move around, and the way we work things, won't make any sense to most people. If it wasn't for you truckers, I'd never be able to do this, so we need to protect you."

"Yeah, well I guess you did that in Helena yesterday."

He glanced at her but said nothing.

"Ah, don't worry about it. I talked with a couple guys that walked the lines in front of the armory."

She grinned and shifted for the grade. "Pretty ballsy there, Sam. I mean, going right in to talk to the Army."

He didn't think of his act as brave but desperate. Neighbors against neighbors, friends facing one another, even families split some wearing the uniform, others in blue jeans. Americans all, everyone armed, and no one understanding why such a thing had been ordered.

The woman glanced over. "You don't have to say anything. I'm just proud to be driving you to the next stop."

She handled the big rig easily. "Coffee in the thermos there. We're all thankful you're doing what you do. Not that I know anything, of course. But there is someone in this part of the country holding the lid on things and if that's you, then thanks. If not, and you get to see him sometime, pat'm on the back for me."

He unscrewed the thermos. "I'd do it. If I knew what're talking about."

She sipped from her own cup as they fell into silence. He thought about the bogus order appearing in the army commander's email. The man had been ordered to seal off I-94 between Wibaux and North Dakota, a move to force a response from Washington. A Lexington first shot heard around the world in a bloody confrontation.

McHale had learned through the grapevine and been driven to where townspeople effectively blocked the troop movement. He walked through the lines, spoke with the commander, and had Angie make a call, governor to governor. He'd slipped away as the crisis reduced itself to hurt feelings and nothing more.

"I've got some extra sandwiches in the cooler. Just behind my seat."

He moved a box aside and saw the AR-15 in its locked rack. "Let me unwrap one for you, too."

Moving around the country by hitching rides with truckers was the safest way he knew but coordinating pickup and drop times wasn't as convenient as having his own wheels. Better than begging rides in truck stops. Josh and Theo Haines used their contacts to move him to and from underground groups, both friend and foe. Many times, he'd met with those intending to take up arms against the United States and split the nation. Other groups decided to fight and keep the country whole. Each time, McHale spoke the same message of evolutionary change, not revolutionary. How many times had he repeated Thomas Jefferson's words: "I hold that a little rebellion now and then is a good thing, as necessary in the political world as storms in the physical." McHale pointed out *little* and *rebellion* were the keywords, not massive and violent revolts.

The big truck slowed for the exit. "Sam? ... Sam?"

McHale came awake. "Sorry. Guess I fell asleep again."

She looked over, her eyes twinkling. "You did, all right. Must of needed it too, 'cause you look a little peaked. You dreamed. I think I heard most of the speech before."

"Hope I didn't bore you."

Her smile warmed him. "Course not. I recognized you, and prayed the FBI got it wrong. You just don't seem like a killer to me."

He was humbled. "Thank you, Sam. I'm not a killer. In fact, I'm not even an adulterer. I am however, one lousy politician and a terrible husband, and I make ass-backward decisions with regularity. I'm hoping the country gets a second chance."

Sam pulled the big rig onto the gravel at the ramp's bottom. Several cars parked along an unpaved extension, all unoccupied.

Traffic passed over the ramp on I-15 as a lonely wind blew through scrub grasses.

He wondered aloud. "You sure this is the spot?"

"This is what I was told. You can come on with me if you want."

"No, but thanks. This will work fine."

She accepted his handshake and held for a moment. "The past is behind us, Senator. What's done is done. You, me, and everyone else need a future. I hope you can find us one."

He nodded and climbed out. With a wave, she shifted, gunned the big engine, and climbed the ramp to disappear south.

McHale walked the length of the half-dozen parked cars waiting for their pool drivers. He stood at the last vehicle and watched the underpass. The side road wound for a half mile, ending at a small substation. Electrical lines, north and south, pointed away and disappeared into the hills. He wondered if the state or the electric company had stationed a guard, and he was under observation. It wouldn't matter soon. In fact, he'd run out of places to talk, and another crisis only waited around the corner.

A vehicle exited from the southbound lanes and turned left, quickly followed by a second turn. Neither driver looked his way. One car from northbound I-15 exited and stopped on the far side of the underpass. McHale moved behind a column listening as tires crunched gravel.

Josh rolled down the window. "Need a lift?"

McHale breathed easier. "New car?"

"Yeah. Wore out the last one." He leaned to the passenger side and pushed the door open. "Best get in. We've got some problems."

Chapter 47

Teague

Wesley Teague watched the sun's rays trace heat mirages off the concrete. He stood in the parking lot on South Valley View in Las Vegas's industrial no-man's-land. The squat building's sign said "ACE Electronics" above, and "For Lease" below, even though a dozen cars filled the parking lot. The phone number went to an answering machine that never returned client calls. The fronds on the long palm tree above his head clacked in a blowtorch breeze.

He card-swiped the reader at the front door. A receptionist glanced up, smiled, and said, "Good morning, Mr. Teague."

"Maya. How are you?"

The empty smile on her face matched his. "I'm fine, sir. Thank you. Have a nice day."

The door buzzed and he walked in. A second door required a retina-and-thumbprint reader. In a narrow passageway, a stout man with an open shirt and gold neck chains watched the visitor behind thick Plexiglas. A revolving door at the end of the hall forced visitors to toe walk, thus preventing more than one person's entry at a time. Neither man exchanged a greeting as the scanner searched Teague's body.

The Colt .45 ACP pistol sat prominently on his hip.

The stout man said nothing. Teague had written the rules.

The room's design gave enough time to destroy the electronics and servers if it ever came to that. The man watched the monitor and held his finger on the dead-man switch. He sounded a buzzer, and the door unlocked into the cool interior.

A darkened bay opened to lead walls lining two end-on-end tennis courts. Power and optical connections dropped from overhead feeds and trailed to hundreds of servers. Small nuclear-powered generators operated silently next door, hiding the huge drain of electricity, and driving air conditioners to maintain sixty-five degrees no matter how much heat computers and people produced. A hacker could only dream about such security and opportunity.

Thirty of the world's best, however, dreamed no longer. Thirty more waited for their shift to begin. No one glanced up as Teague entered the room. Triple monitor banks held the attention of each operator. Keys clicked and murmurs accompanied chuckles and low-spoken expletives. An entire wall of young men and women bypassed changing commercial countermeasures, while another gamed the NSA's cybersecurity systems and peeked inside government computers. The portals often slammed shut the moment they opened, but every failure meant a learned response. Already, no single government agency except the strategic missile defense system remained unhacked in some way. The group worked ahead of schedule and now coasted until its next challenge. In fact, several were playing *HackFlash*, a game to keep boredom away while their new encryption-busting software invaded corporations and government offices.

A figure waved from a glassed-in room.

The visitor entered and closed the door.

"Hi there, Mr. Teague. I didn't know you were coming in this morning."

The young man rose and locked the door behind his boss. Thinning dark hair hung across a forehead matched by sparse whiskers on an unshaven face.

"Thanks, Peter. Where are we at?" Teague noted the man had forgotten to bathe...again. He took the leather armchair and accepted a cup of coffee.

The young man pulled at his keyboard and tapped as he talked. "The Texas grids split this morning. Dallas, Houston, San Antonio, Corpus Christi went dark. They still are. Like the instructions said, we left Del Rio, San Angelo, and El Paso with power. That took a little fiddling. Those are cross grids, and I think the engineers in Austin were waiting for us. It took about an hour of back-and-forth, but we got them, although we did have to fry one of their servers to make them leave us alone."

Teague sipped, then set the cup on the desk's edge. "So, we've got a dark line extending from Del Rio north to the Canadian border. Roughly speaking."

Peter nodded enthusiastically. "Yep. Williston, North Dakota is dark, Montana has electricity, and oh, dude, they're so pissed. You ought to see Facebook and Twitter. They're going crazy. Hashtag—"

Teague interrupted with a wave of his hand. "Good. And what about our problem child?"

Peter sucked a quick breath. "Jesus. How'd you know about that?"

He immediately regretted the words as soon as they left his mouth. "I mean, it's good you know. Saves me a phone call. Just, it was only a few hours ago. I mean, shit. Does everyone know?"

"Everyone meaning who exactly, Peter?" Teague didn't give anyone wiggle room. Even his underlings.

"I, huh, guess the guys running this show. I mean, you and the rest. There are others, right? I mean, there's got to be a lot of others ..." The young man ran out of words and spilled a rivulet of coffee trying to drink.

"Is there something else going on, because if there is, you might as well tell me. You know I'll find out."

Peter's lips worked his teeth as he gripped the arms of his chair. "Yeah, but I didn't know about it till last night, and then he didn't come in this morning. It's Beth Hurley's friend. I mean, like you fired Beth on Monday, right? Sent her back to Knoxville or Memphis, or wherever. But she wasn't the only one pounding down the tequilas and running off at the mouth. She and Donny Porter were like, together, you know?"

"Why didn't I know this before now?"

The young man wiped at his oily nose. "Oh, dude, I would've told you, except I didn't know. I don't know who's doing who out there. They're like a bunch of horney rabbits."

"You should know. That's your job to know, and why I'm paying you twice what they make. And this is the Donny who was going to take over for you when we moved on to Reno. But now, he didn't show up for work?"

"Right." Peter's breaths grew ragged.

"Recommending someone means you take on responsibility for them, good and bad. Check his apartment?"

"Yeah. You bet. First thing I did. Everything's still there."

"What are you going to do now?"

The young man swallowed. "I guess ... tell you."

Teague formed an unhappy line with his mouth. "You've told me. Is there anything else?"

Peter sat up. "Everything's good, really. But what about Donny being my guy in Reno?"

"There are others. What's so special about him?"

Peter swallowed. "He's an LA guy. Great hacker, and the first guy you hired, I mean, after me."

Teague recalled that Dearborn directed Donny's hire.

Peter needed to talk. "A lot of these guys out there are from that world. They know about him."

Teague shook his head. "I'm still not tracking here."

Peter stood and poured the last of the coffee forgetting to offer his boss the pot. "What I'm trying to say is I'm not stupid. Beth had a big mouth she couldn't keep shut. She needed to go, but dude, she was hot, and Donny did what anyone would do."

Teague watch him wordlessly.

"Look, sir, Donny has a lot of loyalty going for him. He just screwed up. Maybe we ought to take that into consideration."

Teague's patience ebbed. "I understand human nature, but what are you trying to tell me?"

The young man danced from foot to foot. "Well, he's my friend and we can trust him. He knows a lot of shit, and I don't think he told Beth anything important. He was only interested in getting into her pants. Besides, she wasn't really into what we do. Donny's good and there's nothing he can't hack. Do you remember the DNA report we swapped on the floater in Frisco Bay? Donny's the one who got into Bethesda's records and swapped them for that senator dude. Now we sort of owe him."

Peter couldn't shut up. "I mean, you remember, right? We were both working with Dearborn in Muroc. This isn't news to you."

Teague's voice soothed the young man. "Maybe it slipped my mind so let's pretend it is news. Tell me what you're talking about."

The young man's breaths left him. "I think I fucked up, dude. I don't want to say any more."

Teague smiled. "Oh, don't worry about it. I remember everything. There's just a lot on my mind and it was a long time ago."

Peter blew out his breath and let his shoulders drop. "Yeah, like a century. I hardly remember it all—"

"So why not refresh my memory?"

Peter blinked, touching the top of his desk, then leaped off the step that was his life. "Yeah, okay. We were working on the research for you and Dearborn. He had us looking around on government websites and shit. You know deep web stuff, right? Archives?"

"Help me out."

"It's like, beyond search engines. Those guys use amateur shit-keywords and concept optimization, you know. If you want to mine deep, you gotta get into RAM, like in a phone or an iPad. Even a digital answering machine. The stuff we want isn't there, but your RAM keeps a record where it was sent for storage, you know. When your phone's asleep or in your pocket, we go in and look around. When we find what we're looking for, we follow the path into someone's laptop or server. Most people don't wipe after a day, so stuff sits there. We go in and take it, do what we need to do, then put it back. No one knows shit and it looks original. Eventually, it makes its way to the end user. We can do the same thing with screwworms ..." He stopped. "You probably don't care about any of that though, right."

"I've got places to be, Peter, so why not stop trying to baffle me with bullshit and just tell me?"

Peter nodded and mouth breathed. "Yeah, right. We were hacking and leaving. Nobody knew we were there. Dearborn was having us grab records from Bethesda on politicians and generals, and shit. When the senator dude had a heart attack, Five-O wanted to get the guy's DNA. Donny and I talked about how to do it, but Donny came up with it, see? We went into the dude's military records. Then we sent it from the hospital to the crime lab using the cell phone for the chief-doctor what-you-call-it ..."

"Chief surgical resident?"

"Yeah, him. So, we sent it and ginned up the signed warrant from the Oakland cops. It's really simple, because as long as you get what you want, nobody backtracks to make sure everything's cool with the dude who started it. Donny and me figured the senator would never get to court, and even if he did, nobody's going to remember who signed what. Right?"

Teague nodded slowly. "What happened then, Peter?"

Sweat beads popped on the young man's forehead. "Well, the shit hit the fan. I mean Oakland got the warrant, and the feds were doing their own digging. We were giving them shit, and still all hell was coming down on the guy. There was stuff going on back and forth—"

"Why didn't I hear this from you, Peter?"

"This was all Donny before we hired him. When he was working directly for Mr. Dearborn. I found out and got pissed. Just when him and me are having it out, we hear the dude got killed. We were relieved as shit, man. I didn't want the information around, but Donny swore he already gave it to Dearborn and didn't have it anymore. I was cool with that."

He looked at Teague's still face.

"I thought you knew all about this."

"So, you're telling me Dearborn ordered Donny to change the fetus's DNA sample with Senator McHale's old military records?"

Skinny Peter juked his shoulders. "If that's his name, but I'm talking too much."

"Who was the baby's father?"

Peter shook his head before Teague finished asking the question. "Hey, dude. I don't know. That's the truth. I just told you, the data's gone."

"But you can find out. You and Donny, right? You can run it though the national database without getting caught."

Peter's eyes widened. "This is Dearborn's deal, dude. I can't hack him."

"Right?"

The box closed in on Peter who began a slow nod of his head.

"So, I'd suggest you get Donny's ass back on his computer pronto and get me the answer."

"Okay. I can do that. Donny's good then, right?"

Teague considered for a moment. "Yeah, he's okay. Get your Reno team to the airport."

"Now?"

"Now. But not you and Donny. I want you guys to work on the archive data. You know where to look, so it shouldn't take all that much time. Get me an answer then get to Reno."

• • • •

Teague slept on the receptionist's couch in the supervisor's office. Dearborn tapped a finger on the desk as he walked in.

"So, what's the latest with McHale?"

The number-two man swung his feet to the floor and stood, instantly awake. "He's still moving around the west, sir. He showed up at Fort Harrison before we could get a team in place."

Dearborn rolled his heavy shoulders. "Too bad. We needed a 'shot fired just to make all this official. That was supposed to be it."

"Yes, sir. We're listening for McHale but he's using one-time burners. The NSA's got him if he goes more than thirty seconds, and we've got the NSA. I've got one of the hackers dedicated specifically to McHale. We'll have him in a day or two now."

Dearborn dropped a briefcase on his desktop. "Well, don't sweat it, Wes. He's a survivor, and you told me to take him out when he was still a senator. I wanted a big splash, but what the hell. Turns out I didn't need it. Twila and Angie are doing better than I gave them credit for."

"Yes, sir."

"I want to use those two hillbillies to get rid of McHale for us, so this just might work out."

Teague barely blinked at his boss' forgotten promise. "We confirmed the big-rig truck companies he's using. Maybe once he hitched around the country, but no longer. The eighteen-wheelers are arranged ahead of time through their underground network. He slips into a truck stop and then he's gone, impossible to track, nothing is digital."

"Is he talking to Angie?"

Dearborn looked up, surprised. Teague usually did not ask questions or look for clarification.

The big man clicked the clasps on his brief but left the lid down. "We're sure he is, but again, probably on a burner. They met in El Paso and then at her book signing. We don't know what was said. McHale's lost weight changed his physical appearance and sparked a terrorist alert from the FBI. I think he just might be sick. The end-of-life kind of sick."

Dearborn nodded at his number two. "Something else bothering you, Wes?"

"We got rid of one of our hackers. She got drunk and mouthy at one of the casinos. El Gordo found out, and I said to plant her. We did. Case closed."

"Damage?" He rolled the cigar between two thick fingers.

"That's still to be seen. I've got a supervisor who should be doing a better job and a hacker who can't keep it in his pants."

"Why not replace them?"

"The supervisor is Peter Quint." Nothing showed on Dearborn's face. "I let him slide because he has history with us."

"I don't care if he's the Pope's kid. If he's a liability, he's gone. Simple."

"Yes, sir. This is on me. I'll watch him."

Dearborn nodded. "Okay, but don't fuck this up."

Chapter 48

Josh

Hard snow crystals rattled at the room's glass. He felt as though he'd just fallen asleep after the short ride from the freeway underpass.

Josh gently shook McHale's shoulder. "It's an hour's drive. We'd better grab a cup of coffee and get on the road."

McHale opened his eyes and looked at the man standing over him. He rasped out an answer. "Okay. Give me just a minute."

The cold room prickled his skin. He glanced at the bedside clock, tired and unrested though he'd slept for nearly nine hours.

When he swung his legs to the iced floor, Josh handed him a mug. "Your voice is sounding rougher than usual. When's the last time you had a checkup, Scott?"

"You mean a psychiatrist, right?"

"I'm talking about your health, smartass. You're looking a little thin there."

McHale pulled his shirt closer. "I'm okay, really. Just a little nauseous, and I'm not all that hungry. Besides, I've gotten used to only eating when I have to."

"I didn't realize how much weight you've lost. You do have money to eat, don't you?"

McHale stood unsteadily and stretched. "I do. Cameras are everywhere, so I'm just careful."

Josh faced him with hands on hips. "So how do you eat?"

McHale sipped the coffee and pulled a blanket over thin shoulders to hide his bony frame. "There's lots of missions. I pay a little and they're happy."

"Missions aren't everywhere. And I know you've been sleeping in the open."

McHale sighed and stood. He placed a hand on his friend's shoulder. "All right. I find plenty of food in the dumpsters."

Josh's mouth tightened into a grimace.

McHale stopped him. "Give me a break, I don't eat everything. Restaurants and grocery stores toss a lot. Once the date expires, they throw it out. So, I eat, and no one knows I'm there." He pulled on his loose jeans and fumbled with the buttons.

Josh opened his eyes wide, like the former high school teacher. ""Two things are going to happen. The first is, you're going to eat before we go. The second is after the meeting in Laketown, we're going to visit a friend of mine. She's a retired nurse."

McHale started to shake his head.

"Don't fight me on this. I can whip your ass with one hand tied behind my back. So just grin and bear it. Besides, you'll like her. She's a Catholic nun in Park City. Nice lady." He smiled. "If you don't get better, you won't live long enough to appreciate my organizational skills and because you're dead, they'll probably give you all the credit. I won't stand for that."

• • • •

Over the previous two years, Josh had reformed the network of resistors and questioners to protect the largest number of people from scrutiny. He isolated each command layer from below and above. In order to share information, he arranged for a small group of young people from his church to handle mass communications through social media, taking a page from the terrorist's handbook.

Josh chaired tonight's meeting in Laketown. Besides the leadership of the twelve states, a small group of dissolutionists from Northern California and Oregon attended. They cast an even darker pall when everyone else stood for the Pledge of Allegiance and they continued to sit.

The gesture wasn't lost on Scott. He rallied from his miasma, spoke, and answered questions. For the next several hours, people tried to understand how their country could turn from the hegemony of the world's greatest country, to the chaos of a third-world nation on the brink of civil war. The antiestablished offered little information and shared no opinions.

Snow covered their vehicles and whipped in the silent night as the cars drove slowly away from the resort hotel. Josh and McHale were the last to leave.

McHale pulled his coat even tighter. "I'm scared, Josh. Some of those people actually believe they can back out of the country, like Las Vegas."

Josh fished out the car keys and McHale held out a hand. "Let me drive."

"No way. I want to make it alive. Besides, you spoke for nearly six hours tonight. You're bushed."

"Nah, I'm okay. You're doing all the heavy lifting. I can drive."

They opened the doors to the blowing snow. "And you're sick. Besides, you've probably never driven these mountain roads."

McHale settled, grateful. "And you have?"

"Remember, I grew up around here. The only reason I left was to find work. Not too many high school teaching jobs in the boonies. Of course, I had to find a wife, too."

McHale's eyes drooped.

"Sorry, Scott. Grab some sleep. I'll ramble on later. I have a feeling we're going to have lots of time to talk."

· · · ·

The first rays of sun fought the valley's clouds over the Wasatch Range as they pulled under the retirement village's porte cochere.

Sister Teresa Marie, a slight woman with veined hands and a weathered, pleasant face greeting them.

"I hope you've always been this skinny, young man. Something tells me you're not well."

She wore blue jeans, an old black sweater, and a small gold crucifix. Her words speared McHale immediately. Several feet of fresh shoveled snow stood sentry on either side of the walkway.

"Just tired, Sister."

She stood back a moment. "Sallow cheeks, yellow eyes. Nauseous and vomiting?" McHale nodded. "Drug user?"

"No, ma'am. Defrocked career politician."

"That explains a lot. You should've stuck with the drugs."

McHale smiled, too weak to laugh. "I just need some rest."

"Excellent. Politician *and* a medical doctor. You don't need me. I'm just a nurse." The small nun stood squarely in his path.

McHale hung his head. "Sorry, ma'am. I wonder if you could take a look? Been trying not to think about it, but I haven't felt well lately. And my clothes are feeling pretty loose these days."

At once, she was concerned and kind. "Of course. Come on in. Joshua? Will you wait in the car?"

She didn't bother with his answer although he managed an unheard "yes" before the door closed.

McHale felt the warmth of the duplex home's interior and yet a chill rumbled from deep within. A crucifix and a yellow three-hundred-year-old image of Mother Mary from the old adobe mission days hung on the walls. He suspected these might be the relics of early evangelical priests in the days when natives owned the land.

After an hour, she emerged with two paper bags from the bedroom and trundled through the snow to Josh's vehicle.

He was quickly out of the car and standing in the snow. "Take these to the lab on Prospector Avenue. I think you know where that is. Tell them stat and be careful of infectious disease. That means you too. Don't open the bag. Stop by the pharmacy. I've already called them."

"Yes, ma'am."

She was already trudging back.

The snow started as she closed the front door.

McHale awoke at six in the evening. Over protests, he'd slept in her bed while she ran an IV into the top of his hand and used a Mac Pro in the small living room.

When he stirred, she called out, "Take a shower, Senator. Don't remove the IV. There's a johnny there for you."

He walked into the living area a half-hour later wearing the open-back sleeper and a terrycloth robe. His head swam in mental cotton.

"I have a feeling you don't miss a trick, Sister."

The deep wrinkles of her face didn't change. "I'm afraid I miss more and more every day. Eighty-five is not good age for those without faith in the Lord."

He nodded absently and sat on the opposite end of the couch from Josh.

The retired teacher closed his newspaper. "So, how are you feeling, Scott?"

McHale tried for bright. "Oh, much better actually. That was all I needed. Just a good day's sleep."

Sister Teresa blinked impatiently. "Have you two ever heard of hepatitis?"

He was no longer "*Senator*." "Are you saying I've got hepatitis?"

"Yes, and it's Type A for now. Communicable but not a death sentence. That does mean those around you get to share. At your stage, it can be cured with medicine and the right food, clean water, and rest. Blah blah blah. You know the drill. Your liver needs to heal. Otherwise, you're going have bigger problems than just looking like poo-poo."

McHale glanced at Josh, who returned to his newspaper with a shrug that said, *Don't look at me.*

"Sister, I can't. I need to keep moving. There's a lot at stake."

She answered matter-of-factly. "Including your life. My opinion is you're in the early stages. That won't last for long. Keep this up and you'll be down a progressive road, and there won't be a recovery without taking you totally out of circulation. You're fortunate to have a friend like Josh. Most people who live on the road don't have that kind of blessing."

"I'm aware of Josh's sacrifice, Sister. Our world would be very different if it weren't for him."

Josh shook his paper. "Hey, come on you two. I'm sitting right here in case you didn't notice. If you get any sweeter, I'll have a sugar attack."

McHale smiled through sallow skin. "And he's humble, too."

Sister Teresa Marie nodded. "He used to be a smart little boy on my baseball team. I'll never forget—"

"Oh, please, Sister, let's not."

She stood. "All right. Dinner will be ready in a few minutes. Scott? You need to make a decision. I have a place for you here though you should be in a hospital. Father Vernon is on a Vatican sabbatical, so he won't be back for a month. He lives in the other half of my duplex. A month might not be enough time though."

McHale looked at his hands. "I'm sorry, and I don't mean to be insulting. But I can't stay for a month."

The small lady swelled to a formidable stature. "No, actually, I'm sorry. Let me clear something up. The fact hepatitis doesn't kill you right away doesn't mean you can continue to run around the country. You are a carrier, meaning you can give it to wonderful people in your clandestine meetings. You could sicken your whole effort in a matter of months if you start spreading this around. You might've already gotten a start."

McHale rocked in his chair. "Oh, boy."

"Right. You could give it to Josh, except I had a vaccine sent over this afternoon."

Josh shook the paper. "I don't like shots."

Sister Teresa Marie sighed. "Big baby. We've got to backtrack and get the people you've met vaccinated."

McHale spoke quickly. "I'll take care of that."

The nun tapped her foot with impatience. "You can't meet with anyone else, because you're a carrier. Get it? You're also facing death from lots of different diseases because of a weakened immune system. If the hep doesn't kill you, your next cold just might. You're rundown. Face it. The war is over for you, at least for a while. Either you sit it out now, or we'll all say how brave you were at your funeral."

McHale looked at the bare floor. "You talk pretty plain, Sister."

"At this age, why mess around? You're staying here. I'll move into Father Vernon's side. I'll supply you with burner phones if that's what it takes."

Josh looked up from the paper in surprise.

She harrumphed. "Give me some credit. I watch movies. But you're not leaving, Scott. There are others who can do what you're doing, at least for a while. You are not important enough to be this country's martyr."

McHale cast a last appeal to an unsympathetic Josh. "I got my shot, so now you do your part. I'll handle the notifications." He grinned. "Bigger baby."

Chapter 49

Josh

Two weeks before Christmas, Josh exited Interstate 5 and pulled under the awning of the Pioneer Truck Stop. Scott took longer to heal than Sister Teresa Marie thought, and Father Vernon was happy to extend his time in Italy. Josh expanded the number of groups he'd been assigned to talk with and tonight found himself in the Willamette Valley of western Oregon.

Even if Josh drove slower this evening, he'd still be a half hour early and that wasn't good. The group might spook if he waited in the church parking lot. They didn't know him by sight but had been told he would be standing in for Scott.

He watched as the attendant topped the tank, then paid, and parked the dark green Subaru. Shivering from the wet night air, he trotted to the glass doors and found a booth. The odor of pancakes and bacon in humid kitchen air reminded him of early morning football practices at East High in Salt Lake City.

Mawkish Days, to be sure. Look forward, not back, Josh reminded himself. Five minutes late to these clandestine meetings usually meant he spent the least amount of time in one place. This decreased his chances of being arrested as a material witness. The funny little no-man's-land between California declaring McHale dead, and the federal government maintaining a fugitive warrant, gave him concern. Josh could be held for the US Marshals, and he could do nothing. A public lawyer wasn't an option any longer and he had no wish to test an already strained legal system.

The waitress, pleasant and heavy hipped, poured more water into his glass. "Positive, you don't want coffee, hon?"

"No thanks, but you could tell me the best way to get to the Methodist Church on Smith Street."

"Harrisburg? Oh, sure. I go right by there on my way home all the time. Its only fifteen minutes."

She put the jug on the table and pulled a pen from a breast pocket. Slowly, using large cursive lines, she drew him a simple map.

"I live on the other side of bridge. You won't have a problem finding the church if you remember to turn at Mel's Tacos. If you get to the middle school, you've gone too far."

He read her nametag poised high on large breasts. "Thanks, Dottie, and the sandwich was great."

She smiled, gave him a flirty tilt of her shoulder, and moved to the next customer. A man rose from a booth near the kitchen and walked to a hidden hallway.

Josh spent several more minutes, then glanced at his wristwatch. It was time.

After dropping ten dollars on top of a bill for just under five, he grabbed his jacket. The rain hadn't let up, but he didn't want to be too late. Before he pushed on the glass doors, Dottie ran up.

"Hey, hon?"

Josh blinked in surprise. "Oh, uh ... the ten included your tip."

She looked disconcerted for a moment. "Not that, but thanks. I think I gave you the wrong church."

Josh's antennae went up. "Really?"

She pointed at the paper. "You wanted the Methodist Church, right? I gave you the First Christian. Same directions, except you go a half block farther and turn right into the parking lot just *after* the middle school."

Josh relaxed. Simple mistake. "Perfect. Thanks."

He expected another shoulder wave, but instead she watched him as if wanting to add something left unsaid. Finally, she nodded and hurried back into the dining room.

He watched her retreat.

She's lived here all her life, and mistook one church for another?

He looked at the looping handwriting and simple lines and thought he might understand. He had taught all levels of high school kids and likely failed them just as this lady's teachers may have failed her. The thought and the rain depressed him even more.

Fifteen minutes later, he turned at Mel's Tacos on Smith Street and crossed the railroad tracks. Her map was perfect. The Subaru passed the First Christian Church with several darkened cars and pickup trucks. He saw the school a hundred yards further and turned into an empty parking lot of rain puddles. Light glistened from the asphalt.

No other cars. Maybe his waitress had been right the first time. He put the Subaru in reverse, just in time to watch a man rolling a large steel dumpster to block his exit.

Josh didn't stop to think. He hit the gas, spinning the Subaru's tires backwards, and shot over the parking curbs and across the sidewalk. Bouncing into the street, he threw the wheel over and shifted, slamming the accelerator again and checking the mirror. Headlights bounced into the street a block behind him, wavered left and right, then accelerated straight.

A trap. Oh my, God. A trap.

At the corner, he kept his foot down and trusted the street wasn't a dead end.

The little car held the corner, but a black pickup truck on high lift shock absorbers did not. He watched in the rearview as the other's skid progressed, bounced over the curb, and stopped in a splashing, muddy half circle. Josh drove even harder, making the next left and then right until spotting the main street two blocks beyond.

He roared into the intersection, then skidded to a stop as his headlights caught a silver Prius slowly motoring under the traffic light. A woman reflected in the headlights glanced at his impatience with disapproval.

He fell in behind the slower car, scouting the road ahead. Double-yellow lines traveled as far as he could see. He waited as they safely passed through without seeing the pickup truck. Then, he flicked his lights and gunned by.

The Subaru hit forty, then sixty in the narrow downtown street. He waited for the truck to burst from an alley. The speed held at seventy blowing through green and red lights until the town grew sparse at the outskirts and he could see a clear highway ahead. Just as he began to breathe again, the big black Ford pickup pulled from a crossroad lot and thundered after him.

Josh watched with incredulity then pressed the pedal to the floor. They were not cops. They were the enemy.

Both vehicles raced south together as the pickup truck gained easily. An unlighted turn in the highway surprised him and he drifted into the opposite lane, his tires threatening to break loose. The pickup driver anticipated and quickly closed the gap.

Narrow Bridge read the yellow roadside sign in a blur.

The mist joined the fog. His windshield chose that moment to cloud. He wiped quickly and fumbled for the fan switch but could see no farther than a couple dozen yards. High headlights filled his rearview mirror. The driver laid on the horn. The waitress had set him up.

His speedometer touched eighty. The two-lane bridge suddenly loomed out of the fog. At the same moment, the truck pulled alongside. He glanced at an angry passenger who pointed a finger and mimed an unintelligible oath.

The steel truss bridge waited with its maw of rusting iron and concrete abutments.

The pickup suddenly slammed into his driver's door, surprising him. He fought the swerve and held the gas pedal to the floor. The truck smashed him again pushing the little car toward the bridge's framework.

As the truck moved in for a third time, Josh yanked the wheel into the big front fender and held. The behemoth wavered then dropped back scraping the Subaru's rear end.

Suddenly, Josh found himself spinning. A tire dropped off the pavement's edge. He overcorrected and slammed into the iron rail. Plastic and glass shrapnel exploded as the car flipped on his side still traveling at breakneck speed. Josh's head bounced off the glass as the airbag detonated in his face. Sparks erupted with a horrible rending until a bridge buttress caught the fender and spun him turtle.

The precipice and a low pedestrian rail lay ahead. Josh flashed thoughts about the cold black water below as he scrapped toward the edge. An upright steel truss suddenly stood in his path and caught the undercarriage in a deafening crunch.

Wheels spun and steam rose as the night became quiet.

Josh's head swam. He tried to understand what had just happened. The bridge road was empty. No devil truck. The seatbelt held him locked in a tight embrace.

As he fumbled for the latch and tried to push the stinging cloth out of his face, four tires stopped a few yards away.

The silver Prius.

The driver wore high heels and knelt down on a bared knee. "My God, are you alright? What happened?"

Josh tried to focus. "I ... I don't know."

"I've called 9-1-1 but they'll take forever to get here. Are you bleeding? Is something broken? The nearest hospital is in Eugene. It'll be an hour on these roads."

"I believe you, especially at the rate you drive." He wondered why he'd said such an extraordinary thing to a stranger and good Samaritan.

He tried again. "Sorry. I'm a little out of sorts. Hanging upside down does that to me."

A thumb in the seatbelt buckle sent him to the roof of the car.

"Careful." The warning wasn't as heartfelt as her earlier concern.

Another chill in the air. "I really shouldn't have said that ma'am. I apologize. Did you see where the pickup truck went?"

"What pickup truck?"

Josh wiggled through the crushed window. She took her arm and they both stood. He flexed a bruised back and shoulder.

She appraised him with caution. "Where do you hurt?"

"My wallet, I think. My beautiful little car didn't fare too well."

She tapped her foot. "And whose fault is that? Especially the way *you* drive."

Chagrined. "That would be my fault, ma'am. If I was a better driver, maybe I could've handled the guy's attack. I think the truck had the weight advantage though. I wonder where they went."

The woman gasped. "Oh, my God"

Josh turned, thinking she'd spotted the hooligans coming again.

"You're Joshua Harrison."

He froze and looked at her ... nearly eye to eye, and he stood over six feet.

She pressed. "You are, aren't you?"

He didn't want to be stranded, and so took the chance. "Yes, ma'am. Who are you?"

"Madison James and no, I wasn't named after the mermaid. You missed the church."

"The two guys in the pickup got in the way."

"They were chasing you. Why?"

"You know, Ms. James—"

"Mattie."

"Mattie. I need to sit down. I don't feel too good. Besides, it's raining, in case you hadn't noticed."

"I'm from Oregon. We don't care about such trifles as rain. Come on. Sit in my car and we can wait for the police."

She started, but he stood rock still.

"I see. The police are a problem, right? Let me call the wrecker. We can get your car off to one side, then someone can take you back to the meeting."

A minute later, Mattie joined him and turned up the heat. "I let Harold know what happened. He's the chairperson. No one wants to drive down here if the police have been called. Sorry, my fault. You ticked me off and I reported the way you were driving."

"Completely understandable."

"It was crazy driving, Josh. You were going to get someone killed."

"I agree and I'm truly sorry."

She blinked away at her irritation. "Tell you what. I'll take you back to the church and talk to Harold. We've got to get you some help, and face-to-face, Harold will fold like a house of cards. I'd stick around except my sister's daughter isn't feeling well, and she's alone. Lori, that's my sister, has to work tonight, so I'm headed into Eugene."

He needed a moment to think. This woman talked fast and took control. He was having trouble following her thoughts.

He closed his eyes. "Sorry about getting the seats wet."

"They'll dry. Now where is this pickup you're talking about?"

He puffed out breath. "I don't know. They must have taken off. When I spun out, he became a blur."

Clipped words came at him. "You stay here. I'm going to set out some flares. Don't want anyone crossing the bridge and running into your car."

"I can set them out."

"I'm sure you can, Joshua, but I said I'll handle it."

Of that, he had no doubt. "Thank you. Mattie. You can stop being mad at me anytime you like."

"That, will be up to you."

A few minutes later, a line of flares marked the wreck. She moved the Prius to the town side of bridge and parked by a closed bait shop. He immediately spotted the broken tree trunk and opened the door.

"Now, where are you going?"

He pointed. "I know what happened to the pickup."

They hurried to the edge of the bank. Ten feet below, the big Ford lay on its side with the driver's door open. Dark river water filled the cab.

He slid down the bank. "I just hope he's not dead. I have a few questions."

A minute later he called up the bank to her. "Empty. They ran. This is crazy. Why would they go to such lengths to catch me, and then just disappear?"

He found no bodies and no trail in the slimy mud.

"Can you make it back up?"

"On my way."

His trip up the slick bank took him longer with two stops to catch his breath.

Once in the car, she turned to him. "I spoke to Harold again, but this is too unusual. The meeting broke up. Nobody wants trouble."

Josh worked his neck around bruised shoulders. "What sort of trouble?"

"There's a time of choosing coming soon, Joshua. We've got a few farmers and hunters in the Willamette Valley, survivalists mostly, who'd love to see our country implode. You know the kind. They love to watch the fires they set. No brains, all brawn. I've heard these fringe elements want to set up a government in their own image. The country has a lot of them. That meets my definition of trouble. I'll tell you; the baby is in terrible danger of getting tossed out with the bathwater. That's why we wanted to meet with you tonight. I heard you were with McHale, but if you're one of these dissolutionists, we're not interested."

"That's not me, Mattie, I promise. I love my country, and we've got problems. All I want is a chance to set it right."

She considered his answer when headlights unexpectedly illuminated the inside of the Prius.

McHale opened the door to see. "It's a tow truck. That was fast."

He stepped out as the truck came to a stop.

The passenger door swung open preceded by a hunting rifle leveled on his chest.

"Hey there, Joshua Harrison."

Josh sidestepped to hide Mattie from their view. "Hey, come on guys. What's with the gun?"

"You just cost me my truck, shithead." A big man stepped out of the driver's side just as the rain began in earnest.

"Why are you doing this? You know we called 9-1-1. The police will be here any minute."

The driver's rancid grin didn't falter. "They take their sweet time around here. You need to come with us."

Before Josh could answer, a voice came out of the shadows. "My Glock has a fifteen-round magazine. You've only got three rounds in that rifle. I'm a crack shot, so I won't waste but one or two rounds on you. I figure to kill both of you and then wait on the cops."

The man spotted her steadying the pistol against a post.

"Now wait a minute—"

Her voice cut like a knife. "No. You wait. You're one of these knuckleheads running around trying to tell people what they should and shouldn't be doing. You're a vigilante punk, and where I come from, we hang guys like you."

Josh tried not to look astonished. This nice woman hung people.

The big man's voice waffled. "Now wait a minute, lady–"

"You know something, I've never especially liked the way people call me 'Lady.' Always struck me as demeaning, especially when I hear it coming from the likes of you. Maybe I'll take my time putting you down. Make it hurt a little. A gift. After all, it is nearly Christmas."

Both men had heard enough and scrambled for their doors. The tow truck reversed as taillights disappeared in the dark rain.

Josh lowered his hands. "Wow, Mattie."

She returned the pistol to the glove box. "I might've needed more than just a couple of bullets my hands were shaking so bad."

"Well, you sure fooled me."

"At the firing range, they told us to pull the trigger until we ran out of ammunition. Somebody probably would've gotten hurt."

"I'm glad you're on my side."

"*That's* still to be decided but we need to get moving. Those bozos will come back with their so-called friends, and we shouldn't be here. The police and a real tow truck will take care of your car. Get your stuff and come on with me to Eugene. You can stay at my place, and I'll sleep over at my sister's. That's where I was headed anyway."

He watched Mattie walk around the nose of the Prius, thinking Hannah, his deceased wife, would have liked this woman. He certainly did.

Chapter 50

Angie

Angie smiled and waved to the La Mesa crowd of several hundred. Tuxedos and once-a-year dresses stood from their dinner tables and clapped in February's kickoff for Carnival, a weeklong tribute to their Hispanic heritage.

She'd pinned back her long dark hair with a turquoise comb, giving her an elegant, movie-star appeal. In the months since her election she'd grown in popularity, with fiery talk and strict budget measures, contrasting her administration with the collapse of the east. She assumed several federal functions such as critical rationing and immigration enforcement to ease the burden on cities and counties. Some cried foul but the population benefited, even if all the while holding its breath. She froze prices and prosecuted gougers. Gas remained available at the pumps with pressure on refiners and food stayed on the shelves. State wages froze and she reduced taxes while factories hired. In the east, corporations ceased the move overseas, and instead went west to the sunshine.

Everything was just as planned.

Security waited in the wings when she eased from the smiling crowd. "We're going through the kitchen, ma'am."

Angie nodded as four Highway Patrol security men formed a moving perimeter. Her chief of detail, Christine Dodd, walked ahead, scanning and assessing. At Ken Litton's suggestion, Angie had fired her former security supervisor.

Christine, only on the job only since Christmas, stopped and helped the governor with a protective, bullet-proof vest.

Angie fitted her straps. "How did it sound, Chris?"

"Good, Governor. It's what everyone needed to hear. Channels Eight and Four got most of the speech, so sound and video bites will be on the late news locally and tomorrow morning's national ABC and NBC. People need to be reassured."

Angie laughed. "You sound more like my chief of staff."

"Just trying to help, ma'am."

"Well, you are. Thank you."

Two Highway Patrol officers jumped to the pavement below the dock to ready their black Tahoes. The two were left alone.

Angie held the straps as Christine tightened the Velcro. "You think this thing is really necessary?"

"Yes, ma'am. Won't stop a high-power rifle but it can defeat most handguns. We all wear them."

"Yes, of course. It's time for the day to be over. I'm really beat."

"I'm just glad it's you in office, Governor."

Angie glanced around. "Why thank you, Chris. That's nice of you to say."

"It's what lots of people feel these days, ma'am. We need calm and commitment to our Constitution."

Critics often claimed Angie abrogated constitutional tradition. "Now, I wonder what you're saying."

Christine reddened. "I'm sorry. I'm speaking out of turn."

"This is important. What do you mean?"

Pots clattered in the nearby kitchen. "I think there's a lot of people wondering why only states east of Denver lost electricity."

"We planned better."

"Yes, ma'am. But there are conspiracy theorists out there saying the country's going to split. I've heard your name tossed around as leading this."

She glanced at Angie. "But I trust you, Governor, and I'm not alone. Any idea repeated enough tends to become reality in people's minds. We shouldn't forget our promises, or our pledges is all I'm saying."

Christine saw both Tahoes pull up to the back. "We need to go, ma'am."

Angie didn't move. "Tell me what you've heard. Please."

The chief of detail signaled one minute to the two men waiting at the loading gate. "Bits and pieces only, Governor. People don't always talk around me, but it doesn't mean I'm not curious. The west has a crystal ball when it comes time to fend off hacking attacks. And of course, we have these little mini nukes. The whole thing is pretty convenient when you stop and think about it."

"And you're saying because I'm benefiting, I must be part of a conspiracy?"

Christine didn't cower. "Not me, ma'am. I voted for you, and I'd do it again. It's just ... the hackers don't target the west. The FBI agents I know tell me we haven't had a real attack since the first six months. Other people are saying it looks weird. That's all. I'm just passing it on."

"So, people claim I created a plan to knock down old power dams, and then build a multibillion-dollar power grid to cut off the east? Then, I somehow hacked the national grid system ... to do what?"

"Not *you*, ma'am. Your husband. They're saying he put it together but let his ... his lust get in the way. They're saying he was killed, and others moved in to take his place. A double cross."

"You believe I had my husband murdered?"

Still the chief of detail refused to back down. "No ma'am, I don't. Otherwise, I wouldn't be working here. I just thought you needed to hear other people's thought."

Angie watched the night through the narrow swinging doors and wondered. If people said that now, what would people be saying in a few short weeks?

"There's nothing we can do about loose talk, Chris. But I've been so busy, I just never noticed. Will you continue to confide in me? I need to hear this."

The younger woman nodded. "Yes, ma'am. I'm always happy to stick my foot in my mouth. Good reason why the Secret Service isn't my employer anymore."

"Their loss, my gain. We'd better go."

"Yes, ma'am." She pushed the heavy door aside to reveal the black vehicles waiting. Christine went ahead but a lone figure caught Angie's eye and her throat.

She touched Christine's elbow. "Before we go, walk with me first."

They stepped into the parking lot and walked into the shadows.

Christine saw the man in dappled light. "Let me check him, Governor."

Her hand went to the opening in her jacket.

"It'll be okay."

"Ma'am, please."

"No, Chris. Trust me. Stay here." She walked the last thirty feet to the figure.

Christine moved for a better angle, holding her pistol low at her side. The men in the two vehicles saw and opened their doors to assume positions. All four stopped when she held up a clenched hand.

Angie embraced her dead husband but gasped softly when he pulled back. "Where have you been, Scott? You're so thin. This has to stop."

"Just a while longer—."

"You've been sick. What is it?"

"I'm just getting over a little infection. Lost some weight but Doctor Joy says I'm not contagious anymore. Still, we need to be careful."

Angie's tense shoulders dropped. "Is that why Joy's been happy as a cat in a bird store? I knew it. How long have you been here?"

"Five weeks, recouping here in San Diego. Joy's been great. I just hope she won't get into trouble for sneaking me medicine. She'd be livid if she caught me out of bed right now."

"Oh, Scott. You've never been good at following orders, have you?"

She glanced at a figure sitting in an old sedan. "Who's that?"

He smiled. "A good friend. He's been helping me and visiting family, too. I took advantage and made him drive tonight. Joy's working a night shift, but I need to get back."

She touched his beard, now completely gray. "You've lost so much weight. You're scaring me. Are you sure this isn't serious?"

"I'm okay, just not the dashing young senator from Camelot anymore. A couple of years living on the road will do it to the best of us." He quickly added, "Sorry. Defeatist crap. What does Ken Litton say?"

"They isolated him. They're still angry about the FISA warrants and the snitch in my detail. Thank God, he told me. All of this would've been much different if I'd been sitting in jail."

McHale's stomach sank. Another life he'd screwed up.

"Did they recall him?"

"Yes and no. When DC's lights went out, the order was rescinded. Something's going on, because Anne Marie told me he's working twenty-four-seven now. Like tonight. He's in Phoenix, meeting Theo Haines. Is there something happening I should know about?"

He wanted so much to tell her but didn't dare involve her. Yet. "It's better you do not know. No conflicts, and plausible deniability if it all goes bad."

"*Bull*-loney," She used their old family friendly expletive. Neither smiled.

He took her hand. The month spent under the care of Sister Teresa Marie had given him a modicum of renewed health, but also a new respect for life. He kissed her fingers without guilt. She squeezed back. He thought of how many lives and careers he'd ruined since he first made a deal with the devil. He could never go back, never plead for a second chance, and never expect forgiveness.

If everyone else is allowed to escape hell, this fate I can accept—

The first bullet ripped into his jacket back and ricocheted off a rib exiting directly over his right lung. The round struck Angie squarely in the chest, knocking her backward, surprised and wide-eyed. An immediate second round, a shotgun blast hit low, bouncing off the pavement and ripping into the meat of McHale's leg. He reached for Angie but toppled into the drainage ditch.

Christine came at a dead run and fired four quick rounds into the bushes. Another shotgun blast struck the tree near her, but she'd already moved. Four tightly spaced rounds from her tiny Glock whacked the dark, wooded stand. The impacts were followed by a high-pitched cry. She never slowed, moving quickly and dropping the magazine on the run. She reloaded in swift, practiced movements, never breaking stride, and fired again and again.

The two California Highway Patrol officers jumped into the first Tahoe and raced to the gap where Angie had fallen. The passenger of the first vehicle laid a stream of fire as they tore through the parking lot, pouring more rounds into the woods. Christine pointed at the thicket and fired repeatedly as the passenger tossed his MP10 inside the open window and ran to Angie. The driver fired his own submachine gun, ripping the thicket into flying leaves and broken branches. The first patrol officer placed the wounded governor in the backseat and was quickly in. The Tahoe's engine roared as tires spun and the second two officers emptied their Glocks. The second Tahoe followed making radio calls to the preplanned hospital.

Christine watched the last muzzle flash, then put nine more deadly rounds into the spot, dropped the mag, and loaded her next. She didn't stop firing or using herself as a target until both Tahoes vanished.

When the retreating siren entered her thrumming ears, she took cover again and steadied the weapon.

She yelled into the night. "Drop your gun and show yourself, Do it now."

A voice called from the dark. "I think you killed Adlai, you crazy lady."

A stumbling giant of a man emerged, dragging a smaller, lifeless body. The big man bled from his shirt's chest, neck, and abdomen.

The other assassin had no face. "You done killed him."

He released a pathetic, animal cry then looked at the holes in his own body. "And you killed me, too."

She centered the sights on his forehead and watched as he let the shotgun slip from his hands. She sprang up and ran in a crouch, watching the wood line, and jumped the ditch at the same instant Josh left the sedan and ran to McHale.

He knelt and pressed his hands on a bleeding chest. "I'll call an ambulance."

McHale's eyes opened. "Angie?"

"I don't know. Oh God, I should've never agreed to let you do this."

Scott watched the sky. Tears of pain and disappointment ran into the wrinkles of road-aged skin. Only overcast clouds this time of year. No stars. June gloom or was it May gray? He could always find stars when he needed them. The time on old Highway 14 when he lay on cold pavement, feeling his lifeblood draining into the night. Where were his stars?

He took Josh by the arm. "Thanks for believing in me. Thanks for being my friend. Don't let evil win."

The words were lost as Josh lifted the gaunt body and hurried to his car. Christine fought to wrap cuffs around the huge man's dying back and glanced up in time to see the car driving out of the parking lot. The distance and the streetlight's reflection hid the license plate.

Chapter 51

Angie

Angie's chest still hurt if she tried to take a full breath. Sitting at the writing desk in the private wing of the governor's mansion, however, let her wear a robe and grimace when she liked. Her private hospital room in San Diego housed a comatose patient who was guarded around the clock in an attempt to throw off another attempt on her life.

The bullet that struck her slowed as it penetrated Scott's heavy winter jacket and ricocheted, so it had not penetrated her vest. She still felt as though a two-ton truck had hit her.

FBI Assistant Director Ken Litton sat across from her and set his cup down. "The question is going to be asked by the US Attorney. You know that."

She smiled at her longtime friend. "I do and the answer will be the same. I needed air and I took a walk. It's simple."

"No, actually, it's not. Your chief of security isn't talking—"

"I didn't tell her not to talk."

"I believe you. I also believe she's taking her lead from you. The CHP guys said they were too busy emptying their weapons into the woods and saving you."

"For which, I'm eternally grateful."

Litton chuckled with a shake of his big head. "Anne Marie and me, too. Let me tell you what I think the federal lawyers are going to say. They believe you met Scott McHale, and he passed information to you of a highly confidential nature ... or you did to him."

"I'm the governor of California and we declared him dead. It's you, the Feds, that have a problem with that. Why would I tell Scott's ghost anything?"

Litton raised his considerable eyebrows. "Because the NSA monitored a phone call from the Naval Observatory in DC. The vice president's residence."

Angie started to explain. "Twila—"

"Don't, Governor. You shouldn't say anything. I've read the transcripts of your debriefing to the attorney general. You'll probably have to testify to the grand jury or in front of Congress, and the last thing you'll want to say is you and the FBI discussed your testimony."

She nodded and looked out the window.

"I'm only debriefing a 134 ..."

She glanced around.

Litton said, "Asset to the Bureau."

"Informant ... snitch."

"A loyal and brave American. I got to tell you something, Angie. I am so damn proud of you. To be called a friend of someone who believes in her promises and her oath of office, who can't be swayed ..." He laughed. "And, I'm going to say it: someone who *stands by her man* ... or the ghost of her man. That's my kind of hero."

Angie sighed and grimaced. "Oh Ken, you're such a romantic, and you obviously don't know all of it, really. I'm nobody's hero."

"The whole western world says differently, and on this, and I'll believe them."

He sipped the tea, wanting to ask about McHale, but of course, he did not. His best friend had been placed on the US Marshals' most wanted-fugitive list once again. California legislation wanted to declared him undead, and Litton, the private man, could believe what he wished, but he was still an FBI agent. He would do his job when it came down to it.

He set his cup down. "We might be close to turning a corner, but we're not out of the woods. So many powerful people have committed so much, they're not turning back. Some multimillionaires saw a way to make a buck. Some terrorists and foreign financiers, a different kind of terrorist, have to be watched, too. We've got one of the world's most powerful cartels running two major US cities with millions of willing and unwilling hostages. We still have a lot of very angry people divided by an invisible line from Canada to Mexico, and we must avoid a shooting war at all costs."

Angie added the next thought. "And of course, we still haven't solved the root of this entire crisis. Hackers killing our infrastructure."

Litton agreed. "This thing is like a perpetual motion machine. Once started, I don't know if we can stop it."

"We have the will, Ken. Many can find that will again, even if they're on the fence now. We need to help Scott, help them rise against this tide."

The effort weakened her and left her pale.

"I didn't hear that, but you've got to get back to bed, Governor."

Angie wasn't done. "Our efforts cannot fail. We need to fight smarter and use all our resources. If this means we give up personal property or positions or even a sliver of our Constitution ... temporarily ... in the process, we do it.

Presidents have asked this favor in the past. Somehow, they forgot when the crisis passed. Not this time. I'll fight to get it back. We need to buy time to give our nation the will to survive. The year is 1776 all over again, and we are declaring our independence from evil."

Litton waved at the nurse outside the glass doors. "I'll be right there with you."

He took her hand. "Now, will you get some rest, for God's sake? Anne Marie will have my butt if she finds you got out of bed to talk to me."

Chapter 52

Teague

The big man paced inside his county offices in Muroc County.

He tensed his arms and flexed his fists. "Angie, shot down in the parking lot by those two hillbillies. I can't believe it. What the hell? Thank God, she wasn't the key to this deal. Is she dead?"

Teague stood impassively. "No, sir. She took a rifle round that penetrated her chest. For now, they put her into a coma to help the recovery. My guess is those two boys were using their antique deer gun. Under normal circumstances–"

Dearborn chewed his cigar. "I know, I know. If she croaks, we'll make her a martyr or something. For now, I want you to buy flowers to pile up in the parking lot. Hire some professional mourners. Get the news crews working. Get to your sources in the media. People like this kind of stuff. We'll get some actors to be interviewed. When will you know?"

"It'll take me a couple of hours to find someone willing to talk. That's where Joy works, you know and everything's on lockdown."

He pounded his fist against the leather chair back. "Doesn't matter. Angie wasn't ever going to be more than a figurehead anyway. Get Brewster from Nevada to the hospital. The timetable stays the same. He'll take over behind the scenes until we get the paperwork updated."

"No problem."

"We need to start marketing him now. He knows how to take orders without all the crap Angie gave me. Get him to lay some of the first flowers."

"I'll call him."

He took a calming breath. "Good. Three decades of planning, and then a couple of hillbillies from Podunk, North Carolina nearly blew the whole thing. We should have the WCG firmly in control by the end of the month. The fences are up, and we got rid of the troublemakers. We'll backdate Angie's approval for the referendum to get the two states together. Jump on that right away. Get someone in her office tonight."

"Yes, sir."

"El Gordo is a loose cannon in Vegas. Make certain the geeks keep an eye on him. I want to make damn sure no one breaks our hold."

"I'm working on it."

"Work faster. The fact Ken Litton is on a plane to Arizona means something's going on. Track him. Get to El Gordo then to Peter Quint. I need to stop it before we have another problem. Offense, not defense. Got it?"

"Yes, sir. I'll call him now."

Dearborn turned to the window, watching the last line of blue before the sky swallowed the day.

He didn't turn around. "Are you still here?"

· · · ·

Teague drove for the LA/Ontario airport. Dearborn's Citation business jet waited on the ramp. At over four hundred knots, the flight would take less than an hour. Another hour, and the plane could be in Reno.

He parked the rental car in the lot at the West Valley warehouse and spent five minutes going through the stages of security. The bored hackers playing computer games had disappeared. People shouted to one another in the bedlam, moaned, and even cried in the dark room. Counterattacks by several nations in concert with the United States fought back. A group of three mined the dark web and added data strips to a central monitor. He saw Ken Litton's name, as passenger on Southwest Airlines, an intercepted cell call for a pickup at Phoenix Sky Harbor, another mobile call to the FBI field office. Also up on board was a call to Anne Marie, Litton's wife. A strip thirty minutes ago showed Pima County sheriff Theo Haines ordering a helicopter to fly to the FBI's Tucson Resident Agency parking lot. A hacked "Finder" app showed a half-dozen police chiefs and several private citizens with digital tags massing on a large, dark screen. New encryption hid the contents of a phone call from the Mexican president.

A young man stood and threw his coffee cup against the lead wall. "I'm out! Goddamn it. The Mexicans kicked me out again."

No one seemed to notice.

A heavy-set man stood instead of sat at his terminal. Snowball cellophane wrappers covered his desk and floor. "Forget them. I'm sending you a link. Grab another laptop. Quick. Try this one."

The man crammed a handful of Cheetos into his mouth. "Paste it to reenter. Don't wait. They're catching everything I come up with. The bastards! Move fast. This is definitely an attack."

"Got it, got it." He was sharing the fight with an invigorated NSA.

Peter looked up and didn't move as his office door closed. "Mr. Teague?"

• • • •

The penthouse looked out over the city of lights, not Paris but Las Vegas with its own Eiffel Tower tucked between high-rise hotels. Not in the highest, or the fanciest, El Gordo, the alias of Hector Beltran Guzmán, changed rooms nightly, leaving his true location a mystery to everyone except to his most trusted bodyguards. Tonight, red dragons and blue lilacs adorned a ten-thousand-dollar rug as the kingpin of the Vegas and Reno takeovers stubbed out his cigarette.

"They do nothing. Weak. If I'd known ten years ago what I know today, Mexico would have elected me *el presidente*, because I bring back what the Yankees stole from us two hundred years ago."

Teague sipped his club soda. "You have the next best thing, *Señor* Guzmán. A money tree, and an ally who will soon give you all of Mexico for yourself."

Guzmán chewed and smacked, his small eyes never leaving Dearborn's emissary. "When?"

"Very soon now. But until then, you need to have patience and let us work the American political system."

"You are afraid of your own government? Not me. Not of prison. Not of any man. Ask the stupid cops and your own politicians that tried to stop me."

He grinned, the dead front tooth malevolent in mouth. "They enjoy resting in a lovely park downtown."

"I understand, *señor*. Dearborn only asks you give him the courtesy—"

"I owe him nothing. I did this. He did nothing." The heavy shouldered man leaped off the couch and strode to the wide, mirrored window. "No one else could hold this city against the Americans. I have done this. The party goes on. I have the city by the balls."

"Mr. Dearborn appreciates and admires your work, *señor*. He only asks you allow him to work similar magic on America."

The man's mouth turned up. "One month."

Wes Teague stood and stretched out his hand. It would be over long before that. "One month. I'll let him know immediately. Thank you."

"Enough work. Let me introduce you to the most beautiful ladies in the world."

• • • •

Teague's escort motorcade stopped at the barbed wire leading out of the independent Las Vegas City-State and into the wilds of no-man's-land, North Las Vegas. In the rearview mirror, he watched as the lead Tundra with ISIS-styled mounted machine guns wheeled away. More trucks followed, and then he was alone. Two men with MP5 submachine guns approached from the shadows as he pushed the window's button.

Both men immediately backed away. One offered a half salute.

Maya smiled at Teague as he peered, pressed, and swiped his way into the dark hall. Forty-eight hours later and the same cyberattack continued. Occupied sleeping bags filled the dark corners.

Teague noticed Peter's darkened office glass and picked up the internal phone. "Maya? Where's Peter?"

"He left a couple hours ago Mr. Teague. He said something about dinner."

"Okay. Call his cell and tell him I'm waiting in his office."

Teague swiped his card at Peter's door, turned on the light and sat. He noticed the missing laptop immediately.

He picked up the phone again. "Did he take his computer, Maya?"

"I, ah ... I don't know, sir."

He swiped his way back into her office. "You know, Maya, I'm beat. If you get hold of him, call me and we'll meet at the apartments. I'm going to grab a few hours' sleep. Looks like you guys have everything under control."

She swallowed hard and tried to smile. Peter's phone still didn't answer.

• • • •

Ten minutes later, Teague pulled into their leased apartment house parking lot and clicked off the headlights. Why would Peter leave at such a critical time? Pandemonium without control could be fatal. He should be there, keeping a lid on these excitable hacker morons.

At nearly one in the morning, Dearborn's apartment complex slept, except for a car idling at the curb. Teague sat watching the twenty dark apartments. He rarely felt fatigue and tonight was no exception.

A light showed on a second-story walkway as a figure appeared. When the door closed, the outside corridor fell back into darkness once more. The figure took two stairs at a time holding an object close to the chest. The passenger in the idling car smoked and waited.

Teague stepped from the shadow. "Hello, Peter. Headed back to the warehouse?"

The young man flinched backward. "Holy shit. You scared the crap out of me."

Teague looked from Peter to the woman passenger.

"Who the hell is this, Peter?" Her voice scratched from too many smoky bars.

His lower jaw opened to suck in more air. "Nobody."

The woman watched. "What the fuck? I'm nobody?"

Teague ignored her protest. "Where are you going, Peter?"

"No place." He licked his drying lips.

The woman threw open her door and dropped a high stocking leg out. "Hey, asshole. Back off here. We're taking a vacation to San Diego."

She turned to Peter. "Isn't that what you said? I had to take off work, you know, and the pit boss wasn't very happy. Don't screw around here."

She walked up to Teague and wrinkled the diamond in her nose. "And just who the fuck are you?"

Peter looked between the woman and Teague. "I just called work, Heidi. All hell's breaking loose. We're going to have to leave tomorrow."

She turned her rage on him. "What the fuck are you talking about? Five minutes ago, you needed to get your computer updated or some shit. Then, we're out of here."

She turned to Teague with a sneer on her face. "What are you, his father?"

Peter stepped between them. "Please, Heidi. Wes is my boss. I thought we could go, but not now. I'm sorry—"

"I'll show you sorry, asshole. It's my credit card holding the Bahia, and it's too late to cancel. Tell this shithead to shove it and let's go."

Teague spoke in soft, almost kind words. "You know, Peter. She's got a point. And you did promise her. Be a gentleman and give the lady your wallet."

Peter saw the look on the other man's face while a Glock Model 27 poked skin in his belt. He handed over his billfold.

Teague rarely smiled. He did now. "Is this a new car?"

A sullen Peter nodded. "Yeah,"

"Fine. Let her have the car, too."

She perked up. "Hey, now you're talking."

Teague turned to the woman. "Miss? I hope you have a good time. Peter will be along in a day or so, but right now, he is needed at work. I hope you understand."

She grinned and slid long legs into the driver's seat. "Cool. Hurry, hon, okay? I'll be missing you."

Peter muttered. "Yeah, right."

When the top finished dropping, she twiddled her fingers. "Ta."

Twin black rubber tracks followed the tail lights.

Teague watched. "A little cold to have the top down, but all in all, that went well. Don't you think?"

"I just leased the car, dude. If she scratches it—"

"I'm certain she'll take care of it, Peter. Even tattooed-and-pierced card dealers can be *very* responsible. I asked you to locate some information for me."

He pouted. "I explained to Donny all was forgiven, just like you said. But this really cost me, dude. I had to front the plane ticket to get him back."

"And?"

Peter should never play poker.

"Look, he'll tell you. I really don't know anything about what he found."

"I'm not going to ask you again."

Peter bounced from one toe to the other. "Really, dude. This is Donny's gig. Let him tell you."

Teague waited the other man out.

Peter finally took a ragged breath and pointed a finger. "You, dude. He found you. That dead baby's got DNA from Captain Wesley Lincoln Teague, US Army. *The kid was yours.*"

Teague's face remained impassive.

"Don't go getting all exercised with the messenger, you know? Donny made sure, so he's got the whole story. He went into the Army's medical records from like, St. Louis or something. They had DNA for all the black-ops guys. So, you got wounded in Bosnia, right? You know Donny was the one who switched the results in the police reports."

Teague continued to stare, saying nothing.

Peter gritted his teeth, an unhealthy anger growing. "I didn't know for sure until last night, so I would've called you, but—"

"Any chance he's wrong?" Teague's voice, barely held above a whisper.

Peter scoffed. "Fuck no. It's right here in my laptop. I wouldn't let him use one of ours."

"So, you're going off to San Diego with a laptop and you've got my information. What were you going to do with it?"

Blood drained from the young man's face. "Oh, no way. I know what you're thinking but I'd never do that."

Two hours ago, he'd told Donny they'd use blackmail to live. Both men knew none of the hackers would survive beyond the next few months.

Teague cracked his neck side to side. "That's what I thought, but it doesn't matter. The only people who'd care about all this are dead. Besides, you wouldn't have gotten a penny from me."

"Blackmail? Oh shit, no. I wasn't going to do anything like that. Honestly. I was keeping it for security. You know, in case anyone broke in."

"Sure thing, Peter. That's really good of you. We're going back to the warehouse and talk to Donny. Come on."

"You know, he's probably up in Reno now. I forgot."

Teague paced his breathing. "That's fine. I've got a plane. Let's go."

Peter stepped back. "No way. I'm not going anywhere with you."

"You don't have a car. Don't be stupid. I'm not going to hurt you."

Teague opened the driver's door as Peter fumbled with his pistol, firing once, twice, and then a third time. Teague drew his own gun and shot once, hitting Peter in the forehead. The lifeless young man crumpled to the street. He walked over and put the next shot in his open blue eye.

Teague holstered the weapon and pulled the computer from dead hands. As he drove to the airport, no police cars, lights, or sirens passed him going the other way. The cops no longer responded to North Las Vegas since funding had been pulled.

He hit the phone button for the pilot. "Steve? Can you fly me back to Reno and then on to Muroc County? I have what I came for."

"Yes, sir. I'll have her pulled out of the hangar and fueled. Thirty minutes at the North Las Vegas Airport?"

"That'll work."

• • • •

Two hours later, Teague shifted in the Citation Jet's leather seat and once again refused a drink. Instead, he asked for more ice and another towel. Encryption had protected Peter's laptop, but hackers like Donny dreamed about breaking another's code. The young man slept on the Citation's couch across from him while Teague read through Peter's documents and emails. Donny hadn't been fearful like Peter, and quickly accepted the reassignment from Reno back to Vegas. They would drop the hacker to assume Peter's job, and then return to Muroc County. The sun pushed a blue line on the eastern horizon.

He dialed the sat phone. "Madam Vice President?"

"Jesus, Wes. Do you know what time it is?"

"My apologies, ma'am. Can you talk?"

She blew out her breath. "Yes. Tom's back at Humboldt for the rest of the semester. What's so important it can't wait until normal people get out of bed?"

Teague sipped at the bottled water and grimaced. "I need to know if Big Jim ordered Juliette's murder."

The phone fell silent for long moments.

She finally spoke. "I know you're talking on a secure phone line, but that doesn't mean much to the NSA. Besides, how could you ask me such a thing?"

"Because I'm aware of your ambition and your relationship, ma'am. I've been with Mr. Dearborn for over twenty years, so I know all about your occasional boink in the back room. I'd appreciate an answer."

"You might be forgetting who the hell you're talking to." She calmed herself and leveled her voice. "This isn't like you. What's going on?"

"There's a lot going on, Madam Vice President. El Gordo's getting impatient, and we're monitoring a lot of cyber traffic that makes me uneasy. Angie Molina-McHale is comatose in a hospital bed, but you're already aware of this. President Swanson raised the domestic threat level, and our hackers are hearing talk of an underground revolution."

Twila scoffed. "That's nothing new. I understand everything's under control. I also heard Scott McHale might've been with Angie when she was shot. Is it true?"

Teague cleared his throat and lay back in the seat to close his eyes. "When the police arrived, there was no sign of another person. Angie will deny she met McHale, as she's been denying all along ... if she even survives. The security agents killed the two assailants, Adlai and Abel Cook—"

"The two mountain men?"

Teague wasn't surprised she knew about them. "Yes, ma'am. Cameras on the grounds caught the whole thing, and there was another person. Two, in fact." Teague wiped at his perspiring face and blinked for clarity. "I understand the FBI is analyzing the data now. They'll know pretty soon with their personal recognition software."

"How'd he get away? My sources are drying up out there."

"Witnesses say a second car drove away before the police arrived. An analysis of blood is being done by San Diego PD. We'll have the identity of one person soon."

Teague glanced at the silent computer in the seat next to him. Blood. DNA. Evidence of distrust at the most basic of levels.

"Twila? My question is very simple. Did Dearborn order Juliette's death?"

She hesitated not wanting to reveal what she knew. "I don't have an answer for you. If I did know something about it, I'd be guilty of a crime, and I haven't any idea what you're talking about."

"I expected better from you, Twila—"

But the line had disconnected.

Chapter 53

Twila

Twila nit the buzzer to alert her security. In spite of the early hour, the man outside her door stepped in. She threw back her covers.

"I want an emergency lockdown ... a silent lockdown. Notify no one outside our compound. Threat level red."

She picked up the phone and glanced at the surprised agent. "I'll explain later."

The man nodded and closed the door. Silent blue strobe lights alerted throughout the Naval Observatory as the emergency protocol went into effect.

A phone rested in her palm. She didn't know what Wes Teague had in mind, but she needed to warn Jimmy. Could this be the end of the dream?

It was true that secrets never outlasted its second telling. Now she must race time.

Even if Swanson could survive splitting the country, the impeachment soon to follow would drop the man onto the dung heap of history. She would succeed him and be in a position to stop any scurrilous inquiry. Obviously, the crime had taken place in the west so her multiple deals with Angie would protect her. People would heap praise high when the electric power came back, and the factories reopened. With McHale out of the picture or at the minimum, as a scourge to be shunned, she planned to take full credit for the legislation. By the time the next election rolled around, the country and its economy would scream along in high gear.

People didn't care how they got there, only that a new car sat in the driveway. The sheer number of lies meant nothing to personal prosperity.

Twila's biggest problem was who to choose as Vice President. A Goldilocks milquetoast would serve her well. Plenty of men and women fit those requirements right here in Washington.

The Seattle advertising agency was poised to make Angie and Twila the most popular historical figures of their day. She would need to move the schedule up and be ready to launch the information blitz. Easy enough to make Angie a martyr if she died, although Jimmy likely already had a contingency plan for that.

She wondered how many criers he had hired for the shooting site.

She slipped a toothbrush into her mouth. Teague had sounded odd over the phone. Pushy and reticent at the same time. There were few secrets between Dearborn and her. Juliette's death notwithstanding. How could Teague have been so careless? She knew all her calls were monitored and of course, recorded and made a mental note to speak with the Observatory's chief technician.

Even if a data trail led back to her, she kept scrupulous exculpatory documents and recordings hidden in her safe. After heavy editing and falsified calendars, all trails led to others. One could never be completely sure of victory, of course, but she loved the gamble, the roll of the dice, much as Jimmy had taught her.

She spit a foamy white into the pink sink.

Penitentiary or presidency?

She recalled Dearborn's words. The quiet blue reflections flashed off her study walls as she sat to use the porcelain.

Jimmy didn't need a warning. He would be fine.

She spoke aloud. "Presidency. I chose the Presidency. Sink or swim, Jimmy. That's your choice."

Chapter 54

Scott

"It's time, Scott. How do you feel?"

The former US senator glanced at his friend. "Joy's pills are a little too good. I've cut back but doing okay."

He looked out from the hillside vantage.

"You know, Josh, I've imagined myself giving up. At times, I even welcomed it but now I'm a little scared."

The two men sat in Josh's replacement sedan. They had started out yesterday when getting an all-clear from Joy but only after she extracted a number of promises from Josh. Now, at two in the morning and a long overnight drive from La Jolla, they sat in a scenic overlook gazing at a small strip mall at the end of a dark ribbon of road. Behind the stores sat a dozen FEMA fifty-foot emergency response trailers, with sides unfolded into makeshift square offices.

"Can't get it done sitting here, Josh."

His friend sighed and turned the key to start the car.

"No, no. I'll walk. Alone. There's no need to get you tied up in a bunch of legal crapola. It'll be years before I walk free again. I don't want you involved."

Josh snorted. "Involved? I've been hauling your butt around twelve states for the better part of two years. Don't forget you're the one who took me hostage in my own home."

They both chuckled.

"I want to go with you, Scott. Maybe I can say something."

McHale shook his head. "Thanks, but no. You'll be so much more valuable away from all this. Get north. Go as quick as you can. The nation is coming apart at the seams, and the city cells need a leader now more than ever. I've never been that leader. You need to carry the message, make sure nobody gets hurt. The first injury will be the catalyst to a fight no one wants."

Josh didn't look at his friend.

McHale puffed out air. "I don't think they'll allow visitors in Supermax, but if they do, try and come see me. If you want, of course. I'd wouldn't mind knowing what's happened."

Josh set his jaw. "I don't think you're giving these guys much credit. If anyone has an ounce of sense, they'll make good use of you. You're not going to sit in some cell while a bunch of lawyers get paid every billable six minutes. There's more in your head about what the entire country is doing than any two dozen of these intel guys."

McHale laughed. "Maybe, maybe not. I only know the time has come for me to stop running and pay up."

He pulled the door open but hesitated. "Listen, Josh. I ..."

"Oh, sweet Jesus. Don't go all sentimental on me. I'll be bawling like a baby."

Both men smiled and shook hands. McHale limped across the road, and down a pathway. Since he'd taken the buckshot to the legs, the limp seemed to worsen. The chest hurt but no real damage had been done. The old aches and pains returned with a vengeance, and he felt his years. By the time he reached the outer perimeter, he breathed through his mouth and needed a handhold to stand. He walked out of the scrub brush and crossed the highway into the parking lot.

A man stepped from the shadows "Can I help you?"

McHale saw the bulk of a ballistic vest under his shirt and a squared-off semiautomatic pistol on his hip.

"I'd like to speak to the person in charge. I'm former senator Scott McHale. If you're a US Marshal or an FBI agent, I'm on your capture list."

The pistol appeared and McHale was spread-eagled on the ground before he could utter another word. Flex cuffs tightened on his wrists as two more agents arrived.

McHale gasped. "Take it easy. Don't rip my stitches. You guys are likely the FBI Hostage Rescue Team. I know your commander is inside. Would you mind letting him know I'm in custody and need to speak? I might be able to help."

One of the men moved him to a sitting position. His touch was gentle. "I recognize you, Senator. Give me a minute."

He stepped away and keyed his radio.

A moment later, another man joined them. "They want to talk to him."

McHale blinked at the bright lights inside the trailer. Black-clad like his men, the HRT commander stood by a whiteboard now covered with a cloth. Across the table sat a US Marine Corps general, his single black star thread-stitched into camouflage BDUs. Also in battle dress uniform, stood a tall, grinning cowboy, hands on hips and laughing like a loon.

"Goddamn, Scott!" Theo Haines shook his old friend by the shoulders. "I thought you were dead. And now you show up in the gol-damnedest, unlikeliest of places."

He turned to the commander. "Come on, Dick. Get those cuffs off of him. He ain't going anywhere."

"He's under arrest, Sheriff. He's also a Top—"

"Ah, bullshit. He walked in here 'cause he's going to help you take back this power plant and our goddamn country. You're in the presence of a patriot, Commander. Do the right thing."

Dick Robillard gave the agent a chin-up command and said, "Senator? You sit. Do not think about getting up. If you twitch the wrong way, Special Agent Monroe there will hogtie your ass and have you in the county lockup faster than you can blink."

McHale nodded. "Duly noted, Dick. How are you?"

"Fine, sir. It's good to see you." Robillard glanced at the general. "We're friends from before the senator became a fugitive. He knows all our secrets and our techniques, so he's not getting out of my sight until this operation is a wrap."

The general, tall and lean, with gray hair cut skin tight around a stern, round head grimaced. "Politics makes strange bedfellows, Commander, but you've made my point well. This should be strictly a military operation. I've got the 31st Marine Expeditionary Unit here, with specialists in protecting and retaking overrun embassies. You're not going to find a finer, more well-trained unit for specifically this kind of operation."

The HRT commander clasped hands behind his back. "The attorney general acknowledges your capabilities,

General. He's also given the three of us discretion how best to integrate and employ three forces with far different abilities and responsibilities."

Haines spoke up. "You guys don't forget now, no one has committed a crime out here. At best, all we got is reasonable suspicion. We can make contact with the facility's manager, but we can't really go barging in and throwing everyone in cuffs. If we get all balled up in some sort of pissing contest now, this will go south fast, and nobody's going to come out too good. I used to be a Marine, and I know killing the enemy is job one. Now I'm a cop. We don't kill criminals. We get'm ready to go to prison for a long time … after the jury decides. There's a difference."

For the next fifteen minutes, all three men talked.

McHale listened silently, then finally cleared his throat. "Gentlemen? Excuse me, but I think everybody's missing the point."

Haines tipped up his broad Stetson with a grin and leaned back. "Okay, Scott. We all took our best shot. Earn your keep. What do you got?"

"Each of you has a specialty we need. We've got to have a police presence, because this is a local police thing. Nobody's better at rescuing hostages than the FBI. We've got to be prepared if this goes to hell in a handbasket, but we have patriots inside the wire."

He looked at the Marine. "General? There's no martial law in the twelve western states. When we get our country back, and we will, if just one citizen dies by the hands of a Marine, we will have lost our soul. We've always counted on you, and always will, but tonight is not your fight."

The general said nothing as his eyes bored holes into the other man.

McHale continued. "All three of you must understand a very important fact. What you do today, good or bad, will become the model, the inspiration, and the rallying cry all over the west, and maybe all over the country. We absolutely can't screw this up. We must be legal and must be Constitutional. Americans need to have a reason to believe the United States remains the best option of all the reasons to stay together. We can't let the Western Central Grid be the start of a second civil war."

Haines weighed in. "I can verify that's exactly what McHale's been fighting all the time he's been a fugitive. He's trying to mend our fences and bring us together. This isn't a simple us against them. Americans have opinions and they aren't afraid to act. It's what makes us great, and dangerous."

The General barely moved as he spoke. "If that's true, why were you the most wanted man in America for two years?"

McHale did not hesitate. "Because I was vain, foolish, and ambitious. And, in the words of a mentor in my past, I let my mouth overload my ass."

He looked at Haines and smiled. "I can help you, if you'll let me."

McHale leaned back and wiped at the sheen of sweat across his forehead.

Haines screwed his eyebrows together. "Are you okay?"

"Yeah, I'm fine." He felt the trickle of blood down his ribcage.

For the next hour, the four men charted a plan. The HRT commander and the general left to have their supervisors work out and practice the details.

At five forty-five, a little over two hours later, a county patrol pickup truck approached the front gate of the WCG compound. A security design of double-wire fencing turned the front gates into a sliding port, much like a high-security prison. The pickup truck passed through the first gate and stopped at massive steel rods extended from the pavement. Similar abutments rose remotely a few feet behind the rear bumper. The vehicle was essentially locked in place.

A security man stepped into the cage. The tower guard rotated the big light, and the vehicle's driver stepped out.

The guard stopped. "Well, hello Sheriff Haines. This is a surprise."

Another security officer walked around the vehicle with a mirror to view the underside while the pickup's passenger, a deputy, stepped out to hold the door for inspection.

Haines laughed and accepted the handshake. "Hey, Bobby. Didn't know you're working here." He did, of course. The FBI briefing was thorough, if not exhaustive. "I remember you were a night owl."

The other man waved away the bright overhead spotlight. "Yeah, I suppose that's me. Sometimes I wish I'd never left the sheriff's office though. I miss the guys."

Haines patted the other's generous belly. "That's always going to be the story, but you were right to retire. Policing is a young man's game, and you know times are changing. Hell, you'll turn out to be the smart one, getting a sweet job like this to add to the pension."

Haines looked around. "This ain't a bad gig at all."

"Pretty boring actually. Especially third shift. But we rotate, and ... say, what brings you out here, Sheriff? Couldn't sleep?"

"Yes and no. I needed to talk to Stanley Crenshaw. It's pretty important."

"Heck, sure. The boss's already in his office."

The guard pointed to the lights on the third floor of the block building. "Talk about a hard charger. He'd even give you a run for the money. Let me call him and get you a pass."

"Thanks, Bobby."

Unseen and unheard around the tens of thousands of yards of high wire, twelve US Marine Corps MRAPs, mine resistant ambush protected armored vehicles moved into place. The muffled diesel engines barely sounded above the gentle desert breeze as they approached, lights-out, using night-vision goggles and infrared devices. Each carried eight Marines of mixed technical and warfighting skills.

Waiting over the land's rise, four Suburban SUVs and "little bird" tactical helicopters with ropes and FBI operators sat ready to deploy. Every team member armed themselves with MP10 submachine guns and single-eye Cyclops night-vision goggle headsets for the predawn raid. The double-wired compound, whether wrapped with razors, mined or electrified, didn't concern the force. The combined firepower and overwhelming superiority of numbers as well as their training could take the entire facility in mere minutes.

Nevertheless, everyone waited as Haines and McHale tried to prevent a war.

Crenshaw reread the letter from the US attorney general, the nuclear regulatory commissioner, and the Senate subcommittee chairman. "I don't doubt the veracity of these letters, Sheriff, but what you're asking is way outside my province. I make electricity, and I've got specific orders and directions. Bringing a reactor up to eighty percent is routine. Bringing all nine up to eighty percent, especially the new ones under test, and all the while sending the wind turbine farm to max output, as well as getting the mirrors realigned for morning sun, is unprecedented. When you add opening the geothermal petcocks all at the same time ... well, you're just wasting juice and putting the whole grid in danger."

"The sectors in the east will take everything you got."

"No, no. They've got their systems' safetied in place. It would take days for us to coordinate—"

McHale, wearing a deputy's uniform, hadn't been introduced, and now spoke for the first time. "Already been done, Mr. Crenshaw. Everything's ready. The grid is ready."

Crenshaw glanced at the bearded deputy, forehead wrinkling, and then returned to Haines. "Listen, Sheriff. Without direct orders from the national director, I can't do this."

McHale persisted. "We apologize for not giving you any warning. But as you know, any leaking information would be exploited by the hackers. There's no telling what their interference would cause. You are the first shot fired in peace to reenergize the country's failed grid system. The letter from the attorney general, and the NRC commissioner, and the Senate Subcommittee—"

Crenshaw pointed his finger. "*That's* who you are. Scott McHale, the senator who murdered his girlfriend. The traitor."

McHale grimaced inside. His face a blank. "Even if that's true, and it's not, I'm not the important one here. You're the key to getting this country back on its feet."

Haines watched as the man's hand went under the desk. "Now, before you hit your panic button, Stanley, I'd like you to make a phone call."

Crenshaw stopped but remained rigid. He eyed both men.

Haines continued. "I've got the governor's number, but it's probably better you dig it out. He's expecting your call."

Crenshaw started a slow headshake. "You two are up to something. I don't know you, Sheriff, except by the television, but you're in way over your head. This might be your county, but the WCG's under the protection of the US Government."

"You're right, Mr. Crenshaw. And you work for the governor. You wouldn't believe the three men who wrote you the letters, and frankly I don't blame you. But you know the governor personally. You're his nephew."

"Everyone knows that."

McHale knew they were running out of time. "Call him. He's expecting you. Use your cell phone."

Crenshaw glared at McHale and picked up his dead landline. "You two wait outside."

McHale and Haines stepped out and pulled the door closed behind them.

"What do you think, Scott? Roll the Marines and the FBI? If he hits the goddamn button, this turns into a shooting war. He's got security forces out there who practice holding this place from terrorists. People are going to get hurt."

McHale glanced at the hall clock. "Let's hope not. If they don't hear from us, people will be moving pretty damn soon anyway."

The clock ticked each second.

Theo Haines paced.

McHale's chest ached. The bleeding rib left him feeling sticky and anxious.

Crenshaw stepped out and examined both men. "Okay. We'll begin the process of bringing all the facilities online. This'll take a while. Probably a week to get up to full output."

Haines dialed his cell and spoke quickly. "We're okay. He believes us, thank God. Code, scarlet and gold, *servare vitas.*"

McHale watched the wrinkles in his friend's broad face relax.

Haines signed off. "And thank the general for me, Commander. We'll talk soon."

He turned to the young manager. "It's all up to you now, Mr. Crenshaw."

The man nodded. "I'll give the heads-up to the crews. Wind and thermal water will take a while, but the sun is always ready to go ... once we get one."

McHale added to the instructions. "Thanks, Mr. Crenshaw. Everyone will be in lockdown until you hit the eighty-percent output on all the reactors. No one goes home. No one makes an outside call."

Crenshaw glanced at his cell phone. No service now. The FBI had worked their magic again.

"Uncle Ray mentioned that. The wife and I had plans ... Everything will be in motion soon. I hope to hell you guys know what you're doing. I still don't understand why you don't let the grids back east know. They'd be happy as hell with just a little bit of warning."

McHale remained stone-faced as pain medication ebbed. "This is just part of a plan to stop a war. There are many people who could bring our nation's recovery to its knees if the word got out too soon."

Crenshaw offered a derisive snort. "You might not need the rebels when the load banks start popping and burning."

He walked back into his office and firmly shut the door.

McHale hoped so, too. The week spent in Muscle Shoals, Alabama with the brightest minds of the Tennessee Valley Authority meant he trusted a lot of young men and women who promised to help him take back the country.

The phone in McHale's pocket vibrated. "Yes? Please put the call through. Morning, Angie. Yes, it's time to make the call to your reporter friend."

He punched his off button as the signal strength went to zero. "Those FBI tech boys are pretty impressive."

Haines smiled. "That reporter wouldn't be the cute little redhead pain-in-the-ass from DC, would it?"

McHale smiled. "One and the same. She's a persistent one, but Angie believes she's honest and knows how to use the information."

"Sure, she isn't reaching for a Pulitzer?"

McHale recalled ambitions and the young. "I hope not, but you've gotta start trusting people again sometime."

Both watched out the third-floor glass as the morning twilight lifted the night's edge.

Chapter 55

Teague

Teague knew time grew short. He had been around long enough and seen the signs in others he recognized now in himself. When the Citation landed at Muroc, he speed-dialed a number on his cell phone.

Dearborn answered on the second ring. "Wesley? Where you at?"

"Muroc County airport, sir. I need to see you."

"You're supposed to be in Vegas holding the psychopath's hand, but okay. I spent the night at Rolling Hills. Have Steve fly you to Torrance. I'll get a car to the airport, and we'll have dinner."

"Yes, sir."

Teague lay back in the Citation jet's seat and closed his eyes. The long night and day took its toll on him.

"Wesley. You still there?"

"Yes, sir. I'll check with Steve."

"Good. And turn on the Sat link. Swanson just figured out a way to slip the noose. For now."

Lovely red hair and a dentist-dazzling smile looked into the camera. "No one was more surprised than President Freeman Swanson when Oscar Serrano took full blame. At a news conference held this morning on the steps to the Justice Building in Washington, DC, Chief of Staff and former campaign manager, Mr. Serrano admitted to a number of crimes conducted without the president's knowledge. These crimes included election financing fraud..."

The link switched to a video showing the diminutive man, dressed impeccably in suit and tie, standing behind a bank of microphones. "I wanted to confirm the rumor that I presented evidence in the form of documents, emails, and texts to the attorney general of the United States outlining a pattern of abuse and fraud during the campaign by the committee to elect Freeman Swanson. I take this action because of the grave danger currently faced by our nation, and to expose the dalliances and unscrupulous conduct of several managers and supervisors who answered solely to me. The president had no idea of these actions until now and wasn't briefed on my testimony."

At this point Serrano offered a shy, if insincere smile. "I'm sure he is just as confounded as many of you. I offered recordings of interviews with dozens of people seeking favors in return for cash, all of which flowed and none of which were reported. The president of the United States was unaware of these transactions. When I advised him yesterday morning, he phoned the attorney general, and I was placed under arrest."

For the next eleven minutes Serrano spoke, took no questions, and explained as an American, he willingly admitted his oversight. He never denied knowing money had been traded for favors, insisted the president never had a clue, and said he'd leave the decision of his own guilt to a jury. When he ended the news conference he left in a phalanx of lawyers and bodyguards.

Crowded into the janitor's closet on the second floor of the Rayburn House Office Building, a man and a woman looked on as the articles of impeachment whirred through the shredder. Another man monitored two waste cans with small fires burning near the lone open window. The case against Swanson vanished in the breeze.

As the ashes dissolved into powder, the woman lifted a phone. "Naval Observatory? May I speak with the vice president, please?"

• • • •

Dearborn, livid and in a foul mood, slammed the phone into its cradle. "We don't need them, Wesley. We never did. So what if a few thousand people die? That's what happens in a revolution. Each death will be on Swanson's head. He just doesn't know it yet."

Teague said nothing as he balanced a computer bag on his lap.

Dearborn fell onto the room's couch opposite. His cigar burned against the remains of a T-bone steak on a tray next to his briefcase. "We still got this. I got handshakes and promises from sixteen of the most critical countries. Screw the rest."

He eyed Teague's computer case. "What's that?"

"One of the untraceable laptops from Las Vegas. You remember Peter Quint from Irvine?"

Dearborn gazed through his cigar haze. "Yeah. He's the one who put together the hacker team for you. Seemed like a bright-enough kid, so what?"

"He's not bright anymore. He's dead."

Dearborn's eyes moved around the other man's pallid face "What happened? Did we...?"

Teague shifted in the chair. "Not we. Me. He was about to take off with some Blackjack dealer and go to San Diego. This laptop has all the plans, orders, and documents we've used and hacked for the last twenty months. Maybe even longer. It's encrypted, but not unbreakable."

"You broke it?"

Teague nodded. "Donny Porter did."

Dearborn stood and walked around the couch. His jaw worked the muscles at his temple. "What's wrong with you? Sick?"

He pulled his coat aside and glanced at his red-soaked shirt. "I'm not sick, but I have been shot. I stitched it up, but it still hurts like a sonofabitch."

Dearborn peered over the couch back but didn't move. "Who shot you?"

"Oh, that would be Peter. I don't think the boy ever fired a gun before. Lucky shot."

"I'll call someone. Get you to the emergency room."

Teague watched him and slowly shook his head. "No. It doesn't matter anymore."

Dearborn screwed up his face. "What are you talking about?"

Teague barked a laugh. "You may be the best organizer I've ever met for putting things together. I respected you."

Dearborn's eyes flicked left. He never recalled hearing the taciturn number two laugh before. "You're delirious. I'm going to get you some help."

Teague ignored his offer. "When did you find out Juliette was pregnant?"

He eased to the side table where his own briefcase lay open. "You and I heard together. Don't you remember? We were at Twila's cabin when Juliette's body was found."

"I remember. What I asked you was when did you know she was pregnant, not dead."

"You on pain meds?"

"You had Juliette killed, didn't you?"

"Now, you're hallucinating."

"Has a truthful word ever left your lying lips, Dearborn? Ever?"

He reached inside his briefcase. "I'm going to call an ambulance. We've got to get you to a hospital."

"Don't."

Dearborn's unseen hand rested not on his cell, but on a .357 Colt Magnum. Teague already had his Glock aimed between Dearborn's eyes.

"For Christ's sakes. You *are* delirious."

Dearborn lifted both empty hands.

Teague accused. "You had Donny Porter hack into Oakland's lab and switch the records."

"Wesley, listen—"

"My turn to talk. Donny told me all about the records and the switches. You really shouldn't have done it."

"Why don't you get to the point? I have no idea what you're talking about."

Teague blinked, suddenly tired. As tired as he'd ever felt. "Good idea. You had Donny pull the data on the unborn child's DNA, and it matched mine. You might've even known Juliette and I were in love and our family was coming along just a little earlier than we thought. You had all these grand plans of making your own country, and me with a family just didn't fit in, did it? El Gordo admitted he killed Juliette."

Dearborn said nothing.

"Killing McHale was just a convenient distraction for you. Two birds, one stone."

Teague took another long blink, and Dearborn grabbed for his Colt. He pulled the trigger again and again. Wood splinters flew and a rush of paper followed. Two bullets struck Teague in the chest, knocking him back. Three missed. He saved one.

Dearborn had never been beaten. He walked around the desk to take time with the last shot. Teague fired a single .40 mm hollow point striking Dearborn just below the nose.

Teague rose and walked to where Dearborn fell. He shifted his ballistic vest away from his sore wound and listened as the man died, drowning in his own blood.

Then, Wesley Teague sat on the floor, closed his eyes, and followed Dearborn into the fires of hell.

Chapter 56

Josh

Howard and Russell Chao occupied the living room of the small Tigard, Oregon home. Howard lived across the river and in better times flew Boeing 757s for United. Russell, his younger brother, drove a patrol car for the Portland Police Bureau and didn't lack for work.

Leaders of the Oregon and Washington cells sat at the dining-room table and in the living room, coffee mugs in hand, in post-meeting conversation. Russell offered his house as a safe, central location. For the time being, anyway. The jobless rate stopped being reported at forty-five percent. Since the shooting of the California governor, tension couldn't have been higher in every state.

Russell smiled at Howard across the small room. "Jeannie's going to have your ass if you continue to wear out her carpet."

Howard, older by ten years, stopped pacing. "Sorry. The wait's killing me."

"Just pretend we're back in the Umatilla stalking that buck elk. I think he's still laughing at you."

Howard pressed his lips together and sat. "I'd give anything if life could be simple again. I'm afraid we're going to be hunting each other before long. God, what a tragedy that'd be."

Others tuned in to their conversation.

Howard looked around wishing he'd said nothing. "Sorry guys, but I always hated studying about the Civil War, you know? So depressing. Families disintegrating, brothers killing brothers. And now look at us. On the brink of another civil war and we're actually part of it."

Josh Harrison, elected leader of the twelve-state coalition, spoke up. "We're lucky to have someone like Scott McHale who understands this is a conspiracy and can prove it. He's willing to put his life on the line to stop people trying to steal our country."

Howard sucked in air. "Maybe that's some of my concern, Josh. I don't know this guy. He's a fugitive killer. He'd say anything to stay out of the gas chamber. You know what they say. Where's there's smoke, there's fire."

Josh pulled his lanky frame from the deep chair and gazed around the crowded space. "I don't believe Scott is guilty of anything except bad judgment. I've thought about this long and hard. You need to sit and talk with him, just like me and some of the others in this room. He'll be the first to admit he's flawed, but he's not a murderer."

Mattie joined Josh, slipping her fingers inside his, a recent development. She'd left the Eugene school system and now led the group of resisters centered in Oregon's southern Willamette Valley.

Her quiet voice commanded attention. "Our history tells us about the men and women who took a chance on an idea like democracy. None was without fault. Some worse than others. I for one trust Josh's judgment about McHale."

Russell refreshed the laptop and looked up. "Me, too, but there's still nothing."

Trees waved in the breeze outside. Josh spoke again. "Scott said he'd try to text a heads-up if he got the chance. Text or email. We'll just have to wait."

Russell fingered his badge case and turned to Josh. "Did all of this go sideways? Someone said they're holding McHale in a jail cell down there. Maybe the bad guys managed to get to the sheriff's office, and all we're doing is sitting here, making it easy for the arrest teams to get us in one fell swoop."

Josh shook his head. "No. I trust Theo Haines. He's a good man, too. He's probably being cautious, not pushing too fast."

Mattie spoke up. "We've got to give them a chance. We'd already be in a shooting war if it wasn't for people like McHale."

She looked at the man beside her. "And Josh. Look at the east. The power's flowing again."

Howard sat next to his brother on the small settee. "We're going to give him all the time we can. It's been six days, and pretty soon the cat's gonna be outta the bag, anyway. Our job is to get everyone on the road and back to the groups with enough time. No matter what, once the word's out, everyone will be in the streets. We've got to be first. We must be the first."

Mattie refreshed her tea. Before she could sit, her cell phone alerted. In fact, every cell in the room dinged or vibrated.

Josh stood and read. "Group page. Forty-eight-hour warning. Theo Haines."

He sought Mattie across the room. "Day after tomorrow. Dawn. We're going to do it."

Her breath caught and her eyes moistened. She spoke as if the others weren't there. "I knew this was a possibility, but I never really believed it until I met you."

Bob, a large, quiet man, pulled on his sheepskin jacket and tucked away his phone. "I'm headed up the Gorge. Who needs a ride? We all have a lot to get ready and not much time."

Josh stood, too. "Before we all break up and go our separate ways, I just want to say something."

He looked around at all the faces he'd grown to know and respect. And the one he loved. "There will be many last-minute questions, some cold feet, and maybe even some desertions. That's all right. Accept it and don't be angry. When Scott first came to me years ago ... well, frankly, I didn't believe him. I almost called the police, but I didn't. Some of you already know how persuasive he can be."

Howard smiled. "A politician."

Josh grinned back. "Yes, and an oddball one at that. He's honest to a fault. When he was offered the world, he refused. Maybe not at first, because he is, after all, human. But in the end, he took a stand, and for these years passed stuck with that decision. It nearly cost him his life many times over. And may still, because he's not a well man. He chose to stand against greed and avarice. He's convinced we have something worth dying for in this country."

Josh reflected then continued. "This might be the last time we're all together, and I just wanted to say you're my heroes. I pray the Lord blesses and keeps you all."

No one knew quite what to say or do. Mattie did. She rose and embraced Josh. The others stood while Russell and Howard, the lone Catholics in the room, recited the Lord's Prayer. Everyone joined in.

Chapter 57

Mahoney

As the leaders in Portland received their group page, four FBI agents in two sedans pulled up to the downtown Las Vegas checkpoint. A third vehicle, a white unmarked van, stopped short as four black balaclava and ballistic-clad SWAT agents stepped out the rear doors. The men took defensive positions behind concrete pots that once held small trees.

Civilian cars waiting to be admitted into Las Vegas stopped to watch. Several read the tea leaves and made U-turns back the way they'd come. Barricades among the building and warehouses narrowed arriving traffic into two lanes. Men armed with AK-47s checked IDs and wrote names. Others, armed as well, lazed about other's gun positions.

A mustached young man stepped from a trailer, adjusted his ball cap and eyed the two cars at the far end of the blockade. He signaled for his men to line up.

Giles Mahoney reached for the door handle.

The passenger in the FBI car remained still. "You think they know about the WCG? Look at all the automatic weapons over there. You'd think they're expecting us."

Many years senior to his young Bureau supervisor, he understood the nervousness. "We're only serving notice. You still okay with letting me do the talking?"

"Yeah, sure. The SAC wanted me to come along, just in case, but I think he wanted you to talk."

Juan Carlos, five years out of the Academy and promoted ahead of the many street agents from the now-closed Las Vegas field office, touched his pistol once more.

Mahoney would give the kid points for guts. "Absolutely no problem. Glad to do it."

A bandoliered guard put his radio down and climbed into a Jeep Grand Cherokee bristling with rifle barrels. The car stopped next to the pavilion in a swirl of accelerated dust.

Mahoney looked forward to retirement with a bit of wistful nostalgia. For nearly thirty years, he said he'd never worked a day in his life. To an onlooker, the statement might seem paradoxical because Mahoney was responsible for much brilliant work in some of the biggest cases of the last two decades. The large, barrel-chested agent chose Las Vegas as his final office assignment, liking the occasional big-name shows and Saturday morning golf. Now of course, Vegas was off limits since declaring itself a city-state. If he was angry about the turn of events, his calm features never revealed it.

Carlos turned to Mahoney. "You know I'm okay with you doing the talking, but I think you should've let someone else do this, Giles. You've done your duty."

Mahoney harrumphed. "I'll trust you to make sure I see my retirement party, amigo. Put your earplugs in and come on. Let's give our new friends the bad news."

They exited the black Ford Crown Victoria. Two other agents, a man and woman, stood by a second car holding MP10 submachine guns. All wore ballistic vests under blue nylon windbreakers with "FBI" prominent in large yellow letters. Their orders were to watch and wait, engage only to save a life.

As Mahoney and Carlos approached the first barricade, a half-dozen armed cartel-gang members fanned out next to their leader. Two men stepped forward and leveled their rifles.

The FBI men stopped.

"Go on back where you come from, FBI. This is our city now."

Mahoney, his voice folksy and reasonable, looked at the far high rises. "Actually, this city's mine, too. We were here before HQ ordered us to leave. Now, I need to give these papers to your boss."

He held out an envelope.

"Go away or die. You choose."

"Okay, then. How about if you give these to your boss?"

The man screwed up his face. "I'm not your messenger boy, *puta*."

Mahoney shrugged and felt his partner tense. He cautioned Carlos with a glance. "Then we have a problem, you see. Your boss wants these papers from our government, and here, you're stopping us doing what your boss asked. Now what am I supposed to do? Call him on your radio. You ask him."

The leader, a slender man with a narrow face and scabs on his forearm, sneered. His eyes never left the big Agent as he grabbed the radio and spoke. Nothing.

He shook the handset. "What did you do to my radio?"

Mahoney lifted both hands. "You been watching me the whole time. Come on, take the papers so I can go home to have lunch with the missus."

Carlos edged his right foot back and readied the pistol under his jacket.

The leader pushed the shoulder of the man next to him.

Mahoney was still smiling as the man approached. "Here you go. You've been served."

The man screwed up his face and looked at the documents.

"Bring it back, pendajo." He took several moments to read. "What is this?"

Mahoney hooked a thumb under the blue windbreaker inches from his gun. "You've been served by the US District Court of Nevada. You are under arrest. You're to vacate these roadblocks and turn yourselves in to the authorities. We've got buses waiting for you around the corner. I mean, heck. The judge'll probably give you guys a break for turning yourselves in. Otherwise, it might be life in prison."

"Are you loco, man?"

Mahoney snapped his fingers. "Almost forgot. You must let all the people you're holding hostage go. Just send them through any of the checkpoints and we'll take them from there. No problem ... man."

More quick, harried conversation among the gang members ensued. Snippets that came to Mahoney confirmed what he already knew from intelligence. Merrymaking, debauchery, and endless parties along the Strip had dried up as food deliveries slowed and the FAA declared the airports closed. Many tried to leave while only a few drifted in now, most often with little money and wanting to be entertained. El Gordo had grossly underestimated his ability to attract rich visitors into an open city with no laws and no constraints.

One of the men whispered to the leader as a third man brought his weapon up to center on Mahoney's chest.

Carlos stirred.

Mahoney whispered under his breath, "Give it a minute."

He spoke in a loud voice. "Now, you should look around you. This is a terrible defensive position."

The leader snorted. "I see two *whores* standing here against my guys who are ready to turn you into hamburger."

Mahoney shook his head. "Do you seriously think the FBI is dumb enough to send me in here without backup?"

The leader squinted at the low building and burned-out car husks and saw no one. "What you mean?"

Mahoney turned to look up. "Well, while I'm enjoying one beautiful sky, a whole bunch of sniper teams are putting red dots on your foreheads."

The men looked at each other as lasers flickered on their shirts in the bright sunlight. They shifted around, the dots finding them with each move.

Mahoney bladed himself. If this were to go bad, it would happen now. "You'll want to get your asses up to the North Las Vegas Airport pronto. Did I mention that's the amnesty gathering point? We'll probably just send you all back to where you came from and call this a draw, 'because we don't have enough jails to hold you."

The friendly smile dropped away. "You have an hour to get up there. After that, all bets are off."

The leader raised his pistol but the roar and blast as an F-16 broke the sound barrier a hundred feet over their heads. Dirt and city dust exploded in a rush of air. The guards' tents ripped, papers flew, and men yelled. As the coughing-and-swearing leader spun to aim his weapon, the explosive blast of a second F-16, even lower than the first rocketed over their heads. Guards clamped hands over aching eardrums. Instead of sniper fire from covered positions, canisters of tear gas and thick smoke landed among the gang members. Men began to choke and cough.

From behind the cloud, the Ford sedan's back tires burned rearward. The leader was first on his feet waving his hand to breathe and watching the retreating target. He shook the crumpled package in his hand, screaming and shooting at the retreating cars. The rounds were wild and missed. No return fire from the dozen hidden sniper positions as civilians scrambled to escape the checkpoints.

The gang leader jumped into his Jeep and drove for the Strip. More than once, he looked in his rearview mirror, fearing the sight of a jet targeting his car. The accelerator pressed to the floor. He wasn't laughing anymore.

Television monitors inside the mobile command post three blocks north showed the images from twenty-two FBI and USMC helmet cams and sixteen drone-operator consoles.

Theo Haines turned to the HRT commander. "I don't think they'll make it to the airport, Dick."

Robillard nodded. "I think we're going to have a fistfight on our hands and it's gonna be ugly."

Haines looked at his watch. "So much for taking the country back without anyone getting hurt. Now, we wait."

Chapter 58

Donny

Two blocks outside the Las Vegas zone, along Flamingo Road at Rainbow, Donny Porter sat at Peter's old desk. He'd returned to work after a neighbor found his predecessor shot to death in the apartment parking lot. The killer hadn't been arrested, but in truth, he was more afraid of Wes Teague than any wacko with a gun. Besides, the new hires were ready to go with the Reno operation piggybacked on Vegas. No shortage of orders flowed through their satellite feeds.

Donny tapped his keyboard and saw a pretty face on a split screen. "Come on, Lana. Orders are orders. I don't give a shit if the Scary Guy didn't tell you. I'm telling you. Peter's dead, and I'm in charge."

She sat in an office on West Liberty near downtown Reno. From early on, the hackers called Wesley Teague Scary Guy.

Donny needed to pay attention to his new job. "This comes straight from ... well, I don't know who it comes from, but I think it's Scary Guy's boss."

Lana's disheveled auburn hair stuck to pasty-white skin. "You *think* it's Scary Guy's boss? Oh, my God, Donny. These guys aren't screwing around. I mean, someone cooked half of my servers. The other half are starting to come up now, but it's all shit. I got a virus like you wouldn't believe."

"Yeah, I know. My servers were down until last night, too. We just got up and going again. You'll be up, too, if you get with it."

Her shrill voice over-modulated the Skype connection. "*Us* get with it. You got all those gang guys watching your back. I've got nothing up here. My gang bangers are a bunch of smelly bikers and a half dozen Cartel guys. Geezus, Donny. They got into a fight in the hotel bar last night and someone died. The cops won't come into this part of town anymore. What are we going to do without cops? We can't even go to our apartments. Tomlin ... you remember him from the Twin Cities? Someone shot at him walking in the parking lot. He's going to be okay but it's like the wild west out there. I can see the real cops from the top floor when they change shifts. They're going home at night, eating dinner while we're sleeping on the floors with the frigging doors locked. The water's off and the toilets are overflowing. Except for the Internet, we got a complete communications blackout. This is total bullshit."

"You shouldn't talk like this over an unsecure line."

Donny had no idea what he could tell her. He thought of Beth Hurley, probably long dead-and-buried for talking only half as bad as Lana. And of course, Peter was dead too, and no one had heard from Scary Guy in a couple days. He thought about a CIA assassin slowly wiping them out.

An idea came. "You want me to talk to El Gordo? I think those cartel guys are his up there."

Lana jumped at the life ring. "You think it might work? Could they be our guards or something?"

"Yeah, sure. Why not? I'll get a message to him."

"I'm really scared, Donny, please. Only the stupidest geek doesn't know what's happening. I want to go home. I think we all do."

"Yeah. What I wouldn't give for my mother giving me shit right now."

He thought about his small LA basement with multiple monitors and rebuilt servers, optical lines, and the neighborhood coffee shop. The warmth, comfort, and safety.

His monitor blinked with a flash message. "I have to go, Lana. Call me in an hour? I'll shoot a text over to the cartel building and get you some help."

"Wait—"

Peter wrote the software, but already the integrity of the system crumbled under attacks from government hackers.

Wind picked up outside and rattled the roof units. The Dark One flashed a message onto his screen. Funny how they'd given names to the new leaders in their life, as if they were characters in a *Call of Duty* game. Scary Guy only visited Peter, and Donny had been fine with that. Scary Guy looked like a serial killer. Everyone knew a third dark team monitored Las Vegas and Reno even if no one knew who they were. Donny thought that was probably where Scary One had gone. Maybe even to where Dark One lived.

Like an evil Hobbit Farm with Gollum and other tribulations. He never wanted to go there.

Now, they'd probably heard Lana giving him shit. The thought loosened his bowels but there was no way he was going to ask for help in Reno. Scary Guy might be terrifying, but the Cartel made serial killers look like pussies.

Given any chance to run, Donny Porter would leave them all. He didn't want his money anymore. He just wanted to go home.

The flash message unencrypted read: "Increased Homeland Security activity. Advise admin immediate. FEMA, FBI, other alphabets gone from home stations. Expect activity in 42 to 96 hours. Relay ASAP." All messages limited themselves to twenty-five-word bursts. In that way, the NSA couldn't shut down. As Donny reread, their hacker program erased the screen.

"What the hell–"

At the same moment, outside his office the heavy lead door suddenly exploded inward. The bald security man flew across the room, instantly unconscious and broken. Donny raced to the glass office wall. Ceiling tiles rattled and fell from the overhead, followed by feed wires and then, total darkness.

Donny hand-walked to his door, wide-eyed in the black, waiting for the battery backups. Red lines of laser beams crisscrossed the big room. As he had feared, the cartel had sent men to kill them. He reached for the panic alarm not knowing what else to do. His addled brain forgot the alarm only brought more cartel. Just then his door crashed inward with a white flash and deafening noise. Hands grabbed and threw him to the floor. He cried out as his wrists burned with plastic bands and a hood covered his head.

Thirty seconds later, the generators came up and the lights came on. Men in Nomex and black vests stood in each corner and the hallway, as others dressed in windbreakers poured through the door, filling the chairs and saving data. Many picked up the string of typed sentences and answered the other side of ongoing conversations. Visual connections croaked as inserted flash drives came to life. Trusted connections all over the world suddenly died under their attack as viruses disabled, and sometimes killed the receiving machines. Tracers from the NSA landed in the computers of several foreign governments, while automatic messages from the State Department demanded those governments' ambassadors report to the secretary of state.

In an odd turn of events, an NSA computer in Washington received a flash. The US Naval Observatory's main server fell offline. Counter Assault Team agents rolled from predetermined locations and entered the vice president's grounds. The Director of the Secret Service led the raid.

Alarms also went off in several other American venues. The NSA coordinated the cyberattack, and most of the hackers were identified. Most importantly, the cartel in Las Vegas and Reno remained unaware their underbelly now bled from fatal wounds.

The Dark One, Big Jim Dearborn was beyond caring.

Chapter 59

El Gordo

El Gordo read the arrest warrants with amusement. "That was our little airshow today?" The man scratched against the gold neck chain while he cocked a cowboy boot against the fifteen-thousand-dollar Carpathian elm desk.

"Yes, my captain. Two jets covered the federales' escape from the checkpoint."

The man ran his finger down the page. "Only two warrants for me but look at Manny. Fifteen! Oh, my, but he is a bad boy."

Both men laughed. The computer blinked off. El Gordo shook the mouse, but the screen didn't come back. He shook again and glanced at the power. The blue light glowed.

"What is going on with this piece of crap?" He slapped the side of the flat screen and cursed. "Call tech support. Get one of those guys up here. I've got a call to Mexico City in fifteen minutes."

The lieutenant snapped the radio off his belt and pushed the call button. The brick failed to respond. "My battery can't be dead. I just took a new one."

El Gordo tried his cell. "Dead. Hit the alert. The Gringos are coming to die." But the alert also used the airwaves, cell towers, and radio translators. All disabled. Some channels worked but the realization came too late for the opening minutes of the confrontation.

The chop of helicopter blades drew both men to the wide plate-glass window. Three huge Chinook helicopters hovered as men slid down fast ropes and onto the roof. Gatling-gun fire from a pair of gunships squelched a few tentative red muzzle flashes from windows.

El Gordo pounded the glass. "Why aren't my men fighting?"

Just then, a shoulder-fired missile arced up from a parking garage rooftop, an ambush set to slaughter any hostage-rescue attempts.

El Gordo pranced and yelled. "Die, Yankees,"

Just as quickly, an arc from an invisible drone intercepted and exploded the missile. A gunship pivoted from its hover, raining horrendous fire upon the launch site, vaporizing the ground force.

"Get down there. Surround the Metropolitan. Kill anyone trying to escape." Recalcitrant revelers now trying to leave Las Vegas had been locked in the facility.

"Yes, El Gordo." The man ran through the door and down a staircase, never to be seen again.

A second gunship engaged and devastated two flat parking roofs, exploding cars, dropping light poles, and rolling twenty-millimeter cannon fire across the flat concrete. Blackhawk helicopters swooped in low and fast, roping two more assault teams into the neutralized rubble.

El Gordo watched as months of work unraveled in minutes before his eyes. He grabbed his AK-47 and ran to the roof, cursing the fat Dearborn and his empty promises.

All over the hundred square blocks of his city-state, simultaneous assaults took back building after building, overwhelming his men. Much of the city choked on drifting yellow, green, and purple marking smoke. The barracks for his troops burned after a dozen surgical airstrikes from drones. He watched as his remaining men deployed from their rally points to corners and blinds in the city. Soon, they were taking the assaulting force under fire with fixed light artillery. A helicopter smoked and landed on a side street.

He gripped a window rail with an insane anger and grabbed a security man. "Go get me missiles and RPGs."

He heard the clank of Bradley Fighting Vehicles and the gunning engines of the Stryker multi-wheeled urban assault troop carriers. When the security man returned with three other fighters and rifle-propelled grenades, El Gordo sent them to the building's corners.

"Shoot and run. Don't wait for me."

The men ran to the roof's parapets as he climbed to the elevator shaft roof. He sighted in on a Stryker and released the grenade. The shot exploded short of the vehicle. The dark-green vehicle rotated its 105mm gun. El Gordo jumped just as the small blockhouse exploded.

He grabbed another RPG and ran to the roof's edge. A Bradley who obviously hadn't seen the shot passed the Stryker on its way to the Metropolitan holding area. El Gordo fired, and this time struck the small tank. The left tread spun off the vehicle and began to smoke. The nearby Stryker turned and fired on the roof corner, but El Gordo had already moved. His men engaged in laying an ugly fire on the assault vehicles below, giving the leader time to escape.

As he ran hunched over down the walkway, an Air Force A-10 Warthog attack jet annihilated the roof and the men. Black smoke billowed with no return fire.

El Gordo swore vengeance on the cold-eyed man who promised this could never happen. America would never assault one of its own cities, he'd said, never kill its own citizens and lay waste to hundreds of millions of dollars in buildings and sophisticated electronics. The man claimed he knew the most powerful in the government and would personally prevent such a rash reaction. Dearborn claimed citizens only wanted comfort, to have their power turned back on and their television cables working. No one wanted to sacrifice themselves in a bloody civil war. So many gladly gave over buckets of liberty in exchange for house subsidies, food stamps, and cell phones.

And, yet here they were fighting like madmen, and for what? Were not some of the neediest and worst-treated the soldiers of America?

Failing to understand, he ran for the basement. The rumble and thuds of the struggle overhead drowned his thoughts. Old diesel generators reverberated to life as the mini nukes failed aboveground. He ran for a locked door marked "Electrical Substation—Danger." A key from around his neck unlocked a second door inside the first, where the tiny, two-seat tram waited. Few people knew of the machine put in place decades before by the capitalist Howard Hughes. The long dead man hated to be around people yet wanted to move around the city. The system ran from several of the old building basements to a site twenty-six miles southeast at the grand old Boulder Dam Grand Hotel. Wesley Teague had said El Gordo would never need to use the key to escape.

The cartel chieftain closed the small hatch and turned a switch as the panel lighted. He pressed the green button and felt the door lock and the tram move down the track. The windowless capsule rocked with a whoosh of displaced air as he gained speed. A Burroughs green-screen computer blinked progress at the five stations. As he approached each, the screen asked if he'd like to stop. He hit the *No* button, and the pod accelerated past. He wondered how long his men would fight. The pod had a second seat, but he couldn't think of a single person he might want to save.

The yellow light flashed "Dam," and the car decelerated. He undid the Berretta from its holster just in case. Squeaks and brake howls accompanied the jerky stop. He sat still and listened. The silence of the old hotel basement reassured him no one waited. He edged the pistol around a silent and dark corner. The hotel must have lost power, too.

As he put one leg out, a gun barrel touched his temple. "Drop the gun, *señor*, or I empty your head."

El Gordo opened his fingers and let his freedom hit the floor. The lights came on and a smiling Marine Corps general stepped up.

"Mr. Guzmán, I presume."

"Oh no. That is El Gordo. I'm Jose Estrella from San Diego. The janitor. I ..."

Marines slipped plastic cuffs around his wrists. The general re-holstered his pistol and dropped the man's arrest photo on the deck.

"You are a sorry son of a bitch, aren't you? You ran off and left your men to die."

The cartel leader eyed him. "Before you start in on me, soldier boy, I want an attorney."

The general laughed. "You're not just a sack of shit, you're stupid, too. I'm not arresting you. I'm going to blow your goddamn head off."

El Gordo's face drained white. "Wait. You can't do that. I know people. I know the whole story. I'll tell you everything, but you must protect me."

The general shook his head at the man. "I don't have to do any such thing."

A second man dressed in a tie and a Kevlar helmet stepped up and stuffed a crumpled paper into the pleading man's breast pocket.

"I'm Assistant United States Attorney Ben Allen, and the general's right. I might not even be here. For the moment, I'm only in charge of ensuring warrants are served."

He glanced at the general then back to the prisoner. "If you make it to trial, my job will be to put you in a maximum-security prison for the remainder of your life. But you are not getting a deal. No way, no how."

The general watched El Gordo. "Come on. Be a smartass now. Those are my men you were shooting at. I just may give you to my tigers and be done with whole thing."

Guzmán watched both men with an open mouth.

AUSA Allen smiled. "Ah, well. Here's your search warrant, Mr. Guzmán. I expect your cooperation and undying gratitude for the next few hours. Properly served."

The general gestured to a young officer who'd had two men wounded in the early fight. "Captain? I'm turning this man over to you. The Assistant United States Attorney has identified him as the terrorist Hector Beltran Guzmán, so-called El Gordo. If he is not, then he is a cartel whack-job trying to escape. If he gives you a reason, I never saw him before in my life. The communications blackout will continue for twenty-one more hours. That should give Mr. Allen plenty of time to debrief this gentleman."

"Yes, sir."

The captain pointed a finger at the defrocked leader, and a man stepped up. "Sergeant? Put him into the Stryker. Bind his ankles and strap him to the bulkhead."

The young Marine turned to the prisoner. "You had better hope none of your idiot amigos try to take us out. We'll all do just fine, but you'll be spam in a can."

El Gordo took deep ragged breaths unused to people who could back up their threats. "Give me a radio. I'll call them off. They'll listen to me. I can stop this."

The captain turned to his boss. "Sir?"

The general shook his head in disappointment. "Damn it. And I was just starting to enjoy kicking cartel ass. All right, Captain. Get him the Sat link. If he tries anything, anything, make sure he wears dentures for the trial."

The general turned to the AUSA. "Is that okay with you, sir?"

AUSA Allen touched his briefcase. "I've got a ton of questions, but I do believe he'd look excellent in a set of new choppers."

El Gordo watched both men as he was frog-marched into the Stryker with a waiting radio.

Allen turned to the general. "Can we check on the Rangers in the Reno operation? I know they're probably grinning ear to ear, too."

Chapter 60

Swanson

President Swanson stepped up to the podium in the pressroom. He'd spent the night walking the halls of Congress, talking with members of the Senate and the House of both parties. Rumors sent talking heads and opinion brokers into a frenzy when the White House refused comment on possible military action in Las Vegas and Reno. His spokesman had been under daily fire for those updates as well Serrano's admissions. So far, he'd been able to keep a lid on the worst of the speculation, but time had run out.

The President buttoned a rumpled suitcoat for the cameras but forgot to straighten his tie. Behind him stood the Speaker of the House, the president pro tempore,- the most senior member of the Senate, and the Chief Justice of the Supreme Court.

"Good morning. I'm aware most of you didn't plan to get up this early ..." Smile and chuckles greeted the president. "So, I appreciate you being here."

He looked toward an advisor who listened to his iPhone. The young woman nodded. "Let me ask everyone to hold their questions. Frankly, I haven't slept much in the last seventy-two hours, and as you have guessed, there's a lot happening."

"Governor Molina-McHale just started a news conference along with eleven other governors in the west. Now those folks know how to get up early."

Polite laughter.

"Nearly all other state governors have remained in communication with our national command center throughout the last day and night. This presser is being fed directly into state capitals, government offices, and our embassies and consulates abroad. This is being done to ensure the free flow of information during the next critical forty-eight hours."

"Governor Wilford Brewster of Nevada resigned late last night and is currently detained at the official residence in Carson City. Lieutenant Governor Andy Mays was sworn in an hour ago.

"As you know the Western Central Grid is a federally subsidized commercially operated joint venture. Last Tuesday the WCG was federalized by my authority."

The room buzzed.

Swanson held up a hand. "You might have noticed more lights on this morning than usual. We had to keep a lid on all operations to lessen the possibility of danger to soldiers and the police. All actions at the WCG were conducted in coordination with the United States Attorney's Office."

He took a ragged breath. "Twelve hours ago, the 31st Marine Expeditionary Unit, Task Force 160, and the Hostage Rescue Team of the FBI, conducted an operation against criminal forces in several locations, including Reno and Las Vegas. There are injuries to American personnel, but so far, no deaths. I'll have better information later."

Reporters' hands shot up.

President Swanson shook his head. "Pundits will consider the timing of these actions suspect, especially in light of allegations directed at my election committee. So be it. But the life of the nation is at stake. My political party and my career are secondary and we're not out of the woods yet."

More babble from the White House press corps.

"For the last sixteen hours, your government has been coordinating counter-cyber-strike activities around the globe in cooperation with other friendly nations. As of this time, it appears most attacks originated internally. This is most bothersome but perhaps easier for us to handle. The National Security Agency is coordinating the operation. We will have more information on that soon, too."

He seemed to age before the eyes of the nation.

"I would like to express my deep admiration and gratitude to California governor Angie Molina-McHale. Were it not for her personal and professional bravery and to become an FBI undercover operative against these evil forces … well, I just don't know what would have happened. A lesser person might have handled these circumstances differently. For many months, she took grave risks with her own life and her reputation. She is a true patriot, and we owe her an unpayable debt of gratitude.

"As you will soon become aware, Governor Molina-McHale's former husband, US senator Scott McHale, was thought to be the nation's first victim of this odious plot. This turns out to be quite true. As many guessed, he is indeed alive."

The room erupted in questions.

Swanson shook his head again. "Please. For the last three years, he worked tirelessly against these forces and at great risk to himself. We owe a debt to him, as well."

One reporter could stand it no longer and leapt to his feet. "Mr. President. Are you describing a failed coup d'état?"

"I'll leave that to historians, Jason. One reason you all are here is because I am enlisting your help to get this story out. Once you know, I trust that your editors and publishers will inform the nation. We're about to get back on track here but everyone must hear the same recounting and understand just how close we came to losing our nation.

"Patriots are rallying in public parks right now. They are standing in front of public buildings, and around federal and state military facilities. These fine people are *protecting* the buildings and the people who work inside. Those are good people. Our friends and neighbors. California has sixteen major rallies alone and estimates over a million people will attend. A lot of people have our country's back, so if one of you gets the story wrong, our world could change forever. Soon, you'll be witness ..."

At that moment, cell phones alerted throughout the room. Reporters reached to turn them off and realized everybody's phone had chirped.

Swanson dismissed the breech of protocol with a smile. "Go ahead, this was planned. Take out your phones and listen to a historical first. Twelve bands of social media are going to carry the message you're about to hear."

As the White House feed flickered to a split screen, he spoke again. "I'd like to introduce you to groups across the country calling themselves '1788.' That was of course, the year the last state ratified our United States of America Constitution, and we became the nation we are today. The title may have been a secret but is apropos to the situation we find ourselves in today."

The same young woman signaled from the side of the dais.

"Okay. Let's listen in. Afterward, I'll take questions."

A gaunt face peered from twenty million screens across the nation. The man's blue eyes sagged, and scars marred the once handsome Latino face. A country kitchen framed his backdrop.

"Thank you, Mr. President, and good morning to everyone. I'm Scott McHale, a former fugitive and currently in FBI custody. I used to be a United States Senator until I screwed up. Yes, I got taken advantage of by evil people, but this was my responsibility, and I must be held accountable just as those others are held accountable. We've seen evidence of their handiwork and been made to suffer because of them, and by extension, me. But I'm not telling you anything new except I take full responsibility for my actions ... and until three years ago, my inactions.

"This message is being sent to many on their phones and tablets, home and work on computers. Those who are at the rallies need to check around and make certain everyone can see and hear. If anyone misses the president's conference or my small part, please replay it for them.

"From these troubled times, true heroes emerged. If you're not at the rallies our president just told you about, get to one. These 1788 rallies aren't a protest, they're a show of our support. The president is behind 1788. Get behind the president and stand with your friends. There are no political parties today.

"Find people with the ugly green t-shirts. These are your fellow citizens who met in secret to get our nation back. These are the new heroes and founding fathers just like in 1788. They're standing next to people in uniforms of blue, gray, olive, and brown—our police, firefighters, and military. There's a lot of them out there. Don't decide our country's fate in the streets or with your fists. No more rioting. No more killing. Let's use our system to set things right. Our Republic."

McHale had taken no pain meds this morning, wanting to be sharp for the camera.

"Let's all agree to disagree on occasion, but let's get involved in saving our nation. The world must see us united, no matter who we are, no matter the color of our skin, where we came from, the place of our worship, how we got here, or the beliefs we hold. Work with your neighbors. We are all Americans, and she needs saving just now. You're about to hear the tale of a country nearly upended by a rotten few. Let's heed the warning and wish ourselves good luck in our shared future. Thank you for this opportunity to speak directly. Mr. President?"

McHale's face disappeared.

The President's news conference ended nearly two hours later.

Chapter 61

Scott

In the two years since the President's speech played around the world, brownouts and blackouts became unpleasant memories. Interstate commerce bounced back when the barricades came down. Large companies that escaped abroad brought back swaths of wealth when major media outlets identified the tax avoiders. For its part, a bipartisan Congress passed a new legislation offering incentives to keep business home and with tax breaks.

Sixteen men and women worked a pistachio and almond orchard of nearly seven hundred acres. Most spoke Spanish and were, or at some time, had been immigrants. Several waited until the time came when they could join America as citizens.

The foreman, a tall man with rounded shoulders dressed in a denim shirt, chinos, and high-topped leather boots, drove his ten-year-old pickup to where a man squatted at the trunk of an aging thirty-foot almond tree.

He pushed the button for the truck's window. "What's it look like, Jorge?"

The younger man tipped up a blue Dodgers baseball cap. "Native coleopterous. Not too bad fortunately. I've stopped them here. I'll treat his neighbors this week."

"Ah, that's good news. This was one of the original trees, you know."

"Yeah. My granddad made me learn every tree on the farm. I think he even gave some trees names."

479

"Yes, he did, and he made me learn them too."

McHale climbed out of the truck and stretched in the sunshine. Any change of weather, he felt the pain. But not today. Today was perfect. Even the limp was perfect.

A horn honked down the valley. The two men watched as a black Tahoe stopped at the small stationhouse.

"Think this will ever be over, Mr. McHale?"

He waved at the driver. "Probably not in my lifetime. At least your two girls can use me as a resource in school. I've got some firsthand information that might be interesting someday."

"I'll let Carol and Gina know. 'Course they're still in kindergarten, so by the time you're getting around to telling your story ..."

McHale grinned. "I'm not slipping that much."

He still had to work to maintain his fleeting weight. The beard lessened the impact of his burns when he met others.

"Will you make it to dinner on Sunday? Angie ... the governor ... will be here. She'd like to see you."

"Yes, sir. We'll all be there."

The family picnic tradition meant an annual BBQ celebration attended by numerous families. Security measures would ensure everyone's safety. The nation had grown safer but was still not out of the woods.

McHale clasped the young man's shoulder and shook his hand, an old politician's habit he couldn't break. He drove to where the Tahoe waited.

"Morning, Christine."

"Good morning, Senator."

"Scott."

"Right. Your cell phone isn't on, correct sir?"

"Left it around here somewhere." McHale made a show of looking around on the truck seat.

"Right. You have a visitor at the house, sir. Now, if you had your mobile with you, I wouldn't have had to abandon my post ..."

"Sorry, sorry. I'll remember next time."

She shook her head. "Sure, you will. I'm heading back. I need to clear the area before you get there. Can you wait for a minute?"

McHale brightened. "I'll race you."

"I'll tell the governor on you."

McHale fitted a straw hat to the back of his head. "You win. I'll meekly follow in your dust, Special Agent Dodd."

She gave him a firm mouth that passed as a smile. "By the way, sir, Brian Peterson called and said he and family will be in around eight tonight. Now stay behind me, please."

He laughed and waited to let the breeze move the chalky dust then shifted into first gear. They bounced along the road until the original hacienda came into view. A figure stood at the hitch post watching their approach. Even from a distance, he recognized Josh.

They embraced without awkwardness. "It's good to see you, Scott."

"I hoped you'd come. I would've visited you but my parole agreement ..." He shrugged and shook the electronic ankle bracelet.

"That's pretty unfair."

"It's less than what I deserved. Listen, I appreciate the notes and letters while I did my time. They really made the whole thing bearable."

The two moved out of the sun, up and on the porch.

Josh spoke. "Don't people realize what they owe you? The chances you took. Right up to your deathbed, and then getting shot for Christ's sake. What do people want?"

"Honest public servants, better than me. More like Angie, though they broke the mold after her. I'm just lucky there wasn't a tree and a rope handy."

Josh watched the sky for a moment and sighed. "You just flat wear me out, son."

McHale laughed. "Can you stay till Sunday? We've got our annual family—"

"Angie called and invited me."

The door to the house opened, and Mattie stepped out. "That was an invitation for two, by the way."

McHale chuckled. "Hey, now. This is really terrific."

Her auburn hair bore a little more gray these days. She was pretty and stern and handsome and a presence like few others. "I hope you don't mind, Scott. I couldn't let this big lug travel without me."

His eyes narrowed. "You guys are ... what?"

Josh moved to put an arm around Mattie's waist. "What do you think?"

"I think nobody ever tells me anything. Theo Haines will be floored. Or does he already know, and I'm the last? We're supposed to pick him up at six."

Mattie glanced at Josh concerned. "Maybe we should get a motel—"

McHale put a quick end to that. "No way. I think this old place has at least a hundred bedrooms. I assume you two share a room now."

Mattie raised an eyebrow. "Yes, and that'll be all you're assuming."

All three grinned at one another.

McHale broke the silence. "Let's get some iced tea."

He waved at Christine. "Chris. You work too hard. Come on. Iced tea."

They sat around a kitchen table many in America had already seen.

Josh spoke first. "I imagine we're not supposed to discuss this, but I understand Twila Crawford was pardoned by President Swanson."

McHale answered. "It's okay, and you're right. After a two-year investigation, and probably a ton of Twila's perspiration, she got a pardon. She and Tom are living in Scotland. I understand the president helped him get the position."

Mattie put her glass down. "I suppose that was nice to make sure they didn't starve, but I wouldn't have been as gracious."

Christine joined in. "The president was making sure Ms. Crawford would forever keep her mouth shut and not make a book deal. He can yank support anytime and tie her up in a new investigation if she doesn't. There's no statute of limitations on treason."

Josh nodded. "It's time for the country to put all that behind us. We still owe a lot to the people hurt by this power grab."

The table fell into an uncomfortable silence.

McHale pushed back his chair knowing he was the source of their discomfort. "You folks drink your tea. I need to check on the new trees up on the hillside. Sort of an experiment with a new breed I got from Turkey. Got a second, Josh?"

Josh touched Mattie's hand as he stood.

Once outside on the porch, McHale spoke first. "I understand you've had some trouble from your hometown."

He avoided saying "church," but both knew what he meant.

"I'd be lying if I said different. There were people who wanted to take advantage of the chaos. Utah, Idaho, Nevada, and Wyoming would be landlocked, but they were sure a new order could be formed, right up to the point of petitioning the federal government."

"There was a lot of that loose talk."

Josh hung his head. "Nearly every cell meeting I attended before and after in those two years had at least one, and usually more people who wanted to start the country all over again. They never bothered to learn their history and wanted to repeat all the ugly days of our young country trying to find a place in the world. I doubt America could survive a reshaping like that today. Those people were the greatest part of the reason for the ten-million-person rally."

McHale put his hand on his friend's shoulder. "Your terrific idea that saved us all."

Josh shrugged. "It took the sweat and guts of a lot of people to pull it off. It's hard to talk revolt when people all around you are singing 'God Bless America.'"

"I wish I could've been there."

McHale recalled the jail and lack of news while the US Attorney and a room of lawyers decided his fate.

"I wish you could have been there, too."

"How's Mattie doing with all this?"

"She's taken some grief. She thinks it's because she's a Methodist and I'm LDS. I don't necessarily agree, but we do have hardheads in both our churches."

"Every family's got hardheads. You guys love each other. You'll weather the storm."

Josh nodded but his face wrinkled in concern. "We're going to move, Scott. I really don't want to leave my 'neighborhood,' but it's not fair to her."

"I understand. Where will you go?"

Josh smiled. "Mattie fell in love with Park City. There's this retired nun up there. You might've heard about her."

McHale chuckled. "A nodding acquaintance. Have you let your families know?"

"Mattie's alone, except for a sister and a niece in Oregon. My brother will survive just fine without me. Besides, it'll give everyone something to talk about. Will you come and visit? I mean once they give you permission."

"I'd be honored. This country would've been a whole lot different if you'd thrown me out that first night. We might have been two or three countries by now, and far worse off. Thanks to you, none of it happened."

Josh laughed and grabbed the front door's handle to head back in. "You want to thank someone? Check the mirror first thing tomorrow morning. That's the guy we owe."

Chapter 62

Scott

The CHP helicopter assigned to the governor's detail took two hours to make the trip from Sacramento to Muroc County's airport.

Governor McHale tucked her papers away and keyed the intercom. "Ted?"

"Yes, ma'am."

"Would you detour over the west end of the Valley? The family planted some land on the upslope, and I'd like to see if the new trees are in yet."

"Certainly, Governor. It's right on the way." Ted glanced straight-faced at his copilot, a twenty-year California Highway Patrol veteran.

The other man's acknowledgement showed only the briefest of tight smiles. "You might need to point it out, ma'am."

"Happy to oblige."

As they circled the land owned by the Molina family for three generations, she pointed up into the hills. "Up the slope until it opens into the valley. There's a little meadow on the south side."

The helicopter climbed until the road ended.

She spotted a tan pickup truck parked off the dirt road's terminus. "Can you put me down there?"

"Roger that, ma'am. Landing checklist, Pat."

The upslope rose into a rich sandy loam catching and holding each year's brief rainfall. The cool ocean breezes from fifty miles away crossed the mountain's top, giving the modest plot's hundred acres a microenvironment which both pleased and left a visitor in awe.

Dust engulfed them as the sleek Bell 525's touched down, and the pilots slowed the rotors.

They understood and didn't bother to shut down. "Let me check out the area, Governor. For security."

The two pilots watched one another, with smiles on their faces.

"Thanks, Ted, but no. I appreciate the offer. You too, Pat. Great flight. I'll get out here and walk the rest of the way."

"Now, Governor, you know we're supposed to ..." But her headset already lay on the seat. She ducked under the blades and walked away.

"That woman is going to get us fired one day."

Ted laughed. "Yeah, probably. But I like her."

"Yep, and she is one hell of a governor."

Angie stopped in front of Scott, who leaned against the door, his straw hat tipped back. A gaunt body, hard from daily manual work, and relaxed in the waning sun.

"Howdy, Ms. Governor. How are you this fine day?"

She looked at him and scanned the expanse. "I'm well. I figured you might be here."

The helicopter powered up. She turned and they both waved at the pilots. They waved back and dropped down the valley.

Angie and Scott watched the aircraft disappear into the waning light. The noise left with the helicopter as the quiet returned to the high desert.

"I like your new ride. It's very nice."

"One of the perks for putting in sixteen-hour days, seven days a week." Gray strands highlighted her long dark hair.

She would remain a lovely woman all her life. "You look good, Scott. How are you feeling?"

"Stiff on cool days but healing fine. Joy is a wonderful doctor, but you already knew that."

They smiled at one another.

He gently touched her cheek. "We did good there, you know."

"We did good in a lot of places, Mijo. You'll just never get the recognition is all."

"Don't need it, ma'am, and thank you very much, don't want it. I'm fine being a pistachio farmer from the San Joaquin."

"And a sexy one, too." The gold flakes in her dark eyes caught the sun's last rays.

"Hmm, you best be careful. You're an unmarried woman. I might have gotten the wrong idea. Let's go for a walk and take a look at your new babies."

"Okay. But just don't tell me you gave them names."

He looked around in mock surprise. "Me? Name trees? Please. That just isn't right."

She laughed. "You named them, I know you did, so introduce me."

And he did. They wandered through nearly six hundred small trees, each of which would one day grow to thirty feet. The offspring of ancient trees from the Mediterranean loved the arid lands in California.

As they arrived back at the old pickup truck, the first stars of the coming night rose just visible in the low east.

She slipped her hand in his. "I do love the desert."

He turned and gathered her up. "And I love you. I seem to recall another time in our past, and the front seat of an old Ford."

"Yes, I remember, too. That was a long time ago."

"Was it too long ago? Too much water under our bridge?"

She smiled into his beaten and scarred face. "No. Not so much."

He lightly kissed her lips. "Angie? Will you marry me? Again?"

She touched his cheek, her fingertips tracing the scarred skin. "Of course, I'll marry you. What took you so long?"

He smiled, kissing the tips of her fingers. "Come on. I'll drive you back to the ranch. We've got company waiting on us."

"You could drive me home, gringo, or if you're man enough, we could stay here for a little while longer."

He took her in his arms. "I've missed you."

She sighed and laid her head on his chest. "God knows why, but me too."

• • • •

The End

Praise for Novels by Frank V. Costanza
Penned under the name, Oliver F. Chase

Levant Mirage "...the perfect storm of ideology, technology and mother nature drag you to the edge of annihilation."

Gerald Baker, US Navy, Satellite Intelligence Officer

Hunt the Shadow "A fast-paced and thrilling plot. Fantastic characters and suspense around every corner."

Verified Amazon Reader Reviews

A Time for Dying "Oliver F. Chase uses intense dialogue, deep backstories, and powerful characters to shape the story. "

Verified Amazon Reader Reviews

Certain Evil released 2024

At the precipice of an extraordinary medical advancement, a lovely young researcher plummets five stories to her death. The coroner decrees suicide. Her parents claim it's violent murder at the hands of the university's president.

• • • •

Camelot Games "...the amount of twists and turns and secrets! It never ends. The suspense keeps showing up and the changes come throughout the whole story!"

The Writing Piazza

Don't miss out!

Visit the website below and you can sign up to receive emails whenever Frank V. Costanza publishes a new book. There's no charge and no obligation.

https://books2read.com/r/B-A-HBPGC-HYKHD

BOOKS 2 READ

Connecting independent readers to independent writers.